Dirge of Titans

S.J.S. Adair

La Tène House
Publishing

Copyright © 2024 by S.J.S. Adair

Dirge of Titans is a work of fiction. The story, all names, characters, and incidents portrayed in this production are fictitious. No identification with actual persons (living or deceased), places, buildings, and products is intended or should be inferred.

No part of this publication may be reproduced, distributed, or transmitted in any form or by any means, including photocopying, recording, or other electronic or mechanical methods, without the prior written permission of the publisher, except as permitted by U.S. copyright law.

All rights reserved.

Edited by Laura Josephsen
Book Cover by Angela Adair

ISBN 978-1-0688718-0-1 (Paperback)
ISBN 978-1-0688718-1-8 (eBook)
First edition June 2024

La Tène House Publishing

To the children of 4 East (1996),
and the adolescents of 4 West (2004),
at the Children's Hospital of Eastern Ontario (CHEO).
You were the bravest people I've ever known.

PART 1

Fate

Chapter 1

ARK

Darkness. It's always the first thing I see.

The edge of the airlock marks the end of my world and beyond it, the vast stretch of the abyss. Ahead of me are thick LED borders, black and yellow stripes and a sign that reads:

Danger! Do not open until the airlock has sealed behind you!

I gulp and breathe out, and the sound of it echoes within my helmet. To be sure, I check behind me. A solitary round light illuminates green around the quarantine lock: all clear.

Before I reach for the lever, I stop.

"Right..." I exhale, tapping down on my wrist. "Let's get this over with."

"*Welcome,*" a cold synthetic voice greets, "*please complete your site preliminary report before leaving the ship.*"

"Okay," I begin. "My name is Ark'Onus of the Eridas Deck. Age: nineteen. Sex: male. I'm a designated repair tech, level 3 clearance. EV certified. Reason for EV: repair of the outer hull of the *Nautilus*-generation ship. We're currently floating by the Perseus-Pisces Supercluster. Reason for repairs, uh... meteor impacts. Investigation ongoing."

There's a pause, and a faint luminous orange light blinks from my wrist.

"*Form incomplete,*" the voice in my helmet reminds me. "*Please indicate the exact date.*"

"Oh..." I reply. "It's the fourteenth of Tyrras, 5034 CE... 1607 hours."

A tiny blue flashing light blinks in the far right-hand corner of my visor. It reflects in my line of sight a distorted image of my misty dark cobalt-blue eyes and loose strands of my charcoal-brown hair.

As I move away from the hatch and closer to the release console, my reflection fades away.

My heart weighs heavy as I stare at the release console.

"Come on, damn it, quit stalling," I whisper.

The echo of each breath I blow out gets louder. My cheeks burn hot, and while my arm steadily hovers over the lever that will open the maw out into space, my chest constricts tightly.

Oh, man. Okay...

My hand flips a red lever to my right, and for a second, the sound of a faint 'pop' erupts from outside the safety of my baggy spacesuit. The sliding door that lets in the vacuum of space seems to retract so quickly it looks like it just... disappears.

Up and over. Every second I waste is another second I have to spend out here...

Lifting one magnetised boot in front of the other, I step out over what appears like the edge into absolutely nothing... and then it happens. The artificial-grav from the ship lifts, and right after, I'm struck by a nauseating surge of vertigo.

Up and down have no more meaning, and the only thing anchoring me to my world is my magnetised boots. As I take one heavy step away from the exit, my stomach does a backflip. It's hard to get my bearings back without throwing up my lunch.

My feet carry me toward a wrecked patch of hull that got torn up in the last meteor scattering. As I hold a normally very heavy drill with one hand, my sweaty palms worsen the sensation of the rough fabric inside my gloves.

The more I grip the handle of my drill, tensing my fingers, the more a raw itch spreads across my hands.

I try to breathe deeper, seeing a thin layer of condensation creep its way around the periphery of my visor. My chest tightens, and I frantically mash my fingers against the console on my forearm to heat the fog blocking my line of sight.

Calm down, Ark... it's not the first time you've been outside, and it won't be the last.

One foot up, one foot down.
Sealed.
Safe.
One foot up, one foot down.
Sealed.
Safe.

The crackle of the comms squawks in my ear, and it throws me off. It's bad enough when the foreman gives a command and you can't see him... but it's nothing compared to the sinking sensation you get when there's static.

Could it be solar interference from a nearby star? The last meteor shower must have done more damage than we thought... I mean, the last one dinged up the outer panels from marble-sized pellets. But the bridge's report shows that the electrical wires are all torn to hell, and just short of the quadrant above the artificial-grav generator. A close call, no doubt about it.

I try to plant my left foot on the hull, there's nothing underfoot. An icy-sharp pain wracks my chest as my body drifts away from the moving ship. I drop my drill, still tethered to a thick metal strap on my belt, and scramble for the lead anchoring me to the ship. For a second, there's a slackness in the tether. My breaths become quicker and panicked.

"Uhhh!" I yelp. No one's close enough to respond, and my heart beats faster and harder.

Like a rug being torn from under me, I hover above the ship as it speeds up below me. One second, two seconds, and then... I exhale deeply as my tether jerks as it tenses. Gods...

Sealed.
Safe... for now.

The harness on my suit catches the floating drill, dangling from my belt like the tail of a drifting comet...

"*...and if we clear up by four, I won't have to look at your ugly ass either!*" a familiar voice barks.

The comm static clears, and through the small lighting on my helmet, it shines on the boots of one of my crew.

"*Ark?*" our foreman, Yan's gruff voice calls. "*What the hell are you doing?*"

"L-lost my footing," I manage, getting back to my feet again. His face isn't visible, but his helmet cocks slightly to the right.

"Glad you're safe. Now, if you're done screwin' around, we need your hands."

"Aye, sir!"

As I reel in my drill, I can't ignore the change in my foreman's voice.

Yan contains his giant six-and-a-half-foot form and copper red hair within the confines of his baggy spacesuit. His gruff voice matches his no-bullshit demeanour: hands on his hips, helmet visor peering down at me. He's always been firm but fair, and today is no exception. I can't make out the details of his face when I look up, but I hear how pissed he is.

Of course...

With drill in hand, I carefully approach the damaged quadrant. The dossier report in my helmet's tiny screen lists off electrical shorts and tile insulation damage. A quick job, but still dangerous.

My helmet illuminates the faded chrome panel ahead, and each screw I undo quickly floats right into my hand. The last one, however, is halfway stripped and refuses to budge.

"Come on..."

I hear a soft *tink* and see the screw prone against my visor. My left hand shakes as I reach for it, and as I do, I'm scanning my helmet for a crack. A small tear. Anything.

After the twentieth time I search, it all checks out. My breathing finally slows as my hand comes down. I've only been out here for a few minutes and nervous sweat already beads down my face. I crouch down. The drill doubles as a fabricator, re-stitching insulation fibres back together.

As I take my eyes off of my work site for a moment, Yan walks past my field of vision as he inspects the others' work. Every once in a while, he reappears, stops, and peers out toward the lower aft of the ship. What's he staring at?

I come back to the panel, and I seal up the wires with a smaller soldering tool.

Mission complete.

My hands shake with the vibrations of the drill, and the metal panel seals back up at my feet.

I hear the hurried inhale and muffled exhale of my breath. When I'm inside the ship, the sound of my tools, the surrounding people, and the chatter of other crew members are commonplace.

But out in the vacuum of space, it's different.

The sounds of my instruments, normally very loud inside the ship, become nonexistent out here, and in the moments when no one is talking on the comms, the silence itself is deafening. It's ... eerie.

The vibrations of my drill stop; the sudden thud of my magnetic boots clings to the outer hull, and the echoes of the chatter from the comms jostle my eardrums, shocking them awake.

I scan my surroundings, and out of my peripheral vision, I see there are other people working on repairs to the same stretch of hull. Beyond that, I don't see much from the lit tubing inside my visor. Only a small area of one square meter is visible on the ground. Now that the work is done, all the nerve endings in the back of my neck settle, and a welcome calm settles over me.

I've got time – and far more of it than the other repair techs.

I reach down to my wrist and press a small blue button, turning off my helmet light. The ground below me goes dark. As I look up, I catch my breath. That once black canvas gives way to a startling array of stars. Like someone drew an inspired brushstroke across the abyss, creating twinkling spheres and faraway galaxies. They reveal themselves in different shades of luminous colour, and the closest stars fly by quickly.

It's a single moment of calm in a chaotic ocean fraught with peril.

"*Report in!*" Yan barks.

I gasp, snapping out of my trance and fumble to switch my helmet light back on, sinking the universe back into darkness.

"*Lemme hear some good news,*" he grumbles.

"*Quadrant 4, complete.*"

"*Quadrant 2, complete.*"

"Quadrant 3, c-complete," I say, voice wavering.

"*Ugh. Quadrant 1, in progress.*"

Ohhh... no two words bring on nervous sweats more than 'in progress' when out on the hull.

"*Gods, man, you taking a nap over there?*" Priam jabs.

"*Oh, yeah, dozed* right *off!*" Kai says, crouched over Quadrant 1. "*Just saw a mess of wires and thought 'hey, now's a great time to do fuck-all.' The hell do you think I've been doing?! Take a look for yourself!*"

Each section, or quadrant, is four meters by four meters, each next to one another in a square. My light, as well as everyone else's, focuses on Quadrant 1.

And Kai wasn't kidding. No wonder it's still in progress: a giant charred hole bore the impact of a thousand tiny meteor fragments. Sure, the tiny pellets are a good source of pure mineral ore, but true to his words, there are dozens of frayed wires and two broken pipes below the thick metal of the hull. If the meteors had gone deeper, it's what all of us techs would call a *really bad day*.

"*Shit. It's going to take another hour to get this patched...*" Kai groans over the comms.

"*Better than getting hit with another shower,*" Yan barks. "*Now batten down! All hands to Quadrant 1, on the double! Priam, get in there with some copper, and, Ark, you an' Kai start soldering!*"

More time out in space means only one thing: the chance of something going wrong goes up.

Anything from running out of oxygen to a tool that breaks or the spike in adrenaline that can make you do something real stupid. The list goes on... and it sucks for the entire team. Everyone's affected, not just the one tech, and it's why every second counts.

"*We'll need the fabricator on the bottom left. Insulation's all torn to shit.*" An unfamiliar feminine voice adds. They must be a new transfer.

Their voices are muffled, and I can't make out each tech's face. The only three that stand out are Kai, crouched over a gas main; Priam, with a wheel of copper wire; and Yan, standing by over the site. As I take a knee and lend Kai my fabricator, Yan's luminous helmet scans over our work, and he motions back toward a fixed point in the sky. Again, what's caught his attention seems far afield from the stretch of the ship, and as much as I want to ask, I know better. It falls in line with the two commandments of the crew:

You don't question the chain of command, and
If you take care of the ship, it will take care of you.

"*Damn it!*" Kai groans. "*The drill bit's stuck! Anyone got a wedge?*"

"Hang on, you can use—" I say as a sudden tremor quakes beneath me. I peer down, and there's a two-by-two-metre divot in a panel outside the quadrant.

Then another tremor. Then another.

"*Meteors!*" Yan cries, leap-running in what would look like slow-motion inside the ship. "*Shields up!*"

I hit my right wrist as hard as I can, activating my *Vinár*-class multi-tool and stinging the bones underneath. Metal unfurls from my wrist, fanning out into a circular shield. It covers me completely as I stare at the ground. My left arm trembles and shakes against the coming debris, and all I can hear is static again.

The comms are dead.

I spin my head; my neck jerks as the dread *thud* of space rocks collides with the outer hull and rattles my bones. The rest of my crew cower below their shields, same as me.

In front of me, Kai inches toward the open gas main, trying to protect it from getting hit.

Too late.

A meteor strikes two meters from my position and collides with the gas main, and all of it appears like it's happening in slow motion. Much like Yan's sprint across the hull.

The impact.

Followed by a brief yet powerful explosion.

Kai shoots like a missile into the abyss. The pressurized gas sends him flying, his tether extends into the void, and there's nothing I can do to stop it.

Seconds painfully stretch to minutes. I don't look away... because if I do, I'm afraid I'll lose him forever. And in this last fleeting moment, from what I see, Kai has only a few moments left before his frayed tether snaps.

I have to do something.

"Man overboard!" I cry over the comms as time speeds up again.

No reply.

Only static.

I leap up and dash toward Kai's anchor, and I attach my tether to his lead.

Gods, I'm dumb...

I switch off the shield on my wrist, hook the drill to the hull, and disengage the magnetism from my boots. I spring down in a squat and ready myself to jump.

It's now or never!

"Aaah!" I shout, springboarding myself upward.

The ship continues moving, so instead of jumping vertically, both he and I are banking at forty-five degrees.

Suddenly, it happens.

His tether snaps.

My hands clumsily grapple his lead as it sputters away, and as I do, Kai stops.

My right arm jerks, and the loose motion of my ball joint makes me think that it's torn out of its socket. Like thousands of knives have pierced my shoulder, a sharp radiating pain almost takes the wind out of me. Like before, my stomach quickly flips.

"Ugh...!" I groan.

Wide-eyed, I feel tears stream down my face as my mouth hangs open. Kai's suspended in the abyss, his arms outstretched.

He's not floating away. I made it in time... thank the gods...

"...*Ark!*" Priam cries in the chamber of my helmet. "*Ark! Where the hell are you?!*"

"*Holy shit!*" another voice cries out. It sounds like Kai.

"Hey," I say between gasps, my mouth dry and chest burning, "I've got you. I've got you."

I tie his tether to mine, right arm in searing agony... but I ensure my words aren't an empty promise.

"*Ark! W-what the hell happened?*"

"Don't worry about it. We're getting you down. Just hold on tight..."

As the words leave my mouth, they sound serenely calm... but everything in my head has gone to shit. But I can't let him know. That'll mess with his head, and right now, we need to get back down.

"*Do. Not. Move,*" Yan cautions. "*We're reeling ya both in.*"

I take a moment and realise Kai and I are being drawn back to the ship. As we inch lower, I seriously struggle to keep my arm at my side. When it drifts off into the nothingness of space, it twists at the socket in my shoulder... like if it were being crushed in a vice. While I can shift it a little, every time is hellish...

"Aye, sir." The words tumble out of my mouth.

At last, my feet touch the metal panels of the hull.

Secure.

Safe.

Priam's separates me from Kai, and he scans me over with a medical wand. I'm close enough to his visor to make out the details of his face... and he looks like he's seen a ghost.

"*Y-you saved him!*" he says, the medic's wand wobbling in his outstretched hand, "*How the hell'd you do that?! How'd your arm not rip off?!*"

"I... uh..." My words tumble out.

I struggle to stand as a sharp pang of guilt hits my chest.

"Luck," I lie, shrugging. "Can't be anything else."

He doesn't answer... but instead, his helmet shifts to the side. As I get back more blood flow to my feet and hands, the pain gets worse.

"*What... what were you thinking?*" Priam asks me, breathless and questioning my sanity.

"I couldn't just *let him* die!" I finally say, frantic and defensive. "I-I mean, you'd do the same for me, right?!"

"*No, I wouldn't have...*" he said with a faint sigh of resignation.

The hell? Did he really say that?

It might've been too faint for the untrained ear, but not for someone jacked up on adrenaline. Like when I trained on the mats inside the ship, all of my senses heighten as my heart beats faster. I wished I heard differently, but the way Priam's helmet lowered gave it away. I think it must have slipped, but the damage is already done. My eyes sting thinking about it...

Yan drags me to the side, startling me as he grips the loose fabric of my suit, pulling me away from Priam. And as I'm drawn in, the rest of the crew tend to Kai.

"*You crazy, stupid, arrogant asshole!*" he says. "*Do you realise what you just did?!*"

I shake my head, wordless and shaky. Pissed. All I can do, in my simple state of mind, is point upward with my left hand. All of it crashes down on my head: the pain, Kai, Priam, and now Yan... my whole body shakes, and a creeping cold spreads through my hands.

"*That's right,*" Yan stresses, "*you saved his ass from oblivion! Recklessly! You jumped off the bloody ship like a maniac! What's wrong with your arm?*"

"Tether."

"*Right...*" he begins. "*Get yourself looked at... an' like I said, I'm glad you're okay.*"

His words carry like a father's or older brother's might, and as they reach my ears, I blink hard and let go of my breath. One that I didn't realise I was holding. His words, normally like sandpaper, were more soothing than I was expecting.

"*Team, how is he?*" Yan asks the group surrounding Kai.

"*He's got a few small tears in his suit that we've patched,*" someone pipes up, "*and a minor O2 leak in the gauge, but nothing serious to report. He should be able to make it back to the ship.*"

"*Good! Ark,*" he says, turning back to me, "*Priam will get you and Kai to the med bay. You've got the rest of the day off, both of you.*"

Oooh, fun, an entire day? Great...

I nod, holding my arm as it gets heavier and more useless.

"*And, Ark?*" Yan says. "*Today, you took care of the ship. I personally don't care how you did it, but you did it. The captain'll be informed of it.*"

Gods... wait, did I hear that right? The *captain*?! The words send a shiver down my spine and butterflies into my stomach... but I still might need to hurl from before.

"*Hey,*" Priam says, "*can you walk?*"

My nostrils flare as Priam approaches. Wordless, I give him a thumbs-up with my good arm and point toward Kai. From what I've seen, he's barely moved an inch since our feet made landfall. I'm uneasy about his condition, but the on-staff medic cleared him.

When Priam approaches, he's already carrying a folded cloth out from his first-aid kit. He points at my arm, and I nod for him to secure my bum arm into a sling.

"*I'm... I didn't...*" Priam says, woeful.

"Forget it," I say, shaking my head quickly. "I've already forgotten about it."

But I haven't. Priam has always looked out for the team, for the crew at large, and I always thought he'd have my back. That's why I assumed he'd save me in similar circumstances.

"*Yeah?*" Priam asks.

"Yeah," I lie.

Would he really let me die...? I don't want to think about it... if I do, all the hurt and anger bottled up inside of me is going to go off on Priam.

And Kai doesn't need that right now.

Priam hands me a grappling gun, one that shoots magnetic tethers to far-flung panels of the ship. Considering the wreckage of our previous safety net, a clear shot to the airlock makes the most sense.

As my hand visibly shakes, I take a shot. Gas escapes both sides of the barrel, and a rippling thread of fabric flies like a bullet toward the airlock. Well, technically, it lands on the post of a comms antenna. If it didn't, the lead attached to the gun would extend out and hit me in the helmet with the recoil. Not fun. I've seen it happen. And with everything else that has happened on the job today, I take my sweet-ass time.

"*Bull's-eye!*" Priam proclaims.

I get he's trying to make nice, but what he said hurt. Badly. It's going to take more than that.

Supported under his arm is Kai, who is moving home at a decent pace. His helmet meets mine. I can barely see his face from the lights within our visors, but we exchange something between the two of us.

What it is, I don't know.

Gratitude?

Probably.

It doesn't take us long to follow along the tether back to the airlock. All three of us step over the ledge and onto the other side of the ship. With my good hand, I release the airlock and disable the magnetism from my boots. We climb down into the ship, helping Kai along, and the manufactured gravity of the ship anchors us to the ladder.

Priam goes down first, next goes Kai, and I follow behind. I climb down, one rung at a time, with one arm jimmy-rigged to my suit. The pain's getting better, now that it's bound to my chest and not flopping about in space. And I haven't lost my lunch. That's a plus.

As we descend, the door above me automatically seals shut. The tunnel leading down makes my suit more visible, its keyhole lights aligning every foot or so toward the bottom. The faint sound of a hiss escapes, mere feet below, and Priam's hand moves away from the release console.

The locker's only a couple of rungs below.

My left arm and feet carry the weight of me and my suit, and I hobble down one last rung. I'm trying not to make the radiating pain in my arm any worse, so I shimmy down carefully until the last sealing doors shut above my helmet.

The locker room is stark white because of the side panelling and the floodlights on the ceiling. It must be hell to clean, but it works really well to determine if anyone is tracking space debris or blood into the ship.

I hop down from the ladder, and Priam's helping Kai with his helmet and gloves. As I take a few steps to the centre of the locker, I melt onto a nearby bench and unlatch my helmet with my free hand.

"I'm going to need your help in a sec," I say as loud as I can, realizing how weak I sound.

The comms shut off once we set foot within the ship, so I sound like I'm talking underwater. My helmet starts fogging up from the humidity inside my helmet. We've been out for a while, and it gets hot quickly in these suits.

I follow Priam's visor, and... good, he heard me.

"You got it." Priam nods back at me.

I need two hands to remove the helmet, and I'm down to one. When Kai is finally out of his gear, Priam walks up to me, looks me over, and lifts my helmet up.

The glint of the overhead lights reflects off of my helmet, and as it catches my eye, my teal tattoo comes into sight. It interweaves lines of artistic knots that runs the length of my left cheekbone. I can also see my matted hair in my visor, like Kai's. And the second the helmet's off, the sensation of the circulating air from the upper vents is freeing.

Oh, gods... suddenly the smell of carbon and sulphur hits me. Like someone burned an animal carcass and rubbed it on my suit, the scent wafts everywhere.

"Ugh...!" I gag, smacking a gloved hand to my mouth.

Hey, if I throw up now, it'll be *way* better than if I still had my helmet on... that happened once, and I *really* don't want it to happen again! What stops me, though, is the smell of chlorine filtering in through the air ducts.

In the three-way battle between my nervous sweats, cosmic burnt steak, and the recycled air, the chlorine wins. Hands down. The barrage of scents is uncomfortable, but I've got it together.

As Priam smacks the main release panel, two heavy blast doors slowly retract into the walls. The first thing that invites me home is the overwhelming scent of flora. Trees, bushes, flowers, vegetables, and herbs flood the locker, and beyond it comes the chatter of our fellow crew passing by the exit.

We step out, and my lungs breathe in the thick air of our deck, and there's a sweet aroma that stays with me. There are a couple of spice trees in the garden module, which leads up to three decks in height. Light creeps through the corridors ahead, and people come and go. The mezzanine comes into sight... and it instantly brings back happy memories of when I was a kid.

Once we're actually on the floor of the deck, two guards on our left and right nod us both forward. And each of them wears light armour vests, tinted grey, and tote a medium-sized shotgun, in case of an invading force. Raiders and the odd pirate, mostly. Nothing we haven't dealt with before. The rounds are non-lethal, loaded with rubber bullets and small electrical charges meant to immobilize.

Then, suddenly, we stop.

"Heh," escapes my lips.

"Ha..." Kai adds, his arm slung over my good shoulder.

"Hehe," Priam echoes.

"Ha!" I laugh.

We all share the same expression. They're as nervously relieved as I am.

Holy shit, we actually survived!

We're alive! *I'm* alive! Death showed up, and I *punched it* in the face!

"... I wouldn't be laughin' if I were you," a voice breaks in between us.

Yan strolls past us, adorned in his spacesuit, minus the helmet. He gives the guards a nod, which they both return, and he glances in my direction, one eyebrow raised.

"Your mother's gonna kill you," he adds, reminding me how mortal I really am...

Chapter 2

Takh'Aliah

2 Hours Later, Cabin 342 of the Eridas Deck, Nautilus, Generation Vessel

I move gracefully from the stove to the sink and from the sink to a roasting pan. The long ruffles of my flowing tunic ripple in the air and cease as I approach the island of my open kitchen counter. I hum as I work, the tune soft and melodic as my right hand works swiftly along a plastic cutting board. As I do, my mind keeps note of the ticking hands on the kitchen clock.

Tick. Tock.

Tick. Tock.

"First Ark, now Ann'Elise," I sigh, grabbing an onion. "They don't stay little for very long, do they?"

Laying my blade down, I tie back a few loose strands of my wavy raven-black hair; and out of the corner of my eye, the sheens of a couple rogue silver hair strands catch in the overhead lights. Before I get back to work, I rub the sweat off of my cheeks, noticing faint stress lines. Ones that I gained before my children, Ark and Ann'Elise, and I made the *Nautilus* our home.

The knife in my hand saws through onion confidently, quickly, and without error. My children won't be returning for another hour. I have time to work some things out.

Tick.

The knife in my hand stops moving halfway through the last onion on my board. My breath catches in my throat, and a sudden gasp escapes my lips.

I look down, and blood trickles out of a nick from my blade. The metallic smell of iron from the cutting board reaches my nose, forcing my heart to beat faster and harder. No matter how much I try to keep calm, to hold a stream of intrusive memories at bay... the dam breaks as I'm drawn back to the day my little girl, Ann'Elise, came into this world.

Tock.

As we ran for our lives, my lungs burned, my muscles ached, and the man I loved led me by the hand. I held my four-year-old child close to my hip. The orbital station was running out of corridor. The rapid sound of burning plasma exiting a gun filled my ears. Our son was crying, and my comforting words barely reached his ears. My heart skipped a beat as we turned a corner... there was only one lifeboat left.

Tick.

"Are you strapped in?" he asked, toppling a shipping crate over as a barricade.

"Not yet... hurry!" I cried. "They're coming; we don't have much time!"

My heart sinks to my feet as a glimpse of sorrow tinged his eyes.

"Luc...?" I said, my voice wavering.

His hand reached down to my abdomen, heavy with our daughter, and I could feel his love through his touch.

"They're not here for you or Ark..." he says. "They're here for me."

Tock.

He pulled away, like sand slipping away from my fingers... and I instinctively threw my arms up and grasped at his arms and the cuffs of his shirt. Sheer panic wracked me, and I trembled as I held on for dear life.

"N-no..." I stammered. "No, you can't leave... not now!"

A horrible, gnawing sickness reached up deep within my gut. My chest felt tighter as I searched Luc's eyes, pleading with him as I did.

Nothing...

The emotions he had held back until now appeared on his ruggedly handsome face. Tired, worn out... but not broken.

"Mommy?" my son called, safe within the pod. His voice fades into an echo, paling compared to the narrowing window I had Luc for.

I watched as my husband quickly looked over his shoulder, his face etched with lines of strain and grief. My gaze didn't leave his, and I immediately sobbed as he pried my fingers from him.

"I love you..." were his last words.

Tick.

His arms shoved me backward into the pod, close to Ark. I watched, helpless, as Luc sealed the hatch on the lifeboat from the outside. Frantically, I jolted back up and wailed on the thick transparent window of the hatch as tears streamed down my cheeks.

"Don't you leave me!" I sobbed loudly, my heart tying tightly like knotted rope... choking me... "Don't you leave us!"

His hand touched the glass, and he backed away... running in the opposite direction, and he disappeared forever as he turned a corner to the right. I cried in terror as our pursuers, unaware of the lifeboat beginning its ejection from the station, dashed in his direction.

Tock.

"M-Mommy, what's wrong?" Ark asked through sobs of his own. Again, his voice sounded distant, like a faraway echo.

Another contraction hit, and it felt like I was run through with a dagger with the speed of a monorail. She was early, and there was nothing I could do to stop her arrival.

"H-honey, you need to stay over there. Look away; cover your ears. Uh... Mommy's going to be okay, but you need to, ah... stay there, baby."

As I scrambled through the lifeboat's med kit, the expression on my son's face stayed with me as the stabbing pain in my abdomen left.

Terror mixed with confusion. I had just lost the love of my life, and I was alone in this... but Ark had also lost his father and couldn't escape seeing me in pain.

All of it was wrong...

"No, I'll help!" Ark protested, visibly shaking.

"Uh..!" I grunt.

Damn it!

"Stay over there!" I said with my eyelids shut tightly, struggling to breathe.

When I did open my eyes, after that contraction ripped its way through me, I looked over to the back corner, where Ark sat.

And in the brief moments of silence, between my loss and agony, dizzy from I didn't know what, I watched as my little boy huddled in the far corner of the pod. His hands were above his head, face against the wall... whimpering so softly I could barely hear.

"I'm sorry..." I said, wincing, "I'm so sorry!"

Tick.

I gasp, back in my kitchen, and far from the hellish visions of my... *our* past and my daughter's beginning. The knife slowly cuts through the rest of the onion. Metal hitting plastic.

Tock.

"Aargh!" I scream, flinging my arms up at the clock on the kitchen wall.

Ripping it off the wall, I heave the damn thing up and *slam* it against the countertop, frantically ripping at its small metal back panel, my nails digging like claws until it finally comes loose. With my other hand, I reach in and remove its entrails: a single battery.

"Yaah!" I howl, twisting my hips as I hurl it against the wall.

Bang!

Gasping for air, I tremble as I brace myself against the counter... freezing as it suddenly dawns on me. What I just did.

"O-oh..." I stammer, my arms heavy.

Straight ahead, against the light shining down from the kitchen lights, there's a two-inch divot in the metal wall of my cabin hallway. As I let go of the counter, standing by myself, tears roll down my cheeks.

What's wrong with me? I'm the daughter of a War Chief. How did I let myself become so irredeemably *weak*?

The front door clicks open.

Tick.

My body stiffens. They're early.

Tock.

"Hey, Mom!" my daughter exclaims, coming through the door. "We're home!"

Tick.

I breathe deeply and stare down at the clock face down on the kitchen counter. My hands rest at my sides, still shaking from before. My lips quiver as I wipe the tears from my face and see my little girl, who, until tonight, was fourteen years old. I tightly squint, fighting the sting threatening to burst into tears.

Okay.... reel it all in.

Tock.

"Happy birthday, dear!" I exclaim warmly.

A phantom pang hits me in my chest. I hate that I can't separate my baby's beginning from my beloved's end.

Tick.

I have to get this under control. They deserve better from me. I'm their rock, and I do not break.

Into the living room walks an almost carbon copy of my younger self. My little girl, Ann'Elise, undoes her long raven hair and shakes it loose. Its fine strands remind me strongly of my husband's soft hair...

I waste no time moving past the sofa and chairs and hug my little girl tightly.

"Mom! Hi!" She giggles. "It's good to see you too!"

"Heya," Ark says behind her.

I loosen my grip and look past Ann'Elise's shoulder, and my son, Ark, strolls through the doorway. I can't ignore the distant expression on his face as he walks by us, hangs his pack on a hook, and disappears behind me. Maybe he went on a spacewalk today?

He *hates* those.

"Hey, pumpkin," I ask Ark, "how was work?"

He doesn't answer right away, but the silence ends with Ann'Elise breaking free and tossing her running shoes to a magnetised mat near the door. Her shoes fall haphazardly, contrasting Ark's neatly stashed work boots.

But before I get an answer, I catch his gaze fixed to the far left of the hall, where I left a dent in the cabin wall. For a split second, his face flashes with concern.

"Uh, it wasn't great. There was a lot of damage to the hull this morning, so they commissioned my team for the job. We couldn't use drones... there was too much damage, so Yan sent us out for a spacewalk."

I was right.

I face him, take two large strides toward my son, and bear hug him as tightly as I did my little girl.

"Ohhh," I say, "that must have been really rough! Supper's almost ready, but I'll get you some tea for your nerves."

"M-Mom, hey!" he protests as I kiss him on the cheek. I catch him roll his eyes, blushing with embarrassment.

"No 'heys'. Sit!" I insist.

As I glide back to the kitchen, a resurging confidence emerges in my step. The melody of Ann'Elise humming echoes from her room, and I expect she's changing out of her gear and into casual attire. I set a kettle to boil and grab a small puck of tea and plunk it into a nearby teapot. Her humming grows louder as she exits her room, and the ache of a smile spreads across my face.

"Oh, Mom! You won't believe it," Ann'Elise says, "but Ark saved someone at work today!"

Tock.

Keep it together, Takh'Alia.

A familiar wave of nausea threatens to overtake me. It's not the same as back then, but it's similar enough.

"Oh?" I ask.

"Ann'Elise!" Ark chides his sister. "Um, yes... I, uh, I did. There was a minor incident on the surface of the keel, but my team and I saw to it. Kai's safe and sound now!"

Tick.

"What happened to him? To Kai?" I ask Ark.

"He, uh... a meteor knocked him off. I went after him."

"You... jumped out into space? Risking your own life?" I ask, composing myself as my hands tremor beneath the table.

"Yeah..." he replies.

Tock.

The recent memory of Luc running from the lifeboat, watching as he disappeared from sight, comes flooding back. And now Ark could have... he might have died, in the same way, for someone else.

"And I heard it from a surgeon at the medic's station on Lagash Deck as I handed him his package. Ark's a hero!" Ann'Elise beams with pride.

Like I have for most of her life, I save face with a cordial mask. By drawing up the subterfuge I was taught by my clan's council, I smile intently at my daughter's words... and my eyes go to Ark's face. His expression is empathetic and quizzical, as if to ask me:

'Are you alright?'

Tick.

No. Far from it... but my eyes soften, and I give him a slight nod. I'm guilty for lying, but it comforts him.

I slow my breathing, trying to quell the shakes, but I can't stop it...

Damn it Takh'Alia, calm down!

Tock.

"That... was a foolish but very brave thing you did today. I'm very grateful you're still alive."

It's not much, but it's all I can muster right now. I keep my gaze on him, and from his expression, he seems to understand my meaning. Ark has always been perceptive to unspoken words, even as a child. The pain of almost losing my son touches him deeply – it's clear in his expression.

"Yeah, me too, Ark," Ann'Elise teases him with a gentle poke to the ribs. "Oh, Mom! I ran a route past your school today, and Amaya got me these runners!"

The whistle of the kettle begins as a slow whine and picks up in pace as Ann'Elise unzips her hung-up pack and brings out a pair of leather shoes... A gift from the woman who looked after my children following Luc's death while the deck's counsellor treated me. For Ann'Elise, it was the first three months of her life. I should be grateful, but those lingering scars of guilt cut deeply into my heart. It's time I'll never get back with my baby girl, all while I was too weak to pick myself back up again...

The clock seems to have stopped ticking, drowned out by a growing howl of the kettle... until suddenly, it stops. A hand gently clasps my own, and when I glance up from my trembling hand, it's my son.

"Hey," Ark says, "I can take over for a bit. You can have a rest if you're feeling tired."

His dark cobalt-blue eyes look back at me, with the same irises I possess, bearing kindness, compassion, and understanding. I don't deserve such a wonderful son... not after pushing him so hard to be strong as a child... and not after keeping my babies at a distance...

"Hey," Ann'Elise pipes up, her voice sounding so sweet and innocent, "it'll be okay. We'll play nice while you sleep."

Her soothing words almost bring up a sob in my chest.

I exit the kitchen, linger in the hallway before my room, and glance back at my children.

"Thank you both for taking over for a bit," I say, bowing gracefully out before entering my room.

Once in, I close the metal sliding door behind me, facing it.

My eyes scrunch together tightly, and I clasp my mouth. Agonizing cries leave me, rising deep from my belly and crashing, muffled, against the wall of my interlocked fingers and trembling hands. I sob, quietly, so as not to worry my children more than I already have. The tremors in my hands have spread throughout my body like a disease, and with every gasp, my whole body shakes.

Guilt overtakes me... and again *weak* for crying over something that can't ever change. And what's more, it's not their fault!

A stream of tears runs down my cheeks, drips down from the curve of my chin, and rolls down the lengths of my wrists. My hand gently hits the hard surface of my forehead, and I lean against it. My head swims, and so I slowly squat, seat myself down on a small ornate rug, and keep my head against the steel of the door. My eyelids are tired and heavy. The deep breaths that rattle in and out of my lungs are painful yet soothing. They slow down, and for a moment, my eyelids shut.

"Aha!"

I startle awake, but I'm no longer on guard. Have I been asleep long?

"Who cares if that's where it goes on the table? Hey, quit it! Gods, you're weird!" Ann'Elise exclaims.

Thinking about my two beautiful children, I can't help but smile. I remember in pieces, patches from my childhood, how I got along with my stepmother's children, and... how she treated me like one of her own daughters.

Again, I'm grateful for the village of people my family has called home.

Okay, Takh'Alia... it's time to get up.

I shift myself onto my feet, feel the creak and crack of my knee and ankle joints, and situate myself on the balls of my feet. I command my thighs to lift me up, bracing myself against the cold metal of the door. As I right myself, I stand, and I remember the burgundy package I left on top of the tall dresser behind me. My fingers reach it, and suddenly my heart flutters; like I was before, I get excited for the anniversary of the day.

Today's her day, and I don't want to miss any more moments in her life. I don't want to be weighed down by any more of this pain and grief I hold on her birthday.

Those days are done.

It's time to move forward.

I wave my hand over a panel near the door, and it slides open. Once I step out into the well-lit dining room, the aromas of my hard work flit across the air.

"Well, I think you're an amorphous crab for dropping out of the competition! You've been training with a wooden sword your whole life!" Ann'Elise protests.

"How the hell am I supposed to compete with torn ligaments? They'd wipe the floor with me!" Ark counters.

"Nooo! Can't they mesh that with synthetics?" she says, her voice determined while her frantic expression gives her away. She secretly implores Ark not to give up.

"Yeah, they can... and I'd be out of work for a week to recover from surgery!" he retorts, cheeks flush and his nose scrunched up.

My hand runs past the island counter of polished oak, and my eyes gleam at the pot of tea Ark prepped. I glance at the table, and my children have laid out the meal, set places, and brought a bottle of red wine. The beginning of a smile draws across my lips at seeing how thoughtful they've both become.

"Oh, hey! Welcome back, Mom!" Ann'Elise greets. "You gotta make Ark give the fighter's ring a chance tomorrow! He's worked too hard to pass that up!"

She pleads with me wholeheartedly with the shrill in her voice and a noticeable desperation deep within her irises.

"Hmm..." I say, turning to Ark, "I could do that, and ask him to best his opponents with a literal arm tied behind his back. I could do that."

Frustration, pain, and exhaustion slip through, show up in the creases of his brow and the defeat marring his face. When he was younger, I pushed him to fight competitively. I did this so that he would be strong and stand before the God of War with courage and honour... but Ann doesn't know the whole truth.

"But... Ark already saved a comrade from certain death. I would say he has nothing to prove tomorrow. My dear daughter, he has already honoured this household well enough until the next festival. Wouldn't you say?"

Ark looks tired, but his spirits seem high. Relieved. That makes me happy.

"Well, um... yeah. Okay..." Ann'Elise replies sheepishly.

"And Ark is a grown man, as you are quickly stepping out onto the stage of womanhood. Honestly, I don't believe I can tell either of you to do anything anymore."

I say this knowing there won't be a next competition for Ark.

When he was only five, I saw Ark hurt another boy. I remember when he came to find me, sobbing, horror still fresh in his eyes from when he struck that child in the side. The boy had fractured ribs, sending him to the infirmary.

"*H-how did I do that?*" he asked me.

"*It's because you're special. Like me and your sister.*"

The fear of hurting others plastered on his face from before fades into nothing.

"Once your arm heals," I say, turning to Ark, "will you help me with the next class of guards? The new ones are clumsy on the mats and could use finesse in their techniques."

"Yeah, absolutely," Ark replies in a higher octave than before, his face alight.

I watch as both Ark and Ann'Elise beam at my words. *Lucas, if you can see us, I hope you're proud of them.*

"Oh," I begin, drawing the purple package from my lap to the top of the table, "I got you something special this year. Once more, happy birthday, dear!"

I never tire of watching her face light up as she receives her gift. Another steppingstone, on a journey we're on together, that I will cherish forever.

"Oh, Mom, it's beautiful! It's just like something you'd wear! Thank you!" Ann'Elise squeals in delight, clasping her hands together. As I catch the glimpse of her eyes misting up, her hurried arms wrap around my neck.

"You're most welcome," I say, disengaging. "I want you to have a great time tomorrow. You said this morning that Natalia and the others were getting excited?"

"Oh, yeah, are they ever! It's all we talk about!" Ann beams in a wide, toothy grin. "It's their first festival too!"

Her smile is contagious, as always.

My daughter sits down, and she grows quiet. A sudden departure from the glee she displayed moments before.

"Hey, Mom?" Ann'Elise asks quietly. She looks up at me with her big beautiful sky-blue eyes. "Um... can you tell me something about Dad?"

Her voice cracks a little as she casts her head down, like she did something wrong.

I'm taken aback but not undone like before. It never takes too long to think of my beloved, on all the memories I've treasured... both before and after he left.

"Well, not unlike our intrepid Ark," I begin, my face hurting as I smile again, "your father was always brave. Reckless, but very brave."

I pause for a moment. Both my children are captivated.

"But one of the most endearing things about him was that he always made a big deal about events – whether it was a date, watching Ark excitedly take his first few steps... or embracing his inner child at a festival."

Chapter 3

Ann'Elise

"Awwwugh!" I yawn.

Every joint in my arms and legs snaps, straightens, and shiver along with everything else in my body. It's all part of being a runner, but I don't mind.

No, I *especially* don't mind this morning because *today is the day!* My eyes widen as an electric surge of excitement runs through me!

The first thing I notice, as I blink a second time, is the star-decorated ceiling of my cabin room. The UV rays from the lamp above me switch on every morning at exactly 6:30 a.m. It does with all our cabins and keeps us all working on the same clock.

I raise my hands up, wiggle my fingers and toes, and giggle softly to myself. When the last of it escapes my mouth, I flop my hands down on either side of my hips in bed.

"Oh, it's gonna be a *good* day," I whisper under my breath, smiling as I do.

Anticipation builds like a fluttering butterfly in my chest, and I think about how my friends and I will go to the festival for the first time. I throw off my blanket as I think of all the attractions and sights I've never seen, and truly, everything is *great!*

Clad in flannel jams and a loose-fitting black tank top, I jump up from my bed and open the sliding door to my room. It's with the press of a button, but it's *very* enthusiastic. My feet screech against the smooth surface of the floor, and I remember to grab the gorgeous, flowy dress Mom got for me. While it's still tucked away, hints of fine white cotton, bronze embroidery, and loose leather straps peek out of the burgundy shawl that holds it. The patterns are a little hard to make out in this light, but the designs themselves make my jaw drop.

I'm definitively wearing that today!

With my dress bundled up and in hand, I leap through my doorway, turn the corner, and find my footing in Ark's unlocked room. As soon as I find myself there, in his room and as nimble as a dancer, I catch him snoring away with his comforter shielding his head. He even deactivated his UV light!

Well, this won't do...

"Ark...!" I whisper, trying to contain myself.

Nothing... ugh.

"Ark!" I repeat, my whisper stepping aside for a louder morning wake-up call.

Still nothing. Hmm...

"Okay, you asked for it," I say. "*Wake up*, Ark!"

A flying dive follows my last very obvious attempt at getting my lazy brother up. For a second, I'm airborne, and then I land near the foot of his bed... overshooting my target by a few feet. So I scramble, readying my arms. Screw being gentle. I shove him awake.

"Wake up, Ark!" I'm practically screaming now. "It's the festival day! Wake up or you'll miss it!"

Ark lets out a low, frustrated growl as his face surfaces from his shield of blankets. His hand reaches for something, but I'm too late in noticing. His second pillow shoots faster than I do, whacking the left side of my cheek and jostling my kneeling stance in that direction. Worth it. At least he's awake.

"Damn it, Ann'Elise, it's still early! I've got an alarm set and everything..."

I straighten myself, glance at him quizzically, and wait a couple of moments. As I do, the sound of a constant ringing blares.

"Oh, look at that," I tease, "*now* it's time to get up."

He groans a second time, loudly, followed by the same assaulting pillow from before. Now Ark launches it at me like a projectile, but it's still a win for me. I get the hint, though, and giggle in the process of a tactical retreat.

I burst from Ark's room and proceed to my next and final victim...

My long legs take wide strides toward Mom's room, and where I originally planned to make my presence known... I stop. Her door's already open.

"Oh?" I say.

Slowly, I peer into my mom's darkened room. It looks like the bed's made, the room's tidied... no Mom, though. I frown, cautiously entering her dark sanctum...

"Morning."

"Ah!" I scream.

Two warm, loving arms wrap beneath my collarbone, and my mother presses a kiss against my cheek. And... my body tenses like a spooked cat!

"How are you feeling today, dear?" she asks, and it definitely sounds like Mom's voice.

Phew...!

"I think I may have had a stroke, but other than, I'm great!" My voice squeaks.

"Wonderful! I saw you venture into Ark's room earlier. Is he awake?" she asks.

"He is now," I say, a devious grin spreading from my lips.

"Ah," she replies, "well, breakfast is ready. I've steeped a senku bark tea for you and coffee for Ark."

My mouth hangs agape. Mom's cooking always makes me happy, and with the festival today, my spirits soar even higher than before!

Before I head for the dining room, I pause and shift my gaze to the copper carafe on the dining room table.

"Um, actually, I was thinking of trying some coffee with you and Ark today. I figured, I'm fifteen, and I might as well start my morning as women do. I'll still have the tea though. I don't want to waste it!"

My mom stops and looks at me with a mixture of parental realization. What it is, I'm not sure, but if I were to guess, it would probably be a cross between motherly pride... and concern.

"Oh, honey, I'd love to share with you!" she begins, "but it is quite strong. Are you sure?"

"Yes," I stress, "today is a day for firsts!"

Mom shrugs, the peace never leaving her face, and pours me a cup of coffee as we both sit down. As I do, the first thing that hits me is the smell of toasted cardamom, cinnamon, and raw beet sugar. I do my damnedest to compose myself as I salivate.

She said it herself last night: I'm a woman now.

And women drink strong, spicy coffee.

I sip the steaming black liquid, and as it touches my tongue, I understand why my family likes it so much! It tastes rich, it smells warm and fragrant, and it doesn't leave a bitter lingering like I thought it would!

"Hm. I could get used to this," I say, trying to sound more grown up.

My mother smile brightly, and for the first time in a very long time, she actually seems at ease with herself. The stress lines on her face almost seem to disappear, the tension from last night melting away. A warmth surrounds me like a blanket as I think about Mom's recovery. A wonderful start to the day.

Beyond the market square of Eridas Deck, the misty community gardens completely transformed overnight. I fix my gaze on the front gate, where a dozen merchant stalls showcase jewellery from different ships in the Fleet and flowing silks and linens from the artisan castes.

"Ann, over here." A faint but recognizable voice rings through the air.

As Ark and Mom approach the crowd ahead, I whip around and face the direction my name is being called from. Among all the other girls at the festival, I'm one of the few dressed for a race.

"Coming!" I reply.

"Well! My Dears," Mom says, "remember to meet me at the dining tent by noon, and you both have yourself a wonderful time."

"Aw, Mom, I – okay," I protest... then catch myself.

"I know it's your first time at the festival," Mom adds, sounding guilty, "but it would really mean a lot to me if I could share this moment with you too."

Call it a sixth sense, but I walk on over to her and give her a tight hug.

"It's okay, Mom. You don't need to explain," I say with more heart and less of my usual fluff. "Just make sure you enjoy the morning too, alright?"

"D-deal. Absolutely!" She trips over her words, beaming at me.

"Great, I'll see you there!"

I can tell that yesterday evening was rough for Mom, being the day Dad died. And... what's a little quality time to help lift her spirits?

Mom nods graciously, and Ark waves his hand goodbye, cutting a path of his own.

"And try to stay out of trouble!" Ark yells from further away.

"Isn't that *my* line?!" I shout back.

Without another wasted second, I spin around again and race toward my friend.

"Welcome to the party," Natalia greets with a broad smile.

She brushes a hand through her short silver hair, hands falling to the sides of her ornate blue-and-white-patterned dress. Behind her calculating azure eyes, she seems just as giddy to be here as I am.

"Yes! Finally! Phew." I readjust the weight on my shoulders, my pack jolting against my back. It contains the dress from Mom, trinkets Ark salvaged, and my water bottle.

"Come on, Arjuna is waiting for us by the track. She said she wanted to place some bets before your race starts," she says as her eyes sparkle with calm excitement.

"Oh-my-gosh, you're adorable!" I squeal.

She blushes, quickly following me toward the fairgrounds.

Of all the introverts Arjuna and I adopted on this deck, Natalia is, without a doubt, our favourite.

The large habitation module of Eridas Deck garden became a bustling square in the span of one night. Some merchant stalls I recognize, lining the main path toward the elevator chute. Traders dealing in essentials, grocery stands, that kind of thing. But this... the smells, the throng of people moving in every direction, the new stands set up on the edges of the garden's walkways... I can't help but catch my breath, as *everyone* in the crowd is having a wonderful time!

"... and I am pleased to welcome other fairgoers today, each of you from different ships of the Fleet..." A booming, masculine voice comes from the centre of the garden. The man speaking is Hyueon, chief of Eridas Deck. He stands out, raised on a metal platform above the crowd.

For a second, we stop, halted by a large swath of our crew members and other visitors from the Fleet.

"Without further ado, we of the bridge and the council declare the first day of the Festival of Lumina open! May we celebrate a thousand more years together along the starway paths, free from the rule of the Republic!"

Everyone around me is cheering. Natalia whistles with her finger and thumb, and I get enveloped in the contagious excitement around me!

"Yeah!" I shout, clapping along.

I'm not sure *why* we'd want to be free from this 'Republic', but from what I've gathered over the years, it's not a great place to live: they don't migrate from system to system like we do, they're planet-bound for the most part, and the people in charge suck ... well, now that I think about it, maybe that's reason enough.

<hr />

"Hey! Over here!" Arjuna's voice carries over the sound of spectators.

Perched on the outer rail of the track, she waves at us both, legs kicking playfully against the fabric of her dress. The white stitched patterns lining the hem of the skirt come across as mysterious, like glyphs from a long-dead language. My mouth goes agape as we get closer, seeing the purple-dyed silk contrasting against her shoulder-length strawberry blonde hair.

"Good morning, ladies!" Arjuna beams at us, lifting off of the rail.

"Oh, it's going to be!" I say, stretching one leg behind me, butterflies fluttering in my stomach.

"You've got this," Natalia adds, her hand rising for a high five.

I return it, wobbling off balance as I do. "Whoa."

"*Careful* now," Arjuna chides, "we wouldn't want you all banged up before the race starts! We bet a lot on you to get first, considering how fast you are on the job!"

"Hehe, don't worry, I'll give it my all!" I lie.

A whistle from the judge's seat sends Arjuna and Natalia off the track.

"Alright! Runners, take your places; race is about to start!" the starter shouts, clearing off the last stragglers from the track.

Phew. Okay.

I give one last wave to my friends before finding my spot. The last thing I do before getting on all fours is tie my hair back into a tight ponytail. My bangs fall to the side, and I find the blocks with the back of my shoes.

Arjuna's right. I've been a courier for over a year, and now... it all comes down to this.

A race against other couriers from ships all across the Nomadic Fleet.

"Runners, on your marks..." the referee calls out "... get set..."

The stands go quiet. As I plant my hands down on coarse rubber, a couple of guards argue near the starboard exit. They seem tense...

No. Focus. Clear your head.

As the starter raises his gun, I brace my feet brace against the blocks, ready to launch off.

Bang!

Like on the job, I blast off like a rocket, and time slows down around me. Every muscle in my body electrifies, springing to life.

My feet fall rhythmically against the silicon track like the faint sound of drums in the distance, each of my arms swinging in sync with my hiked-up knees.

"Go, Ann!" Natalia's voice rises above the crowd. It's rare, and my spirits soar.

The ribbon's one hundred more meters away. It's faint, but it's in my sight. There are only a few of us in the lead now, and my lungs burn. As I pass the third leading runner... my heart sinks like a rock.

I purposely slow down.

"*Don't go for first,*" Mom said to me years ago. "*But don't settle for last either. Strive to succeed... just don't let them find out you're different.*"

My tear ducts sting as I let up, falling behind.

I was only thirteen when Mom cautioned me. It felt like I was betraying myself. I kept asking her why... with a blend of fury in my flushed cheeks and the irritating tears running down my cheeks.

"*Because being different is dangerous... no matter where you are,*" Mom said.

As much as it hurts, she's right, and I'll never forget it.

The third runner to my right loses pace, falling behind me real fast.

It's just me and another girl sprinting ahead. Her face is a mixture of agony and determination.

I envy her.

Snap!

The ribbon ahead of me gives way, the girl in front carrying it with her for a couple of steps, and I watch as she slows down, leaning over to catch her breath.

Aside from the burning in my lungs, stopping feels like the end of a quick jog. I take a couple of deep breaths, place my hands on my knees... and pretend to be tired. Ugh.

"Ohhh," Arjuna's voice says, "you were so close!"

"Yeah..." I say, and a fresh wave of heat hits my cheeks.

"Second isn't bad," Natalia counters. "You gave it your all; you should be proud of yourself."

Ohhhh, crap...

"Aw, thank you!" I say sweetly as Arjuna buries her face in her hands.

"Welp... what's a few trinkets worth of barter, right?" Arjuna says. "I'm still glad you placed high."

Yeah... it's hard to miss Arjuna's eye twitching even a kilometre away. And yes, I disappointed her... but I had to.

I won't make Mom cry.

Sweat drips from my brow like raindrops, and as the referee comes over, I arch back up and meet him face-to-face.

"Congratulations on second place!" he exclaims, handing me a shimmering chrome medal.

"Thank you."

Not my best... but I'll take it.

"And... there we are," I say, tying the shawl around my waist. "All done."

There's a long mirror in one of the circular changing tents, a little way from the vendor stalls. It took a while to change out of my smelly track clothes and slip on the gift Mom gave me. Now that it's actually on, I crane my neck forward, eyes fixed on the woman staring back at me.

"Wow," I blurt out.

It's a long-sleeved white dress, loose and flowing down to my wrists, where leather straps weave together into snug bracers. I stare down toward my feet, where the hem of my skirt's dyed a light burgundy, and above it are bronze threads woven into ornate linear patterns. As I lift my gaze up the mirror, I linger on the neck trim, lowered just below my collarbone, where a similar etching of bronze decorates a crescent over my chest. And to finish it all off, Mom gave me a dark burgundy shawl that I wrapped several times over my midriff. Its extra fabric flows down opposite sides of my waist, ending a foot above my ankles. As I examine it closer, my breath catches, following the intricately woven designs on the overlapping fabric. Its highlighted design matches the colour of my skirt's hem.

The best part? It breathes better than my track outfit!

"Hey!" Arjuna's voice rings into the tent. "Are you almost done? It's torture to wait by the stands and not grab a bite."

A loud, monstrous growl echoes from inside the tent... and it's coming from my tum.

"Almost th—I mean, a-all done!" I say, tripping over my words.

I burst from the changing tent, squinting immediately. The lamps high above the module simulate late morning... and my stomach threatens to go on strike as a million appetizing smells fill my nostrils.

"I'm so sorry; it took a few tries to get my shawl on. But what do you all—"

"Holy shit..." Natalia interrupts me, her draw dropped.

"No kidding!" Arjuna adds, stunned, looking me up and down. "It's exotic, like *good* exotic!"

I flinch a little at her last words.

"Did your mom make that?" Natalia asks, awestruck.

"I don't think so," I reply. "I've never seen her sew before, but I think she said last night that she was very specific about the design."

"It really suits you!" Arjuna gushes.

"Aw, thanks!" I say, smiling with a rising heat in my cheeks. "But seriously... you said you're hungry, and my tum is eating itself. Let's get food!"

"Behold," Natalia calmly says. She raises her hands, holding up three still-steaming meat skewers.

"You sorceress, where did you get those from?" Arjuna asks.

Natalia's already got a skewer in her mouth, staring at Arjuna deadpan, then points to her right. "Thinking ahead," she says, mouth unapologetically full.

"Good idea!" I beam at her, accepting the stick. "Thank you!"

Arjuna reaches in for one as I bite down, ravenous... and...

"Oh, geez, this is *good*," I say, chewing a bite.

Natalia flips me a thumbs up, grinning, and swallows.

"Okay, good call," Arjuna adds. "Now we can explore for a bit!"

Behind Natalia, people pass us by, each holding cones of savoury crepes and fruity pastries.

"Sure!" I say, bobbing my head.

As we set off, a melodious tune floats through the air.

"Do you hear that?" I ask.

"Let's go check it out!" Arjuna urges.

Natalia and I follow Arjuna's lead, weaving past both stranger and kin. In the centre of the garden, where the chief gave his speech, a large crowd is gathering. In the centre sits our deck's shaman, Narubis the Sage.

In his hands, he strums a tune on a wide-based lute, finger-picking the odd string as three other musicians play along with him. And, as they perform, Narubis recites a story into song:

From out of the ether,
A thousand ships they scattered,
Toward foreign stars they sailed,
Blue nebulas and new constellations,
They charted the course of the gods,
Finding safe harbour on solid ground,
While the travellers parted skyward,
They sailed to faraway horizons,
Oh, children of the void,
Your song is the starway.

It's a comforting tune, one I grew up listening to from story-keepers in the streets. It's similar to other tales told about giant leviathan-like creatures that live and die in the vacuum of space and are supposed to guard the Expanse of the Ancients: a desolate collection of stars where the first Terrans were supposed to have come from. In tales, these creatures are described in many ways, but they all have one name collectively.

The Ominii.

"Ooooh! Ann, look at this!" Arjuna says.

On the way to food-cart hopping, I grab Natalia's hand, zigzagging through the crowd toward the merchant stalls... and a bobble instantly catches my eye.

Hanging from a long iron rod are several necklaces, shimmering against the synthetic sun of the overhead lamps. But the one Arjuna is pointing at is gorgeous!

Mom would say the pendant is 'ornate'. The necklace enshrines a dark blue gem housed in interwoven silver and threaded with a shiny cord. Its label reads: *ethically sourced from asteroid salvage*.

"I need it," I say, almost as a gasp.

"Ohh, you like this one?" the shopkeeper asks.

I nod slowly, breaking contact when I feel a sudden *thump* against the merchant's counter.

"Heya," Natalia says, her arms flopped down on the edge of the stall.

Over her shoulder, she holds on to a silk shawl, dyed a beautiful shade of emerald green.

"See anything you like?"

Arjuna leans in, already decked out in two different styles of necklaces and a pair of teardrop gold earrings. The designs seem like they might have come from a Republic mining colony, imported by Fleet merchants. Those pieces are usually very rare... since few Republic exporters will engage with the Fleet, let alone do business with them. I mean, I could guess as to why, but I think the biggest reason is that they don't trust how easily we travel through different pockets of space, never settling planet-side. But, the longer I stare at Arjuna's earrings, the more their authenticity holds up.

As she rests her chin on her palm, a new bronze bangle of hers sparkles in the noon light. She cocks her face toward me, as if to say *buy it*.

"This one," I say, glancing from Natalia, to Arjuna, and then finally the shopkeeper. "I'll take this one!"

"Very good!" the balding old man exclaims. "What are you willing to trade?"

Before I can reach into my pack, Natalia shuffles ahead of me, gently places a hand on my shoulder, and slowly shakes her head. "I've got this," she says. "Consider it a birthday present from me."

"Wh—" I protest, interrupted by her hand against my lips.

Natalia drops a small plastic bag of medical supplies on the counter, causing the old man to jump.

"Oh, my, that'll do!" the shopkeeper says, laughing to himself.

"You didn't have to do that," I say, hands clasped and my cheeks flushed, "but thank you. It's beautiful!"

"The blue gem stands out with your dress," Natalia says, smirking warmly, "and matches your eyes. Happy birthday."

"I love it." I beam. "Thank you again!"

"Huuaahhh!" A fierce voice erupts across the duelling square, mere feet from me.

Clink!

Two pole arms strike and make a loud noise, following two large men darting back and forth from one edge of the ring to the other.

"Knock him out." Natalia raises her voice, hands cupped in front of her face.

"Yeah!" I add, jumping up with a single raised fist.

Alongside the beating of drums and a low-keyed flute, the two combatants harry one another, spears pointing in each other's direction.

"Go, Lorrus! Kick his ass!" Arjuna cries, slamming a clenched fist down on the hide-covered duelling mat. "Oh, what the hell was that?!" she shouts, dismayed. "Stab him back! Quick dancing around and *cut him!*"

A thin spray of blood decorates the hide mat in front of me.

Shit's getting serious...

My heart pounds fast, and with it, a prickly sensation flows through my veins. I follow the two combatants, and for the first time, I realise that they're wearing protective helmets and thin leather vests. Their feet scuffle along the mat, and beads of sweat drop like rain on a tightly bound drum.

Sweat beads down my face, hitting the canvas mat. I reach a hand to my hair, and the wavy strands on my head frizz up. Maybe it's the mugginess of the garden or the extra bodies around the ring, but I was hot before I even started watching the fight. If my dress weren't made of cotton, I think I'd be dead.

As large drops of blood splatter onto the mat, inches from my face... something clicks.

"Wait a sec," I whisper to myself.

If I have to hold back when I compete... how would Ark hold back in a ring? Would he be able to?

"Is that why he's afraid to... oh." I stop myself, a sickening knot forming in my stomach. "I don't think he can."

I sigh deeply, thinking about last night. How horrible I must have sounded...

"Yeah! I knew you could do it!" Arjuna's voice hollers.

I'm drawn back to the end of the match: there's one man down, cold on the ground, while another stands triumphantly above the other. The referee holds the victor's left hand up, his other hand loosely clutching his bloody spear. The referee releases his hand, walks slowly over to our corner of the ring, and removes his mask.

The champion of the match, Arjuna's brother... of course he's my crush. Of course.

The way his mask falls with his hand, how his loose hair falls like a wetted mane, and how his dark brown eyes sparkle... it's, uh... hot. Like, wow...

As he approaches, my eyebrows rise.

"Hey, what did you think?" A husky, masculine voice escapes his lips.

My heart beats faster. I try to say something, but... my mind goes blank. Nothing's coming out.

So I straighten myself up, dust off my dress, and my friends shoot a mischievous grin at me...

"Hey, bro! That was insane!" she says, turning her face in his direction. Even at a side glance, her beaming expression is hard to ignore.

Lorrus jumps down from the fighting ring, and as he comes down to our level, heat floods my cheeks.

He towers over me, probably at six-foot something, and I quake a little in his shadow. He's broad shouldered, two years older than me and...

oh, gods, his shirt is still off... he's standing like sheer perfection before me, glistening!

"Hey!" he replies. "This is my second-last match for the day, and I've got some extra time on my hands before the next one. What are you ladies up to now?"

"Well..." Arjuna says, "we were on our way to the firing range to, you know, try our hand at getting a prize. You should come with!"

I'm floored. She literally just asked my crush to come with us. Damn it, Arjuna!

"Absolutely!" Lorrus replies. "Do you both mind?"

Oh, shit, he's talking to me... well, he's also talking to Natalia, but he's talking to me too! Shit!

"The more the merrier," Natalia assures, nudging me.

"S-sure thing," I say, my voice barely containing my excitement.

"Great," he says, "let's go!"

He slings his tunic over one shoulder, sheathes his spear in a back-strapped holster, and pauses. He gazes down at me and slowly raises his hand near my face.

"Here," he says.

He runs his hands across my brow, straightening a few loose strands of my hair, and I'm too embarrassed to meet his gaze.

"Thanks," I squeak.

"No problem. You look so refined in your dress that I thought you might appreciate it," he says.

I slowly turn toward Natalia and Arjuna; both of them shoot me expressions of amusement and a sisterly victory for their group. Me, though... I'm dealing with what's probably a permanent blush on my cheeks.

They both suck... but I love 'em both.

Wait... he said I look *refined*. Me! He said that to me!

"Come *on*, you two; the range isn't going to be open forever!" Arjuna says.

There's a teasing pitch in her voice, and while my cheeks are flushed, I squint at her. "On my way!" I say.

"Hey, Ann." Natalia points outward. "My sister's up there."

Sure enough, two hundred meters from the fighting rings stands a large wooden stage, and on it dances her sister, Euphemia. I watch as she spins, twirls, and lunges in almost perfectly synchronized choreography with the other eleven dancers on stage. Their dresses appear similar to mine – all of them seem intentionally flowy. They almost mesmerise me with how their dresses ripple through the air. The accompaniment of a fiddle and nylon-stringed guitar only add to the appeal of their dance.

"Ohhhh," I say.

"... No, she's looking at me!" a voice protests in the crowd.

"*No*, she winked at *me*! You're ugly as hell!" another retorts.

I snort, covering my mouth as I walk past the stage.

Then... I remember Ark's words, something like:

"If anyone tries to whisk you away, you tell me. No, I'm not going to break their arms! Do I think you're someone worth marrying off? Well, yeah, but not right now! You're fifteen! Also, what would Mom say? Or worse, what would she do?!"

That's a horrifying thought...

But, as Lorrus holds my hand and we watch the performance together, I wonder... how would he look at me if I were up there, in this dress, trying to get his attention?

"Hey!" Arjuna raises her voice, waving me over. "We're almost there; keep up!"

"We will!" Lorrus replies.

I gaze up at him, and he tilts his head in Arjuna's direction.

"Shall we?" he says.

"Okay!" I say behind a cracking mask of composure.

Sure enough, only twenty paces away from the dancers' stage is a wide rectangular shooting range. The lines aren't as long as the other attractions, but, as Ark informed me before we left home, they get busy fast.

"Come on!" Arjuna said, from where she's saving a spot at a vacant booth.

As Lorrus and I approach the booth, my eyes wander to the stand. At the far back is a large metal target hoisted against the wall of the booth. It's well loved, covered in several scattered dents.

"First prize is a blue rabbit!" the shopkeeper calls. "Anyone who hits the bull's-eye gets the prize!"

"We'll take that!" Arjuna replies as Lorrus and I approach the booth.

"Very good! Who's going first?" the shopkeeper asks.

I reach my hand up to a couple of loose strands of hair by my shoulder, twirling them in a circle.

I've never fired a gun before, and Mom was always against keeping weapons in the cabin. But... everyone's watching, and Lorrus is here! I can't just say *no*.

"I will!" I blurt out.

"Good, here you go," the shopkeeper says.

He lays a 1.5-meter hunting rifle in my hands, and as I hold it, the first thing I notice is how heavy it is. It seems old... like *really* old. How am I supposed to fire this thing?

I sigh, take aim, and pull the bolt back on the top, reading the diagram on the wall. I quickly pull the trigger...

... Miss...

"Crap," I say.

"Hey," Lorrus say, "would you like me to give you a few tips? I've shot here before."

Fuck, yes.

As I look back at my friends, their shared expression shows they're thinking the same thing.

Hells, yes, give me pointers!

"That'd be great!" I say.

"Okay," he begins, moving closer to me, "try moving your feet further apart, like this. Now, relax your shoulders and hands."

"Won't I drop the gun?" I ask.

Suddenly, his arms wrap around my own, supporting me.

"Nope. I've got you," he replies.

Eeeeep!

"What you want to do now is stare down the barrel, but with both eyes this time. Next, you want to control your breathing, like when you're on a courier run."

Oh, shit, he notices me! Ah!

"Take a deep breath in, slowly squeeze the trigger, and keep your aim. Let your breath out and squeeze all the way back."

I do as he says, adjusting my footing and loosening the tension in my shoulders. I take in one deep breath and narrow my gaze down the barrel at the target. I squeeze the trigger, raggedly blow out, and fire.

"That's a miss," the shopkeeper says, his voice deadpan.

"Damn it!" I cry.

I blow out a deep sigh, and then crinkle my nose. How can I suck so bad? I was actually *trying* to hit it!

"You know what?" Lorrus says. "How about I get that rabbit for you?"

"That'd be great!" My voice squeaks again.

The rifle goes from my hands to Lorrus's, and I step back toward my friends. The grin on Arjuna's lips says it all – she's impressed by her brother's approach.

"Here we go," he says, standing *way* more confidently than I was mere seconds before.

"Hey, Lorrus!" an unfamiliar voice exclaims at an adjacent booth. "You got this, man!"

"Oh," Arjuna says, "his friends followed us!"

Lorrus quickly glances back at me, a little less confident this time, but I believe in him. I stand where I'm at, hands behind my back, and sway slowly from side to side.

I nod and say, "That's right, you do got this!"

He smiles and returns to his target. As he fires, there's a slight tremor to the rifle. The rubber round goes off.

"And... that's a miss," the shopkeeper says.

"Ohhh..." Lorrus groans.

As he does, I move away from the girls and approach him. "You know," I say, "at least you tried, and I really appreciate that you did!"

A part of me melts as he smiles at my words.

"Thanks," he says. "Hey, Arjuna, do you or Natalia want to give it a go?"

"Nope," Arjuna says, grinning from ear to ear, "but I *do* want to go visit the Fortune Teller!"

"You ladies haven't been there yet?" Lorrus asks, sounding confused.

"We've not," Natalia replies, "but it would be good if we stopped to visit Kinsharla before the day's end. I'm curious as to what she'll says."

⤳⤳⤳ ⬳⬳⬳

Once more, we navigate the fairgrounds together, but this time Lorrus, my crush, is walking right beside me. His left hand grazes my own, and more heat immediately radiates from my cheeks. I stumble a bit in my dress along a cobblestone path, and as I do, his hand braces my own and entwines his fingers with mine. Words can't fully describe where I am at right now. I'm so happy I could float off into space!

As we approach the Fortune Teller's tent, just up the tier, Ark's over the bend in the path. He's sitting with his friends, one of them talking loudly and the other nodding in response.

"Noooo!" Alyssa, Priam's girlfriend, cries, and I freeze in my tracks. As we approach Ark's group, she flees the flaps of the tent, sobbing.

Chapter 4

ARK

5 Minutes Earlier

This is a stupid idea.

"We're here! I'm going first!" Alyssa, Priam's girlfriend, exclaims.

As we walk toward the Fortune Teller's tent, I hoist Kai up with my good arm, keeping pace with my friends. He staggers a bit as we go, so I try not to walk too fast.

Priam utters a muted groan at Alyssa's words, but he smiles brightly and waves her on.

"You're a mess…" I say to him, only after his girlfriend disappears into the tent.

"I'm not meant for any of this…" Priam mumbles. "What if she says I'm not meant to be a tech?!"

"Then you're not meant to be a tech," Kai says matter-of-factly. "You can't fight your own destiny. I mean, do you seriously want to live a cursed life?"

Priam sobers up by half a drink. His eyebrows rise, and his lips purse with realization. "*No*, I do *not*."

That's the thing: what Kinsharla says almost always comes true. Her predictions don't cover the grey areas. What's more, her readings are more geared toward the matchmaking end of the festival… It doesn't help that she listens to *every wind of gossip* on this ship.

She travels every deck, picks up who's interested in whom, and has the gall to churn out a prediction based entirely on her observations. It's this reason, right here, why I have been so hesitant to have my fortune read...

"Oh!" Kai says. "I heard that Leah and her boyfriend are migrating to a different ship. Who do you think'll cover her shift?"

I breathe out a sigh of relief, which leads me to reason number two: Leah. This woman has done everything short of stalking me to ask me out. Don't get me wrong – she's not unattractive; I'm just not interested in her as much as I am other girls. She's the reason I skipped out on getting my fortune read last year... I can't skip out again, but this year appears to be a safer bet. Now that Leah has a boyfriend, I'm scot-free.

"There aren't any new transfers," Priam replies. "Someone's gonna be working double."

As he says this, Lorrus's head bobs up the terrace toward the tent... hey, wait, that's Ann'Elise!

Are they holding hands?

"Noooo!" Alyssa cries from within the tent.

"Hon?" Priam replies, out of her earshot.

Bursting like a shot out of a cannon, Alyssa rips out of the folds of the tent. As she flees, she covers her face and sobs loudly.

"Hon, wait!" Priam calls out. "Sorry, gotta go! We'll chat later!"

Kai and I watch blankly as he runs off, past the crowd and toward the festival gates, a good stretch behind Alyssa.

"You wanna go next?" Kai asks.

"*Hell, no*," I reply.

Kai shrugs, enters through the flaps of the tent, and disappears. As the flaps settle, the sound of footsteps on smooth metal grows louder and suddenly stops. Coming up the stairs, Ann'Elise looks quizzically back at me.

"Hey, Ark!" she greets. "Is everything alright?"

I stare blankly at her and shift my gaze to Lorrus. They *are* holding hands. When did this happen?!

"What on earth?" Natalia adds softly, following Alyssa's sprint.

Natalia faces me, and her deep azure eyes lock onto mine. My arms and legs squirm with the intensity of her gaze and... wait, is she blushing?

"It's good to see you. What happened?" she asks sweetly.

"Alyssa had her fortune read... doesn't seem like good news," I say, my brow creasing.

"Ohh," she replies, her eyes tinged equally with understanding and concern.

"It must have been an *ill omen*," Arjuna exclaims dramatically. "Why else would she have bolted away like that?"

"Or maybe she heard something that she didn't like," Lorrus adds.

This guy gets it. I'm still in the dark as to what his intentions with Ann are, but I definitely dislike him less.

"Have you gone in yet?" Ann'Elise asks.

"No," I reply. "I... wanted to go last."

"Hmm..." Arjuna purrs. "For a man who single-handedly saved another from oblivion, destiny seems to be your only opponent!"

I shrug and awkwardly place my hands in my hoodie pockets.

"The legend grows." I say the words as blandly as I feel about getting my palms read.

"Hey!" Ann'Elise interjects, her voice determined. "Ark has his reasons for waiting! Right?"

"*Exactly,*" I reply, matching her energy.

Ugh. My reasons are super lame, and today is probably the *best* day to get this over with... it's bad enough I cancelled my spot in the sparring ring with my arm all banged up, but really, as I'm thinking about it, what's the worst that can happen?

"You're up."

My head jerks toward the tent, and Kai exits the flaps. The first thing I notice about him are his sunken eyes. He didn't have those going in.

"Is it that bad?" I ask, my brows tensing.

"Eh, sort of," Kai groans. "It's not bad... more confusing. So no, not 'Alyssa' bad, but not great."

I want him to share more, but I remember that we're not supposed to. From what the elders taught us, "*The seeds of destiny we're given are for us alone. Unless bound to another, our destiny is a secret.*"

"If you want to talk about it later... what you can, I mean, I'm here," I assure him.

"Thanks... but seriously though, you don't want to keep her waiting," Kai stresses. "She sounds testy today."

I understand why. She's probably seen more people from different walks in the Fleet on this day than any other in the year. As I ponder this, I face Ann'Elise's group, then Kai again and nod.

It's now or never.

I make my way from the waiting area outside the tent to touching the flaps of its entrance.

"Come in," says a voice from within. I take a bold step forward, and the heavy flaps hit my back.

Now that I'm inside the tent, the smell of incense is the first thing to draw my senses. Mom often lights incense for Dad, on a mantel on our bookshelf, but this smells *very* different from that. Something between roasted cinnamon and burnt cat hair...

What I notice next is how dim this old tent is. There's a natural beam of light streaming down in the centre, and the whole enclosure can't be anything over four meters in diameter. It's cramped, uncomfortable, and more claustrophobic than a space suit.

"Ah, yes, Kai said you are a reticent one." A soft, haggard woman's voice echoes. "It's good to finally meet the eldest and only son of Takh'Alia."

"It's, uh, a pleasure to meet you," I say, trying to be polite as I advance toward the light.

"Oh, please, sonny, I'm sure this is the last place you'd like to be today. Or any day" – she laughs – "but the strict tenets of the crew are clear. To hold your place both with your family and peers, you must visit this tent at least once in your life."

"Yes," I reply.

"Well, I'm sure your future is nothing to be afraid of, seeing as how our lives as crew members rarely ever change. And to be honest," she says, nearing the light, "I rarely ever give bad news."

"Do you think Alyssa would agree?" I say defensively.

"Oh, it wasn't bad," she replies. "It just wasn't what she wanted to hear."

That's one point for Lorrus and Ark. Woo.

"That's always the trouble," she says. "We never want what we don't want to hear, especially with a future that is unchangeable. But enough about that... as you're probably aware, I'm Kinsharla, and from what I've gathered from your friends, you like to be called Ark."

"Y-yes," I stammer.

"Excellent!" she exclaims.

Kinsharla looks to be a woman of about seventy. She hunches over in linen robes laced with silver trim, a hood covering her light grey hair and a silk bandage over her left eye. Her dark brown right eye meets mine, and she peers back at me knowingly.

"It's the price for the sight... an eye for an eye, if you will," Kinsharla explains. "Now, come closer and let me have a *good look* at you!"

My whole body shivers at her words, but I do as she says.

"That's a good boy," she says as I draw closer. "Hmm... there's a lot going on here..."

As she says this, she raises both her hands toward my face. She doesn't touch me, but her hands hover a couple of centimetres from my ears.

"Now let's see..." she says. "Oh, well, my vision's blurry but... uh..."

Her mouth hangs agape, and I can almost feel her hands tremble a short distance from my head. It's like I got a slow punch to the gut, and what little nerve I had coming into the tent is slowly disappearing...

"Yes?" I ask, trying to move the reading along.

"AAHHHH!!!" she screams.

As I jerk back, her frail hands clamp down on my wrists, seizing tight like a death grip! I'm shaking, terrified, as she continues to wail. I try jerking backward, but every time, her fingers dig deeper into my flesh. Even worse, her right eye rolls into the back of her head.

"Ohh, son of the Traveller, your path is marred by shadow! Everything you know will be lost to you, and your walk will be laden with unspeakable suffering! Your feet will touch waters, sands, cold steel, and vast forests, and your crown will cover a thousand stars. How the ancestors will weep! How they pray alongside heart-stricken gods for the blood to cease running, and... oh, how they rejoice when they see what rises from smouldering ashes. What once was will die, and what is dead shall live!"

I don't speak. Her words stop; her hands are icy and glued to my wrists. My hands form into balled fists, and I want nothing more than to flee from this horrible place like Alyssa did!

"Umm.... Oh, uh... yes. Right..." she says, her right eye in its rightful place.

She stares at me with utter bewilderment, embarrassment, and... something else.

Horror, I think.

I'm not sure what to say, and she's as confused as me... what the hell just happened?!

"Wh... I don't..." I manage.

Her right eye flickers down to my wrists, and in shock, she releases me. As I recoil, I look down and two large thumbprint bruises form alongside the beginnings of four fingerprints on both of my forearms.

"You, uh... tell the next party I'm out for the next couple of hours... maybe more. That was... a lot."

I don't say anything and nod.

As soon as she slumps back down on her dusty pillow seat, I trip on a rug as I quickly escape.

"No, seriously what happened in there?!" Ann'Elise asks again, her voice getting louder.

"I said we can't talk about it," I reply with a dry mouth.

My voice sounds subdued as I speak, and even as we walk together up the terrace to meet with Mom, there's an unmistakable weakness in my bones now.

"That's stupid!" she replies.

"I agree," I counter, "but even if I could share, I really don't want to. Not right now."

What the hell happened in there...?

As we pass by large, towering trees and thick fruiting bushes, the only things I remember is the look on everyone's face. They all shared it.

Shock.

I remember Kai staring at me, stunned; Ann'Elise and her friends all looked like I saw a ghost... and Lorrus stared at me as if I were pulling a fast one... until he realised I wasn't joking. Each of their facial tattoos seemed to contort in reaction to me, however the hell I appeared. Even with the inked lines that run the length of my left cheek, it didn't shelter my expressions that showed how I felt in that moment, let alone now. Thinking about it makes me lower my head...

It was Ann'Elise who seemed to mirror the horror I carried with me.

"Are you okay, though? Really?" she asks.

"I... yeah," I lie. "It's just like Alyssa; I heard something I didn't like."

Way to underplay it, ya idiot...

In the end, we're all superstitious. Sort of. And I'm no exception. Behind the crew's ornate and symbolic tattoos and simplistic wares, we're all steering a ship surrounded by the otherworldly. With it comes both its wonders and its sheer terrors alike.

"Oh, there's Mom!" Ann'Elise pipes up.

As she says this, I lift my gaze from the path ahead to near the top of the terrace. Sure enough, waving us over is Mom, her other hand resting on a wooden table. It sits nestled in front of a large brazier and tavern. Many people come in and out, and the scent of Eridas Deck's local cuisine slowly waves the fog from my mind.

As if on cue, my stomach growls like I haven't eaten for days...

"Hey," Ann'Elise says as we walk toward Mom's table, "whatever the hell it was, I'm sure you can handle it!"

I'm not sure in what universe I can handle 'blood that will not cease' or 'unspeakable pain'... but I know she means well.

"Oh, absolutely!" I say, putting on a brave front.

We stop in front of a metal gate, and as we approach, it disappears into the ground. Once inside, we're surrounded by other fairgoers and revellers. Standing by the second table on our right is Mom. She walks over to us and gives me a hug and kiss on the cheek.

"Hey, honey! Did you have a good time?"

"Oh, it was fantastic!" I lie enthusiastically.

"Right!?" Ann'Elise joins in. "My friends and I saw *everything!*"

"My goodness, that's so much!" Mom gestures for me and Ann'Elise to have a seat, and we all settle in. "I already ordered ahead. We've got drinks and snacks coming soon."

"... What did you order?" Ann'Elise asks.

"Lavender mead," Mom replies with a grin.

I watch in sheer amusement as my sister's face lights up in sudden realization.

"Ohhhhh," she says.

Not a moment too soon, Vylka comes back with a large pitcher and three clay goblets. They're accompanied by a bowl of warmed olives, soft cheese, and toasted rosemary bread.

"And here you go!" Vylka motions with a courteous smile. "Enjoy!"

"Thank you!" Ann'Elise says cheerfully.

I sit back and watch as Mom pours us each a cup, passes them around the table, and positions the pitcher in the centre.

"To your first Festival, dear," Mom says, raising her cup toward Ann'Elise. "I'm so glad you've had a wonderful day today!"

As she says this, while Mom seems tired in this moment, she seems nonetheless happy. A warmth spreads through my heart, and I can't help but smile.

As our cups clink, the entire table shakes. Violently.

Less than a second later, a loud explosion echoes from the top of the garden's ceiling and roars downward. My eyelids expand, and my whole body tenses. Ann'Elise and Mom have the same reaction.

We're all frozen in position. My gut tells me to scan for the exit, but it's too far out of sight. I take a second to look at the other people at the tavern, and they're all petrified.

Wait. That means the explosion is *inside the ship*. It's not an outer hull impact; it's *inside*!

"...W-what was that?" Ann'Elise asks.

A second, louder explosion wracks the entire hold of the garden, causing me and everyone else to shudder. The din that follows turns Ann'Elise as white as a sheet.

Popping sounds, coming from above and near the garden's exits. They're small at first, and they sound increasingly more controlled and rhythmic. No, they sound less like popping and more machine-like.

"Gunfire..." Ann'Elise gasps, and shouts, "T-that's gunfire!"

Chapter 5

KAEL

I can think of a million better ways to spend my time... honestly, I'm not in the mood to burn out one more *goddamned* rat's nest... but I have to make my quota. It's their own fault they showed up on our sensors, anyway... and for unregistered illegals floating around in our space, I can't simply sit by and watch.

I peer down at the metal plating of my boots, then to the lustrous metal panels of the APC.

"*You're twenty seconds to the LZ, Commander. Vanguard's burning hot;* Nautilus *hostiles have been engaged.*" Captain Seijin buzzes in my ear.

"Copy, *Rugia*, bracing for impact," I reply.

I look up, and along the exit bay corridor stands my personal squadron. Like me, they're fixed in by heavy restraints, buffered from the impending breach. Unlike the rest of their regiment aboard my ship, I selected these men by hand. I trust them more than I trust anyone else, and that they have my back.

"Keep it tight and make a hole to the bridge" I order.

"Sir!" they reply in unison.

Like every other time, the roar of the retro burners on the APC fire, and a familiar recoil shakes my men and me as our craft slams into their vessel. The laser cutters pierce through their flimsy tin can in less than a second and suddenly... the exit bay pops open like a champagne cork.

"*Go! Go! Go!*" my sergeant barks, echoing through the comm in my ear.

I watch as my squadron pours out, single file, rifles in hand and at the ready. But I bide my time, waiting as my lieutenant is the last one to disembark the APC.

"Godspeed," I say over our closed circuit.

The words sound hollow as they leave my mouth. I spring up, hoisting extra ammunition into several weighed-down pockets, and straighten my skewed chest plate with my free hand. The other carries an identical white enamelled rifle to those of my men, loaded with first-contact piercing rounds of plasma and lead.

"*Red carpet's rolled,* Commander," Sergeant Lacan reports over the comms. "*Sector one is clear. Proceeding to two.*"

"Copy," I reply.

Okay, it's showtime.

Out of ritual, I take my first ammo magazine out and tap it twice to my helmet. It barely echoes. The magazine is full to the brim, and I stow it away.

The second my feet touch the flooring of the *Nautilus*, the racket of their alarm system floods my ears.

"*Hostiles in sector six, return fire!*" Sergeant Lacan's voice accompanies the sound of single shots fired. "*Barricade's up. Sending a volley.*"

A sudden muffled blast echoes in my ears. Even though each sector I pass through is clear, there's a pair of our units guarding corridors at every checkpoint. As I calculate each step into secured territory, hostile melee weapons scatter about the wings.

Spears. Swords. Short daggers. Non-lethal shotguns. There's one fatality hunched over, wearing primitive clothing and loosely holding a bolt-action rifle, and it resembles an ancient Remington. God, this is embarrassing...

As I walk one sector away from the kill zone, the first thought that pops into my head are those damn conscription papers...

The muscles in my brow throb; my jaw tightens, and my teeth ache under the pressure.

"*Fan out; sector twelve is a large habitation module. Stay sharp,*" Sergeant Lacan says.

I'm down the corridor from the module mentioned in the comms, and it surprises me how these rats keep such a craft so well maintained. The ceiling and walls of the corridors are a bright eggshell white, polished enamel... maybe a type of archaic polymer used for interior siding, and even the floors are a well-polished brushed steel. It really is a pity.

"*Twelve's clear. Moving to the bridge. Stairwell's still hot; send a volley,*" he adds.

Another blast echoes, louder than before, and it vibrates my eardrum. My daughter says I'm almost completely deaf, but even that's not enough to retire you early these days.

As I step out past the first bulkhead, one of the hostile fatalities catches my eye.

She's a civvy. Unarmed, wearing some kind of trinket, and a thin emerald-green shawl covers the waist of her blue and white dress. Very ornate... these people are full of surprises.

I slowly drop to one knee, keeping my distance, and tilt her head from side to side with the nozzle of my rifle. Her short silver hair flits freely across her brow, most likely tousled from the engagement, but it appears well combed.

I examine the dark green shawl. It's woven, and it's barely stained by a plasma charge through her chest. Then there's her eyes.

They're vacant, unresponsive, but the lustrous azure surrounding her dilated pupils must have made her stand out. That, and with her mouth agape... I think she saw it coming.

Again, I think to my family... and, for a second, to my daughter. What if it was her on the ground, unprepared for an assailing force?

No, thinking about it makes me sick, and the headshrinker already has her hands full as it is.

I get up, walk past the cadaver, and treat her like a simple variable in the equation: an element of resistance and a physical reminder of that consequence.

The large habitation module is vast, and my senses take in the various details of the environment. The air is thick, like a giant humidifier rests either at the belly of this room or hangs above it. Up above, an old synthetic cloud generator cloaks beams of artificial sunlight from above.

They're innovative; I'll give them that.

Next, there's a residual smell of different foreign foods; spices and all of it mingles with the smell of sulphur and smoky charcoal. If the body count rises, the smell of iron won't surprise me.

There's a torn-up and scattered attraction hosted in a zone for agriculture. Not the best place for one, but the *Nautilus* is a thirty-first-century generational vessel. It wasn't built to be luxurious.

"*Status report.*" My lieutenant checks in. "*What's the situation topside?*"

"*Gamma Squad broke through the bridge, and we've captured their captain,*" my sergeant replies.

Checkmate.

I take one walkway up an elevated elliptical terrace and find a dilapidated tent charred by incendiaries and mottled by plasma rounds. It's downhill from my current position: some sort of watering hole with kicked-over tables and a torn-up sun sail. A shrill *clink* follows, and the vibration of a metal object hits against my left boot. At my feet, there's scattered copper cups and cracked clay jugs. The smell from the ground resembles honey. Strange.

"*Lieutenant,*" my sergeant squawks, "*there's strong resistance coming from the stairwell and the ship's life rafts. They're unarmed, but we're taking heavy casualties! They look like civvies! Permission to engage?*"

"*Do* not *use lethal force, Sergeant,*" my lieutenant barks. "*We've axed enough of their people; be discreet, for God's sake. That's an order!*"

Now I'm curious. Do these nomads have a secret stash of arsenal, ones that weren't covered in the dossier? We'll see how this plays out.

As I march past toppled stands, scattered linens, and the effects of basket weavers, above me is a wooden archway in the centre column of the module. It hoists a banner in a language I can't read. Ahead of me is an open bulkhead leading up to the stairwell where my men have dug in.

"*L-Lieutenant! There's a female civvy; she's taken down my men! Request back up from Iota Squad! Kappa Squad! Somebody hel—*" Sergeant Lacan hollers over the comms.

I switch to a private channel on my helmet's radio.

"Lieutenant," I say, "what's the status of Gamma Squadron?"

There's no static and no immediate reply. This is doing nothing for my blood pressure.

"Bastards!!" a voice roars from behind.

I don't think. I twist, quickly, narrowing my body to the imminent threat to my rear. My heart beats wildly, my mind like a steel trap. A tall young man dressed in a linen tunic charges at me with a spear.

"Commander!" one of my men cries out.

My assailant gets closer, his face menacing and his weapon poised like a primitive warrior. I take this in for a microsecond, and I'm not amused.

The heat from my rifle buzzes like a loud hum, and just like that, he goes flying backward. I absorb what little recoil I get from the offload and stand defensively with my gun pointed at the fallen idiot.

"Stand down," I say to my men.

The man below me twitches, coughing up blood.

I slowly approach him, kicking aside his spear, and stop short of his boots.

One less feral rat.

I shoot my rifle once, and three rounds dim the light from his irises.

"That's how you neutralize a hostile," I say.

And once more, a crackling comes from the comms, ringing in my ear.

"*Copy, Commander, we—take cover! She's at the foot of the stairwell; don't let her get through! I said take—*"

Goddamn it.

"You men, on me," I order.

How hard is it to apprehend a single woman?! What a nuisance...

I flag a small contingent of four units following behind me.

We race up the stairs, sidestepping men sporting the insignias of my squadron, and a trail of blood leads to the very top.

And as I get there, the annoyance plaguing my mind bleeds into every aching muscle in my face. Dozens of my soldiers lay dead, scattered across the corridor, men and women armed to the teeth... and yet...

There's a woman wearing flowing robes stained with blood. She's crouching over someone else... a younger woman, maybe fifteen or sixteen. And in the defensive woman's hand is a dagger dripping with the blood *of my men*.

"Drop it!" I bark, aiming my rifle as I approach.

I ought to gun her down *right now* for what she's done, for what resistance she has put up. Cobalt eyes, wild with fury, glare back at me. She poises her dagger, unwavering. Her glare shifts uncomfortably between me and my men. She has no way out, and the only means of escape is through me.

The static of my comms crackles again, but as I lift my hand to answer, the crackling muffles. In its place, the sound of boots contacting steel draws closer. They're soft on landing, purposeful... quick.

"Get away from them!" A booming masculine voice echoes.

A spectre of a man leaps into the periphery and serpentines his way from one end of the corridor to where my men and I are, and while my men ascend with truncheons in these close quarters, the assailant moves like a man possessed.

I watch, rifle raised, as this young man tears through one of my men like paper. The dagger he wields cuts, not recklessly, but with meaning. He doesn't go through my men's armour but through the weak spots. Under the biceps, between the plates, and knocking one man over... slitting his throat.

I'm not letting another one of them die here!

"Make a hole!" I shout.

By reflex, my men stand down and take point on the woman in the corner. I draw my blade, a standard issue combat knife, and fly at him. My hand swings at his arm, another sending a blow to his ribs.

Miss.

He counters by throwing a blow of his own, cutting through the air with animal-like ferocity!

I strike upward, aiming to disarm him, and when I think I have him, he blocks with a downward strike. But as he does, I get a good look at his face... and I wish I hadn't. The blood drains from my face.

"Vaughan...?" I whisper.

My face stings with a secondary physical blow to my cheek that sends me stumbling backward, like I got hit with a large iron frying pan. I crumble to the ground, quickly, and I stare up in horror. I try everything I can to cart myself backward, but it's no use. Fury and judgement looms over me now, and my heart breaks as he towers over me...

A loud *thwack* resonates in the corridor, a stunned, blank expression washes over my executioner's face, and he too crumples to the ground at the butt of my lieutenant's rifle.

"Ark!" the woman cries, the dagger in her hand shaking. She doesn't leave the young woman.

"Drop the weapon!" my lieutenant barks. "Drop it now!"

The woman's dagger *clangs* to the ground, and I don't take my gaze off of the man who almost killed me. Though he's unconscious, his eyes haunt me. I could have stopped him... no. I was unwilling to take his life... and I still am.

Chapter 6

Takh'Aliah

I wake, my vision blurry as a splitting headache further brings me to my senses...

As I raise my head, I see the surface of a chrome desk. On top of it is a small box with a glowing yellow phosphorescence. The sheen on the desk's surface is made more lustrous by the blinding light of an overhead lamp. It's pointed right at my face and makes the pain in my right temple worse. I try to raise my hand to shield myself from its rays... but it doesn't move. I try my right. It's stuck too.

"Ugh!"

No matter how hard I struggle, viciously try to shake my wrists and ankles free... it's no use.

The rattle of my breaths coming and going through my mouth increase, and whatever haze of vision I had before is quickly disappearing.

"Good. You're awake," a deep masculine voice says.

I try to make out the figure saying this, but there's too much light obscuring my vision. Judging by where the sound is coming from, he's in front of me.

For a moment, I stop breathing.

The adrenaline in my veins brings to the surface the last few moments I can remember...

Running. Slashing. Fire. Blood. They hit my daughter, and...

"Ark!" I cry.

"Calm down," the same voice chides soothingly. "This will go a lot easier if you remain calm."

It all comes flooding back... the explosion, the gunfire, the... oh, gods... they attacked the ship! This man, whoever he is, if he has my children, I need to do as he says...

I nod, taking a deep breath in and painfully exhaling. Sweat beads from my forehead and rolls down my cheeks.

"Good," he says, unfazed.

The overhead lamp adjusts to the centre of the desk, revealing the other person in the room.

The man sitting across from me is upright, silhouetted by the surrounding dark. What catches my eye, however, is the painfully familiar memory of his attire: the same overcoat that reaches up to the top of his neck, the terracotta-brown and white trim matched with thin silver metal shoulder marks, each running horizontally, and two running vertically down his arms. His very image reminds me of when I was younger, the... things they used to do to me, and the people like him who both observed me and *tortured* me... It's bad enough that this sterile room only serves to throw me back to a time I had no autonomy and no choice. My body involuntarily jerks as he crosses one leg over the other. And overshadowing all of it is a burning heat rising from my gut.

"Where are they?" I ask, barely containing a shout. "Where are my children?"

The man takes his time, tilting his head to the side. "First, some ground rules. I'm going to give you three answers to three questions, and only that. What I will state is that you're currently on board the *RSS Rugia*; you have been detained by mandate of the Department of Migrations and Resettlement. My name is Kael, I'm a commander serving on this vessel, and you're now in federal custody. You may ask your questions."

I draw a ragged breath, glaring daggers at him. "*Where* are my *children?*" I reiterate through clenched teeth.

"What are their names?" he asks.

"My son is Ark, and my daughter is Ann'Elise."

He waits a moment, diverting his gaze from me, and reveals a blinking blue light on the side of his right temple. It might be a telepathic module...

After four seconds, his eyes meet mine again.

"We have two youths in detainment right now; they go by those names," he replies, "but like you, they're both in our custody."

It's bittersweet. I'm small in this moment... defeated... my head becomes heavy and hard to hold up.

"Why would a federated vessel, whose goal is colonial resettlement, be so concerned with me?" I ask.

"That is a good question," he says, "and deserves a thorough answer."

I flinch as he gets up from his seat, and he paces from one end of his side of the desk to the other.

"In a routine operation, yes, they would have rounded you up and the rest of your crew and thrown you all in the brig below. Your captain and his senior staff violated Terran settlement protocols, not the lower crew. And yes, you're right; normally we only hold commanding officers and the captain of a Nomadic Fleet's vessel accountable for violating these protocols. Charges of vagrancy through our territory, that sort of thing... and by this point, the Republic would have assigned you and your children colonial re-designation numbers for resettling on established worlds, based on genetic aptitude," he explains.

My chest tightens, and my mouth is suddenly parched.

"Which brings me back to you and your children," he says. "With the rest of your crew, we can trace their lineage back two thousand years, back to the first settling of Haradrun after the exodus from Holy Terra. They all have a genetic paper trail... except for you and your children," he says. "In fact, this variable fascinated my science officer so much he did a thorough analysis on the samples collected from you three, and the results were... interesting." He narrows his eyes at me. "There are only a handful of reasons you wouldn't show up in the books or why your blood is so different from our own... and even humans produced from a Foundry have a pedigree, if you can call it that."

Even if I weren't tied up, I don't think I'd be able to get up... I'm so terrified I can barely breathe.

"This leads me to believe, at least, that you're the product of an experiment within the Republic, or associated with one," he concludes.

A tremor runs through my body, and with these restraints, it's like I'm a caged animal...

My head sinks down further to my slightly exposed chest, and whatever pride or accomplishment I held before has bled out onto the floor.

"I... I'll give myself up," I say, my head hanging low, "please let my children go... they're not what the Department of Science needs; it's me."

The tightness in my chest constricts with the very thought I may never see my babies again... but it's better if I return to a cell to be dissected and studied than them...

Seconds pass. He doesn't say anything, so I lift my head and as I do, I pause.

I stare up at him, and Kael does not bear a malicious countenance on his face, but neither does he appear sympathetic to my pleas. I follow his hands as he raises them onto the desk and clasps them together.

"... I'm in something of a predicament," he says, frowning, "and I can understand the position you're in right now, as hollow as that might sound."

I'm too stunned to talk. My brows flex into a confused scowl, and he diverts his eyes to the left again. His blue device doesn't blink.

I'm awash with a thousand horrible thoughts; every vile experience I suffered in captivity warns me not to listen to him, but as he faces me again, I notice something in his expression that betrays him: pain. The next thing he does is flick off the small box on the desk, switching off its yellow phosphorescent glow. The tag "audio log" is now dimmed.

"This might be hard to believe, but I find myself in a very similar place," he continues, his face away from me, "and because of this, I have a proposition for you."

I stare at him, unbelieving. I want to trust this man's words... but like back then, it could cost me everything. And now, it could cost me my son and daughter too. I glance down, only for a second, and square my gaze on him. "Why are you helping us, risking your position and even the lives of your men?"

Now his eyes fall... what's happening?

"I have two children, like you," he says, "and I love them *dearly*, and one of them... he... his life is at stake. I don't think I can do much for him if I don't act now."

My knees shake, and my head bobs.

"I'm willing to pull a couple of strings and expunge the data my unit collected on you and your family before it's logged away with the Department... but it will come at a price," he says.

His sympathetic expression fades into despondency. I consider his words and stare at him with indignation and impending shame.

"W-what do you want me to pay?" I ask, fearing the worst from him.

Once more, I'm taken aback as Kael looks at me, almost like a saddened father might.

"I never said it was *you* who has to pay this price," he replies.

Chapter 7

Ann'Elise

"Hey!" I scream again. "Let us out! Damn it, I said let us out!"

I beat my bruised fists against the enamelled steel of the thick door in front of me; and each time, they ache a little more.

※※※

"Let me go!" I cried, both of my arms held by two armoured guards. "Who the hell do you think you are?!"

A trickle of blood ran down my arm as they took me down a blindingly lit corridor. They dragged me along, down a winding corridor, and suddenly they stopped.

"Open it," the guard to my left said.

The metal door slid into the wall to the left, and Ark was inside.

With no warning, one of the guards gave me a rough push between my shoulder blades, and I stumbled forward.

"Ann!" Ark cried.

As I struggled to get to my feet, I lunged back at the guards with guttural fury, and the open doorway sealed shut. My body crumpled against the hard metal.

"Ann!" Ark repeated.

"W-why are they doing this?!" I sobbed.

Red anger pulsed through me, and I screamed bloody murder at the top of my lungs. It wasn't only rage though... I was absolutely terrified...

As I got to my feet, I banged against the metal door loudly, each fist more forceful than the last. I remembered looking behind me, only once, as Ark paced back and forth in this two-cot cell.

"Ann, are you okay?" he asked, his face pained.

"No!" I wailed. "No, I'm not fucking okay! They strapped me down, they took my blood, they did things to me... what the hell do they want with us?!"

Ark glanced down, covering a small bandage on his inner elbow. They'd done this to him too...

"Mom," I said. "What did they do with her? Did you see her?!"

"No... I lost her back on the ship. I'm not sure if she's with us or not..." he replied, his head lowered.

"W-we have to get out of here!" I shouted, crying again. "We have to get back to the ship!"

"You can't keep us in here!" I shout, banging the door until smeared patches of blood streak behind my fists.

"Ann, stop..." Ark says, defeated. "It's no use."

I stare at him, stunned with disbelief, as droplets of blood drip from my fist to the ground.

As I'm standing here, doing everything I can to get us out of here, my older brother is crouched in the corner on one of the two cots. It's more than I can stand, and the rage in me only builds...

"Why shouldn't we try?!" I shout at him. "We can't give up!"

I want to fight them, whoever they are, with every bit of fight I have in me, and Ark... he just wants to quit...

My chest is heavy, and my bloody hands shake. My cheeks stop burning, and instead I'm overwhelmed. There's a foreboding pang in my chest.

"I-If Dad were here, they wouldn't have found us!" I cry.

My back hits the wall next to the door, and I close my eyes as tears freely fall down my cheeks. My body drags down to the cold metal floor.

"How do you know?" he says.

Again, I'm shocked. This hurts differently.

I never met Dad, and the only bits I have about him are from Mom and Ark... but for him to say that to me, especially now...

"At least he wouldn't give up!" I say through gritted teeth. "He'd keep fighting!"

"What would we be fighting against?" Ark says, his voice rising in anger. "We don't know who these people are, and what's worse, they *know* we're different."

I stare at him. "How are we different?"

He frowns at me, huddled on his stupid cot. "It's the reason you can run so fast, why my reaction time is quick, and how Mom crushed a man's face in *with a single fist* like it was paper! *That* different." Ark holds his knees tighter.

I stare at him... and with all the surrounding chaos, something clicks.

"*What makes us different is what's written into our blood,*" Mom said once. "*Our people call themselves Thetian, or 'Children of Iron'. And ever since the gods formed us on Mars... the Terrans have always been afraid of us.*"

"Because we're not Terran." I fight more sobs.

"Yeah," Ark sighs, "and it's the reason Dad's not here."

My lips quiver, there's a scratchy, dry sensation in my throat, and my face contorts into a scowl.

Mom's fierce. I didn't fully understand *how* fierce until today, but she can fight. So...

"Why didn't she prepare us?" I ask, staring at the ground, "Why didn't she warn us?"

"She thought we were safe," he says, sternly, "and she was doing the best she could. And even if we fought Terrans from the Republic back, she said that if they found us out, it's over."

I tremble, and I slip away from the fear of these horrible people and back into the familiar rage that drove me before. "Mom wouldn't say that!" I bark. "You're lying to me! She wouldn't give up hope!"

"*I'm* lying to you?!" Ark snaps back.

"Yeah! And why the hell are you saying this now, of all times?! Mom would've trained us to fight, to repel those godsdamned people who *killed my friends*!"

An image of Natalia's terror-stricken face flashes before my eyes. I gasp as the events of the attack on our ship flood my mind.

In the chaos of the attack, we lost Arjuna in the crowd at the festival grounds. While Mom tried to lead us out, the sound of screaming filled the air all around me. The security sentinels were powerless against the invaders' rifles that shot beams of energy at them. Behind me, Ark carried the rear, and holding on to his arm for dear life as we ran was Natalia.

When we had almost reached the exit, Ark let out a blood-curdling cry as Mom cut down an attacker to our left. I turned back in his direction, watching as Natalia crumpled to the ground, her face frozen in terror, her hand tightly clutching Ark's sleeve, blood quickly pooling around her body.

I shrieked as Mom took me by the hand and tore Ark away from Natalia's death grip.

"She wanted us to live a normal life!" Ark shouts.

I sob again, crushing my face against my hands. I wail and scream, hunching over as wave after wave of delayed sorrow reaches up from my heart and out into the air. Once it's all out, I back up against the wall again and crumple into the corner, shielding my arms over my head.

"Ann..." he says, his voice softer this time, "I'm sorry, I—".

"Don't talk to me." I spit the words out like venom.

Heeding my words, he says nothing. Not after ten seconds, or ten minutes.

The air in the room decompresses as the door swings open, startling me.

I don't get up, though. Not with two masked, armoured guards with rifles aimed at us both. I glare at them. Two more guards enter and take Ark up by his arms. Like before, he doesn't resist...

It makes me sick.

"Maybe they'll make you disappear too!" I say bitingly, watching him leave.

The only reply he gives is one last sad look before the guard behind him prods him with his rifle, and they take him out of the room.

In defiance, I get up and turn my back to him, facing the opposite cell wall. There's a beeping noise as the guard punches in a code.

Gods... what did I just tell him...! I mean, yeah, I'm pissed. But he's my brother!

I circle around before the door closes so he can say I'm sorry and I can take back what I said...

But as I do, he's already gone, and the door slams shut again...

Chapter 8

ARK

"Maybe they'll make you disappear too!"

Her words linger. Even as they throw handcuffs on me and take me by the shoulders down winding corridors, her words cut me deeply...

"This way," one guard orders.

They lead me toward a large two-panelled door, and on the right-hand side, it reads: *interrogation room*. My mouth goes dry, and all I can think is... this is it. This is where they'll end me... and I don't even know who they are.

The sliding doors open from both sides, and the nozzle of one of the guard's rifles prods me to enter the dimly lit room. I proceed, shaking, and they sit me down in a metal chair and bind my cuffs to the table. Both guards exit the room.

"Ark..." a soft voice calls to me.

"Mom!" I cry. "Are you alright?!"

She's cuffed to the table, like me, but what makes my blood run hot is how much fight has left her eyes... So I struggle in my seat; I wrestle the cuffs against the table... I want to go to her, to hold her and get her and Ann'Elise the hell out of wherever we are!

"So," a man across from me says, "you're Ark."

I try to gauge his appearance, but the small light on the table barely illuminates the edges on the man's face and hands. I stop struggling and watch as, with a flick of his hand, the silver on the table becomes a black screen.

"Ark'Onus of Eridas Deck, if I'm correct," he says, "crew member of the *Nautilus*, registered with the Nomadic Fleet. You and I first met when we raided your ship."

He waves his hand again, and the long light on the lamp brightens the rest of the room.

This is the man who *threatened my mother and sister*. The man I almost killed...

I glance back at Mom, and I tense more. She looks subdued, cornered.

I'm not even sure what he did... but if I weren't in these cuffs, I'd kill him.

"As I've said to your mother, I'm Kael, a commander on board this Republic ship, and my function is to re-designate migrating people, unassigned colonists, and peoples who otherwise do not exist in our system."

His words hit like a punch to the gut.

"You should know that you, your sister, and your mother are in a very serious situation... and I'm here to discuss with you the possibility of a solution," he says.

"What *kind* of solution?" I say, catching the defiance on my own lips.

He pauses for a second, but his stare doesn't leave mine.

"An opportunity has made itself available, and it directly affects you," he retorts.

"Ha!" I scoff. "If you're going to extort me, or any of my family, you must understand that the Fleet doesn't make deals with someone twisting their arm."

"I'm aware," he counters, his voice harsh.

As I search Mom's expression, I waver, as her face has become as pale as a sheet.

"Ark, this is very important..." she breathes softly.

The concise way she speaks makes me shiver. Furious, I direct my gaze at the man across from me. "What do you want?" I ask him.

"What I want," Kael echoes, "is one life for another."

I blink. What does he mean? Whose life? My life?

"Here," he says, waving his hand over the desk.

The black of the table brings up several holographic files, and there's a dossier of a young man in the centre of it all... and the person in the photo staring back at me looks just like...

"I have a son," Kael says, "and he's facing conscription. My son, Vaughan, is not fit for military service. Not physically, not mentally, and they'll use him as cannon fodder... but that's where you come in."

The very doppelgänger pictured on the table haunts me, right along with this man's words.

"I'm asking you to take his place," Kael states carefully.

"How?" I ask, not really wanting the answer.

"You'll assume his identity," he explains, "take on his name, his station in the GUILD Republic, and his fate with the military... and in return, I'll spare all three of your lives."

Like I'm on a spacewalk, my stomach does a backflip. "W-what will happen to them? How can you guarantee this?" I ask, cursing how weak I sound.

"They'll receive new records and colonial re-designation," he explains, "and I'll fabricate a backstory to suit this narrative."

"Wait," I say. "What kind of narrative?"

Kael exhales deeply, placing his hands together on the desk. "Again, whatever will suit the narrative," he stresses, "whether your mother is an old flame of mine, your sister a love child, or that my son, in this version, is your mom's flesh and blood instead of his own departed mother's... again, it's going to be whatever I can swing with my men. All I can say for sure is that your mother and sister will have lodging, matching colonial designations of their own, and assigned work in their colony."

I want to be indignant... I want to finish what I started in that *damn stairwell*... but I'm chained to a desk, with my mother's and sister's lives in my hands.

"Hold on," I begin. "Why does your military need your son? They can't be that desperate, can they?"

Kael raises an eyebrow and rubs his hand over his face. "Yes, they are. The GUILD has been fighting a war with the Thriaxian Kingdom for over five years now... we're not doing well, and we need more bodies on the frontlines."

"The Thriaxian Kingdom?" I repeat. "Who are they?"

"Xenos," Kale spits. "Aliens who attacked our frontier colonies."

Wait, hold on... aliens?

As I check with Mom, she's as confused as I am.

"You've never encountered them before on migration?" Kale asks. "Well, they're brutal. Merciless. They appeared out of nowhere and attacked us, unprovoked. They annihilated an entire star system in the Azores Dominion."

That name sounds familiar. Dad used to talk about that place when I was really young, and to this day the Fleet trades with that area of Republic space.

"So yeah," Kale adds. "Aliens exist, and they hate us. All Terrans, Republic or not. So we're fighting to push them back to their core worlds, solidly on their own turf, to prevent another Silesian Incident."

"Do you know why these aliens attacked you?" Mom enquires, visibly shocked.

"No," Kale replies. "And I don't want to find out. I just want them to pay for the millions of lives lost."

My hands shake as he explains this, and as I think about all of the innocent deaths, the thought of Vaughan's fate pops in my head.

"What will happen to Vaughan?" I ask. "I mean, your actual son?"

"It'll take care of it..." he says, his voice sharp, "but by the end of this, everyone is going to pay some sort of price for this arrangement."

His words linger in the back of my mind. If I say 'no', that's it... we're done for.

But if I say 'yes'...

Like peering at a mirror, I study the person I'd be sparing... this young man named Vaughan.

"I will..." I whisper, barely audible to my own ears.

"What did you say?" Mom asks.

"My answer is yes. I'll do what you say to save their lives," I state, louder than before.

I'm not sure if Kael's relieved by my cooperation or distressed.

"If... if you do this," he begins, "the person you are right now, Ark, no longer exists, or *ever will exist*. Not to me. Not even to you own mother or sister."

He leans in closer, his stern countenance unwavering.

"Are you good with that outcome?" he asks.

"I've m-made my choice," I stutter.

He leans back from the table and settles in his chair. He doesn't seem distressed... maybe resigned?

"Good," Kael says, waving his hand over the table again.

As his hand moves out of the way, a single document replaces every file in the open dossier that had been there moments ago.

"It's a conscription paper," he explains, "by signing on the dotted line, you're agreeing to replace your destiny with his."

I examine the page more, and the lingo is hard to understand. Words like 'in perpetuity', 'notwithstanding execution', and 'His Excellency's Republic Guard' confuse me.

Fuck it. I meant every word.

"Do you have a pen?" I say.

"Wait." Mom speaks up, her words laden with terror. "You don't have to do this! You have a choice!"

"No, Mom, I don't," I say. "This is the only way."

She tears up, struggling against her own restraints... and when I glance back down at the table, Kael's hand leaves behind what I asked for.

"Sign here," he instructs.

There's a box that says 'Given Name', and the one to the right of it says 'Last Name'.

"Do people in the GUILD have last names?" I ask.

"Some do..." Kael replies, almost as a curse, "but most don't. In that box, you'll put down 'Colonial Designation 634-AFZ'. It'll be the same for your mother and sister."

I do as he says, filling out the first box as 'Vaughan'. As soon as I finish, the translucent document disappears into nothing, and Kael rises from his chair.

"*Ark'Onus...*" Mom says to me.

Before I can say anything, two guards march through the door and detach my mom from the table.

"I'm so sorry!" she cries. "I'll make this right!"

Her bound hands reach to me as they take her away, and two more guards enter the room. They stand on either side of me, and all I can do is watch as she disappears behind closing doors.

Now that she's gone, the weight of what I agreed to crushes me.

My head drops close to my hands, and I weep against the cold metal of my handcuffs.

"Eren," Kael says, "what's the status on the machine?"

Eren winces, waving a hand 'so-so'.

"They haven't repaired it since the last mission. Can't guarantee results, sir," he replies.

"Shit," Kael spits. "No, it's fine. We have what we have. Bring it in."

I stare up at Eren, then back to Kael.

"Bring what in?" I ask.

"Right. There's one last thing," Kael explains. "In order to survive basic, or any life after this moment, your memories are going to be altered."

I freeze, realizing what he said.

The door opens again, but this time an older man in a lab coat shows up with a team dragging a trolley behind them. On top of it is some kind of computer, medicine tubes, electrical probes... and a thick-gauge needle.

"That applies to your mother and sister as well," Kael says.

Part 2

Crucible

Chapter 9

VAUGHAN

Pain is the last thing I remember. Tiny fragments come and go, and as I'm sitting in this shuttle seat, I'm not even sure how I got here.

Wait... how did I get here?

There are two rows of seats going down a navy-blue aisle, and against the hull are arm-length portholes. Outside of them, stars fly by from right to left. There are constellations out there I can't make out or even name.

Name... what is my name? Is it Ar—

"*Goddamn it! What have you done to me?!*" I screamed, having banged my head against a sterile padded wall.

"Augh!" I groan.

An agonizing wave surges deep within my head. I bury my face in my hands, and when I remove them, a trickle of blood lands on my palm.

My hands shake...

"*Ahhh!*" I cried, hands and arms bound.

I remembered pieces of a chair, a restraint on my right hand, and a long, thick needle exiting the side of my head. Blue and red lasers circle and dart around my scope of vision until finally, there was only darkness. As the light of the room faded, my body convulsed.

"Hold him down!" *a faceless man said* – *accompanied by other men in white lab coats.* "The synaptic protocol won't hold if he doesn't stop regressing like this! Are you deaf?! Restrain him!"

Why did he say that?

I try to dig further only to be met with another wave of pain and disappearing fragments from the recesses of my mind's eye.

Then... I remember. I remember Kael, the man who almost killed my mom but who's also my father?

Someone, possibly him, mentioned that an invading force scuttled a captured craft. The people that had lived on board this ship were now scattered or dead.

But... why? What happened? I grasp at fragments, but I can't remember everything...

My dad, who raised me until I was four, but who's also not my father?

Mom making supper for Ann'Elise and me. Both fathers are missing.

The deal I made to protect my sister and mom, my family, but I remember it differently – all of it blended through the memories of the man I now call Father. Everything blurs, and two distinct realities take up space in my head, while it all struggles to keep from spilling out of my nostrils.

I bleed from my nose again.

"Errgh!" A second pang wracks my head.

I'm two different people wearing the same face.

Electrical discharges crackle in front of a canvas of black as I close my eyes, and to make it all end, I try to stop thinking altogether.

I scan the cabin, and I scan for someone else here... no one. I'm here by myself. While I'm holding one hand to my throbbing right temple, I leave my seat and check underneath it. Maybe there's some sort of clue there: a wallet, ID papers, something.

I peer down... nothing.

My legs carry me up slowly, and as I lean against the head of my seat. There's an overhead compartment above me, and when I open it, there's a single illuminated pad within it. I snatch it, eagerly trying to find some sort of answer as to why I'm here, who I am, and how I got here...

My hand falls from my head, and I examine an illuminated paper-thin sheet. On the surface is my reflection: a shaven face, chestnut brown hair, a fair complexion, and dark cobalt-blue irises staring back at me. I orient it, and it fills the screen with text, save a picture in the top left corner. The photo is of a young man, dressed well with a stern look about him, on what appears to be a legal document.

"By mandate of the GUILD Republic, Congress and the Elect House Council of the Senate, we hereby conscribe the following citizen," I read, "Vaughan..."

I read the text again, circling back on the name. I glance back at the picture and flip the sheet around, my reflection visible on the back. In haste, I pitch it around again and fixate on the photo.

That's me. I'm him. I'm Vaughan. *That's* my name.

Unlike before, my head doesn't hurt. I think I'm on the right track.

I check the overhead storage again, and there's nothing else there. Just this sheet.

"Attention passengers," a voice says above me, *"we are approaching Port Yegevni. Please take your seat and secure yourself in."*

Doing as the PA says, I strap myself in. A phantom memory lingers on three straps being tightened across my chest... and like my whole body starts shaking. I try to distract myself and peer out the window again. Suddenly, an *enormous* shipyard comes into view above a large moon tinted red with swirling white clouds. Large multi-decked ships come and go from several thousand terminals, and I can only make out a small fraction of this station.

No sooner do I strap in than the entire cabin lurches forward and halts. There's a sensation that comes with this, like your stomach drops into your boots, but it doesn't make me lose my lunch. I don't even remember having any lunch to lose, anyway.

A chime sounds over the PA, and the door at the head of the cabin suddenly slides open.

"Offload!" a masculine voice barks.

I freeze. I focus toward the end of the cabin, and from out of the doorway, a tall, broad-shouldered man appears. He wears pressed terracotta-coloured clothes with a closed collar that touches the top of his neck, and a white trim runs down the length of his coat-like tunic, which extends past his knees. His hands rest at his sides, his body impatiently rigid.

"I said *offload*! Last stop, *recruit!*" he growls.

"O-okay!" I reply.

There should be more items on me, maybe a satchel or ID, but all I own is this sheet. I clutch it to my chest, unbuckle from my seat, and hurry to the front of the cabin.

"Good, good! His Excellency likes eagerness," the coffin of a man says, "and trust you me, we're gonna need all of that goin' forward. Now git off my ship, and show that pad to customs!"

I pass the man, who dwarfs me by two feet, and head through a passage module that leads to an open airlock. Beyond it is a well-lit terminal hall, leading up.

"Customs is that way," the man grunts. "Now get a move on!"

I scramble, hurrying up the terminal walkway, and glimpse a red moon falling below the periphery of the bridge. When I finally get to the customs kiosk, there's a large desk at the end with a square metal arch to its left. Once I make it to the end, the hiss of the bridge's airlock startles me as it closes behind my feet. Ahead is a middle-aged woman wearing the same colour uniform as the man, but on the tops of her shoulders are silver plates. I remember someone calling them "shoulder marks", but I can't recall who. Before I approach, I notice that they have two dark grey lines that run through the middle.

"Papers, please," the woman asks.

Her eyes are mildly sunken, disinterested, but not without some modicum of discipline.

"This?" I ask, showing her the only possession I own.

"You got it, Ace," she replies, her tone almost sarcastic. "Pass it over, and I'll scan you through."

I hand it over, standing a foot away from the desk. As she takes it, her gaze doesn't leave me until the sheet is firmly within her grasp.

"Okay," she says, "do you affirm your name is Vaughan, citizen of the Colonial Dominion of the Nebulous Reach? That your homeworld is Korvingshal VI and that your colonial designation is 634-AFZ?"

"... Yes," I say.

She stares at me squarely, squints at the sheet in her hands, and faces me.

"You need to be sure, recruit," she stresses. "If your testimony is false, or you have falsified information on your record, the penalty is death."

I swallow hard, not sure what to think.

"Yes, it is!" I say, much louder this time.

"Good," she replies, typing something on her keyboard, and she closes her hand, holding my sheet upward.

The sheet disappears into thin air.

"Welcome to Port Yegevni," she greets. "According to your papers, you're scheduled for genetic screening before we can ship you off to basic. Standard procedure. Pass through here, and wait with the others in the atrium."

I obey, passing through the metal gate and into a much larger room. Once I get there, I'm immediately surrounded by the hum of a large crowd of people. I wait at the edge of the atrium, hands awkwardly by my sides as I watch different circles of people talk with one another.

Some women congregate together, wearing lace and silk dresses the likes of which I've never seen before, and other women wear patched linen tunics and flax leggings, and a few have similar bust-length, high-cut leather and synthetic jackets. As for the men, the division is similar, with some guys wearing smooth fold-over coats over dark slacks and tall black or brown boots. Others wear the same rough material as their female counterparts. Their jackets differ, with some trimmed with fur, others not, and they have outlandish hairstyles and facial tattoos that remind me of—

My head throbs, but not nearly as bad as before.

It's the first time I consider what I'm wearing. I glance down at the cuffs of my jacket and at my pants. From what I can tell, it seems like a mixture of rough flax slacks and hardy boots, but my jacket is smooth... like some guys here who look like they own an entire planet. For all I know, they might.

I'm not sure what this means, but from what I gather from the crowd, it places me *somewhere*. Though I'm not sure where exactly.

But the last thing I want to do is mingle, and I also don't want to be an outcast right out of the gate. I wonder what my dad would say, what words he would have to give me. Maybe something like:

"Make your presence known. Be yourself, but conduct yourself with the decorum of the party, whatever that looks like."

And my mom... she'd be very to the point, in life and with other things: keep your centre, strike first, and let the gods remember your name.

"*My man* Vaughan!" a chipper masculine voice says to my right, making me jump. "It's been years! How have you been?"

As I peer over my shoulder, two girls and one boy approach me, all of them dressed *very* well. They sound familiar... but I can't place names to match their faces.

"Hi!" I say, feigning excitement.

"We didn't think you'd enlist, but we're glad you did," one girl with shoulder-length blonde hair says, sporting a navy blue high-cropped jacket. "Chloeja has *not* stopped talking about you since we got here! How come we don't see more of you?"

Oh, shit.

"Um," I say, "I, uh, haven't been very well these last few years... the colony's climate does a number on my joints."

From what I can recall, that's not technically a lie. I remember being both fit and in ailing health.

"Ohhh. Well, depending on where they ship you, it could be better or worse!" the blonde girl teases.

"Heh heh." I laugh nervously.

Great. I can't put a face to whom they're talking about... I remember something about a girl named Chloeja from a long time ago... but nothing recent. *Come on, Vaughan, what does she look like?*

"Vaughanie!" A charming, feminine voice rings past the ear of one of my, her... uh... our friends.

The speaker is a young woman, maybe about twenty or twenty-one, with messy ear-length raven-black hair. Her exuberant eyes are a golden shade of green, and her tan skin contrasts with the light colours of her clothes. Like some of the other girls I saw earlier, she's wearing a white lace dress with a halter top, with her shoulders covered by an even higher cut fine cloth jacket cropped above her bust line.

Her name matches a younger version of the face I remember from a long while back.

"Chloeja, there you are!" a boy welcomes. "We were just talking about you! Did you cut your hair already?!"

"Nothing bad, I hope! And yes, most basic barbers essentially use garden sheers and kerosene," she replies, hands resting on her hips. "So! Where is he?"

My stomach flips as she says this.

"He's, uh, right here," the blonde girl points out, waving her hand in my direction.

Chloeja rests her arms at her sides and looks me up and down. "... You're Vaughan?" she says, her eyes narrowing. "You seem different. Have you been well?"

"Oh!" I reply. "I was telling everyone I've been sick this last bit. Because of the climate on Korvingshal VI?"

"Oh! Yes," she adds, "it's a tropical hellhole. Thank God you still have both of your lungs!"

Phew! Fuck.

"Right!" I reply. "So! How have you been?"

She tilts her head to her left and brings her hands together. "We'll catch up more soon. They just called your name at booth thirty-one, and you're up next on the chair!"

Her words make me flinch.

"Oh, don't worry; my lab tech was very gentle, and they're very good at what they do," she says with a grin.

Chapter 10

XHYR

"You're off to Naval Academy," I say, checking down a roster, "and you're off to the Heavy Infantry Corps."

I match registry numbers to the faces of new recruits, past the one-way window behind the sample collections lab. Most of them seem eager to fight, and there's that thirty per cent in the periphery. I scan the room from the tinted window, and I can count on one hand how many people would rather be anywhere else. These are the same folks, dressed minimally, simply, and often in clothes made by their own hands.

Colonists. My people, at one time.

Amidst the incoming data stream and mixture of fresh meat, there's the tiny hiss of the sliding door opening behind me; and accompanying it, the *clack* of stiletto heels. As I twist around, the temperature in the room drops by an entire degree.

A woman walks in, wearing a finely stitched black dress what comes down a couple of inches above her knees, sporting a silver necklace with a single sapphire jewel. Cube-like. Her white lab coat almost seems to flow behind the tapered hem of her dress, and in her hands is a single transparent sheet, an illuminated holopad.

"Good *morning*," she greets. "I don't believe we've had the pleasure."

She meets me halfway into the room, like a House noble would... so I take the hint and leave my post.

"I gather not," I say. "I heard the Department of Science was sending a veteran..."

"They're not wrong," she replies, giving me a smirk.

Could just be me, but the way her steel-grey irises gleam behind her glasses seems almost... threatening. Not actively, but like something I'd expect from my men: a cunning killer instinct.

"And no, we haven't had the pleasure," I reiterate. "I'm Major Xhyr Talthor."

"Ah, so *you're* my liaison. Wonderful! Well, in that case," she begins, "I'm Doctor Rachael Vayne, of the Minor House of Arcturus."

As she curtseys using her lab coat, my eyebrows rise at the mention of her name. Not from the name of her House. That, I don't give two shits about... I mean, *who* she is.

The same science officer who *repeatedly* throws out the book on ethics.

The very same woman who created fifty-two different medical treatments, all derived from mad experiments.

Yeah... this is gonna be fun... what the hell is management thinking, sending me someone with *this much* prestige *and* notoriety?

"The pleasure is all mine," I manage to say, bowing in turn.

She smiles and walks right past me, left of the boardroom table and pushed-in chairs and toward the observation terminals.

"I... started testing for genetic aptitude at 0600 hours. So far, we've had three thousand recruits tested and processed, awaiting their post," I say, keeping my accent in check. "I've collected the data the analysts asked for."

She doesn't answer, and instead flits from one terminal to the next, scanning the data like she programmed an algorithm to work the info in her head. Hell, knowing her, she *may* have.

"How many recruits have made the cut for the project so far?" I ask.

"None," she says casually.

I stand in place, watching in horror as some of the best the Republic has to offer are so easily dismissed.

"None of them are?" I repeat, noticing the pitch in my voice escalate.

She stops in her tracks and glances back at me with blatant annoyance...

"They've trained you well, Major," she says, "but I don't expect you to grasp the full magnitude this project requires with the number of folds in your brain."

Ouch... How in the hell did I deserve that?

"It turns out," she adds, "we can't simply rebuild a subject that's already broken down. Conformity, it seems, presents an ever-consuming issue... so, no, we're not currently looking for cohesion alone. This isn't the Legion, after all."

Neat. It's been only a couple of minutes, and I hate her already. Notwithstanding, this lady knows how to balance the meter between instilling fear and respect. I gotta admire that.

"No, what I want is an *apex predator*. A regal lion. Or a powerful orca. The stoic wolf. Major, I'm looking for *the* cornerstone to build my temple! You must understand, nothing else will do."

She strolls away, her parted bangs and high-tied ponytail of charcoal brown flowing behind her. She examines the terminals again, and she stops dead in her tracks.

"Major," she says, "do run this test sample again."

She points her finger at Y-112587, the reading being less than five minutes old.

"Yes, ma'am," I say.

I meet her, shoulder to shoulder, and punch in a command at the terminal to re-sequence the sample.

The numbers come back in, and the DNA analysis appears exactly the same. To me, anyway.

"Run it again," she orders.

Again, I comply, punching it in.

"Again," she says, drawing closer to the monitor.

I do as she says, twice, three times, four times, and I'm dumbfounded as the numbers are *identical*.

The steel grey sheen of her irises illuminates against the glow of the monitor, and when I investigate what the fuss is about, she's staring directly at the genome sequence map layout.

"Interesting..." she says, adding to my confusion. "Have *this* subject brought in! I'd like to take a good look at him."

"I'll see the *recruit* in."

Before I can make the call, she shoots me a disapproving scowl.

Chapter 11

Rachael

There he is.

After years of combing, seeking, I've found it. The sliding doors to the room part, and like a shining ray from the heavens, my specimen makes himself known. He walks in, escorted by a lightly armoured grunt, and is left at the foot of the entrance like an abandoned kitten. The doors close behind him, and the room returns to a tranquil dusk, save a scattering of blinking lights and other screen projections.

I sit myself dead centre of the observation quarters' boardroom table, and, of course, Major Talthor remains standing. It would seem it suits his brutish clout.

But this young specimen... he stands, so lacking in any constructive confidence, and yet he harbours an entire universe of possibilities.

"What's your name, young man?" I ask.

"... Vaughan," he says.

"Speak up, recruit!" the Major barks in that guttural tone of his.

"Vaughan!" the specimen repeats. "My name is Vaughan! Ma'am."

"Of course it is," I reply, standing up from my seat, "and where, may I ask, are you from?"

Oh, he's cast his gaze down. Why ever so?

"Korvingshal VI," he says.

"Ahh, another mineral colonist! Lovely," I reply with a grand hand gesture. "Major, I do believe our ranks are in dire need of some resiliency, are they not?"

"Yes, Doctor," the good bulldog replies.

The corners of my mouth upturn into a smile. This truly is momentous!

"Come, child," I say. "Let's get a better look at you."

Yes, there's a drop in his confidence as he walks closer, the tick expressed in the rubbing of his index and middle fingers over his thumb... but only in his right hand. The left is as rigid as a steel beam.

He stops, a mere centimetre from the edge of the table. While the major may regard this specimen as an unshaped lump of clay in *desperate* need of shaping, firing, and filling with purpose, I notice something else entirely: potential.

So, having gauged my hypothesis, I dive into my prescribed method. Now, to elicit the proper stimuli.

I catalogue *everything* this specimen offers: from the sheen in his dark cobalt irises to the tightening muscle and sinew above his clavicle. The faded alterations to the skin below his left cheek, while some may consider a defect, tell an interesting story of a tattoo that was removed. Again, what window do his eyes possess! Not the substance of their colour, nor what cones or rods make up his irises, but, oh, what an enigma they present. The shape and scope of his lips are ... oh, now look what I've done; he's squirming.

Success. I shift to my right, where the major stands, to see if he shares in my victory! But when I regard him, he seems as uncomfortable with the variable in my experiment as the specimen himself.

How very dull...

"He may go, Major," I instruct.

"Guards!" he bellows.

There is a sort of nuanced appreciation I have for the military chain of command. One officer says "leap", and those given the order jump. And without question.

Truly, there's power to this.

I watch, eagerly, as the same guard who walked my specimen in shows him back to the petri dish. Once the major and I are alone, I circle around to the other end of the boardroom table and face him.

"I want him at the top of the list." The words fall off my tongue like a statement of fact.

"... Doctor?" he asks.

"Is what I said unclear?" I return.

"No, no," the major says, his face all muddled up and reeking of confusion, "it seems to me that this recruit doesn't bear any notable qualities, and he has no notable connections with a Major House. Let alone the skill set from a Minor House. The Korvingshal System is a poor sector of the Azores Dominion, and while his father, Kael, is a commander, he's only served a handful of years in a survey fleet. I'm confused because there are several more qualified recruits in the wings, hand-trained by masters-at-arms their entire lives."

"Ahh," I reply, "so *now* my theorem requires the stamp of pedigree to quantify success. Of course, how silly of me. Why hadn't I thought of that before?"

I tease, but it seems like the major is quite serious.

"I'll be frank, Major," I explain. "It doesn't matter. He could have landed at this port with a silver spoon in his mouth, like some others, or been thrown onto our doorstep from a prison colony that is, honestly, too full. No, what I'm interested in is the full scope of what I can extract from this specime—"

The major gives me a slow, narrowing stare.

"—recruit. What I can extract from this recruit, and how he fits the mould of that *predator* I mentioned earlier. And, again, nature in all of its fury is a far better leveller than the social guises we use to make sense of our external world."

With that, I snap my fingers and materialise the holopad I left on the table back into my waiting hand.

"My work here is done," I announce, "and there is still much to do before the day is out."

While I beam excitedly toward the major, he stands in increasing discomfort as he continues to say nothing.

"I appreciate the data you've collected; you've been most useful, Major." I speak with a tone that suggests I'm grateful for his compliance.

"Doctor." He nods before he takes his leave.

As the doors to the corridor part for me, the squeaky sound of the major's feet scuffle along the polished onyx floor.

"I hope to see you next time the station has a new batch of recruits," he says through mild vocal strain.

His veiled lie is not a clever one, and what's worse, it's shielded in his own ignorance. So I face him with my holopad clutched to my chest.

"Oh, quite the contrary," I say in a heightened pitch. "You'll be coming with me."

The transmogrified shock on his face is well worth every syllable I spoke.

"Ma'am...?" he asks, his tone denoting purposeful respect.

Must I repeat myself a second time, you oaf!? The ire painted on my face causes the major to recoil his neck away from me.

"Yes, like I said, you're coming with me. Given your past skills as an instructor and given your time serving alongside the Legion, you've been selected as my drill sergeant in the next stage of the plan," I explain.

"That, that was years ago," he says, holding back his words. "I haven't drilled in ten, and the last time I served as an operative was when Daniel was restructuring the ranks."

"Exactly! Your experience, track record, and adherence to detail," I return, raising an eyebrow of approval, "speak volumes, no matter how far back that may have transpired. Your ability to get results is, without doubt, absolutely necessary for what is to come!"

The room is positively electric, like all the strings are connecting and all the gears are aligning.

"Drill sergeant would be a significant demotion from major," he retorts.

"Rest assured, it'll only be temporary," I assure with a devilish smile, "and once basic has wrapped up and the chaff has *burned*, your role will only increase in value."

Now it's the major's turn to squirm, like the specimen before him. Oh, how I'd love to be an extracting code of cypher in his mind right now! Might he be regretting his high academic and field performance?

Perhaps now, yes.

But, oh, how much he is a vital cog in a divine machine that is almost ready to switch on.

Chapter 12

Vaughan

Day 1 of Basic Training

It's a strange sensation, travelling through a wormhole. Patchwork memories remind me that this isn't my first time travelling across several parsecs in less than a couple of minutes, but I remember how every time, the sensation is awful...

As I'm strapped in, clutching at my restraints, every tiny hair on my body stands on end. The weight of a truck presses down on me and the sensation of free-falling envelopes me *at the same time*. All the while, my spine tingles as a swirling blue and dark red ellipsis ring permeates away from the empty space we pass through. A long-forgotten fact floating around in my head knows this is called an Einstein-Rosen Event, or an ER Halo, or just the 'halo' of a wormhole. While we pass through it, I can't help this uneasy feeling, like I'm being scrutinized. Not by the two hundred recruits around me, or the sergeant at the front of the cabin, but by some unseen force reminding me we've violated the laws of physics... the sensation reminds me of a whisper, but I don't actually hear anything.

Then the halo collapses and dissipates from the reflection in my nearest window, and the unease subsides. I search around to see if anyone else is as unnerved as me, but half of the people I've met are either laughing in hushed whispers or completely deadpan. Hell, even Chloeja to my left nodded off through the crossing!

"*Attention,*" a gruff voice announces from above, "*we've entered Nostrean low orbit. Prepare for re-entry.*"

When the pilot said this, I wasn't expecting the additional G to hit me so quickly.

As the pressure builds on top of me, the hull around me shakes, and through my left-hand window, a large planetary horizon rises from the porthole's bottom edge. There are patches of blue, white, and grey as the growing sphere enters the corner of my eye, but everything fades as I grab tightly onto the padded restraints on both of my shoulders.

"Welcome to Nostro, Cadets," the sergeant up front bellows. "It won't be long now before landfall!"

No sooner does he say this does the ship creak and groan against the loud roar of the ship's aft engines. I have mixed memories of smoother trips with my mother, and one time I flew on a dingy between two Nomadic frigates.

When was that...?

As I try to remember more, a dull pang hits my temples, but not as bad as when I first arrived at Port Yegevni.

Some of my peers scream at the rattling in their seats. Most of them are like me: holding on for dear life but keeping everything bottled in. And there's Chloeja, who's... yeah, she's still asleep. Of course she is.

The roar ahead of me gets louder, immediately stops, and the ground below me shudders. The restraints keeping me in swing upward.

"All out!" the sergeant barks.

The doors to my left fly open, flooding the hull with light. In no time at all, Chloeja exits through the opening. I don't hesitate, and I follow her lead.

As soon as I fall from the deck down to the frost-covered ground, I regain myself... and freeze.

I take a deep breath, icy air stinging every corner of my lungs as I stare up at an impossibly large blue sky. I quake, imagining that if I take too large of a step, I'll get sucked right up into it.

"Keep it moving, Cadet!" the sergeant cries mere inches from my ear.

I startle, shift my eyes forward, and follow Chloeja and the others into a converging straight line.

"That's right, keep those feet of yours moving! Instructor ain't got all day!"

The sergeant's voice echoes behind me as I keep pace with the herd, and like them, I'm wearing faded terracotta reliefs, designed the same as the officers in my periphery... only not as flashy. I linger for a moment on how the odd sergeant wears a single white stripe along his coat and neck collar. The shining metal on their shoulders is etched with an insignia of a bird of sorts. Lining his sides are several pockets. Other officers have the same uniform but different stripes.

We don't have any stripes, shoulder marks, or anything unique on our reliefs.

What we have is a common look – a complete departure from the unique clothing everyone sported at Port Yegevni. I can no longer make out who can afford what, who is more well off, or who had a harder life.

In this rushed procession, we are all the same, and I'm thinking that's exactly the point.

I try to keep pace, despite the unfamiliar burning in my chest and the weakness around my knees. An encroaching shadow eclipses us, blotting out the rays from the sky above. I stare up and take in the obstruction... and what I behold is a metal wall, fifty feet high, with taller fortifications further back. Ahead of me and everyone else in line are two wide-open doors. They look built for giants.

As I pass through, tight bands of marching cadets fully suited in power armour drill with large bulky weapons. Their mechanical whirring and boot compressions drown out the footfalls of our issued boots as we proceed into the centre of a large marching square. Every detail of the muster is exactly as my father recounted it.

"And halt! Section off, line two!" a harsh feminine voice directs me.

I startle but do as she says, breaking away from the line ahead of me, and stop right behind the last person at the front. The hurried shuffle of boots makes the sound of stepping on cornstarch against the frozen ground behind me, and beyond a head or two, I can make out the outline of a raised platform.

"A-ttention!" a voice to my left booms. "Officer on deck!"

Everything stops. The shuffling, murmurs, and fidgeting all around me ceases *immediately*. All save the echo of a single pair of boots clacking against a metal pathway. I hear it rounding the corner, and the man who steps up to overlook us all is the same man who scrutinized me back at Port Yegevni.

"At ease," the man says with an almost acrid annoyance.

Everyone around me separates their stance by one footstep, and I quickly do the same. As we do, the soft falling snow cascades around the man dressed in the same reliefs as he was in that darkened room from before.

"As I've said many times in my years of service, the first and last words out of your mouths will be 'sir'. Am I understood?"

"Sir, yes, sir!" I say in unison with the other cadets.

"Good. My name is Xhyr Talthor, a retainer of House Rurik. I'll be your drill sergeant for the next few months and will ensure that as few of you will die in service to the Republic Guard... as is necessary," the man booms with little effort.

"As some of you know, Fort Durran is not your typical outfit. You won't be used as cannon fodder, nor will you be sitting pretty at the helm of a very expensive Republic starship. No, His Excellency has devised that by the make of your DNA, you're destined to be the tip of his spear... If the Legion is his scalpel, his dagger in the shadows, then every one of you will be the hammer that goes where no one in his armed forces dares to go."

Looking for a familiar face, I spot Chloeja further into the crowd. Unlike before, her focus is steely and straight ahead... it actually creeps me out a bit.

"Having said that, I see *far more* square pegs that must fit into round holes than pegs that already fit... and as God is my witness, you *will* fit into the round hole of this outfit. And... if you belong to a Noble House, you are not excluded from this chastisement. In fact, you can and *will* learn a thing or two from your colonial counterparts. They've seen things that'll make your blue blood curdle, and by the end of your service, *so help me God,* so will you. Is *that* understood?"

"Sir, yes, sir!" we echo.

"I'm sorry; you're going to have to repeat that in my good ear. I *can't hear you!*" he booms even louder.

"Sir! Yes, sir!" I strain, matching the surrounding pitch.

"Alright. I'm done looking at you lot. Go get yourself presentable and immunized. Can't have whatever diseases you're carrying infect my outfit. Dismissed."

"Next!" a shrill, booming voice echoes ahead of me.

I take a step, single file, as another sharp pain stings both of my wrists.

"Next!" the voice repeats above us, over a metal canopy.

With each step I take walking through one immunization stand after another, I wince as my wrists bruise even more. I thought the pulmonary and muscle mass tests were invasive, but this is torture! By the last injection, a fever already wreaks havoc inside my head. The chill of the air worsens, and my muscles weaken as I catch a duffle bag thrown at me.

"Cadet," one of the corporals shouts at me, "what is your dysfunction?!"

"I-I'm fine!" I reply.

"You're *what?*" he stresses.

"Sir, I'm fine, s-sir!" My speech warbles.

"Aw, shit. Medic! We got another one. Get him to the infirmary hold before he hurls all over my boots."

"Yes, sir," a softer voice replies.

I break out of line, my knees shaking as the antibodies and mRNA solutions from *millions* of different worlds attack my sheltered immune system. Gentle arms hoist me to my feet, and a complete stranger frees my duffle bag from my hands as I stumble away to a steel bunker etched with a red emblem above the door. I can barely make it out, but it's shaped like some kind of bird holding a solid cross in its talons.

"Doctor, you were right." The medic's feminine voice rings out into the hall. "634-AFZ had an adverse reaction."

"Ohhh, did he? What a surprise." A familiar voice grates against my mind. "Well, do lay him down on this gurney. There are a few more tests I'd like to administer while he recovers."

Blinking seems to help ease the blurriness, and the image that hovers mere centimetres above me is... the scary lady from the port?!

"Ah, yes, my specimen returns to me," the woman says. "I'm not sure if you remember, but I'm Rachael Vayne. Outside these walls, you'll have to refer to me as 'Doctor', but for today, we're going to make an exception."

Her words are as icy as they are inviting. I don't like it.

"Now, let's see here," she says, adjusting her glasses as she guides a long lamp over my torso. "Oh, dear, you really are fighting quite hard, aren't you? Let's explore what else is at work."

A deep foreboding sinks into my chest, like the lamp itself is pressing down on me.

"Ahhh," she muses, "I knew your lungs were quite remarkable. Oh, if only you understood what it is I'm seeing right now! Are you aware that pockets of your lungs produce oxygen from excess CO_2? Perhaps not, and you might not realise that the steel alloy in your bones has completely replaced the calcium found in most Terrans. Very *interesting* indeed. And highly unusual. Now, don't be frightened... these are *just* the qualities that make you an asset."

Shit...

Her words seem to come out as a purr, quizzical and dripping with entertainment. And here I am, lying helpless on this stretcher.

"Well, since your boosters are so wretchedly out of date, you're going to have to spend your first night here instead of at your barracks. Not bad for you, since it'll be a reprieve from the hard bunks you'll be issued from now on. Oh, don't give me that look; someone will keep a close eye on you! My lab assistants are both competent... and devout. You won't find a more trustworthy team to take care of you!" she says with a wink.

Seconds later, Rachael gets up and leaves my tiny room. Now I'm completely alone. The lights dim, save a couple of blinking red and blue lights on the walls, but the realization that I'm alone for the first time since Port Yegevni finally sinks in.

Then it hits me.

My name is Vaughan, but I wasn't always called that. But I can't remember what my name was before.

The man I recall as my father, Kael, isn't actually my father.

My mom and Ann'Elise *were* in danger, but I traded *everything* for them.

I *have* a father, but I'm certain he was murdered when I was young.

They scattered all my friends to the four corners of the universe... or they killed them.

And they destroyed my home, the *Nautilus*. The ones who wear the same uniform as me... they destroyed it.

As these thoughts and emotions churn within me, I clutch the blanket Rachael laid over top of me tight to my chin. I roll over, curling my legs close, and sob... like I did before they took Mom away...

Chapter 13

VAUGHAN

Day 2 of Basic Training

A shout jolts me awake. My eyes flash open as a surge of adrenaline shoots through me. As I lay in bed, I blink, and stare at the dim lights hanging above me.

The raised voice sounds like it's coming from the other side of my room's window. I lean up in bed with weak and shaky arms and peer outside.

The odd head bobs past my line of vision, followed by what I think is a drill sergeant, barking clear orders.

"About-face!" a sharp, feminine voice hollers. "Left-march!"

Parade. I rub my hand against my sweaty face as I remember seeing a parade march... but I can't say when.

It's hard to breathe, and when I sit up, my chest tightens. As my jaw and brow muscles ache, I turn in bed, watching the blinking lights on the wall to my left. Centre of the wall is a monitor that reads all of my vitals on a screen, including oxygen, heart readings and pulmonary. I think that has to do with my lungs.

Rachael... did she find out I'm a Thetian? Does she know about Mom and Ann?

While I rest my back against the wall, the heart monitor does a quick jump. I pull my legs up close and clutch my sheets tight against my knees. It wasn't enough that they killed my father; they had to burn down my home too.

Damn them...

My breath catches in my throat as my eyes burn.

"Damn them...!" I wince, placing a hand to where Kael and his men drilled a needle through my skull.

The fragments of my memories, once like a dream, start converging into solid recall. And with it, all the clarity of the wrongs done to me and my family. How the GUILD murdered my father, tore Ann and Mom away, and sent me to this frozen wasteland. The only thing that's completely blocked from me is the name I had before I became 'Vaughan'.

Oh, gods... what if Mom and Ann don't remember what I do? What if they don't remember anything we've been through, the life we've had on the *Nautilus*... or Dad?

"Argh!" I seethe, looking down at the stretcher. A phantom pain spreads up my forearm where Natalia held on tight.

She was right there next to me... trusted me, and in a second, she was gone. Cut down by Republic soldiers. Cast aside by their *cruelty* and *apathy*.

"I'll kill them..." I exhale a shaky breath. "I don't care how many I have to; they're dead."

It's not like it'd be hard. I tore through Kael's men on the *Nautilus*, breaking open the floodwaters of my wrath.

As I think more, it's not just my injustices that rage in my heart... it's someone else's.

"What?" I whisper.

It doesn't seem altogether clear, but Vaughan's memories... the original Vaughan, his struggles to prepare for military service surface in my mind, mingling with my own fury. His consecutive failures, his fruitless training, and the desperation on Kael's face. The GUILD's transgressions extend to Vaughanie, the same as me. What's true to me blends into what my mind's eye tells me is real...

But what is real?

"I-I don't know..." I stammer softly, a knot in my stomach forming.

No. Stop it. I'm lost if I sink any more than I already have.

Okay. I'll avenge you too. I'm not sure what Kael did to ensure you survive, but your memories are mine now, and I'll make the GUILD pay for what they've done.

"How though...?" I say softly, peering out into the empty infirmary room. "How do I even begin to fight back?"

Before I can think, the door to my room opens.

"Good morning, Private," a soft feminine voice greets. She sounds familiar.

I snap to attention, a fresh surge of adrenaline coursing through me, my back pressed against the wall as my legs fall straight on my stretcher.

"G-good morning!" I reply.

The young woman examines me, her keen baby-blue eyes examining the readouts on my vitals monitor, and she shifts her gaze to me. She smiles, and it catches me off guard.

"You've improved a lot since yesterday," she says, sounding relieved, "you were in such a state that we didn't have a chance to be properly acquainted. I'm Corporal Reilah, a medic on base and one of Doctor Vayne's assistants."

"Oh," I reply. "You helped me in here yesterday, right?"

Reilah smiles broader, bobbing her head. "I did. How are you feeling today?"

Her kindness is disarming, and I hesitate as I search for my words. "I... I'm okay. I think. My head really hurts, and I can't move too much."

She nods as I speak and takes a seat next to my stretcher. "That's to be expected. You were running a pretty high fever yesterday, but it seems like your body's building up immunities to the vaccines nicely. And, faster than normal, actually!"

Because I'm Thetian?

"The only oddity I can tell is that your blood pressure's a little higher than normal," she continues, her gaze directed to my vitals, and she flashes her eyes at my empathetically. "Are you homesick?"

The question cuts through me like a knife. I flinch, a wave of vulnerability crashing down on me. I'm not even sure how to begin answering her.

"Yes..." I sigh, trying to keep all my mixed emotions together.

"That's normal," she assures me. "Some cadets have never been away from their families, and for them, basic is the first time being on their own. For me, it was really tough when I was conscripted a few years ago because I grew up on an agricultural world."

"How so?" I ask.

"The colonial world I lived on, Jaskandir III, was like one great big farm, and family was never too far away. Then, when I got my conscription papers, I shipped off for processing, and my genetic aptitude aligned me with healthcare. So, I became a medic."

As Reilah explains this, she reaches over to my bedside table and hands me a paper-thin translucent blue sheet. Its likeness is identical to the document I had at Port Yegevni.

"This is *your* holopad. It's part of your assigned gear and can hold pretty much any book you can think of. For basic though, you're only allowed two books. No, three. The *Code of Conduct for New Recruits*, the *Durranir Bible* and... this."

Reilah presses a button on my holopad and downloads a book titled the *Codex Republica*.

"This book basically serves as an encyclopaedia of the last two and a half thousand years. From the reign of the first emperors of the Old Empire in the late twenty-fourth century to the start of the Hylii War with the Thriaxians within the last few years," she says.

"The Thriaxians?" I repeat as I remember Kael's explanation on the *Rugia*.

"That's right. I'm not sure how much you know from... Korvingshal VI," she says reading from my chart, "but this should help fill in the gaps before you have class in a couple of hours. And don't worry—the time and directions for your modified schedule are already programmed into your holopad."

I nod as a gracious smile spreads on my lips. "Thank you."

Reilah returns the smile and checks my vitals a final time before issuing me a salute.

"Ma'am?" I ask as she stands in the doorway. "What does the GUILD stand for?"

"Like... morally?"

"No," I clarify, "I mean the abbreviation for GUILD. I've seen it on documents, and in this book, but I can't tell you its full form."

She looks at me funny, like even if I've been living under a rock, I should *absolutely* know what the name represents.

"It... stands for the Galactic Unified Integral-Fief League of Dominions."

"Ah," I reply, "that's a mouthful."

Despite my previous lack of understanding, Reilah smiles warmly at me. "It is, yes. Hence the abbreviation."

The base complex is a maze. Fort Durran has corridors that twist and wind dizzyingly. To make things worse, no matter how I orient my holopad, I can't find my lecture hall. Even as I left the infirmary, ready to go in my reliefs, the map pointers and confusing directions on my holopad had me travelling in circles.

"Come on..." I sigh, jogging frantically.

It's bad enough that they pulled me from regular duties, and now this.

"No, wait... okay." Sweat beads off my forehead and down on the front of my reliefs. "404, 405... here."

Before I touch the panel to room 406, I wipe my face with my elbow, sweat staining my left forearm.

Just take a second. Breathe. Stand up straight... you can do this.

After I've calmed down, I hit the door panel, and it opens up to a well-maintained semi-circular lecture hall. There are five rows of seats parted by a path leading to a raised podium. Standing behind it is a corporal I've seen next to Xhyr and a few other instructors.

"*Cadet,*" she says sternly, flicking her short sandy-blonde hair out of her eyes, "why are you late?"

I gulp hard. "I couldn't f-find the lecture hall, ma'am."

Her face contorts in disgust, and she slowly scans the room in front of her. "These cadets had no trouble. What's your name?"

"Vaughan," I reply, more feverish than before, "634-AFZ, ma'am."

"Vaughan... I'll remember that. Take a seat," she orders, giving me a half-hearted salute.

"Yes, ma'am!" I exclaim, vigorously returning the salute.

I don't have to search far as Chloeja's head pops up, and she quickly flags me down. There's a quizzical air about her as she stares me down, but behind it is a tremendous amount of concern.

"Where have you—" she whispers, leaning low to our shared desk. Before she can finish, the corporal ahead of us slams her hands down on her podium.

"Right! It's come to my attention from High Command that not all of you are informed of the reasons for your conscription, nor the enemy we face. This, I will remedy, curtailing your collective ignorance."

The corporal leans against the surface of the podium, scanning the room.

"For those who don't bunk in my casern, my name is Corporal Nevanor 748-UTP, and I thank you not to repeat my colonial designation when addressing me. Now! Can anyone tell me *whom* we are fighting against? And when you speak, state your full name."

As Nevanor says this, she glares at me. "Except for you, Vaughan. I already know *your* late ass."

I cast my head down, and Chloeja spits a mild *tch* in my defence, sizing Nevanor up.

There's a brief period of silence, then a woman with long platinum-blonde hair stands up, clearing her throat as she does. "Lynette Alvarah," she begins, "we're fighting the Thriaxians, ma'am."

"Spot on. Now, while I have you on your feet, can you tell me why?" Nevanor presses.

"Because of the Silesian Incident. The aliens killed twenty-five million colonists five years ago."

My mouth hangs open. Twenty-five *million*?

"Correct," Nevanor replies, motioning Lynette to take her seat. "Without warning, the Thriaxian Kingdom invaded the Silesia System in the Dominion of Azores and massacred those innocent colonists. So we launched a counter-strike all the way on the other side of the known universe, engaging them in their backyard. We've been at war with them ever since."

My chest constricts as Nevanor lectures. Her expression is grim.

"And, for you history buffs in my class," she continues, "you're all aware that a merciless Thriaxian assault is what caused the fall of the Old Empire, sparking the Great Exodus to our now capital world of Haradrun in the thirty-fourth century."

A memory flashes before me: Kael telling me about the Thriaxians on the *Rugia*, and a disjointed memory of watching the news on Korvingshal VI, illustrating the destruction of the Silesian star system.

"These jellyfish assholes have come back to finish the job. All I can say to them is 'good luck'. His Excellency the President-General calls on us, loyal Terrans, and we answer the call. As the drill sergeant this morning said, we *will* contain the Thriaxian menace... and bring an end to the fight on the doorstep of their core worlds, no matter the cost. I certainly don't have to tell you all that they've fucked with the wrong species."

There's a collective energy of camaraderie in the room. The large man across the path from me squints, nodding, and when I turn to Chloeja, she has the same focused ire on her face.

It's the same gut emotion I carried with me about the GUILD since this morning: vengeance.

"On the topic of species, this is what a Thriaxian looks like." Nevanor dims the lights.

Above her, the projection of a humanoid figure comes into view.

"This is a scale model of a Thriaxian cadaver, kept on ice." She steps to our left. "As you can see, they're humanoid, bi-pedal, standing at about seven feet tall. They're lithe in build, with elongated limbs, and their skin pigments range from dark purple to pale blue. From what we've recovered, Thriaxian feet and hands are very aquadynamic, which makes sense, given their natural habitat is water. It explains the gills too, found right under their back jawline. The puzzling thing is, they have a secondary breathing system in their chest cavity... and frankly, the academics are out to lunch as to why. I can't tell you. And lastly, they have very small mouths and several shoulder-length tendrils that protrude from the crown of their heads... and that's pretty much the only hair you'll find on their bodies, if you want to call it that. We think this subject in the projection's a male, but it's hard to tell."

Like when Nevanor told us about the Silesian Incident, I'm awestruck as I stare at the life-like projection.

"Ma'am" – a voice breaks my train of thought – "Chloeja Nadjidhar of House Tamir. How are we supposed to fight these things if their natural environment is aquatic?"

Nevanor nods at Chloeja approvingly. "A fine question. So far, our theatre of war with the Thriaxians has mostly been in planetary orbit of their worlds. Standard naval tactics with fighter-craft dogfights, carrier to carrier. When we do engage them on land, their forces are heavily armed with multi-legged mechs. In that department, we suffer."

My gaze returns to the Thriaxian hologram.

"Ma'am," I say as I stand, "what weaknesses do the Thriaxians have?"

"Question of the hour, Cadet," Nevanor replies. "As far as we can tell, the Thriaxians are like water-breathing mammals. Except their bones are made of a cartilage-selenium hybrid and can break easily when out of water. The trick is to get them *out* of their power armour, no matter the variant they wear. Yes, they're frail on land, but the power armour they wear is *very* sophisticated. They surpass our technology by tens of thousands of years... maybe more. Could be why we've only ever seen a couple of their carriers in the orbit of their worlds per engagement."

I blink as she says this. The GUILD has been the boogeymen of my people in the Fleet since I as far back as I can remember. But, the way Nevanor talks about the Thriaxians is unnerving... and the fact of their brutality is unquestionable. If I thought the GUILD was a force to be reckoned with... the Thriaxians are much more so.

"Where are the Thriaxians from, ma'am?" I ask.

"The Pavo-Indus Sphere." Nevanor collapses the projection and brings up a map of tens of thousands of galaxies.

The projection zooms away from the collection of galaxies labelled *GUILD Republic* along a threaded web of celestial bodies named the 'Perseus-Pisces Sphere'. It scans toward a group called 'Laniakea', made up of smaller spheres named 'Hydra', 'Centaurus'... and skips over the *forbidden zone* of the 'Virgo Sphere', until the map shows the 'Pavo-Indus Sphere' in space.

"For those of you who don't know, the Virgo Sphere is the graveyard of the Old Empire. Where Holy Terra resides, and the former seat of power of the emperors. Before the Thriaxians destroyed everything and moved in," Nevanor points out. "But yeah, the Thriaxian Kingdom covers the expanse of the Pavo-Indus Sphere, and aside from the odd survey team's data we have there, our cartography maps are sparse on their inhabited worlds."

Now it makes sense...

"Hell, if we knew where their homeworld of Hal'Darah was, there'd be nothing stopping us from nuking their cursed planet from orbit," she adds.

I take my seat, drinking in the facts of the lecture, and compare it to what I was told on the *Nautilus*.

The elders and the shaman of Eridas Deck told about the 'Expanse of the Ancients', before planet-bound Terrans settled new star systems. And, if the leviathan-like Ominii are real, living in the voids between spheres, it would explain why the Fleet never migrated to the spheres in

Laniakea. It'd be too dangerous. Other names in my people's mythology come to mind, like 'Dead Space Void' and 'Realm of the Gods'... and if the GUILD is right, those gods are aliens.

That expanse is *Virgo*. The ancients are the people who ruled from Earth.

But if the Fleet always travelled close to the edge of this sphere... why didn't we encounter the Thriaxians, like the Terrans in the Silesian System did? Why didn't they attack the Fleet?

"Do they know about us?" I whisper, staring off into space, until I catch Chloeja squinting at me.

"What are you talking about?" she replies in a hushed tone.

I catch my breath, and before I can explain, the sound of a chair scraping against the metal flooring grates against my ears.

"Ma'am," the giant man to my left begins, "I'm Yuri. Err, designation 566-KNL. What about the Nomadic Fleet? Are they aware of an alien threat while they migrate on our frontier borders?"

I perk up as he talks. It's the first time someone from the GUILD mentioned my people, and better yet, taking the spotlight off of me and asking the questions I would!

Nevanor raises an eyebrow and crosses her arms. "Oh, yeah, them," she answers sardonically. "Well, I'll say this: don't hold your breath. I'm sure those pests in the Fleet wouldn't be aware of *any* threat unless someone came by to swat them."

What?

"The Fleet is a nuisance at best and a joke at worst. Technologically, they're stuck two-thousand years in the past, so what good could they offer? And no, to my understanding, the GUILD hasn't allied itself with the Fleet in any way against the Thriaxians. And why would they? The Fleet is *useless*, filled with vagrants, amateur merchants, and feckless travellers. They're like pirates and salvagers, minus the cut-throat mercenaries. At least pirates will cause enough of a ruckus to keep the Republic's navy on its toes... but yeah, no, the members of the Fleet are just a minor annoyance. End of story."

The lecture hall echoes Nevanor's biting words along with snickers and giggles. From whom exactly, I can't tell.

My heart sinks to my feet. I've never heard the Fleet smeared and dismissed like this before. I had no idea the GUILD thought of us like this.

I want to be calm, but I'm not. But, if I speak out, I'll give myself away... it'd all be over.

"Alright! Class is over; now get to your next activity, on the double!" Nevanor barks.

A symphony of chair legs scraping against metal resonates around me. Chloeja shuffles past me, pats me on the shoulder, and follows the crowd. When I finally get up, I'm met face-to-face with Nevanor.

"Vaughan," she begins, "do you take issue with my lecture?"

"What do you mean, ma'am?" I ask as I frown.

"The way you were staring daggers at me, I'd swear I insulted your mother, talking about the Fleet like I did. Care to explain your grievance?"

I sigh, running my hand over my face. "I... admire their way of life, ma'am," I reply, suppressing my rage. "That's all."

"Is that all?" she says as she squints at me.

"Yes, ma'am."

Okay... How much trouble would I get in if I decked a superior?

"Hmm. Carry on, Cadet." She walks by and looks over her shoulder at me. "Remember this: as admirable as they may seem, they lack the grit we need to fight the Thriaxians. Opinions aside, that's the brass tacks. In this war, or any other, you either fight or you die. There's no third option."

The next activity on my holopad says "personal time". A map function on the sheet directs me to a common room between the caserns, and when I get there, it's mostly devoid of other cadets like me. On top of that, I can't shake this overwhelming sensation that I'm alone. I've had it since Port Yegevni, but not this bad.

As I slump down in a leather armchair across from a central coffee table, all of the information from the lecture keeps gnawing away at my thoughts.

How powerful and expansive the GUILD Republic actually is.

The way they view people in the Fleet like vermin.

Their enemy, the Thriaxians, are as formidable as they are mysterious.

And, as I flip through the *Codex Republica*, I don't find anything on the Thetians. Is that because Mom, Ann'Elise, and I are the only three left?

My world has expanded immeasurably bigger and even more terrifying.

Beep.

"What's this?" I hold up my holopad.

There's a notification in the top right-hand corner of the screen, and it says: "new message."

My mouth hangs open as I press the icon. It's a video letter, and the sender is...

"Mom!" I gasp, holding the holopad closer.

Before I press 'play', the video begins with a picture of Mom and Ann'Elise sitting on a small balcony, overlooking a wide river. Several tropical trees, palms, I think, shade them both in the background, and the sky behind them is a deep cerulean blue. Compared to Nostro, it's like paradise.

With bated breath, I hit 'play'.

"Hey, pumpkin." Mom greets, smiling softly. "I want you to know Ann and I are doing well. We're having a hard time remembering everything before we landed in Korvingshal VI, but it's slowly coming back."

The blood in my veins goes cold... What do they remember? Or what do they *think* they remember?

"We must have been off-world for a while, because coming back felt... well, disorienting. But Kael helped us back to our living quarters near the shore of the Borean Sea, and we've been back to work since the *Rugia's* conflict with a Fleet vessel."

As Mom explains this, she taps two fingers on the table she and Ann sit at... like she did when all three of us were on the *Nautilus*, letting us know she was omitting information when we were out in public.

She knows the videos are being censored.

"We miss you already, Vaughan," Ann'Elise adds. "It's weird not having you here, but we appreciate everything you're doing for us. And I've always known you're a fighter at heart. I believe in you!"

I sob, immediately homesick.

"Make them pay!" she continues... and taps the table twice.

Ann'Elise isn't talking about the Thriaxians... she means the GUILD. Mom nods as she says this, and the same fire in my gut as this morning rekindles, but not as hot.

I will. I'm not sure how, but I will make the GUILD pay. I promise.

As they talk about their jobs, there's a familiarity to what they did on the *Nautilus*. Ann still runs packages in the city of Borealis, and Mom operates a self-defence studio near the beach. It's more than strange how these details appear both new and eerily familiar in the recesses of my mind.

On one hand, what they're telling me is mixed. I can't tell for sure what's true in our memories together until I actually reunite with them again. And on the other hand, Kael kept his word: Mom and Ann both appear unharmed, living a life far away from the war I'm about to be flung into... he wasn't lying.

All of this adds up to one thing: the memory-altering machine Kael and his men used didn't do a complete job. It worked in the way that it gave us a convincing cover story... but it seems like Mom and Ann remember more from our past, like I do. But my old job as a repair tech, the organic aesthetic of Eridas Deck, and the friends I had... all of it's vague and murky.

But a sudden realization hits me: they don't know my original name either. Or, maybe they do, but they're relying on their implanted memories.

Okay... So long as the GUILD is monitoring our videos, I'll have to wait.

"Vaughan," Mom says, "what you're doing right now is very brave. You had every reason to stay afraid, yet you kept moving forward. I see your courage – Ann and I both do. I'm proud of you... and if your father were here, he'd be honoured by your actions."

I smile softly as Ann nods, starting to cry. I try my best to hold back my own tears. And, on top of that, she says 'were', like my actual father is dead. It could be read as if Kael were *physically* there... but I remember how my mom speaks, and in the inflection of her voice, I know the difference. Kael didn't take that away from us...

"Never forget, Vaughan," Mom continues, "that the future belongs to the brave."

Tears stream down my cheeks as she says this. That's a Thetian saying, one Mom would tell Ann'Elise and me over the years on the *Nautilus*. They remember... at least I think they do.

For now, it's enough.

Before I can hit 'reply' on my holopad, the sound of a heavy feminine sigh comes from the couch to my left. My concentration broken, I peer over the top edge of my sheet, and there's a familiar young woman with long platinum-blonde hair, accompanied by an equally familiar giant of a man.

It's Lynette and Yuri.

"Well... fuck," she says between sobs, "isn't that a low blow?"

I slowly dry my tears with my sleeve, trying to be inconspicuous.

"He's not worth it," Yuri says, patting her on the back, "and what kind of scumbag would send you a 'Dear Jane' letter two days into basic? A lowlife, that's who. And a flighty one at that."

"Right?" she says, smiling weakly. "It's so stupid. It was an arranged marriage, but we were engaged for three years, Yuri. Three! He couldn't be bothered to tell me *before* I shipped off?"

"Mm," Yuri grunts, "you don't need a coward in your life."

As Lynette dries her eyes, she nods softly, glances my way, and catches my gaze. "Oh," she says in my direction. "Hey, friend. Someone break your heart too?"

I blush, hurrying to dry my face, and quickly put down my holopad. "N-no, I... I haven't seen my family in a while," I admit.

"Ohhh, I'm sorry. Come over here; all three of us can suffer together!" Lynette grins through dissipating tears, patting an empty seat on the couch. "That *is* what basic is all about, right? Teamwork through hardship?"

"I... guess so." I collapse my holopad with a tap.

As I slowly move seats, Lynette taps me on the knee. "You're Vaughan, right?" she asks.

I nod, reaching across Lynette to accept a handshake from Yuri.

"Yuri," he says, his voice a mixture of gruff baritone and congeniality. "Well met."

"You too." I return his firm handshake. "And Lynette?"

"Yes, sir," she says, shaking my other hand. "It's good to formally make your acquaintance!"

As we sit back, the loneliness I felt before starts to dissipate.

"I'm... sorry too. About your 'Dear Jane' letter," I say.

"Ugh, yeah," she sighs, more irritated than hurt now, "but Yuri's right; my ex-fiancé is stupid. And a coward! You wouldn't break up with a girl over video letter, would you?"

"Absolutely not!"

"Didn't think so. Plus... arranged marriages can be a pain." Lynette groans.

The Fleet side of my memories tell me this is a very strange concept... but the fuzzy memory implants echo that this isn't uncommon, especially for GUILD citizens belonging to Noble Houses.

"It sounds like it," I reply. "So... was it political? The engagement, I mean."

"Uh, yes and no." She squints. "I liked the guy, Dominic, but my father set it up. My father's a marq, like Chloeja's dad."

Right. That memory of her is pretty strong.

"That's a duke or duchess's retainer, right?" Yuri asks.

"Yep. It's kind of like an earned rank of nobility for one of the eighteen Houses," she clarifies.

Yuri sighs, leaning back with his arms behind his head. "Well, that's one thing that doesn't exist on prison colonies: political marriages. I'm sure the wardens would get a laugh if that ever happened..." He starts to chuckle.

"A... prison colony?" I repeat. "What were you in for?"

Yuri's cheerful demeanour ebbs away. "Nothing. My record's clean," he says wistfully. "The only crime I committed was being born to political prisoners on Uteinax... a frozen rock in the Dominion of Rurik's Landing."

Lynette rubs his massive back sympathetically, and my heart aches for him.

"That's incredibly unfair," I reply as my voice breaks.

"No, that's life," Yuri says, shrugging, "and it's always unfair. But you can do things to change it."

"Like volunteer for military service?" Lynette asks.

Yuri bobs his head, agreeing with her. "A uniform's a one-way ticket to freedom. Sure, you gamble with your life, but it's better than almost freezing to death, going hungry, or working in labour camps. It's better than being a slave."

I thought I had it bad. Yuri's never known what freedom is, not like I knew it on the *Nautilus*.

"I get it." I say, leaning in to the conversation. "It seems like everyone's options are limited, whether you're a colonist or a Noble."

"That's a good way to put it," Lynette says, "considering we're all fixed in place by the institution. Since a Noble House can't advance and overcome another in the GUILD, their only option is to cooperate. And this is true for any of the Houses that govern us, whether they're Minor, Major, or Exalted."

It's like we're all on board a single vessel. And this ship we're on is leading us to the Thriaxians.

"Fight or die," Nevanor said. *"There's no third option."*

It's not enough to survive, get out of the military, and get back to my family. Mom and Ann are part of this world now, here in the GUILD, like I am. And like Lynette and Yuri are.

I need to get through basic and learn to fight. To embrace it... and not run away this time. And if I come out alive, I can protect my family in the Reach... and...

"We'll get through this together," Yuri assures us, "because that's what friends do."

Friends?

"Yeah! War-besties!" Lynette cheers, high-fiving Yuri.

Can I really trust them?

"So! Vaughan!" she says, facing me. "How long have you known Chloeja?"

"Since we were kids," I say, thinking quickly. "I'd say maybe seven years. Ish."

"Oh, that's lovely! I only got to know her over the autumn, at one of her dad's galas."

Wait. How connected is Chloeja? I don't remember much about her contacts with any Nobles or other children of marqs.

"Which one?" I ask, pretending to be in the know.

"If I remember, it was a naval celebration of some kind, on Amritsar Tau... a planet somewhere in the Nebulous Reach. Your neck of the woods! Her dad's a rear-admiral in the 12th fleet, and it was kind of a meet-and-greet between officers and their families. Mine's a full admiral in the 27th fleet, and that's when and where I first met Chloeja!"

"Ah!" I exclaim. "I take it you two hit it off?"

"Sort of," Lynette explains. "She's a charming conversationalist, and we have some things in common... but she's also kind of intense. Like, scary intense."

"Didn't you say she won an award for swordsmanship?" Yuri asks.

"She did! Everything from modern fencing to Historical Imperial Martial Arts. I heard she broke a girl's rib once... something to do with a pommel," Lynette says, shuddering.

Before I can confirm this in the list of my fuzzy memories, she gently slaps me on the back.

"But you, Vaughan, you must be very familiar with Chloeja's affairs, you being such a close friend of hers, right?"

No... not that part of her.

"Oh, yeah, of course," I lie.

Okay, not *entirely* a fib. There are patches in the back of my mind of me holding a rapier, practicing swordplay with Chloeja... up until last year.

I wonder... with my actual experience with a blade, how might I square up against her in a fight?

Chapter 14

Chloeja

Day 4 of Basic Training

I'm falling, headfirst, vertically, through a sea of blue-tinted clouds. I blink, blood rushing slowly to my head as the rough grip of a blade in my right hand presses into my palm. My arms wobble gently against the current of air streaming past my bare feet, and my free hand grazes my naked body. I don't think this strange, especially with all the lessons the blade has been whispering to me for the last three months. He's a wise sage, to be sure.

'Good. Well, let's hope the rest absorb these truths as well as you have,' the blade utters through my mind.

"The others?" I ask out loud.

'Yep. But it's about that time, and the ground is getting closer. Best wake up,' it says.

"Wait, what?" I reply.

The remaining blood in my body surges from my limbs directly to my skull. A pounding headache echoes in the grey matter of my mind, and the clouds grow darker. Sensation fades from both of my hands, and I gasp as I let go of the leather-handled blade. It flies away, upward, spinning madly. I want to scream, but every time I open my mouth, no sound escapes.

"Waaake uuup!" A new, grating voice near the ground booms up at me.

"I saaaid..." it says, followed by a deafening air horn.

"WAKE UP!" a grainy masculine voice shouts.

I jolt awake, flinging myself up from the thin covers of my cot. I pat my chest and breathe out a sigh of relief. My undershirt and panties are still on... it was just a stupid dream. Another air horn blasts against the hushed murmurs of everyone else in the barracks.

"We said WAKE THE HELL UP!" This time Nevanor's harsh voice screeches, followed by the abrupt kick of her boot against the cot to my right.

"Parade's up at 0400 hours, and every one of you's gonna be out! No time for lollygagging; get your asses out to square! Double time!"

I glance at my uniform, folded on top of my footlocker, beyond my cot. I grab the leggings first, slinging on both pant legs in a hurry and hoisting them up. As I reach for my coat, I fold one layer on top of the other, like my retainer taught me. I fasten the coat length up to the top of my neck, and as I do, I slam my feet into my boots.

"What the...?" Yuri's voice behind me questions.

"How did I do that?" another voice chimes in.

"Have I been fastening this thing on backward the whole time?!" the first cries out.

Before I rush for the only exit to the barracks, I look back to the cot in the far corner: Vaughan's. Again, he's not in it... Where the hell has he been bunking?!

"H-hey, Chloeja," Lynette stammers, halting me, "you know me – my uniform wasn't to code these last two days. How did I fasten it like this?!"

I don't say anything. It's like no one in this barracks has ever had a lesson beamed into their hippocampus before. It happens *all the time* at academies in each galaxy of the Republic. I wouldn't put it past Xhyr to download us with a program or two in our sleep, to help speed training up. He might've also done it to mess with our heads and determine how we do under pressure. On the other hand, Lynette might've just grown into the outfit and is actually learning how to be a better soldier. Who the hell knows?

"I, uh-um... n-never mind," she stammers again.

"Good. You're in my way," I say coldly.

She nods and falls in line.

"I-it's not possible!" another voice behind me cries, further back in the line.

"I'm a goddamn genius!"

The cocky air of a core world princeling grates against my ears as I slip out through the flaps of the barracks' exit. My breath catches in the air of the frozen wastes, and as we jog out to formation, the parade square comes into sight.

We all line up, like always, and as the last of us file in, I see him. Shuffling in, front of the line, is Vaughan. A scowl tenses above my cheekbones as I stare at him, and what draws my attention once more to the front is the same thundering pair of boots from day one.

"Officer on deck!" Nevanor's voice rings out.

My posture stiffens, hands at my sides, face forward. There's no snow today, and a few small beams of sunlight cut through the overcast sky behind the metal stand.

"At ease," Xhyr commands us, followed by a uniform widening of our stances. "You are *all* too squishy," he says after a pause. "Several megaparsecs from here, those jellyfish bastards are glassing *Terran* worlds." Xhyr spits out his words like venom. "Republic outposts, colonial trade vessels, and *civilian lives* are at stake, people! You think the Thriaxian Armada is going to sit tight while you learn to fire a rifle straight?"

"Sir, no, sir!" we say in unison.

"I didn't think so. The thought of civvies getting blown up makes me sick, sicker than looking at all of your collective squandered potential every single goddamn morning... so, Corporal Nevanor?" Xhyr turns to his subordinate. "What do you reckon I ought to do with this sorry lot? The blue bloods think they're hot shit, and the colonial dogs continue to lick the blue bloods' assholes, despite the fact they belong to the same consecrated outfit! How shall we learn them?!"

"Sir, combat drills," Nevanor says in her siren's tongue, "and the obstacle course, sir!"

"Mmm! A fine and noble idea, Corporal! That will *indeed* grow spines in all of you, harden you up like a true Terran warrior, and, by God, make you work as a well-oiled machine. If one of you is weak, then *you are all weak*. Corporal Nevanor, learn these cadets some manners."

"Sir, yes, Drill Sergeant, sir!" Nevanor's voice echoes.

Xhyr takes his sweet time leaving the stand, waltzing off until only Corporal Nevanor remains dead centre.

"Cadets, drop and give me fifty!" she barks.

"Ma'am, yes, ma'am!" I say with the rest and quickly drop low on all fours.

Unlike yesterday, most of us are lowering and rising in sync with each other for every push-up... fascinating. Lessons at the academy were like this, where no one fell behind the bell curve, but it's another thing to witness it in military training. As this crosses my mind, I'm also reminded of how the process is not one hundred per cent effective. Three cadets ahead of me struggle to keep up, and for all intents and purposes, they never will. Then my gaze settles on Vaughan.

I notice him strain, like he hasn't done much of this before, yet he still presses on.

"My, my," Raleigh whispers to my left, "Vaughanie's finally decided to show up! Didn't think colonists would get special treatment here, did you?"

"Shut the hell up," I hiss. "You feel like doing laps around the base again?"

"And strut myself like a prized rooster in front of all the heat-packin' hens? Please, sir, may I have another?"

"Ugh..." I sigh, lifting myself up. If it's one thing I can't stand, it's princelings like him...

"You can move faster than that! Hustle, children, hustle!" Corporal Nevanor's voice rings out.

As she says this, I'm trailing behind another cadet, swinging one arm in front of the other across a long stretch of monkey bars. Below us is a heinous cesspool of... well, I'm not really sure. It looks offensive and smells awful... I'm not sure *what* exactly the stuff is; all I know is that Nevanor lovingly called the mire 'Olga's Pit'.

"Wa-ahhh!" a voice wails ahead of me.

"*Fear* is an excellent motivator," Nevanor booms. "It will push you further, force you to test your limits... but don't let it consume you! Use it, like any tool we give you, and make it an extension of yourself by *conquering it*!"

Out of the corner of my eye, I can see the outline of someone losing their grip. Bad move. But... all I hear is another palm slapping cold metal like mine and no one taking the drink. *Focus, Chloeja.. you do not want to end up down there!* The person ahead of me drops to safety, and as I grab at the last rung, I follow suit.

Safe.

Having reached the end, I notice a long line of people wait for their turn on the obstacle course. In our small group of fortunate soldiers, none of us has plunked into the mire behind us. For those on the circuit, the encouragement on every new cadet's face soars as they cross.

"Well, now, this won't do," Nevanor purrs, grabbing a pole from the snow-covered ground. "I made this too easy. Some of you are going to have to think faster on your feet!"

The pole in her hands extends to a cadet in the middle of the monkey bars. Raleigh is the first unfortunate bastard to get picked on, and after he yelps from the corporal's quick jab, he falls sideways into the thick quagmire below.

I stand in place, shocked. Not that the fucker didn't deserve it, but even I wouldn't stoop *that* low. And the worst of it is that he's not the only victim. The corporal pokes at one cadet, then another, and every time, each one falls and gets engulfed in sludge. A separate group forms, slinking off filthy and shivering as an arctic wind hits us from the north. God, she is a rotten bitch... and suddenly it dawns on me.

"Vaughan," I say out loud.

I scan the cadets on the rungs, further back in the line, and in our own group. Nothing. A trickle of adrenaline courses through my veins, and the thought of Vaughan actually getting *stuck* in the mire threatens a strong panic in my chest. I glance back at Corporal Nevanor, having the time of her life at the very edge of the pit... and right next to her is... him!

Vaughan's at the back of the line, near her! Phew.

"What's that?" Lynette asks, holding her arms close to her chest.

"*Nothing*," I stress through gritted teeth.

Regardless, I peer back at Vaughan and... why does he look like that?

He's a few metres away, but painted right across his face is a big ol' 'fuck-you' frown, and it's being directed right at the back of the corporal... *Wait, what are you doing now?* It's hard to make out, but he whispers to someone from another casern, and it spreads to another. What the hell is he doing?

Oh, shit.

The next thing that happens is Vaughan grapples Corporal Nevanor by the legs and hoists her up, followed by a sudden yelp from her.

"W-what the?! Cadet, unhand me!" she screams.

Vaughan doesn't do this. He heaves her backward, and another cadet grapples her arms, and if that weren't bat-shit enough, a third cadet waves his arms solidly from side to side, discouraging the rest of them from intervening.

"Fair play!" the man waving his arms booms. "And no fuckery in this outfit!"

Vaughan inches closer to the mire, and he... is that asshole grinning?!

Wait, he's not going to...? No, yep. He is. They are. Ohhh, son of a...!

My mind argues with what I am seeing, and what that entails is Vaughan potato-sack tossing the corporal feet-first into the slop. My mouth drops agape as she screams. There's silence, followed by a sickening *bluap*!

... What the fuck did I just watch...?!

I take my gaze off of the pit as the corporal surfaces and stare straight back at Vaughan. From the expression on his face, I can tell he immediately regrets doing what he did. I mean, of all the stupid, idiotic, reckless—

"Woo!" comes a cry from behind.

"Justice!" another shouts.

"No fuckery!" a cadet to my right echoes.

There's a unanimous sigh of relief from the cadets hanging from the metal bars, followed by the roar of applause around me.

And Vaughan... he's not grinning anymore. While everyone around him laughs their ass off, he's the only one whose eyes are as wide as plates. His shoulders shrink, and he inches further back into the crowd, and before he disappears, I swear I'll never forget the expression plastered all over his face... the one that says: "what the hell did I just do?"

I grin and fold my arms loosely in front of my chest as Corporal Nevanor awkwardly claws at the crumbling bank to get back to land. Amidst all of this chaos, it clicks...

Why didn't I think to do that?!

Oh, that would've been *so* satisfying...

"L-laps! Ten of them! Now fuck off and get out of my sight!" she says, voice cracking.

<hr />

Hours later, nothing actually came of the incident at Olga's Pit.

"Gather round," Corporal Nevanor says, pointing to the large circle in the mustering field. "For those who have never practiced in one of these, this is a psy-ring. Once you have entered, you will sustain damage, get tired, and draw blood. However, none of it is real."

Except for a handful of people in the crowd, everyone else seems dumbfounded by the notion. Not me though; I've sparred in one of these before...

"Casern Iota and Gamma, you've been selected for melee weapons training. Today, you'll not be needing to enter the armoury. We're going to start off with sword practice, and once you all enter the circle, a specific design of blade will generate in your hand, based on your brain's choosing. Savour this time! Tomorrow, you will not be using this circle, and you'll draw actual blood. Mark my words, the medic will be sick of you if you do not pass proficiency within the next two days..."

That's another advantage a few others and I have: we've been schooled by a master-at-arms since we were old enough to walk. *You mark my words, woman; at least one of us is passing proficiency today.*

"Vaughan... you're up first." The Corporal's words seethe. "Chloeja, you're his opponent."

The surrounding energy resonates with anticipation as I lightly jog toward a large white circle, to the centre of the mustering field. As I get to the edge, Vaughan parts from the opposite crowd and hesitantly crosses the white threshold.

The corner of my mouth draws into a smirk. In our past, Vaughanie was never very adept at swinging a blade, and in every single match on my estate, I'd win by a staggering margin. I remember he said something about weak arms or a poor constitution. I'm recounting this, the muscles in my face relax. This isn't going to be a fair fight... I should probably go easy on him.

"Cadets, the program is live," Corporal Nevanor said. "And! If any of you other apes enter this holy sanctum, I'll be sure to pistol whip you myself... *especially* after the events of today!"

Oh, I believe it.

I keep my focus on Vaughan as my feet shuffle through the gravel of the ring. At least he still looks like he did back then: unsure and unprepared. Now, let's see what I can come up with...

A second is all it takes. A heavy corded grip weighs in my right hand, and as I glance down, there's a familiar rapier I've trained with at the academy. There's even an engraved emblem of House Tamir. As I face him, in Vaughan's hands is a blade I've never seen before...

"What the hell is that?" Raleigh bemoans. "Get ready, Vaughanie; Chloeja's gonna lob your wrists clean off!"

Vaughan's sword has the general appearance of a rapier, but heavier. Shorter. It's curved, unlike the blade in my hand, and it has no knucklebow or back-guard. And, what's more, he has the gall to wield it with two hands! Ugh... yeah, I was right. This is going to end *quickly*.

But... why is he staring at his own sword... the hell is wrong with him now?

"Cadet!" Nevanor barks. "Vaughan, secure your shit and get in proximity!"

He raises his eyes at me, like he remembered something important. He pats his right shoulder... for good luck, I guess? Who knows?

... Oh, God, now what?! He tightens his stance, slowly raises his sword, ringing the ever-living shit out of his grip, and slowly glares down the point of his sword at me. I've seen others shoot that look at me, and the duels were *always* exhilarating. Well, okay...

"Oh, Vaughanie," I say, more melodious than I intended, "if you wanted to go, all you had to do was say so."

I inch closer, keeping my heels barely off the ground, assuming a stance where all he can do is pierce my right thigh or shoulder.

"En guard!" I cry, raising my left hand behind me.

Vaughan, however, draws his blade up into a crossguard, completely exposing his right shoulder. And—

"Aaauuugh!" Vaughan shouts.

Everyone stops cheering as he swoops his sword down low, bending almost to a crouch, and knocks my rapier off balance with an upward cut. I take a sharp breath in and find my footing on the balls of my feet as I'm constantly checking Vaughan's. Him? He's got his boots firmly planted in the gravel.

"Hyah!" I return, getting my footwork in, one foot over the other, in this *very* bizarre dance.

I keep my gaze on his, noting when he brings his sword up in a brief high-guard and how he shuffles his right foot forward with a downward strike. I pirouette, deflecting his blow and attempting a backhanded strike with my left hand.

He fucking blocked it! Vaughan's wielding single-handed; now I have the advantage—

No. He shifts up to my shoulder, grazes his hand along it, and elbows me square in the cheekbone.

"Ahh!" I cry.

There's a brief second of stars, followed by a radiating heat on my face, but I shuffle backward and evade a sharp pivot of his blade. I block it, repelling his strike. I keep my feet moving, dodging one heavy swing after the other, and as I do, my gaze locks onto his... Behind them is a burning hatred I've never seen there before. It's not directed at specifically at me, no, but it *is* intense! I've never seen this before... not when we were young, not when I left for the academy, and certainly not these past few days. *What the hell happened to you...?*

I aim to land a strike, his right hip locked with my left, and I swing my rapier upward!

I stop... his feet stop moving. My chest stings every time I breathe, and I feel it: the frosty edge of his sword pressed against my neck. The rest of the cadets are silent, and what breaks it is one drop of blood after another falling to the coarse gravel in the circle.

He... defeated me. What? How?

"Vaughan," Nevanor says, "you're the victor of this round."

I crane my neck to look at her, but not before Vaughan's blade glides away from my skin. She's shocked. Impressed... mildly. I'm not sure what's worse – her mixed approval in this moment or her usual guttural disdain.

"Woo!" Someone cheers behind me.

"You're the man, Vaughan!" Raleigh's annoying voice cracks as he cheers.

A gradual applause follows; each clap of their hands might as well be a backhand worsening the throbbing in my right cheekbone.

You know what? Fuck this.

"Hold it!" I cry, the echo of my voice resonating deep within my chest.

"Is there a problem, Cadet?" Nevanor asks.

"Rematch," I shout. "Change of weapons. Alturion duel."

"Hmm..." the corporal hums, casting her gaze onto Vaughan and back at me. "Granted. As you are, though."

A deep breath escapes me. The weight of my sword leaves, and there's an automatic tightening around my waist as the psy program changes: the familiar straps of a dagger sheath. Finally, some fucking justice.

"Ma'am," Vaughan asks, visibly confused, "an Alturion duel?"

"Affirmative, Cadet," Nevanor answers. "The computer's given you both daggers in accordance with an unofficial House duel. Cadet Nadjidhar has requested Alturion rules: the match ends with a killing blow."

That's more like it.

The blood drains from his face as Nevanor says this, and he cautiously peers over to me. *Yeah, you may have trained behind my back, swung strange weapons on your backward colony, but I've trained my whole life to use a blade like this... you're in my world now, asshole.*

I reach my hand behind my right hip, draw a straight-edged five-inch-long dagger, and bring it vertical to my chest.

"Honour to the strongest," I say, enunciating each word.

Vaughan mirrors me, that look of uncertainty creeping into what little confidence he had before.

"To the bravest," he counters, narrowing his eyes.

Again, the crowd hushes as we draw closer to one another, stopping short a couple of feet apart. I draw my blade up, side by side with my upraised left hand. I keep a foot of space between my hands and watch as Vaughan shifts his hands, undecided on how he's going to hold his dagger. He settles on a stance: a far outstretched left hand, and in his right, he's pointing the blade at me.

I'm not going easy on you this time.

My left knee bends, blocking a pointed strike with a wave of my left arm, and in return, I slash at his overextended hand. Vaughan curls it inward, but with his right, he takes a couple of jabs to my centre, but I block each with quick deflections.

Now it's my turn.

I rush forward, punch his blade downward with my left arm, and shift my weight to throw off his defence. Then I slice sideways across his chest, shuffle into his backward retreat, and jab upward, landing my dagger between his fourth and fifth ribs to his left.

I'm so close that I can sense his body seize, and he crumples downward like a rag doll with his forehead into my chest. I lower myself closer to the ground and hear his dagger drop to the ground as I watch him convulse.

"Rule number one, Vaughan," I say in a low whisper, "show mercy, and you die."

I rip my dagger from between his ribs, and he utters a desperate, stifled groan. I rise, shove him to the side, and face the corporal, who's standing front and centre with the crowd. Now that same expression of intrigue she gave Vaughan before aims right at me. One eyebrow raised and everything.

Damn right.

"You're the victor, Chloeja," Nevanor announces, "and by convention, the honour is yours."

Like before, I raise my blade to my chest and ceremoniously stain my coat with Vaughan's blood before sheathing it. As I do, Nevanor presses a button on her wrist. A surrounding dome of energy crackles and dissipates around me. Vaughan's prone on the ground, but at least he's breathing again.

I bring a hand up to my face and notice that the bruise on my right cheek has vanished. I run the same hand down the long contours of my neck and feel no cut or lesion.

"W-what...?" Vaughan gasps his words at my feet.

"Simulation over, Cadets!" Nevanor booms. "You'll all get your chance, but the drill sergeant's scheduled everyone for the tanks!"

My face constricts into a grimace at the mention of the word 'tanks'. If she were referring to driving an armoured vehicle, floating around on anti-grav pads, I don't think I'd mind... but these last two days, when the corporals said 'tanks', they meant body-sized cisterns filled with God-knows-what... and drugged sleep leading to the things of nightmares...

"Now haul ass!" Nevanor ordered.

"Yes, ma'am!" I join in with the rest.

Vaughan whispers his reply, on his knees and slowly getting to his feet. As he orients himself, he pats the area where I stabbed him and keeps his hand over it.

"Are you still in pain?" I ask.

"No," he says.

His gaze, first pointed at the ground and searching the air, rises to meet my own.

"Where... did you learn to fight like that...?" I ask.

"I—" Vaughan begins.

"Cadets! Do *not* make me repeat myself! You've had your day in the sand; now fall in!" Nevanor barks at us.

"Ma'am!" I reply.

Before I fall back in, I look over my shoulder to see if Vaughan's keeping pace. And he is. Good. But with everything that happened today, I'm going to get those answers. Things still seem... off. I can't be the only one who sees this... I mean, what's Drill Sergeant Xhyr making of this?

Chapter 15

XHYR

Day 5 of Basic Training

My chest expands, and I draw out an exasperated sigh. It's not even a week yet, and I'm compressing weeks of basic training with years of black ops into thirteen days. Goddamn it...

I impatiently wave my hand in front of the door to the alpha deck of the R&D bunker on base. It opens quickly, beckoning me in. The buzz of synthetic light blinks and glows, and standing in the midst of it is a familiar silhouette.

"Busy day, Major?" Rachael asks from inside the room, with me in the doorway.

I step through it, and inside the room from wall to wall are dozens of paper-thin screens, most of them larger than thirty inches, all pressed up against the back wall, facing me.

"Yes, it was," I grunt. "A lot of square pegs getting wedged into round holes. Worst of it is, a good lot of them are splintering, and they can't be used as pegs."

"That's to be expected," she rebuts, her voice unconcerned.

With my curiosity piqued, I walk closer to Rachael's spot, and like she has been from the start, she's watching all of them... all sixty-five of the cadets active in training.

"How do you find the synaptic relays affecting standard operating procedures?" she asks.

"Much improved, but it's coming at a cost," I say. "We had a large transfer of cadets to the Heavy Infantry, and some others weren't even cut out to be officers... no matter what their genes say."

"How many?" she asks, gliding from one screen to another.

"Thirty-five."

She doesn't say anything, but I'm not exactly hiding the impatience coming out in my tone of voice. The drop in numbers pisses me off... but on top of that, Rachael isn't even as excitable as she normally is. She even seems... calm.

"Who are they?" I ask, pointing to the screen she's staring at.

"These," she exclaims, "are the cadets in casern Iota. They're taking quite well to the modified algorithms. It's interesting how the beta and delta waves can be so... intricately interwoven. Don't you agree?"

"It's something," I reply. "I'm curious how they're imbibing these programs."

"Which ones?" she asks.

I shoot her a concerned look. "*All of them*," I stress. "I mean, these last two nights, we've been teaching them how to engage in urban combat, mixed martial arts, black ops stealth regimens, specialized weapons skills... and this – what's this program you're running?"

Rachael's expression perks up. "Ahh!" she exclaims. "This piece is the code I've been working on for the last three weeks! And judging by the pattern of the brainwaves onscreen... I'd say the program is moving along well."

"Even if they're not aware of it?" I ask.

"The catalyst is making it *seem* like it's their idea," she says, "using embedded code to make them think they're drinking in years of experience in a single night's sleep."

That's the first departure from Legion espionage and black ops synaptic programs: those were all voluntary, given up to being moulded into scalpels, used in the dark. For my conscripted cadets, there's nothing voluntary to speak of. And... even if I disagree with the matter, Rachael and her methods are a part of my corps, this corps on the base... and that comes before God Himself.

"Good," I say, perusing the same screen as Rachael. "Them accepting these, uh, chemically and digitally logged courses – that's... one more 'pass' on my checklist."

Out of my periphery, I catch her shift her glance to me, but I don't budge.

"Ohhh," she says, sounding intrigued, "and what benchmarks are you specifically looking for?"

As the last word escapes her, I bend back from the screen and right my posture. "First," I begin, "for how well they fail. Next, how they persevere and how they disobey."

"Ah, like today," Rachael muses, as though she were scrolling through an old video in her head. "I'm assuming we're both talking about Vaughan?"

"That's the cadet," I say.

"At weapons practice today?" she presses further.

"That's part of it," I explain, "but no, earlier than that. I'm talking about the incident at the mire. Vaughan should've been punished for tipping Nevanor in the muck, and mind you, she was horsing around first, but he reacted. He reacted well, executing civil disobedience for the good of his unit."

"I believe I understand," Rachael adds, "and that would improve the future squadron's morale?"

"To an apex degree," I state definitively.

The sheen from her glasses flickers twice as she tilts her head toward me.

"There are others too, demonstrating either the practical application of these programs, or at least porting over what training they had before entering this outfit. Chloeja, for example," I explain.

"Oh, yes," she purrs, "one could even say she found the quickest way to Vaughan's heart: through the fourth and fifth ribs. Imagine what she'll do, what they'll *all do* by tomorrow!"

That's... one way to put it. What I didn't share was how Vaughan and Chloeja handled under pressure and how they reacted to a situation they couldn't possibly win.

"We'll see how their colours come out in the wash," I say, smiling, "and I'll show 'em myself."

"Give them another day." she replies. "The preliminary synaptic programs still need to take hold and... there is a risk of rejection with the rate of data saturation. Oh, no, don't be concerned; it's simply a natural part of the process!"

Shit.

"How natural?" I ask, immediately regretting that I did.

"You forget, Major," she says in that oh-so-familiar tone of condescension, "we only need twelve. That's twelve elite fighting soldiers, programmed better than anyone in the Legion... Well, I mean we need thirteen, but twelve that pass the gauntlet and one particularly *exceptional* cadet. Daniel himself has high hopes for the program and its imminent success. Poetic, coming from the Republic's spymaster, wouldn't you agree?"

... Wait, what?

"Oh, shoot," Rachael says, glancing up and to the corner, feigning an absent mind, "you weren't supposed to hear that part. Silly me... but you asked."

I did. Only twelve... but...

"Xhyr," she chides following a chuckle, her tone softer, "I can almost guarantee you're not going to disappear after this! It's not like you know too much... but I will say, not unlike before, your background proves an invaluable asset to this up-and-coming squadron. One that comes with an integral job opening, and evidently one that you match the description for perfectly. *That*, I can say, would be deadly to refuse."

She says all of this by wrapping it up with a smirk.

Well... shit.

Rachael's been... no, someone higher than her has been railroading me since Port Yegevni. She mentioned Daniel, the director of the Legion... I'll bet anything he put her up to this. Maybe not this stop on the ride, but he'd definitely be the one to lay the tracks for me.

Fine.

"Doctor Vayne," I say, "I go where I'm told. If His Excellency, Daniel, or whomever wants me to vaporize alien scum, that's what I'll do. If they want me to man a naval craft again, I'll do it. I go where I'm told, and I look after my unit."

"Good answer!" Rachael says.

I'm, uh... not sure if she's being sarcastic or not.

"Yes, well," I begin, trying desperately to change the subject, "when I asked R&D about the projected models, they said they came up with a solution for the square-cube problem we were having with the frames. Did you have a chance to read the report?"

"You mean this one?" she replies, her eyes alight. "Yes, engineering had a time with some of the earlier prototypes... the Juggernauts used by the Heavy Infantry are one thing, with their smaller builds. But I can confidently say we've improved them. They said it had something to do with the alloy, refinement, that sort of thing."

It's on track then... very good.

"And, Major," she adds, "try not to worry too much about the rest of the cadets. Yes, they're not all going to make proficiency, but they're going to find a new home regardless. You'll see!"

Chapter 16

Chloeja

Day 6 of Basic Training

Three seconds.

For three seconds, I watched as another cadet hung motionless from the chrome rafters right in front of me.

As the fourth second strikes, I'm immediately jerked aside by Nevanor as she sprints past me. My gaze is still on Raleigh, his lifeless eyes downcast, contrasting the purple on his cheeks. I shudder as Nevanor dashes through my line of vision, jumps up, and takes a single slash at the hanging rope with her dagger.

Raleigh drops to the ground.

The sounds around me appear muted, and several more people rush past. Three medics and an MP scramble to lift him onto a fabric gurney, and leading the way out is Nevanor.

"Make a hole!" Her voice thunders.

I take a step back, along with everyone else, as if by instinct. The crowd blocking the door makes way for Nevanor and the other NCOs bolting from the dorm. Even as they leave, I replay those three haunting phrases that brought me to this room:

"*Oh, fuck... oh, fuck... oh, fuck...*" I heard near the entrance.

"Quick gawking!' A grating masculine voice resonates behind me. "Muster starts at 0500; now shove it down and move it out!"

I turn around, quickly, and notice Corporal Ylud, the second drill sergeant to our casern. The sense of urgency swells around me, and not a single one of us hesitates.

"Cadet!" Ylud barks over my shoulder. "I will break you in half if you do not *hustle your ass!*"

Out of the corner of my eye, right before I join the others, I glimpse Vaughan standing motionless by the doorway. I'm not sure what he does next, as I'm keeping pace with the rest. Not for one second, two seconds, three...

"Sir!" Vaughan replies.

As two sets of boots clap the metal floor behind me, I release a stifled breath. I can barely make ends of what I witnessed or how I actually feel about it... but why did Vaughan just stand there?

It doesn't matter.

I can only guess what was going through his mind, seeing what he saw...

"I mean, what kind of life is that?" Lynette says out loud to us at our table in the mess hall. "What's he going to do if he actually survives operations out there?"

"Who the hell knows..." I reply, diverting the pain in my brow with a throwaway answer.

"Chloeja, they *augmented* him," Lynette stresses. "That's the life Raleigh has now! Do you even know what that's like?!"

Augments.

Across the GUILD, doctors and scientists reverse engineered android cybernetics for Terran augmentation: a frowned-upon practice, moulding machine and man together. But, because of ethics laws, the Terran receiving it is never fully 'aware' ever again. Sure, the lights are on, but no one's home. And... they do that to prevent even the possibility of smart machines... that, and being altered physically simply makes you less Terran...

"I have some sort of idea," I reply.

Lynette nods as she takes her time eating her eggs Benedict. In fact, everyone around our table has a shared atmosphere of melancholy. Like me, though, they're not likely to express it. As Ylud and Xhyr said this morning: shove it down, and move forward.

In between my own forceful bites, Lynette stops and keeps her gaze beyond Shao-Shi and Yuri at the edge of our table.

"Hey, do you think Vaughan wants to sit with us?" Lynette asks.

I follow Lynette's gaze, and there he is, eating alone.

"If he's by himself, I'm sure he has his reasons," Yuri's gruff voice interjects.

"He... maybe he just needs a pick me up?" Shao-Shi suggests. "I mean, you did literally skewer his left ventricle in training."

"And it was a simulation," I reply sharply, "meant to prepare him and everyone else here for whatever's out there. We have to be ready, and honestly, he'll thank me for it later."

A deep sigh leaves me as everyone else finishes up what's left of their plates.

Vaughan.

For almost a week now, we've trained at Fort Durran, and right from the start, I could tell something wasn't right with him. No... even before that, when we were all processed at Port Yegevni, I noticed it then, too.

I mean... where the hell is that kid from seven years ago? He was always sickly, afraid of everything, coddled by his father, could barely lift a training sword, and constantly stumbled over his words.

Now? He almost decapitated me in the first two swings in the simulator, and Shao-Shi's reprimanding *me* for being too harsh! Unless he's using performance drugs, Vaughan should not have *such* a ripped physique, nor should he be so familiar with a sword. Period.

And, okay... so he's as aloof as before, but he's not awkward. Not anymore. His silence is a *mystery*, and maybe I'm overthinking this entire thing, but Vaughanie talks differently than before. His voice is less refined and has almost no regional twang to it.

"I'm going to get more coffee," Yuri offers. "Anybody else need one?"

"I'll take one," Lynette says.

"Me too," Shao-Shi says between bites.

"I'm good," I reply, covering the top of my untouched mug.

And! What the hell is with all of those lapses in his memory? Did he get bonked in the head or something? Fall down a mineshaft? You'd *at least* remember something like that if you did.

I mean... the whole reason I'm here is so that his ass doesn't get killed out there! Even if we split up, I'd find some way to pull strings... so... why the hell am I even here in this outfit if he doesn't *need* protecting?

"Hey!" I said, years ago on Amritsar Tau, my homeworld.

Back then, I was always climbing trees and wearing pants more suited to noble boys my age. My hair was longer, and it remained that way until I enlisted years later.

"W-who said that?" a young boy, maybe twelve years old, replied.

"Up here!" I shouted, waving to the boy while hanging upside down. "Come climb up here!"

I remember how he stared at me, awestruck, or maybe unbelieving.

"Are you allowed to be up there?!" he called back.

"Nope," I said through a grin.

"But you're going to get in trouble up there!" he protested.

"I'm already in trouble!" I replied. "Come on! What's the worst that could happen?"

The tree wasn't that big, and he got about halfway up before getting stuck. As he clung stationary like that, I pouted and swung back up on my branch to sit. I shimmied over toward the trunk to where the boy had fixed himself.

"You're not very good at this..." I said plainly. "What's your name?"

"Vaughan..." he said with his face planted in the trunk's surface.

"Nice!" I said, grabbing a lower hanging branch. "Well, Vaughanie, I'm getting you out of this tree!"

"T-that's not my name," he replied.

"It is now, Vaughanie! Now stay there, or you're definitely going to fall out," I said.

"What's your name?" Vaughanie asked.

I got to a parallel branch to his, balanced my bare feet close to the trunk, and tapped him on the shoulder with my free hand. He shuddered, and as he peeped over his shoulder, his left eye met my right.

"It's Chloeja," I said, "and seriously, if you're going to be hanging around here more, you're going to have to learn to climb better!"

That day, I learned that his father, Kael, was at my family's estate to swear fealty to my dad as our retainer. In the years that followed, Vaughanie didn't always come around, and his dad told me it was because of poor health. But one summer, three weeks after I turned eighteen, he came back.

"Hey," his soft voice greeted me.

With a rapier in hand, I stopped swinging and faced him. "Hey, yourself," I said. "You look like you've seen better days."

Vaughanie was taller, but he seemed leaner than when we were kids. His face was more emaciated, now with dark circles under his eyes.

Regardless, he still found some reason to smile, even now. His head lowered, he shuffled his feet and glanced to the other side of the stone courtyard I was training in.

"You left a sword out for me?" he asked.

"Of course I did," I said, slapping the side of my blade against my shoulder. "You need the practice."

"Ugh... do I have to?" he asked.

"Yeah, you suck at it," I said, half in jest, "and you won't get better until you push yourself."

I remember how he picked it up, like it weighed more than he did, and mirrored the same stance as me. We fenced with rapiers, intermittently for years, so that when they called, he'd be ready.

"En guard!" he said, pushing off with his right foot.

Each movement of my feet was calculated, calm, and measured to the effort his sword resisted against mine. But this time, unlike before, his footing wasn't everywhere. He had been practicing...

But, after a clumsy pirouette on his part, I got the advantage, shuffled in close, and tapped the side of his ribs, causing him to drop his sword.

"Ugh!" he grunted, followed by a laboured cough.

I tried rushing over to check him over. Instead, he raised his hand up at me.

"I'm fine!" Vaughanie growled, his eyes darting away. "It's just... harder."

I nodded, backing away and letting him get back on his feet.

"They're going to conscript me," he said with a wavering voice.

"What?" I asked. "Even in the state you're in? The Republic Guard's still dragging you in?!"

"Yeah. Dad's been trying to fight it, but he lost at the last tribunal."

"Shit..." I said, throwing my sword to the ground, "so that's it?"

"Pretty much," Vaughanie confirmed. "There's nothing I can do."

I hated those words. Not that they came from him or that he hadn't tried to fight it, but that he was just another pawn in the admiralty's grasp. As the wind blew that afternoon, I ran my fingers through my long cascading hair, and I knew exactly what to do about it.

"Well..." I began, "then you're not enlisting alone. I'm coming with you."

"What?!" Vaughanie blurted out.

"You heard me. I'll be damned if I watch as they snatch you up only to have them water some foreign planet with your entrails! I'm signing up too, first chance I get, and I'm going to make sure you don't get your ass killed!"

"W-what about school?" he asked.

"I'll go after my tour," I said calmly.

"Wait, what about your dad?!" Vaughanie asked, seeming genuinely mortified for me.

"Oh, don't you worry about my old man," I said. "For one, I can handle him. I've done it all my life. And two, if he forbids it, I know for a fact he'd be breaking the law. You can't deny voluntary service to the Republic Guard."

Vaughanie didn't say anything more. His face told me he had a million uncertain thoughts plaguing him.

"So," I said, "that's that. Even if they volun-tell you, and they drag you through the mud, I'll be there to pull you back up! If they ship you off to train with the fleet, I'll secure a transfer. Trust me. I've got your back!"

⋙ ⋘

I ask myself again, staring at Vaughanie in the back corner: why am I here? As I'm sitting here with a frigid coffee in my hand, all I can think about is how everything I remember about my childhood friend lies askew with the man at the end of the room. And God help me, I'm going to find out why.

Chapter 17

XHYR

Day 7 of Basic Training

I let them down...

    The sun's peeking out of the near constant snowy clouds, coming in through the window and casting down on my bunk, and all I can think about is Raleigh. The kid acted cocky, first lie. Tried to clothe himself in his holier-than-thou Noble House persona, and he almost got himself killed. When you're drilling, instructing, or what have you, that gnawing deep in your gut doesn't die. I should've learned him better; he'd still be cocky, but it'd be real.

    I'm sitting at the edge of my cot, one foot in a boot, the other without. Determining to do as I say and as I do, I shove all that garbage deep down in a corner. The head-shrinker can do her job again.

    Later, though, not now.

    I shove my other foot into the free boot. I draw those laces up, tight with full tension, perfectly interwoven. As I get myself up, there's a slackness of my coat against my shoulders. I peer down the line of my white undershirt, straighten it out, and notice the contrast of my dark skin against the fabric. I fold one end of my jacket to the left and overlap the other to my right. I glance up to a tiny mirror above my night stand, and two tired hazel irises stare back at me.

    I won't make the same mistake twice. I've only got six more days, and when my time is up those thirteen cadets won't need a drill sergeant anymore; they'll need an instructor. And the rest... when they ship out to new homes, they'll be ready to meet them. They won't try to take the easy way out, won't give up and despair and get processed as an augment for continued service.

He's the last example.

"Cadet," I command to Shao-Shi, "hand me that banner."

"Sir, yes, sir!" he replies, less awkward in speech than yesterday.

He ain't graceful, but he moves like he has a purpose. Within seconds, that flagpole and banner are within my grasp. He don't even wait around like he used to; Shao-Shi falls right back in line. To his sides and behind him are forty-something cadets remaining, each toting unloaded assault rifles and ammo.

"Thank you, Cadet," I say. "It has occurred to me that while some of you are not shooting straight enough, running fast enough, or duelling each other hard enough, that is a reflection on me. From now on, less than a week before all the checks are marked, I will *personally* demonstrate every exercise you need to undertake until the final evaluation. Am I clear?"

"Sir, yes, sir!" each and every cadet thunders back to me.

"Perfect," I say. "Now follow me and keep pace! Five kilometres in fifteen minutes is the goal, and I will show you it can be done. Now move out!"

I turn, the flagpole in my hands aimed skyward, and the trail away from the marching square is ahead. The pole weighs a little over a quarter more than the rifles held by the cadets.

They get that it's heavy. That's the point.

My boots dig into the frosted gravel, and I launch forward.

"Left, right, left right left!" I sound off.

"Left, right, left right left!" they echo.

"Alien menace is a sonuvabitch!"

"Alien menace is a sonuvabitch!" they repeat, weaker.

"Gonna wipe them out; gonna head on home!"

"Gonna wipe them out; gonna head on home!"

The cadence is music to my ears... and when I turn the bend and check my right, everyone's got their rifles glued to their hands. Today's gonna be a good day.

"Keep stable, Cadets," I caution, pacing between active simulation pods, "until now, you've fired rifles at inanimate objects, slashed blades, and grappled one another like you owed them money! But in here, remember to keep your balance. These scopes don't auto-correct, and for good reason: you *must* hone these sensitive instruments with the utmost care, like your very life depends upon it. No, scratch that, like the life of one of your own in your unit depends on your sensitive, detail-oriented touch!"

I stop mid-row, catching Shao-Shi and Lynette keeping stable while launching pixelated cannons at Thriaxian heavy armour in VR. Yeah, their brains are in the program, but the motions in the makeshift cockpits are very real.

"Whoa!" Yuri's gruff voice raises an octave, adjacent to my right.

With him being the sizeable grizzly bear that he is, tumbles – and tumbles hard. His pod flips a whole ninety-five degrees to the left and stays there for a moment until the program resets and rights him back up.

"Cease simulation!" I shout.

A uniform whirring, clicking, and powering down resonates across the darkened chamber.

"Keep your visors on," I continue, "and keep them on observation only. I'm jumping in."

"Sir, yes, sir!" they cry.

Two pods down the aisle, I jump into the first empty simulator and sink into the padded cockpit chair.

"Program override, authorization Major Xhyr Talthor, X2-754C," I say to the machine.

"*Instructor authorization confirmed,*" it says back. "*Launching combat simulation.*"

A sudden electrical surge rattles the back of my head, sending shivers down my spine. The visor disappears in my field of vision, and replacing it is me strapped inside a spherical cockpit. There're tiny indicators on the concave screen, but my sight is on the large bogey flying straight for me.

Before I press a single button, I check if all the cadets are linked in, seeing what I'm seeing. Forty-two active cadets out of forty-two.

Go time.

Each of my hands grips down on the dual throttles, and I slam down on the pedals at my feet. The sphere jars me, banking to the right as the Thriaxian craft ahead launches a volley of plasma beams at my twelve. The cockpit edges closer to the arid ground, and I spring the sphere upward, putting up a second set of shields. From my arsenal, I launch two guided missiles and follow up with a plasma charge from the port-side barrel. Most important, though, I want to show them that you *keep on moving*.

"Remember this: in combat," I say out loud, "if you lose your balance, and especially if you get knocked on your back, you're dead. So keep grounded. Always poise your attacks forward, evade with finesse, and strike with divine vengeance!"

The gyroscope display on my monitor shows that I do a barrel roll, but I keep tight to my seat. The whole time, I don't take my gaze off the bogey. Readouts onscreen show one missile hit, the other was deflected, and the plasma charge pierced its armour. These hands of mine send out another volley, and readout shows both are a direct hit, and the fucker's done for.

Easy-peasy.

"Logging out," I command the machine.

"*Confirmed*," it replies in stereo.

Everything goes black again, and I reach up and lift the console off of my face. The last thing I recall before booting out is the expression on each of their faces, all of them in the bottom left of the display.

They all appear both inspired and comprehending. I'll take it.

I swoop my legs out from the pod, get my footing, and stand at attention.

"All of you," I say, "commence a second round, and this time, don't any of you hold back."

The cadets all pile, one at a time, into the trainees' mess. I don't say a peep. They're all keen to rush in on account of their hard work and a desperate need for chow. As I stand by the door, counting heads, my breath catches.

Two of them are missing.

"Corporal," I say to Ylud, "make sure they eat quick and kick 'em to R and R. I gotta see to something."

"Sir!" he replies, saluting, and runs after the thirty-eighth cadet in the mess.

I tap the headset to my ear, and it emits a soft *beep*.

"Sir?" It's Nevanor's voice.

"I got two cadets AWOL, Vaughan and Chloeja. Have you seen them down by the barracks?"

"I did, sir," she says. *"Vaughan was tending to a wound from target practice, needed a change of uniform before mess. As for Chloeja, she should have fallen back into exercises."*

Hmm...

"Do me a kindness," I ask, "an' take a peek at the window of Iota casern. Don't engage; just give me the intel."

"Copy," she replies.

The comm in my ear goes quiet, and now I'm left to figure what the hell those two are doing.

"Sir," Nevanor says, *"Vaughan's still in his undershirt... Chloeja's at the door... her arms are crossed, looks pissed."*

What the?

"Heh, lover's quarrel, sir?"

Not in MY outfit!

"Stand by. I'm coming over to deal with this," I say through gritted teeth.

"Copy..." she says back.

I double time it to Iota casern, the very blood in my veins boil hot. My face aches from my clenched teeth to every fucking muscle in my skull! The HELL is wrong with them?!

As I circle around the bend, thinking of how hard I'm gonna beat both of them shitless for fraternization, I proceed to the only closed door in the dormitory's quarters. I get to it, and it ain't exactly closed. It's ajar.

So I peek through. If I'm gonna charge them with something, I want to be sure.

Chloeja approaches Vaughan with considerable speed. She pins his neck upward with her forearm and lifts his shirt up with the other.

If I charge them now, the punishment will be light. Confinement and maybe re-education. It's not textbook fraternization yet, and by God, it won't come to that.

I reach down to push the door open, catch them off guard...

"You can't be him... who are you?!" Chloeja shouts.

My hand's against the door, but I don't budge it. I'm gonna let them keep talking.

I peer through the crack, and while I can only see the back of Chloeja's head, Vaughan seems genuinely terrified.

Hmm.

"W-what do you mean?" Vaughan stammers.

"I mean, you are NOT the Vaughanie I remember. He had a scar, *right here*," she says with an accusing tone, pointing directly underneath the boy's ribcage. "He got a scar, falling out of MY tree, and it's not there! What the hell have you done with him?! Talk!"

"Stop!" Vaughan says, struggling against her forearm.

"Well?" she presses.

"Listen. My name *is* Vaughan... I'm not anyone else."

"Bullshit!" she screams. "You may look like him, but you're *not him!*"

And... there's that expression again, seething from the dead space in Vaughan's eyes. I didn't forget it when Nevanor showed me the video feed from his duel. Yeah, he was fighting more than this girl that day. I'd seen it before, in other men under my command... all of them looking to set the world on fire.

"I-I don't remember all of who I am," Vaughan stammers, tears threatening to fall down his cheeks. "All I know is that the GUILD either took or killed my father, slaughtered my friends, and hid away the only family I have in the world! *Your people* did this! *They* took everything away from me, everything that made me who I am!"

His words hit me in a soft spot. It's the same story I heard of any recruit, dissident... or victim what crossed paths with the Republic.

"Where *is he?*" Chloeja stresses. "Where's Vaughanie, the real one?"

"His dad said he's safe," Vaughan says. "Beyond that, I'm not sure. He didn't give me those memories before he sent me here..."

Holy shit... the doc was right. They, well, we scrabbled his head.

"I... I don't get it," Chloeja says, loosening her grip. "Why would Kael send you? Vaughanie knew I was coming... why?"

I watch as Vaughan shakes his head, probably running out of answers.

"To fight in his stead," he replies, "because Kael said that his and your Vaughanie was... is too weak for any kind of combat. And despite what his dad could do for him, the GUILD was going to draft him anyway, even if it meant he'd end up augmented like Raleigh, or worse. Kael didn't want that."

Chloeja finally lowers her arm, dropping Vaughan to his feet. "Okay," she says.

"Okay," Vaughan repeats, "now what?"

Chloeja draws a sharp breath, her head fixed in his direction. "I'm here by choice. I volunteered to make sure Vaughanie was safe... so now *you're* going to watch my back, and keep me safe instead. Do you understand?"

"Yes," Vaughan says, "but how do I know I can trust you?"

"You don't," she replies, "so think of it as a business agreement. I keep your secret, and you keep my ass from getting killed. No one backstabs the other... that's how we can foster trust. Deal?"

Heh. I watch as she puts her hand out, and I glance at Vaughan, who's still unsure. Until...

"Deal," Vaughan says, accepting her hand in a shake.

I softly walk away and duck into the nearest open dorm. After I hear their footsteps in the hall, leaving out the front, I tap my headset.

"Sir?" Nevanor answers.

"The situation's under control. Let the cadets Vaughan and Chloeja through to mess."

"Understood," she says.

So... now I know. Rachael suspects something, and fusses over Vaughan like a prized lab rat... but she won't find out more than what she discovers herself. Not from me.

Hell, who knows what she'll do to him if she has the entire story? Well, I ain't willing to find out. He fights good, perseveres, and more or less respects the chain of command. That suits me well enough. And shit, seeing as the good doctor has so many secrets up her sleeves, what's one up mine?

Chapter 18

VAUGHAN

Day 13 of Basic Training

Of course, on the last day of basic, on a planet that only ever snows for ten months out of the year, it rains. This, coupled with climbing a tall obstacle course wall facing the billowing grey clouds above, I don't have only myself to watch out for... and close to arm's reach, Chloeja's scaling a foot shy of me up the slippery wall.

"Oh, *no!*" she cries *disingenuously*.

Damn it!

My arm shoots out like a spring, and I grab her by the ankle. Against the heavy droplets, every muscle in my left torso and arm strains heavily as Chloeja swings right, pivoting a good thirty degrees, and catches her bearings at an angle.

"Phew, that was close," she says, righting herself.

As she takes a step up with her right, I let go of her left ankle, and my right hip pops back into place.

"Vaughan!" Xhyr's menacing shout reaches up to me. "Are you seriously looking to piss me off *this early in the morning?!* Quick fucking around with your acrobatics and *climb,* goddamn you!"

Ohhh, he used my first name... I am, without a doubt, on his shit list, and if I were Xhyr, that's exactly where I'd fall. It's not like this is the first time he's caught me covering for Chloeja, and each time, I'm the one who pays.

Like at grenade practice.

As we're all ducked behind an earthen rampart, tossing grenades into a char-pocked field of snowy drifts, I hear a loud 'clink' to my left.

"Whoops," Chloeja said. "Live round, weak toss..."

Fuck!

I grab that damn thing, hurl the explosive charge through the air, and lunge at Chloeja, hovering over top of her.

"Fire in the—!" I said.

Then 'BOOM', right in midair, that damn near shattered my eardrums.

"Cadet! You stupid, arrogant bastard!" Nevanor growled in my direction. "What has possessed you to loose a grenade so late from the pull that you see fit to endanger every soul around you?!"

"I-I hesitated, ma'am!" I said as I winced at how pathetic the lie was.

"You hesitated!" Nevanor repeated. "Clearly, you know more about when to toss a grenade and how, so I *won't even bother* drilling the rest of you for this exercise. Cadet, you are in charge of this exercise. You tell them the how and when. Your superior insight into the safety and wellbeing of the outfit is *extraordinary!* In fact, get them to double the pace since you do indeed know better!"

I didn't have to look to either side of the firing range to feel everyone's stare, like daggers, pierce me. Everyone's, except for Chloeja's. When I faced her, she shot me a flash of bemusement. A curl of a smile on her lips. It was the expression of someone who said through demeanour alone:

I own you.

So... yeah. As I'm drenched in the rain, shaking as I grind on forward, I glance up at Chloeja, who makes it to the top of the wall. Right now, there's only one thought living rent free in my head...

I hate her.

"Company... halt!" Nevanor orders.

At the end of a fifteen-kilometre march, we stop a few paces from a wide-open field.

Minutes before, the rain stopped.

"Form rank!" she continues.

I shuffle in, with haste and purpose, and stand side by side twelve other remaining cadets. As I stand at attention, I peer out into the distance beyond the field of sparse snow and greenery toward the horizon and the sky. For the first time since I got here, the dark and unforgiving grey clouds of Nostro gave way to a deep turquoise blue. And hanging right below the cloud level are three Destroyer-class battleships.

"Attennntion!" Nevanor barks, her voice hoarse from overuse. "Officer on deck!"

At the very mention, I straighten, heels together, arms at my sides.

To the left, Xhyr steps out of a large arched building. Like the first day, he's dressed in the full uniform of a major. He marches lateral to us, centre stage, and stops right in the middle, facing me.

"At ease," he says.

I shuffle my feet further apart, my arms loosely folded behind the small of my back.

"Cadets," Xhyr says, "today is the last day I will guide you as drill sergeant... you're all trained now. So, from now on, I will be your instructor of your specialized trade."

The ground below me shakes. Xhyr and Nevanor stand fixed in place, so I don't budge.

"Look to your left," Xhyr continues. "Now look to your right. What you see is all that remains of the one hundred recruits posted to Fort Durran. All of you, from this moment forward, will hone your prowess with me as pilots."

The rumbling stops, and while I want to double-check who remain with me, I keep my eyes forward. To my left, Shao-Shi and Yuri passed proficiency; they and Lynette made this last week bearable... but if they pulled Chloeja from rank... no, I don't want to think about it. After everything she's put me through, she'd better still be here...

"As of today, you are no longer cadets with brains being stuffed with neuro-programming. You won't go through drill like a private. Today, you are all lieutenants and pilots... but more so..."

Neuro-programming? What does that mean?

He turns his back to us and points at Nevanor. Immediately, she dashes far afield to our left, back where Xhyr came from. As soon as she's out of my periphery, he faces us all again.

"Today, you are all Titans."

My eyes widen as a monstrosity of metal emerges from the earth behind Xhyr.

Titans, he said... that perfectly describes what I witness towering before me: a metal humanoid resembling the bulk of a tank with the thin frame of a long-legged fighter. It doesn't stop rising until it stands at fifty... no, maybe sixty feet high!

The air draws through my gaping mouth and catches in my lungs as I continue to stare.

"Before you is the Amata-class X-5 Series Xenomech. This," Xhyr says with his hand outstretched, "will be your warhorse, a true extension of yourselves on the battlefield. Take care of it, and it will take care of you."

A tingling shudder runs down my spine as he says this, reminding me of a phantom memory of a near identical sentiment.

"One might think, why, Instructor, isn't this just a suit of power armour like those issued to the Heavy Infantry, geared one hundred and twenty times to scale? To which I say, yes, it is," Xhyr explains. "It is a colossal suit of power armour, adapted for combat in the air, sea, land, and combat in the vacuum of space. That... is exactly what we need. To send the Thriaxians packing, we need monsters... to defeat monsters."

My heart grows heavy as his words sink in. I remember fragmented lessons, briefs about the Thriaxians: the high-pressure environments of their ocean planets, the advanced military technology we've uncovered so far, and cadaver reports on their vulnerable physiology on day two. But this... it sounds strange in my head, but this feels real. Very real.

"Vaughan," Xhyr calls out my name, "and Chloeja, step forward."

My neck snaps to attention.

She's here... oh, thank the gods!

I blow out a sigh of relief as I step forward from formation, and Xhyr takes a step toward us both. He glances to my left and locks gazes with me, front and centre.

"You two will man these mechs today, complete with a test flight and combat exercises," Xhyr ordered.

"S-sir!" I squeak.

"Sir!" Chloeja answers, steely in her resolve.

Xhyr nods to us and stares past our shoulders. "As for the rest of you, it's time to watch and learn... so clear the hell off my tarmac!"

"Sir!" voices boom from behind.

The departing sound of boots on soft earth peters out to my left. Two men, dressed similarly to Xhyr, come out from behind the legs of the mech in front.

"Lieutenants," Xhyr says to us both, "give the NCOs your coats. You won't be needing those anymore."

I do as Xhyr says, unclipping and shrugging off the last evidence of me being a cadet. And, like I was stowing it away in my trunk, I fold it tightly into a square and hand it off. One warrant officer accepts it, reaches over, and grabs one to my left.

I turn and witness Chloeja standing at attention. Like me, she's dressed in a black tank top, standard issue leggings, and two silver dog tags. Geez, how does she wear that better than—oh, shit, she's looking at me.

I crank my head forward again. With arms outstretched, the most haggard of the two warrant officers gestures for me to take the contents from his hands. Without thinking, I accept it... and what I hold seems like a chest plate.

It's painted black, bearing a central insignia of a downward pointing sword aimed toward a semi-circle of laurel leaves. It's finished with brushed steel, and when I flip it over, I find that it has three silver plug-in ports. The weight of it in my hands jogs a memory of spending several weeks training with this very piece of armour and how it works in the field.

Wait, several weeks? How is that possible?

"Suit up," Xhyr says. "Test flight begins at 1400 hours. The sleep-wave programming's been hammering tutorials into your memory cortex the whole time, so activating the suit should be a piece of cake."

Oh. That makes sense, I suppose. That means... wait, that means...

"Ah," I whisper as my lips tremble.

The realization hits me like a hard slap across the face. They tampered with my mind. Again.

A sudden wave of nausea hits me as I stare at Xhyr. My hands ache as I ball them into fists.

"Son of a *bitch*," I utter, soft enough that no one else can hear me.

I do as I'm told, like a good piece of military property, and put the chest plate on overtop my undershirt, and as if by instinct, I double-tap a green button to the right side of the armour. The fact that it's second nature *because* of sleep-wave emissions... no. Not now; get it together. Calm down...

My chance will come. I'll have my revenge, but not yet.

A soft mechanical hum comes from below my neck, followed by a series of tiny clicking sounds. I turn to Chloeja, and from her chest plate unfurls a complete pressurized suit. The shape of it, while sleek and formfitting, reminds me of shattered memories. Ones where I worked along the surface of a spaceship.

My suit reaches down to my arms, tickling my skin and leaving goose bumps behind. When the clicking stops, I try moving my arms and legs.

Like I saw on Chloeja, the suit clings tightly to me, but it doesn't restrict my movement.

"Like riding a bike," Xhyr says. "Now, check each other's life support gauges. As you know, this is part of standard operating procedures for aerial-and space-stationed forces and an invaluable part of working within a well-oiled squadron."

"Sir!" Chloeja and I say in unison.

She faces me head on, I notice how her suit hugs the curves of her hips and thighs. I didn't think it was possible, but she looks much more like a badass dressed in full armour.

No. Wake up. This bitch literally *stabbed you in the heart* and is currently *extorting* you to keep your secrets. I remember what Xhyr said: secure your shit...

Don't think. Act.

I take a step toward her, force my mind to recall *everything* from the last two weeks, and inspect the sensor gauges on the top right panel of her chest plate. Next, I scan up to the lip of her suit's neckline, ensuring the integrity of the oxygen intake valves, and I check the seams along each side of her suit's smooth fabric.

"All clear," I say.

As I drop my arms to the side, Chloeja mirrors me, checking all the same functions. She runs her fingers along the seams with much more force than I used.

"All clear," Chloeja says.

"Good," Xhyr replies. "Vaughan, you're going to pilot this mech, and, Chloeja, you take the one at the far end of the tarmac."

"Sir!" we both say.

For the first time, Xhyr raises his hand and salutes us. I return it, raising my hand to my brow. It's strange, uncommon, but not unwelcome.

"Get your asses back here alive," he says while walking away to the observation tower.

With my foot stuck into a solid metal stirrup, I hold on tightly to a retracting lead raising me high into the air. The lead ends close to the entry point of the mech's open cockpit. The pull stops, and my heart skips a beat as I stand dangling fifty-eight feet above the ground. The control tower and observation deck loom to my left, and I shift my gaze straight ahead to a dark and empty cockpit. The afternoon sun flashes past me. It only illuminates the control consoles and the edge of the seat. Like stepping out into the vacuum of space from the safety of a roaming ship, its insides call to me from an almost ethereal place...

"Ugh." I shudder. "Here I go again..."

So I gather my resolve and enter the goddamn robot.

My foot comes loose, and the whine of the lead retracting fully into the mech grates against my ears. When I sit down, the cockpit door quickly seals shut in front of me. Only a second later, an all-encompassing screen surrounds my periphery, and the layout is immediately familiar to me: it's exactly the same as the simulators.

The cockpit itself is almost perfectly spherical, giving me a bird's-eye view. Well, maybe three hundred degrees. The aft behind my seat is the only blind spot I have. Once I find my seat, I reach for the restraints and buckle myself in. As I shuffle my feet, feeling around for the pedals, I knock something hard on the floor. I reach down, and it's a black-tinted helmet, matching the make and shade of my suit.

I don't think twice; I just put it on.

Once it's on my head, the hiss of a vacuum seal to the neck portion of my suit almost pops my eardrums.

"Welcome, pilot." A robotic feminine voice envelops me. *"Please lean back into the chair to begin start-up procedures."*

I follow along, resting back until I hear a loud *clank*.

"Take a deep breath in, and hold it," it says.

Okay. I shrug my shoulders, and I do what it says. I breathe in—

"Aghhh!!" I cry.

Three large needles piercing my back sends me shaking. A flashing memory invades my mind – a long needle retracting from the surface of my skull, me flailing, and then an inescapable amount of pain. It vanishes as fast as it came. Now, back in the present, my lungs strain against the radiating pain flowing throughout my body.

"Breathe again," the voice calmly says in my helmet.

"Ugh... Ugh..." I sharply exhale, one breath after the other, fighting the urge to vomit.

"SERUM injection complete. All clear for G-resistance and performance enhancement."

W-what?

"Vaughan, keep your head cool." Xhyr's voice says in place of the OS. *"Your ECG's spiking. Think back to protocol delta and secure your shit."*

The second he mentions it, my mind floods with neuro-programming from past days: calming techniques, autonomic pain relief, and focused control of reducing my blood pressure.

Okay...

Again, I breathe in through my nose. I enter a kind of trance and press my index finger to a specific nerve behind my collar bone. The heavy, staggered breathing from before slowly decreases as I shut my eyelids. Once I open them again, something feels... different.

The first thing I notice is an unprecedented level of focus.

I'm aware of every single blue sensor on the concave display; every button and every control on the two consoles at my hands appear tangible and fully laid out. And time slows right down by... a lot.

"Operating systems online," the soft robotic voice says, the words more enunciated than before. *"Beginning startup protocols and tri-core reactor ignition."*

A growing roar reverberates behind me, like it's coming from the maw of a synthetic eldritch beast.

A rubber cup encompasses my face, fitting snugly to my mouth and nose. I breathe deep, but it's muted against the heightened sounds flooding my ears.

Right in front of me, a rectangular image flashes on. There is a symbol in the centre – an equilateral triangle within an inverted triangle within a larger one. There's text appearing, one line at a time, and it reads:

GUILD Republic Defence Systems
Special Forces Branch of the Titans
"Illis Qui Minatur in Tenebris... Audeamus"

I'm not sure what that last line means, but before I can try to take a guess, the text goes away and the insignia blurs in front of a line of descending program commands. The strings of code stop, and a line-by-line list of checks starts appearing on the screen.

>*Reactor core temperatures... check*
>*Antigravity exhaust panel integrity... check*
>*Life support systems encapsulated to pressure... check.*
>*Relay power to primary and secondary weapon systems... check*
>*Secondary aerial and aquatic propulsion modules... check*
>*Armour plating interlock and pressure integrity... check*
>*Pilot vitals and CNS secondary kinetic controls enabled... check*
>*All systems go*

"Lieutenant," Xhyr says to me, *"your call sign is Cronus 1. You are clear to launch."*

My hands gently rest on the dual controls at my sides, and each finger finds their place just as directed by what seems like several years of instructed theory. I ease the consoles forward, right foot to the fourth pedal, and press the auxiliary thrust buttons.

There's a moment where the display shows a small, gentle descent ahead of me, and then...

A sudden heart-stopping thrust upward has me anchored to the back of my seat. In front of me, there's nothing but the deep azure sky ahead, and to the far bottom right of the spherical display, the tarmac and everything else below me quickly disappear.

The display shows wisps of cloud pass by, and beyond them, the four battleships I saw earlier, but now they're much, much larger.

"Unit has exceeded sound barrier. Skeletal frame bearing at nine G's."

"Ehhh!" I'm muffled through the mask.

Despite being half as sick as I'd expect, I feel... strange. Not like there's something off, either with me or the mech around me. There's a surge coming deep within my chest, and it comes with a thought.

No, a memory.

It's foggy at first but becomes clear as day and as quickly as a flash.

I remember flying, in my mother's lap, peering over the navigation console as I held on to the top of a single stick helm. Whatever the vessel – a lifeboat, a yacht or a laser-class starship – I remember the sensation of going between one ship of the Nomadic Fleet to the other. I remember the acceleration, the possibility of exploration, and the direction to chart my own path.

But all of it, each a mosaic that pieced together a perfect work, was freedom. And that sensation back then was... now is, in this seat... exhilarating.

"Ahhh! Haha hahaha!" I shout, the corners of my eyes misting up.

"*Cronus 1,*" Xhyr says, "*you're approaching the test ceiling. Decelerate and bank starboard.*"

"Roger that!" I say, retracting my hands and easing off my foot.

It doesn't matter if I'm instructed, corralled, or marshalled where to live in this moment. Right now, I *have* that freedom I had when I was younger, safer, and... more sure of myself.

Whatever they do to me in training or anything else beyond that... they can't take that away from me.

Not ever.

My left hand shifts forward and my right pulls back, banking the Xenomech in the air. I stare at the parabolic path on the HUD and type a quick command on the buttons at my fingers. I lean forward as the mech takes a dip, with three marked points of tension tugging on my back.

The G's decrease in my descent and as the tarmac nears on the display, and another mech mirrors my approach hundreds of metres away.

That one must be Chloeja.

"*Auto landing sequence initiated,*" the OS tells me. "*Engaging plantar retro-thrusters. Antigravity reduced by five per cent.*"

The hull around my cabin shudders as my forward momentum slows to a stop. Across from me, through the display, the mirror of the mech I'm in slowly lands parallel to me. Flames escape the thick feet of the beast, as I imagine the same does for mine.

"*Three... two... one... contact,*" the synthetic voice confirms.

A dull, resonating *thud* echoes inside my cockpit, and even with my helmet on, its resonance is loud and clear. And, opposite to when I took off, the mech around me rises slightly to its feet.

"*Phase one complete, Cronus 1,*" Xhyr says. "*Stand by for phase two.*"

"Copy," I reply.

With the deafening silence around me, the only thing my ears pick up is the muffled sound of my breathing.

In... out.

In... out.

In...

"*Cronus 1, open comms to frequency twelve,*" Xhyr orders.

"Copy that," I reply, flipping a lever with my left hand. "Twelve is open."

"*Confirmed,*" Xhyr says. "*This next exercise is going to be a duel. The first unit to make contact with ballistics or melee wins the match.*"

I blink and zoom the display closer to the Xenomech on the other end of the tarmac.

"*Cronus 2 will be your opponent. And remember: while you do not have live rounds, this is not a simulation. If you are fubared in the air, or on my tarmac, it's for real.*"

Brief, fierce images of Chloeja pirouetting and slashing at me with violent speed back at the simulation ring resonate heavily in the back of my mind. I clutch my left ribcage, where the phantom pains resurface...

"*Pilots, prepare to sortie,*" Xhyr says. "*Over and out.*"

"Copy," I reply, in unison with Chloeja.

Her mech bolts into the air with a swift jump, disappearing from the surface of the tarmac and the aerial scope of my display.

The sortie's already begun, and I'm still grounded...

It's now or never...

I pull back the controls and engage my foot on the fourth pedal.

Just like that, I forcefully sink into the cushions of my seat, keeping my hands steady as the spherical display shows only the blue of the sky.

"Engage targeting systems," I command the OS. "Ready ballistics and primary cannons."

"Confirmed," the robotic voice replies. *"Ballistics and railgun online. Scanning for Cronus 2."*

The once soft blue lighting inside the cockpit changes to an ominous shade of red, and scattered across the concave display before me are several scanning target sensors.

A loud beeping sounds in my left ear, and Chloeja's unit comes into sight, bearing fifty-four kilometres north-northwest and above.

Target acquired.

I press my right foot down further, increasing my altitude and catching up to her velocity.

"Particle charge detected," the OS notifies me.

As if by reflex, I press my left thumb down and manoeuvre a toggle with it. Instantly, a white and black panelled arm rises, shielding my left flank, and emits a transparent oblong soft blue shield.

One second later, my mech rumbles as several particle charges hit my shield and absorb it.

"Shielding down by two per cent," it tells me.

My brow tightens as Chloeja's mech gets closer on the display. Once her unit becomes more visible, she extracts a blue-glowing sword. It's magnetically repulsive, but if I'm struck with it, I lose.

"Engage sidearm!" I shout.

"Engaging."

A smaller camera shot in the far middle right of my display shows the generation of a black carbon fibre sword, firmly in the grip of my mech's right hand. I move the left arm to grab the lower half of the handle and brace myself.

"Show mercy, and you die." I recall those icy words she said to me.

"Ahhhh!" I cry, bringing my sword toward her in an upward slash.

My entire cockpit shakes as she rushes toward me, deflecting my blow.

Damn.

I shift in my seat, readjusting the controls, and circle around. I press down on the shoulder ballistic missiles, targeting locked on to her quickly shifting unit.

She evades two missiles, blocks one, and cuts the last one in half with her sword.

"Now *you're getting it!*" Chloeja exclaims. "*It's not enough to just exert brute force... you have to come at me with the sheer rage that comes with a killing strike!*"

She returns a volley, launches two missiles, rockets upward, and hoists her blade upward, assuming a high guard. The targeting sensor shows she's approaching fast.

I cut the rear anti-grav, punch the retro thrusters, and drop like a meteor. I press two buttons on my left control and shift left.

"*Countermeasures deployed,*" the OS says.

A series of flashes and bursts blanket the concave screen, and from out of it, she lunges at me, bringing down the hell of her blade.

I burst thrusters from the right shoulder, evading her attack, and swing right to her rear.

My sword strike misses as she cuts upward, repelling another strike.

As the ASI on my console climbs, showing increased acceleration... the altitude keeps dropping.

She keeps her sword anchored against mine and frees her unit's other hand, swiping it away from my blade.

I try mirroring the attack, hoping to block her sword with an upward sweep of my unit's right arm...

There's a flash, and I shake in the confines of my seat... but Chloeja's unit banks past my right. I follow her, watching her mech free fall into a spin.

"*Mayday, mayday!*" she cries. "*Starboard anti-grav panels fucked; I can't maintain altitude!*"

A single dualistic thought crosses my mind:

If Chloeja hits the ground, at this velocity, she's a smear on the tarmac. Or, more like a molten crater. And... if she bites it, my secret dies with her. No more loose ends. My family's safe...

But... what kind of person would I be if I let her die that way?

Could I even live with myself?

With the SERUM coursing through my system, this one thought takes up a fraction of a second in real time, but with that fraction, her mech is that much further away from mine.

Gods, I'm dumb...

"Hang on!" I cry, slamming my foot down on the metal floor.

"Maximum G's reached. CNS and cardiovascular system compromised," the OS warns me.

"Shut up!" I yell. "Cronus 2! Chloeja! Burn your retro thrusters!"

"*C-copy!*" she replies.

Her mech inches closer, the ground quickly coming into view. I reach out to grab her unit and try to break her fall.

I miss. She's *just* out of reach.

"No choice..." I say, punching a command into the console with my right hand.

"Shoulder thrusters self-destruct selected. Are you sure you wish to continue?"

"Do it!" I shout, keeping the mech's arm outstretched.

"Initiating thruster self-destruct in three, two..."

A sudden burst shakes the whole of my cockpit... but I make contact with her unit's arm and clasp down hard.

I'm not letting go.

A groaning sounds from the metal frame around me as I pull Chloeja toward me, and once I have a hold of her, I bank my unit so that she's on top of me, and I aim the back of my mech at the ground.

I only have four of the original six thrusters on my unit's torso. This is going to be close.

"Full power to all aft thrusters!" I cry, keeping the pressure of my mech's arms on Chloeja's.

"Acknowledged."

My chair vibrates madly, jarring the injection sites on my back and causing them to eject and re-insert twice for every second that passes. As my eyes well with tears, I grit my teeth and brace for impact.

"Warning, low altitude. Warning, low—"

I'm not sure if it's the SERUM... or a strange trick of the mind... but I swear, the second my mech stops moving, time stops altogether.

Well, mostly.

What I sense most is the air knocked out of me, a creeping dizziness, and a sharp, radiating pain that starts from my back.

Well... at least Chloeja should be safe. And with no one for her to extort, so are Mom and Ann'Elise.

But what I witness is Chloeja's mech in my arms warping and distorting as the concave sphere of my mech's display starts to crackle and fizz out into visual static. The screen turns a solid blue. The hexagonal panels that make up my cockpit pop out of place as a convex shape forms behind me. As everything slowly crumbles around me, a single display panel dislodges and flips toward me.

I want to move my arms, shield myself from it, but they don't budge. The panel nears my helmet, and then...

Everything goes black.

"Gah!" I gasp, staring up at the tile work of a ceiling. It looks familiar. "Where... am I?"

"Hey," a familiar voice answers. "You're in the medic bay."

I blink and rotate my head toward the source, and sitting against the only free chair in this room is...

"Chloeja," I say, trying to get up, "you're not dead!"

"Take it easy," she chides, placing her hands up. "You went through the gamut; just lie still."

I take a second to process what she said as I sink back into the cot.

"And yeah, I'm not dead," she adds, "so... why is that?"

"Why is what?" I ask.

"I mean, why did you save me?" She peers straight at me. "Not that I'm not grateful, but you didn't have to. It, uh... might have saved you a lot of trouble otherwise."

"I'd be lying if I said I wasn't conflicted." I speak plainly, for the first time in a long time. "I couldn't watch you die like that. It's not in me."

Chloeja turns away, her hands in her lap, still wearing the same black Xenomech pilot's suit from earlier. I watch as she scans the room, like she's searching herself. Her golden green eyes settle back on me. "Thank—"

"S-sir, you can't—" Reilah protests, her voice muted behind the door. "Of course he's a student of yours but – sir! I have orders not to... y-yes, sir! I will, sir!"

I watch down the length of my cot as the sliding door to my room opens and Xhyr marches with speed and purpose toward the foot of my bed.

"Sir!" Chloeja stands to attention, saluting him.

I try to do the same, straining my left arm to brace myself as I raise my right.

"Put your damn hand down, Vaughan," Xhyr says, "and for God's sake, lie back down! You damn near caught a thirty-tonne mech, and you lived to tell of it."

I do as he says, and he slowly cranes his head toward Chloeja, pausing a moment.

"At ease, Lieutenant," He finally says.

"Sir!" she exclaims, sitting back down.

"Right, then," he says. "Vaughan, do you have *any idea* how much your little stunt cost the Republic taxpayers this afternoon?"

The blood drains from my face. "I do not, sir," I reply, "but I will find out for you."

"No, NCOs find things out for me. I trust, since the damages to both Lieutenant Nadjidhar's and your mechs are tallying in the billions of credits, that you took that into account when you... and I quote from Corporal Nevanor... 'Recklessly cannonballed yourself into the newly paved tarmac.' End quote. And! After surveying the site, I can say this was *very* accurate."

"Sir, I –"

"Major Talthor," Chloeja says, jumping from her seat, "sir, this is my fault... it was my mech that malfunctioned in flight. I should have double-checked the shoulder thrusters in pre-flight... the responsibility rests with me."

"Oh?" Xhyr says.

"Yes, sir," she assures. "I'm the reason the lieutenant is bedridden, immobile, and... possibly concussed."

I raise my good arm, checking myself, and feel rough bandages around the crown and brow of my head.

"If you're going to expel someone from the program, let it be me," Chloeja pleads.

My blood runs ice-cold as she says this.

"Settle down," Xhyr says, waving his hand dismissively. "No one's getting expelled."

I sigh quietly, and she slowly sits back down in her seat, not saying another word.

"Now, Vaughan," he says, staring down at me, "you assisted your opponent in a graded duel. What possessed you to do that?"

"At the velocity Chloeja was falling, she wouldn't have survived," I reply.

"We train you and her to eject from a compromised Xenomech. Standard operating procedures."

"I took that into account," I insisted, "and the risk was too great."

"But your opponent—" Xhyr begins.

"She belongs to *my* unit! Sir!" I interrupt, keeping my voice level. "And if anyone else in my charge is liable to die on my watch, I'll do it again."

Xhyr raises his eyebrows at me... but it doesn't seem like he's indignant. More like... he's amused?

"Okay," he says, "I have noted your insights for my report. As I have yours, Lieutenant Nadjidhar."

I follow his movements as he heads back for the door, and I jump a little as he glances back at me.

"I'm glad to see you ain't dead. As you two were." He exits calmer than he arrived.

When the door finally shuts, a rattled sigh escapes my lungs.

"Well!" Chloeja says. "You get points for bravery today!"

"Not for a lifetime?" I ask, a queasy sensation churning in my gut.

"Yeah, you wish." She laughs. "But I must be going now. Shao-Shi was saying all our results are back in, and there's going to be an after-party at the mess."

"Ahh, very good," I reply. "You have fun with the rest of the unit. I mean, even if I could hoist myself out of bed, I seriously need rest after today."

For the first time since Port Yegevni, Chloeja smiles. She nods, excusing herself with a gesture I assume noblewomen give when they leave: a bow and a ceremonious curtsey... but it's an odd sight in her suit.

She walks toward the door, slides it open, and turns back toward at me. "I meant to say before: thank you. You kept your promise to the letter."

My cheeks flush from her words, and unsure what to do, I nod. "You're welcome," I say, smiling.

Before she disappears through the door, she pauses. "Out of curiosity," she asks, "why did you agree to take Vaughanie's place?"

As Chloeja faces me, I breathe deeply, sitting up slightly in bed. "They... the people in the GUILD were going to kill my sister and mom," I explain. "I couldn't let that happen, so when Kael gave me the choice, I took it."

She stares at me, her eyes softening. "It doesn't sound like much of a choice," Chloeja replies, her arms held loosely in front of her.

"No, I didn't think so either," I say, catching the vulnerability in my words.

"It's quite the decision you've made, given your reason... maybe one day you can tell me more about it?"

I nod slowly, wondering how and when I could ever broach to anyone that I'm a Thetian.

"Okay," Chloeja says, smiling warmly, "rest up, Lieutenant."

She disappears for real this time, and the door to my room slides shut behind her.

Now, completely alone, I gently rest my head back against my flat pillow. And, as I can barely keep my eyelids open, I think about everything that happened today.

I piloted a sixty-foot-tall robot.

One I *flew* and *fought* in it.

I saved someone's *life* today! And I'm pretty sure she hates me less now – or maybe not at all. That'd be good.

And! Xhyr didn't rip me a new asshole for... oh, gods, the tarmac...

As my eyelids grow heavy and I slip back to sleep, I remember the duality between soaring free and the tempered rage fighting in a Xenomech brought me.

In all seriousness, I hope the tarmac is at least functional...

Chapter 19

Rachael

Two Hours Later

The tarmac is a bloody mess... I can't stop staring at it from where I'm perched high on the observation deck of the comms tower.

I have to say – it was one of the hardest things I've ever had to watch: seeing near perfection come to life, only to have imperfect Terran hands muddy the results.

"Do you like your job, Xhyr?" I say with clarity and purpose.

I heard the door open to the main floor not more than two minutes ago. Clearly, the oaf has no guts to address me after the mishap, and frankly, I can't blame him.

"Yes, ma'am." Xhyr replies, sounding candid but unbowed.

I slowly turn away from the travesty of the crater below, facing him. There is some solace in how little he's budged from the elevator doors... there is that.

"Would you like to keep your job?" I ask, noticing the octave in my voice rise one decibel sharper.

He blinks.

That son of a *bitch*! He hesitated!

"Yes, ma'am."

"Ahh, I thought that might be," I reply, "so I find myself perplexed – no, more than perplexed to witness, two perfectly calibrated machines nearly destroy themselves, my lab, and my *precious subjects!* How do you expect me to account for margins of error when I specifically factored all of it in?"

"Ma'am?" Xhyr asks.

"Cronus 2's shoulder intake thrusters" – I readjust my glasses – "were inspected to within an inch of their lives. I've had technicians swear *blood oaths* to me confirming their integrity."

"I don't follow," Xhyr says.

Both my eyebrows rise... not at his verbal ignorance, but at the thin veneer of calculated confidence coming across in his voice. *Oh, sir, don't think that I can't see past your mask.*

"Someone *sabotaged it*, Major!" I shout, loudly. "After my assistants both flogged the diagnostics crew and salvaged the crew's work, we found a single transmission coming from the tower. This very tower! And what's worse, if the roster is in fact accurate, the XO supervising the comms deck was *you*."

"Yes, it was," he says, seeming unaffected.

"Well! You could have said something earlier. Who was the culprit?!"

"Me," he says, his face deadpan. "I ordered Cronus 2's shoulder thrusters to blow."

"Major?" I ask, mortified that he would risk my hard work. "How am I supposed to process this?"

Now he takes bold steps toward me. In the light of the moons, his dress attire appears more lustrous, with the red cords coming from under his left shoulder mark, the dark silver marks themselves, and the brass buttons at the cuffs of his sleeves.

"I did what I had to, as an instructor, for the success of my students. I assessed the risks, made the call, and reaped the rewards. If I may speak so boldly, we all have today."

"How avant-garde," I sneer, a storm of fury forming in the pit of my stomach, "but do I even have to remind you of who oversees this project? Let alone how *vital* our success hinges on the thirteen?!"

Oh, *now* he squirms. Of course.

"His Excellency the President-General," Xhyr says with a kind of fearful reverence.

"Correct, Major," I reply. "I must stress this to you, that I am not truly in charge of Project Titan, but the one who sent me. Now understanding this, if God Himself sent me, what *does* that make me?"

"Ma'am?"

"His *prophet*, Xhyr. His *prophet*. And I've been sent here, to this planet, with a purpose. I chose you to help me fulfil that purpose."

He doesn't say anything but drops his jaw for a moment and recollects himself.

"So, that being said, did I make a mistake, Xhyr? Did God's prophet choose badly when I selected you?"

"No, ma'am!" he retorts, but interestingly enough, not from a place of fear.

"I didn't think so. Now get your ass back to those children," I say with disgust, "and do your job."

He doesn't protest, nor say 'ma'am' for the millionth time. No, instead he salutes me, and that's it. Even his gaze stopped searching me... like they found what they were looking for. There doesn't seem to be a hint of fear in them, not like on Port Yegevni, and he doesn't even bring up the possibility of an investigation. Not that there'll be one, but still.

I watch him leave through the elevator doors and disappear altogether. Now, setting all of my ducks in order, I flip open the holopad in my hand. It materialises, populating with the preliminary data from the battle this afternoon. As I scan the document, a metallic creaking in the distance echoes through the room. I look, and the recovery crew is very careful hoisting Cronus 1's mech from the centre of the crater, as they should be.

As I glance back down at the measurements, algorithms, and code, a smile creeps along my cheeks.

The Serotonin Exoskeleton Receptor and Umbral Meta-Stimulants, or SERUM, worked as I dreamed it would. Not only in repelling G-force, but in the synaptic readouts from both of my specimens.

Where Juggernaut mechs are slow, lumbering machines, a Xenomech moves *exactly* how I designed them. The frames are agile, the command-to-interface functions are almost instantaneous with the direct pilot-to-console interface, and all of the cardiovascular buffers stop the pilots' hearts from being crushed under all of those G's.

It's the perfect combination... and most importantly, it works.

Of course, I'll let them know of the short-term effects of this miracle drug, like night-sweats, headaches, and dehydration... but that's all they need to know.

"Oh, how wonderful it will be, these next two years of research..."

Part 3

Audeamus

Chapter 20

Chloeja

2 Years Later

The drop. Just thinking about it sets my blood on fire. The warm water from the shower head above me runs over my head and soothes my skin, but it can't calm the rage in my veins. The water cascades off my shoulders and streams down past my waist and legs, and I keep myself anchored with one arm leaning against the shower wall. I'm not even at the brief yet, and already I'm planning five steps ahead, calculating risks with the coming drop, and going over melee techniques. In orbit, and on the surface.

I sigh, press my hand against a luminous blue plate against the wall, and feel the creeping chill as the water stops. As I hop out, the cool air of my cabin slaps my naked skin, but I take my time grabbing a towel. I unceremoniously throw it over my head and start wringing my short hair dry... ish.

As I grab my uniform, folded neatly on the surface of my desk, I glance at a small picture angled toward me. It's a graduation photo of me and the other twelve on Nostro. We're all wearing our long dress coats. It was a rare day when the sun was shining, rising out of the west, and standing by the seat of honour near the middle is me... having earned my gold commander's shoulder rope.

I look closer at the photo. Vaughan's placed in the seat of honour, wearing the dark blue shoulder rope of a captain. For a long time, I wasn't sure what to make of Xhyr's decision.

I had trained my whole life under a master-at-arms, outperformed every cadet on Nostro... and yet Vaughan was given leadership of Cronus Squadron. My hand touches the glass on the picture frame, and I regard the image warmly. The truth is, even though I thought I deserved it at the time, over these last two years, Vaughan proved me wrong. He worked hard too. All of his actions led up to his promotion... I admit that.

The second I grab my form-fitting tights from my uniform pile, the phone app on my holopad rings.

Who the hell would call me at this hour? It's 0400 hours standard time!

With my black tank top in hand and my dog tag chain hooked on my middle finger, I glance over to the picture on the flat, paper-thin and translucent blue holographic screen...

Aryana Yazdani, Ashkaad Galaxy, Dominion of the Gemini Pale

"Ari?!" I say aloud.

What the...! A civilian call? How did it get through the comms net?!

Still half naked and mostly damp, I pat myself down in a frenzied haste. I dash my towel down and hustle to get my arms through my tank top, peeling it past my breasts and down to the seam of my leggings. All the while, the *cling* and *clank* of my dog tags rattles with the swift moments of my arms.

"Answer it!" I cry.

"Hi!" Chimes Ari's oh-so-cheerful voice. "I didn't catch you at a bad time, did I?"

The real time video shows Ari, sitting with her ankles crossed, her knees facing to the left, on a silver patio chair. In her periphery, I can see the rest of the matching patio set, placed on an elaborate mosaic of stonework, and beyond her, an extravagant garden enshrines her: the picture of a noble lady.

"Oh, noooo, not at all." I stress my words while trying to save face. "To what do I owe the pleasure?"

Ari giggles on the other end, and close to the bottom edge of the screen, I catch wisps of her white embroidered sundress rippling in the wind.

"Well! You know my brother, Aras?" she asks.

"I do. He's in the Legion, right?"

"Yes, and very on point for what I want to share with you." As Ari says this, her gaze trails off. "He... they informed Aras that there's a potential threat in your zone of deployment... I'm not sure what that means, but it sounds serious."

"A new threat...?" I ask.

She nods and attempts to keep a calm face. Ari's a poor actor... her eyes give her away.

"He said he couldn't say much more than that to me," she says, "but when I heard, I had to tell you. So, uh, whatever's out there, be careful."

"Oh, sweet Ari, you know me." I say, beaming a wide grin. "When have I ever been careless?"

Onscreen, she crunches her nose up into a scowl, and her calm, stately arms tense at my words. "That's the problem, bestie; I do know you," she emphasises, "and what Aras said sounded... serious. So, if only for my peace of mind, be more aware of what else could be out there."

A deep breath wells up in the space of my lungs, and I slowly expel it from my lips.

"Alright. I'll be more prepared," I assure, "and I'll pass it on to my XO and CO. Thank you, Ari."

Her posture visibly relaxes, and the protest in her face melts away, revealing a complexion of relief.

"I'm glad," she says, leaning in closer. *"So... tell me more about this boy you keep going on about."*

"Oh, uh," I say, turning away and to my right, "that's not... it's not entirely appropriate."

"Come on!*"* Ari pushes. *"I prattle on about every suitor who walks through my father's hall. The very least you could do is tell me his name! Or her name; I won't judge."*

Before I can say anything to my defence, a blinking red notification appears in the top right-hand corner of the holopad screen. It reads: *New text, encrypted line.* Without answering her, I press it.

"It's my XO," I say, breathless as I read who sent it.

It's from Vaughan, and all that it says is **"Where are you?"**

"Oh, my, *that is* scandalous!" Ari says, visibly blushing.

"N-no! That's not what I – I have to go!!"

"Wait, what?" she says, blinking repeatedly.

"Can't explain! Thank you again!" I blurt out.

My left hand's fingers smash against the formless hologram; my friend Ari's avatar quickly dissolves into nothing, and all that's left is a wristwatch.

No more time.

I snatch the watch from my desk, dash for my cabin's exit, and the jingle of my dog tags follows me while they're still in hand. The door to my quarters opens, and as I burst out of it like one possessed, I squint at the difference of lighting. I cut right, slinging my dog tag chain over my head one-handed. I manage a jog along the white-panelled corridors of the Republic Carrier *Nineveh*.

Other personnel come into focus, approaching me to my left. Most of them are well dressed, showcasing the elegance of long military coats, identical to those from basic training. And all of them seem so proper... and here I am, dressed in ten thousand credits worth of gym wear. And, in their finery, they all seem to take their sweet time getting from point A to point B.

I don't have that luxury.

"Hey!" someone says past my left ear. "Where's the fire?!"

As I glance over my shoulder, I find that person is the ship's second officer: Commander Lorne Freydas.

"Can't talk!" I exclaim, turning to face him in a dead halt. "Late for brief!"

"Well, get your ass gone, then!" Lorne shouts back with a wave. "And slow the hell down, will you?"

"Aye, aye!" I say with a wink.

I orient myself again in the right direction, swinging my arms into an enthusiastic jog... slower this time.

The next corner I take, I leap over the lip of a bulkhead gate and take a sharp left. Just ahead, three doors down, is the entrance to the briefing hall. With zero finesse, I slide my boots along the fine polished surface of the corridor laminate and straighten my stance as I come face-to-face with the sealed door in front of me.

Fuck...

I take a second, then another, staring at the door, and wonder what to say to my XO.

"*Well, sir, I had a very important call from a very close friend, and* that's *why I'm late!*"

... Nope...

"*I have* vital *intel about the next mission, and* that's *why I'm late. I'm a good soldier.*"

Yeah, no.

Just, knock and let yourself in. You're the queen bitch of Cronus Squadron; now act like it.

"Okay," I say under my breath. I raise a half-clenched fist up, parallel to the door, and knock twice with the knuckles of my fingers.

At first, nothing. Not after one second... two seconds... thre—

"Come in," a strong, assertive male voice says.

"Sir," I reply, stepping through the doorway.

The lighting in the briefing hall is dim, so much so that I can't make out any faces when I enter...

... all except for one.

A couple of feet to my left, addressing the front of the squadron, is Vaughan.

He stares at me, expressionless, silent... and I'm sure he's holding every word of reprimand for a one-on-one later. After the operation. But, to my surprise, he raises his hand and salutes me. I don't hesitate to return it.

"Take a seat, Commander," he says, lowering his hand and gesturing to the front row.

"Sir!" I say, bowing my head before finding my seat.

On my way to the far back of my row, Xhyr sits with his holopad open, and unlike Vaughan, his face is an open book... something to the tune of '*how the hell could you be late? Did I not teach you, above anything else, punctuality?! You're the commander of Cronus Squadron, for Gaaawd's sake!*'

Or something like that.

※

"Scans show a higher radioactive signature on floors three and four, and there's a possibility of hostile units gathering in larger numbers around the primary gates. This means the reactor is still up for grabs, and we'll come in through the top," Vaughan instructs.

A strange thought floats through my head as I'm comparing stats and following Vaughan's speech and hand movements... and I'm not sure if it's natural confidence or something of an ego he's grown, but I don't think he's looked hotter than he does now... weird.

I mean shit, maybe Ari has a point.

A computer changes slides on a projection in midair, like a holopad, and as Vaughan points at the screen, the operation strategy proceeds.

"Talmorah, like most Thriaxian worlds, has mostly water covering its surface," Vaughan says, "About ninety-nine per cent, so anything besides a direct landing on the surface installation is going to be an uphill battle. During the drop, keep your head and follow me. It'll be just like the others."

As I nod, trusting, I glance back at the dossier in my hand.

The part of the meeting I missed outlined the reason for the operational assault: breaking defences, gathering intel, and sowing chaos – and all to lay the red carpet for infantry drops and securing a beachhead. We are the hammer, indeed.

"We'll be using cloaking shields during the drop, so the orbital batteries shouldn't detect any vector faster than Mach 12. Once we're in the upper atmosphere, we'll be clear to switch to shock panels."

The onscreen simulation stops, and the only lights in the room are dim half-circular lamps jammed against the walls and the ceiling. The glow of Vaughan's holopad illustrates the same black tank top and leggings I wear, with dog tags and all. But, when I look at him again, he doesn't appear like he's wearing anything for the gym.

He looks like he's built to spill purple Thriaxian blood.

"Any questions?" he asks, his gaze lingering on the front row before surveying the back.

Again, there's silence. I turn to my right, seeing Lynette, and to my left is Yuri. We all share the same thing in common: mutual assurance of operation success. Hell, even as I crane my neck, Xhyr seems pleased. A feat, to be sure.

Suddenly, Vaughan aggressively collapses his holopad into nothing.

"Suit up," he commands.

Shivers run down my spine as I stand, side by side with my comrades in arms. Like before in my cabin, my blood is on fire, and nothing can shake my resolve.

Chapter 21

VAUGHAN

I still hate public speaking.

I don't care how long it's been or how I save face by showing everyone a relaxed demeanour; it's something I wouldn't miss. Even without Chloeja's ambition and drive or Xhyr's almost arrogant air of confidence, my Titans respond well to the resonating calm of my voice.

"Any questions?" I ask, surveying Chloeja and Xhyr first, then the rest of my squadron.

What I get from Xhyr is that half-crooked smile of his. Good, because that means I didn't miss anything. As far as he's concerned, the operation will go as planned. He's dressed, as always, in the formal wear of a Republic Guard Officer: the long, past-the-knee jacket dyed in iconic terracotta, two shoulder ropes distinguishing his new rank as colonel, and four bars etched into his shoulder marks. The rest of us pilots sport titanium marks too, but only on a fully assembled pilot's suit.

Chloeja, even though she got in late, was attentive during the brief... more so than she's been in the last couple of months. It's like she's scoping the room and checking Xhyr's reaction.

With no hands raised, I take the holopad in my hand and collapse it shut by forming my left hand into a fist.

"Suit up," I order.

My twelve squad members and Xhyr stand at attention, raising their hands in salute.

"Sir!" they holler.

I return their salute, and as soon as my arm drops, I lead the jog to the back of the briefing hall. I don't watch as they fall in, but the footfalls of their boots against the smooth metallic flooring reassures me.

The door ahead of me slides open, revealing the open-concept design of the armoury. At the end of the room is another set of sliding doors, sealed shut, but to the right is my locker.

I open it, and inside is my assigned chest plate, the one I received on my last day of basic. I grab it confidently, fit my head through the hole between the front and back pieces, and latch them together at the sides.

The only one out of our squadron I don't see is Xhyr, who is well on his way to the bridge. From what he's guided us through together so far, I say he's a damn good air boss.

Again, setting the example, I activate my armour with the press of a button and generate the rest of my suit. The clicking sound of nano-integrated fabric assures me, and as I hear the sound grow with each pilot doing the same, I focus on the rack in the middle of the room.

We're all given a small arsenal in the event we ever have to leave our mechs. Be it emergency or need... we're always prepared.

"Six magazines?" Yuri asks Lynette.

"Six full," she replies. "Five grenades?"

"Copy!" Yuri's gruff, enthusiastic voice chimes above the rest of our chatter.

I approach the multi-levelled shelves of typical arms: short-barrelled rifles, pistols capable of ripping through atomic bonding, a select number of grenades, plasma-charged wrist shields, and, of course... thirteen specifically made daggers. They each have unique engravings etched above the small hilt, and below them is an engraving of our first names... just in case, in the heat of the moment, one of us grabs another's dagger by mistake. I'm sure most of us would rather sleep with our blades on the ship, but operating procedures forbids us from carrying *any of this* past the armoury.

So I grab what's necessary and strap it to the fittings and clips lining the belt of my fully formed pilot's suit.

Five grenades stowed against my lower back and a pistol holstered to my right belt. Last, a collapsed shield equipped to the wrist guard of my left forearm.

Among the equipment checks, I take my short-frame rifle and load it with a magazine of repeating ion charges. The cartridge *clicks* into place with a quick slam of my palm and draw the loading mechanism back. Once satisfied, I lash the rifle to my right thigh. Aside from my dagger, I've used this tool the most.

"Commander," I say, "line the kids up."

"Sir!" Chloeja replies. "You heard the man. Form rank!"

The lieutenants don't answer back but thump their metal chest plates with the titanium plating of their gauntlets. They act as a single unit, the very sound in the air a martial reply to her command. And, without hesitation, they line up in two columns before the sealed door behind me.

One row of five to the left and six on the other, and the first row is complete when Chloeja herself falls into rank.

"Gauge check," I say calmly but with discernible authority.

"Sir!" my Titans answer.

Every pilot checks the readings on each other's left wrist displays, follow their fingers along the seams of each of their suits, and check for any tears or signs of wearing. I wait until the last pilot stops patting down the other and fold my arms comfortably across my abdomen.

"All clear?" I ask.

"All clear, sir!" they respond.

Chloeja falls out of rank, facing me. "Captain," she says, "if I may?"

I nod and let my arms fall loosely to my side. Like the first time she and I boarded an X-5, she gives that same meticulous look as she checks the readouts on my wrist, scans me over, and pats the areas of my suit that are more sensitive and susceptible to wear. This time though, like in past months, she's not as aggressive in her task, and I... I don't know. There's a tenderness about her now when she gets this close to me.

"All clear!" Chloeja exclaims. "Good for another parsec."

"Thanks," I say.

As Chloeja falls back, I regard the rest of my squadron. "Titans, who fights the Thriaxians hand to hand?"

"Audeamus," they reply.

"Who wields the iron rod of His Excellency to stars unknown?"

"Audeamus!" they echo, louder.

"Who stares into the abyss and laughs when it stares back?" I roar.

"*Audeamus!*" my Titans cry.

My heart swells with pride. Each time we drop, I understand a little more how Xhyr must feel being our CO ... and it's empowering.

So I waste no more time, and I smash the release button to the hangar behind me.

"Fall in for drop," I order.

"Sir!" they shout in unison.

As the large blast doors to the hangar open, I jog ahead to an extensive network of catwalks, and far above are the vast ceiling lights, hanging two to three stories up. In terms of colour, the catwalks and the walls project little light from their dark gun-grey hues. For size, you could park two large infantry drop ships, each with a five-hundred soldier capacity, and that's including their traditional bulky power armour.

My gaze drops from the ceiling as I keep pace. An invigorating shiver runs down my spine as the repair techs come into sight. They stand by each of our thirteen respective mechs, waiting for us to board.

"Whoa, whoa, whoa," Chloeja says mere steps behind me. "Horatio, what possessed you to put *that* on your mech?!"

Out of the corner of my eye, I see her pointing up in abject disgust at his spoils of war: a decorative horn protruding from the head of his mech, as well as gold and silver Thriaxian armour plating bejewelling the tops of its shoulders.

"A *badass spirit*, Commander!" Horatio hollers back. "My charm and wit alone can't terrify the jellyfish, now can they?"

"Ha! That charm of yours could strip the paint off of a Thriaxian warship," Serena jabs back, interceding on Chloeja's behalf.

"Mm, I won't argue," Horatio says with a shrug, "but the message still comes across."

"And that is?" Chloeja asks, her tone tiptoeing around how rightly gaudy the unit in question looks.

"Fuck with Horatio and find out," he replies with a broad, cocky grin. The way he folds his arms, appearing both pleased and accomplished, only adds to the wince Serena and Chloeja share.

"Oh, the only thing they're going to find out, Horatio, is that the only thing worse than your taste is your manners. I mean, shit, it barely meets tactical code," Xalpha adds, passing me.

"*That's the point!*" Horatio stresses loud enough for the whole hangar to hear.

More of the squadron fans out across the rest of the hangar, and as I get two steps away from my mech, Yuri passes me from my left shoulder.

"If it's fear you want them to feel, paint it in their blood." He says matter-of-factly, "Look at mine."

One gangway down the catwalk, I glance up, and Yuri gestures with his outstretched hand toward his mech; decorated in intricate designs of war paint is the faded purple-hued blood of Thriaxian soldiers.

To this day, I still don't ask how he smuggles that much back on board...

"Heh, all you young folks think about is clout and valour..." a familiar, sage voice says ahead of me, and I watch the lieutenant about-face. Sure enough, it's Oreiga. Or, as he's lovingly known in the squadron, the Old Man. His moniker, or pseudo call sign, came about on the last day of basic, when the Heavy Infantry gave us a single transfer. Being thirty-nine, the oldest out of all of us, the nickname stuck.

"I used to see this a lot when recruits would transfer from the Heavies to the Titans, but it was always the hotshots with the racy nose art what got blown up first. Me though," the Old Man says as he leans against the right-facing rail of the catwalk, staring up at my unit, "I came to rely only on victory marks. It keeps a low profile, bolsters the pilot's ego just so, an' shows off if you truly are an ace or simply a cocky kid playing war."

The Old Man pushes himself up and places his hand below the cockpit door. Normally, it'd be a faux pas to touch another pilot's Xenomech... but he's making a point, and Horatio could benefit from another lieutenant's words.

"Take the captain, for instance," he says. "Simple victory marks: twenty-three in score. That's good enough for me."

"Ah, you can keep your simplicity, Old Man!" Horatio retorts. "Me, I'll stick with making a point!"

The Old Man and three other repair techs shrug collectively.

"Eh, I tried," the Old Man sighed, "but enough about that. I'll see y'all in the drop."

Xalpha, Horatio, Serena, Chloeja, and I give him a silent salute, and he hops back into a jog toward the end of the catwalk. Everyone else disperses, except for Chloeja.

"Sir..." she says, "about the start of the brief..."

"It's a one-off, Commander," I say, "just get your head into the mission."

"That's what I mean, Captain; it *is* about the mission," Chloeja stresses.

"Explain," I reply, my brow tensing.

"It's not much, but I received a piece of civilian intel about a hostile element in our quadrant. She said it's serious, but she lacked any real details."

"Is your source credible?" I ask.

"She is. The woman received it second-hand from a Legion operative."

"Recommended course of action?" I enquire, bemused as she lights up at the question.

"Higher alert. Maybe it's a new Thriaxian unit prototype, some experimental pulsar weapon variant... we should stay frostier than usual."

"Copy that," I say. "Thank you, Commander."

"Sir!" Chloeja exclaims, saluting and disappearing with the rest of the squadron.

Now it's just me and my mech.

The Old Man wasn't wrong: I, we, take great pride in the only warhorse we each possess.

Before I activate the latch to the cockpit, I trace my fingers along the victory marks and then next to deep scratches in the armoured plating.

My first close call, and a lesson well learned.

In fact, when the repair techs insisted on buffing out the plating, I actively refused. While they may not have understood, they've since respected my sentiments. And as a whole, I've gotten along more with the repair techs than any other division of the ship. After all, they're my sort of people.

I get them, and they seem to get me.

Later, when they asked about it, I said that I wanted to remember how close I was to death... and that it wouldn't get another chance like that again.

I can't afford another brush like that. Not while Mom and Ann'Elise are out there.

The pressure from the latch against my Xenomech increases, followed by a deafening mechanical *thud*. Two opposing doors open wide, one flinging up, and the other down. Like the first time I entered one, the insides are dark, but now I'm anything but afraid.

<hr />

"*Take a deep breath in, and hold it.*" A familiar, synthetic voice instructs me through my helmet.

I do as it says, and a sudden, uncomfortable sensation radiates from my upper back.

After basic, Doctor Vayne surgically installed port receptacles in the backs of the squadron: one in the spinal column for brain to OS interface and two arterial ones near each shoulder blade. Each circular chrome port helped mitigate the pain of the needles, but they also engaged the SERUM that much quicker into our bodies. Now... it's bearable.

"*Breathe again.*"

Without the shock of the pain, I breathe out, and... yeah, there's that aluminum aftertaste.

"*SERUM injection complete. All clear for G-resistance and performance enhancement.*"

Outside the display in my cockpit, a brief, shrill siren echoes from my mech's audible sensors to my ears. The ceiling lights change colour to a darkened blue.

"*Attention. Depressurization for drop in T-minus sixty seconds. All NCO personnel, evacuate the hangar immediately,*" a scripted, synthetic voice says from outside speakers.

The mechanics give us one final send-off, a salute for each of the thirteen Xenomechs they care for. Ophelia described it once: "They do this like a parent would for their child, or a spouse for their partner."

Either way, at least I appreciate it. It's a warmth we don't normally get in our line of work.

Once their job is done, they fall out starboard side to the maw of the hangar.

"*Operating systems online,*" the OS says from inside my helmet. "*Beginning startup protocols and tri-core reactor ignition.*"

Outside my helmet, my mech groans, and within seconds, it grows into an encouraging roar. The familiar enclosure of rubber covers my mouth, and the smell of surgical anti-septic enters my nostrils.

The centre console of my cockpit illuminates with our unit's motto on the screen, and I linger on the last word shown:

Audeamus.

"Let us dare," I say aloud to no one but myself.

"Hangar depressurization underway. Standby."

The blue lights above me flash as soon as the hangar blast doors seal. Below my feet, the optics on my concave display show large bay doors sliding apart. The lights immediately go black, and below me a startling array of stars is illuminated. It's strange... seeing the vacuum of space open up like this would have scared me to death a couple of years ago. Not so much anymore... and if I'm being honest, not at all. Since the first few missions, I look forward to each and every drop.

It's enthralling.

What snaps me back to attention is the sound of soft beeping coming from my centre console. Pre-flight checklist's almost done:

>Armour plating interlock and pressure integrity... check.
>Pilot vitals and CNS secondary kinetic controls enabled... check.
>All systems go.

A soft thunder quakes below me, and in an instant, I grab the dual controls at my sides.

"Good morning, sunshine." Xhyr's gruff voice resonates in my helmet. *"Everything's showing green from up here. Squad's clear to drop... over and out."*

"Roger that," I say, my voice muffled against my mask. The comms feed ends, and I switch to the main channel with the squadron. Now, amidst the loud sound of my breathing, everyone's listening for me to give the word.

With seconds left before zero hour, my steady breaths are the only thing that breaks the eerie silence around me.

Three.

Two...

"Drop," I command my squad.

Crack!

The restraints holding my mech's shoulders propel me down, and for a split second I see the open bay doors, head-on, in the flash of an eye. All at once, adrenaline surges through me as my stomach lurches up into my lungs. Ignoring all that, I press two buttons on my right control throttle and bank ninety degrees, aiming head first toward the azure sphere in my display.

Like a meteor, facing the light side of Talmorah, we accelerate into planet-fall, one G after another.

"Initiate cloaking panels," I order my unit's OS.

"*Confirmed. Shock shielding disabled; light refracting enabled,*" it replies.

My hands squeeze tightly onto the controls, angling the unit closer to the planet's low orbit for entry. On a second screen, I bring up my squad's mech vitals and stats: they've all cloaked up too.

To my nine is one of three orbital batteries, too far away to target the *Nineveh* but coming up real fast. So far, no readouts of activity... a *much* better start than the first operations.

"*Target locked,*" the OS says, seeing the HUD zero in on a pinpoint of white wisps in the azure blue. "*Commencing silent drive propulsion.*"

I dart to another quadrant on the display, and I note the rapidly descending number of kilometres toward the mesosphere.

I quickly tap the rear cam display, and it shows the battery is inactive, with no signs of particle charge targeting me or other squad units.

No question now: we're in the clear.

Ahead, thick storm clouds churn and flicker with bolts of lightning. It's normally risky weather to fly in, but honestly... that's exactly how we like it.

The display shows the lower stratosphere fade and disappear, the dim light of the local white dwarf evaporating into the periphery, and the intensity of the lightning growing.

"*Passing into the troposphere,*" the OS tells me. "*Target facility locked on.*"

As the clouds and electricity dissipate around me, the darkened waters below rage with a torrent of crashing whitecaps. And...

... there it is.

At the epicentre of this ocean, the target comes into full view on my HUD.

"Open comms channel," I tell the OS.

"Acknowledged. Cronus Squadron channel open."

"All pilots move into formation," I instruct, "and Cronus 9, make us a hole."

"Copy that!" Xalpha replies, her mech accelerating past me.

In my display, she materialises a large particle rifle in both of her unit's hands and aims it at the nearing facility below.

"Firing charge one," Xalpha exclaims. *"Firing charge two!"*

One blinding flash after another engulfs the entire convex display. It slowly dims, and a thin narrowing beam of light leads toward the surface. A few kilometres below me, one particle beam explodes over the target, and another hits further into the facility.

"Weapons hot!" I order. "Bank hard and retro-burn down!"

Before banking upright, I fly past Xalpha, and immediately put on the brakes.

Twelve G's turn into fifteen real quick, and even with the SERUM, it feels like I'm slowly being crushed, but even this goes away as the anti-grav thrusters burn hot.

"Surface contact imminent," the OS cautions at me.

... Now.

"Drop cloak!" I shout. "Engage shields, and prepare to sortie!"

"Sir!" my squad confirms.

Seconds from reaching the enemy's new skylight, a faint white rippling envelops the entire display of my cockpit and shifts to a faint solid blue. The hole Xalpha made comes into sight, fifty meters to contact, and as I take one breath... two breaths, hands glued to the controls, I slip through the opening.

A loud screeching erupts beneath me, followed by a loud mechanical *thud*. The low groan of hydraulics rearing my unit upward permeates my helmet. And before I get my bearings, I unsheathe a particle rifle of my own, aiming it forward.

On both sides, large grey pillars with geometric lines of glowing blue illuminate the large room I'm in.

The HUD isn't showing any hostile units.

Even as Xalpha and Chloeja make landfall a hundred feet from me, there's no activity on the display.

"Fan out," I order, scanning the large corridor ahead. "Keep tabs on our nine and six."

"Copy," Chloeja and Xalpha acknowledge one after the other.

Tension builds on my foot as I press down on the right peddle, proceeding into the dimly lit chamber. As I walk my unit out, the tremor of four, five more contact descents shakes my cockpit. That's eight of us, and the geo-locator on my display shows five more falling through the pipe up top, and it shows Lynette touching down last.

The red combat lights fill my cockpit, and a flashing sight on my HUD zeroes in on a target to my ten.

"Take cover," I shout. "Hostiles engaged!"

Chloeja ducks behind a large pillar at least a hundred feet in diameter, and scattered across my HUD are several glowing fields that show up out of nowhere. The way these fields appear, they seem like the tiny wormholes our ships come out of in space...

Out of them comes the sickening hiss of Thriaxian particle beams. Firing them are fifty-foot-tall automatons, each of them silver-chrome plated and crawling their way into our offensive line on six mechanized legs.

"Light 'em up!" Chloeja barks. *"Cronus 9, 5, suppress these assholes; I'm going in!"*

"Copy!" Xalpha and Shao-Shi both reply, brandishing their rifles in the direction ahead of Chloeja.

As a barrage of automatic particle beams rage across the octagonal room, Chloeja's unit serpentines in my display to the right, left, then forward with two long pulsar blades drawn. Each of them emanates white from the fusion of plasma, and she lunges forward in an X-strike.

"Die!" she cries, slicing through, propelling her mech upward, retreating backward into a flip.

One more pawn off the board.

"Cronus 2," Yuri growls over the comms to Chloeja, *"duck!"*

Her unit crouches low as another automaton skitters in, blasting one particle charge after another, until a thin beam of energy blasts from Yuri's long tactical rifle, clear on the other side of the room.

"Headshot!" he declares.

"Nice one!" Ophelia says, stepping beyond him and repelling a shot away from Yuri with her shield.

A blinking crosshair zeroes in on my screen as a bipedal Thriaxian mech emerges from the dark corridor ahead. In its hand is a long pulsar blade, glowing phosphorus yellow. I know them all too well...

Sentinels.

Two clicks on my right console and my rifle collapses into the void of quantum storage; in its place is a pulsar blade of my own. My knuckles tense from the tight grip of my hands, and with a deep feral rage, I accelerate my unit toward the Thriaxian mech.

Unlike the grounded steps from before, my unit glides through the air, my blade angled high in an eagle-guard. There's three mechs' worth of space between us, but in that gap is a hurricane of automaton beams and return fire with our enclosing approach. I can rest my laurels on their robots... but it's the Thriaxian pilots I reserve my wrath for.

Target distance is a hundred feet, fifty feet...

I grin as I allow this jellyfish bastard to enter my space, and I simultaneously shuffle right, pivot my mech one-eighty, and bring down my blade on the Thriaxian unit's back. The plating is thinnest there, closest to their cockpits.

Thunder invades my ears as ionized fusion energy crackles against alien metal, shooting up sparks and molten alloy in all directions. I keep the sword in my hand level, checking for any more encroaching hostiles and check my scope for any movement from the enemy.

No movement.

So, to be sure, I lunge my unit forward one step, raise my blade parallel to the ground over the Thriaxian mech's cockpit, and drive forward on both of my controls. There's a moment of resistance and a muted crackle at the point of impact, followed by a pressurized geyser of water and spray of purple staining the hands of my mech.

I think I understand a bit more why Yuri paints his mech in their blood: it's both a determent... and a reminder of justice well executed.

"Squad," I call out over the comms, "status report."

"Sector 1 cleared," Yuri confirms. *"Hostiles neutralized."*

I switch up my sword for my rifle, the weight of one weapon disintegrating as the other materialises into my Xenomech's hands.

"No casualties to report," Chloeja adds, *"just some shield damage from the last volley."*

A sigh leaves me at her words, and the tension in my brow releases. "Copy that. And Cronus 5, what's the integrity of the payload?"

"Payload's secure, sir," Shao-Shi replies, *"no radioactive leaks detected."*

"Good job; let's keep it that way," I say. "All units, move to phase three of the operation. Keep it tight, and follow my lead to the reactor."

On a small area map in the corner of my convex display, all of Cronus Squadron forms a vertical column down the expansive corridor.

Me in the lead, and Chloeja in the rear.

As we leave the antechamber, a question lingers in my mind: How would the Heavies have managed this sortie?

With all their combined firepower, with only power armour and Horatio's "charm"... I'd say poorly. An entire division of fifteen thousand... gone. Ground to dust by Thriaxian engineering...

... which only fills me with more purpose. We fight them back, and we save scores of Terran lives. In my mind, there isn't a higher calling than that.

<hr />

We pause our slow march toward the reactor before a thin stretch of tubing, about two mechs in width.

"Through here." I motion, highlighting the luminous corridor ahead on our HUDs. "The reactor's ahead."

"Sir!" the squad replies.

As my mech sets foot inside the narrow ventilation shaft, the top part of my display starts to shimmer and blink. Most of the shaft is transparent, capturing the faint glow of the lighting against the ocean that surrounds it. And in it, large alien sea creatures swarm close by: ones that are recognizable fish like salmon and tuna, and others that resemble wide, elongated serpents with giant fins... hundreds of times larger than our mechs.

"Here there be dragons," Shao-Shi says over the comms.

"Don't get poetic now," Yuri gruffly interjects. *"The only dragons in this ocean are* us.*"*

"Oo-rah!" Horatio adds.

Oreiga chuckles, but I'm with Shao-Shi on this. We don't know much about what the Thriaxians keep in their facilities, let alone what they're willing to use against us.

No sooner does this thought cross my mind than the luminous corridor ends; the faint blue of illuminated pillars and obelisks come into focus on my display... as well as three humanoid mechs standing between us and their reactor.

Ahead, they simultaneously brandish their yellow pulsar blades, which protrude from their right arms.

"Hostiles, twelve o'clock!" I shout.

"Roger," Chloeja says. *"Cronus 4, 7, send 'em a nice parting gift."*

"Copy that, Commander!" Yuri and Oreiga reply enthusiastically.

Both men came up to my three and lean in against the siding of the poly-glass corridor, and each whip out a missile launcher.

"An RPG by any other name," Yuri says, followed by the releasing hiss of a mortar, *"wouldn't sound as sweet."*

BAM!

A flash of light and a spray of metallic sparks shoot from the sights at our twelve. Out of the corner of my eye, I see Yuri's mech disintegrate the launcher and materialise his particle rifle.

"Hey, Shao-Shi, how's that for poetry?" Yuri says, the smile on his face easy to imagine behind his mask.

"Stunning," he replies, backing Oreiga and me up. Once Shao-Shi's at our line, Yuri bolts ahead.

"The commander sends her regards!" Yuri cries, firing one particle beam after the other, his oval shield guarding his left.

As the sparks clear, the HUD shows that Yuri *annihilated* the target on the right and rushes the centre one. Their shields are looking pretty bad, but it's the one on the left that has my sight locked on.

With one control, I summon my pulsar blade in my mech's right hand and fire one beam after another in my left. The Sentinel ahead of me dodges one round, two rounds, and gets nicked with the third, throwing him off balance.

I have my shot.

My left hand types furiously, jerking the control to support the blade in my right. I angle in, shuffling forward, and left-slice the head clear off my target.

Now!

As the Sentinel's arms flail, I twist my mech's body ninety degrees and plunge the blade directly between the enemy machine's shoulder blades. I finish, slicing right, spraying the torso of my mech with more purple Thriaxian blood. The water from their life support systems leaks out, and all I make out from the opening in their cockpit is a shaky metal-clad arm.

It wavers and falls limp down the side of its mech.

"Clear!" Xalpha exclaims. *"No hostiles in the periphery."*

"Copy," Chloeja replies. *"Cronus 6, 12, bring out the payload."*

"Roger," Janessa and Rasmus answer.

"Squad, fall in," I say. "Keep the defensive line on the ventilation shaft. We'll be out soon."

"Sir!" the squad shouts back.

My display focuses on the corridor, and I watch as most of the squadron takes post. With no other way in or out, Janessa and Rasmus unpack the rectangular charges strapped to their units' backs.

"No soft intel to collect?" I ask Shao-Shi.

"No, not so much as a terminal jack-in or wireless frequency. The Legion wasn't kidding when they said a data scrub was almost impossible... but I took some pictures, and maybe the Science Division can use them."

"Copy," I reply.

With the line secure, I gently shift the controls in my hands and veer my gaze toward the reactor. Janessa gets to the central console and carefully places down a twenty-thousand-megaton nuclear bomb. My gaze follows Rasmus as he does the same.

Of course, it'll wipe the facility off the face of Talmorah. But more than that, it'll cut the resonating power relay to the batteries in orbit. Once blown, the 4th Republic Fleet and the rest of the Terran regulars can storm the planet en masse and take possession of the few fortifications it has further away on the coastline.

"Charge set," Rasmus says to the squad.

"Same here," Janessa adds. *"It'll blow at your Command, Captain."*

"Roger that," I say. "Let's waste no time. Everyone, fall back to the evac zone. We're almost home free."

"Sir, yes, sir!" my squad says back.

⋙⋘

The feet of my mech break thrust and land on the outer lip of the entrance on the facility's roof. One pilot after another follows me up. The last to land are Shao-Shi and Ophelia.

"*Nineveh,* this is the captain of Cronus Squadron," I say, "On my mark, the 4th fleet has clearance to proceed to planet-fall on Talmorah."

"*Roger that, Captain,*" Xhyr says back to me. "*Relaying instructions to the fleet now and sending you their channel. Everyone in one piece?*"

"Copy, safe and sound," I reply, and there's audible relief in Xhyr's sigh.

"*Acknowledged. Get your asses back to hangar.*"

"Copy that." I end the transmission and flip back to the squad's line. "We're go to lift-off. Clear the zone, and head back home."

"*Sir!*" the squad replies, more or less in unison.

My fingers clank against both controls in my hands, I switch comms to my unit's OS.

"Prime thrust for planetary escape," I command.

"*Confirmed. Firing reactor cores for optimal escape velocity,*" the OS replies.

My unit slowly bends down into a mid-kneel, and suddenly...

The SERUM kicks in as my stomach does somersaults. The G counter on my screen shoots from two to nine in a matter of seconds as I accelerate into the lower atmosphere. As the nausea sets in, I stare down at my feet, and on the bottom of my display is the rest of the squadron following behind and quick on my tail.

I shove back into my chair, and the force of ascent eases up.

"Commander," I say, "you want the honours?"

I stifle a laugh as Chloeja draws out a long, satisfied sigh.

"*Oh, Captain, when* don't *I? And to nuke alien scum? Oh, yes, the honour's all mine,*" she purrs.

One transfer of codes later, a small box on my screen shows the status of the nuclear charges, and in seconds, we'll be clear of the blast radius. So I tap my helmet and activate the tint to maximum on my visor.

"*Hey, Commander,*" Yuri says, "*what are your thoughts on their hospitality?*"

"*A fine question, Lieutenant,*" Chloeja replies, enjoying this far too much. "*Well, no refreshments upon entry... can't say I'll recommend.*"

The box on my screen reads:

Live charges, nuclear detonation detected.

"*Zero stars,*" Chloeja adds.

A blinding flash of light wraps around the sphere of my display, and my mech jostles as I continue to climb. After a few seconds, I activate my rear cam... and behind the metal flame-emitting heels of my unit, a massive explosion of water shoots up below us. Maybe a few hundred feet high.

"*Woo!*" Lynette cheers. "*Closed for renovations!*"

"*Permanently,*" Yuri adds, sounding pleased with himself.

Out of the blue, a repeating beep catches my attention.

I glance up toward the top of the convex display, and my HUD's showing five large spacecraft. It seems like they're hanging there, suspended in the middle stratosphere. My sight can't identify them... maybe they're too far away...

Or it's...

"Patch me through to the *Nineveh*," I say to my unit's OS.

"*Acknowledged,*" it replies.

"*Hello, Captain, you've reached the* Nineveh's *resident Sky Daddy... now what is it?*" Xhyr asks.

"The 4th Fleet is awful close to our evac zone. I didn't give the go-ahead; when did they depart?" I reply.

"*Captain, the 4th never left their post. They're ten thousand kilometres out from the* Nineveh, *waiting on the admiral's go-ahead. Can you identify the crafts?*"

"Negative," I say, reconfiguring my sight on the five large crafts getting bigger in my display. "Wait, they don't look like Republic crafts... they—"

"*Captain,*" Horatio interrupts on our squad line, "*I'm picking up a bogey, flying in fast, descending altitude. Sight's picking up three signatures...*"

I freeze.

"*They're Thriaxian craft. Unknown classifications.*"

The sight on my screen is useless, but I can make out five crafts, now identifiably Thriaxian in make.

"Bank west!" I order. "Evasive manoeuvres! Stay away from those carriers; they're not ours!"

The lighting in my cockpit glows ominously red as the targets Horatio picked up near my sights.

Even with all the SERUM in my veins, my brain feels caught in a vice.

"Colonel," I say, flipping the channel to Xhyr, "requesting backup from the 4th and 5th fleets. We're outnumbered."

"*Got it,*" Xhyr replies. "*Hold strong for twenty minutes. We're on our way.*"

"Copy that." My voice wavers.

"*Stay alive till then,*" Xhyr replies. "*Over and out.*"

Get it together, Vaughan. This fire won't die by itself.

Both my hands slam back into the seat of my console, cutting thrust and re-angling toward the hostiles in a free fall. As my fingers move wildly along the controls, Chloeja's words come back to me:

I received a piece of civilian intel about a hostile element in our quadrant... it's serious.

"Commander," I message Chloeja directly, "take the heavy hitters and defend the units' ascent. I'm going after that detachment with Shao-Shi, Yuri, and Lynette. Angle the squad's exit away from those carriers."

"*Roger that, Captain.*" While usually confident, her voice carries the same tremor mine had with Xhyr.

"We've got this," I say to her, pushing my panic down. "I've got this."

"*Copy!*" she replies, ascending above the defensive circle with Oreiga and Xalpha.

"Cronus 3, 4 and 5, you're flying with me," I command. "Our targets are those three unknowns."

"*Let's ground 'em!*" Yuri roars.

"*Got it!*" Lynette and Shao-Shi say together.

I glance quickly to the level of shielding I have left: 46%.

Not bad. I've fought through worse.

The HUD's showing the three Thriaxian mech units approaching my detachment with only a couple of hundred kilometres between us and them. The one mech in the middle appears slightly bigger than the other two... a sentinel model I've never seen before.

That one's mine.

"Cronus 3 and 5, take a dive and engage the flank supporting craft. Cronus 4," I say to Yuri, "you're my wingman... we're taking out their leader."

"*With pleasure.*" Yuri snorts.

One quick flick of the channel, and I'm broadcasting to the entire squadron.

"Pilots," I say, "prepare to sortie."

"*Audeamus!*" they cry.

I shove my controls forward, slam down on the acceleration, and summon my pulsar blade in hand. My body sinks into the back of my chair, and Shao-Shi and Lynette dive downward with cannons armed, serpentining for a downward volley. Then...

The Thriaxian detachment splits off.

The two support units veer off in opposite directions, disappearing from sight, leaving the middle unit exposed.

"*Shit! Lost targeting!*" Shao-Shi strains on the comms.

What are they planning?

As the remaining Thriaxian mech remains, nearing my scope, I engage the second arm and ready my strike.

I go in, take a swing...

And the mech in front of me cuts thrust, pivoting in midair, falling right into my blind spot.

"To my aft!" I shout.

"*On it,*" Shao-Shi returns.

One shot fires past my right. And after the second particle beam narrowly misses my head, I pitch the mech upside down, feet in the air, shifting thrust to the back.

"*Damn it!*" Yuri groans. "*He's fast! The hell kind of model is that?*"

Above me, the Thriaxian mech extends glowing translucent wings and draws a single blue blade... like a sentinel.

I expect him to get closer, take advantage of my descent, but instead, hundreds of particle beams escape from behind him and shoot toward us.

"Brace for impact!" I lower my left arm and bring up the hexagonal shield against the onslaught.

Crashing, screeching sounds come from the contact of the blasts.

When the blinding white charges fade out, the Thriaxian mech is gone.

"*Where is he?!*" Yuri exclaims.

Beeping floods my cockpit, and for a second, my sights capture the hostile unit accelerating up into the clouds, past Yuri and me.

"*Captain!*" Lynette cries. "*He's on my six! Keel side!*"

"Copy, approaching to intercept." I drop my sword for my rifle. "Shao-Shi, close in with a harpoon!"

"*Firing!*" he shouts.

An otherworldly echo wracks my head as Shao-Shi aims the rifle in his mech's hands and blasts a neutron beam straight at the Thriaxian Ace... but in a background of clouds, he disappears again.

"Detachment, get behind me," I order. "Don't break formation. He's trying to pick us off."

If he thinks he can hide in cloud cover, our sensors can—

A single beep goes off in my cockpit before the Thriaxian Ace materialises to my left. Streams of subatomic recombining material follow in his wake. Time slows to a crawl as I attempt to draw up the controls at my palms, followed by one powerful thump of my heart. A pulsar blade is seconds from hitting my command capsule...

... I'm done for...

...

"*VAUGHAN!*" Yuri screams in real time.

A split second later, his mech is in my left periphery, impaled by the Thriaxian's blade.

"... Yuri?"

Except for broken static, there's silence... followed by a massive explosion that throws me back.

"Yuri?" I repeat, my hands shaking.

On my screen, Yuri's comms go blue. His signature's gone.

A flash of Natalia getting shot, a gun pointed at my mom and sister, my father disappearing in the wake of blasts... all of them bombard me as my chest tightens. Yuri's video feed, pained, afraid for me, is the last I see of him.

He's gone...

"Yuri!" I scream, firing wildly at the Thriaxian Ace, only to have him fly further from my sights.

"*No...*" Lynette whimpers.

"*Bastard!*" Shao-Shi howls. "*Come back, you coward!*"

"W-wait, stop!" I shout. "Don't engage! Both of you, fall back with the rest! I repeat, do *not* engage!"

After one, two backward rolls, I reignite thrust and head straight for Yuri's murderer, flying past Shao-Shi.

Transfixed on the Thriaxian Ace, I hear, in the background, Lynette hyperventilating over the comms.

"Fall back, Lynette," I order a second time. "Now!"

"*S-sir!*" she confirms... changing course and ascending into the ionosphere with the rest.

I focus everything toward a single point: the Thriaxian Ace. A *demon* of sheer malevolence.

A deep, raging fire burns inside me as he gets closer; I don't even care that he's charging up for an attack. The particle charge at my right does the same.

Out of my left swoops in Shao-Shi, aiming in for a forward strike of his blade. The tremor in my hands gets worse.

"Get out of my way!" I roar. Before he can attack, I slam Shao-Shi's exposed left shoulder downward, sending him off course below me.

As he falls out of sight, the Demon's beam slices right through my shielding, causing my left arm and shoulder to shatter into a million pieces...

... But not before I fire my shot.

As sirens blare around me and navigation systems go haywire on my screen, I glance up to find the beam I shot took half of the Demon's head clear off, damaging its optic scope.

It's more than a struggle to get my mech stable, since I lost two of my thrusters, and even keep my hands steady enough to break through the last layer of the atmosphere with what propulsion I have left. As the sky above me blackens into the endless void, what makes my heart sink is the Demon turning about, falling into a retreat.

"No..." I say. "No, get back here."

Sparks spray at my helmet as another error pops up on my screen. I can't even read what's wrong as my enemy flies off toward the nearest Thriaxian carrier.

"Come back and *fight me!*" I shout.

Before I can accelerate faster, my screen showing three G's in low orbit, one explosion after another spans across my display. The small fleet of Thriaxian ships ascend with us, but as beams shoot from behind my left and right, a familiar group of Terran ships hovers past me. Following them are tens of thousands of personal fighter craft, engaging similar Thriaxian ships that are defending what seems like a collective retreat. It's the 4th fleet.

Xhyr kept his word.

Seeing superior numbers in Terran naval craft, I cut the thrust to my unit. Now I can't help them even if I wanted to.

I can't help them. I couldn't help him. I can't –

"*Cronus 1,*" Xhyr's voice calls, "*Cronus 1, do you copy?*"

"Yeah," I say in a muted tone.

"*Guide your unit up; the* Nineveh's *top of your twelve.*"

"Roger," I reply, reaching a shaky right hand to the auto-dock panel on my screen.

The maw of the *Nineveh* encloses my mech, and the nav systems have full control.

When I finally surface past the catwalks of our hangar, some of my pilots have stuck around, still wearing their suits. I can't make out the expressions on their faces very well, but a lot of them look shocked. The mech must be in worse shape than I thought...

"*Captain,*" Chloeja's voice says, causing me to frown more, "*are you alright in there?*"

The pupils in the reflection of my helmet are as small as pinholes. My teeth clench behind the rubber around my mouth.

No... no, I'm not.

Chapter 22

XHVR

Three Days Later

They found less than half of him, floating on the crashing waves of Terran-occupied Talmorah. And to be exact, there were pieces of Yuri fused to his chair, like the charred remains of his head, torso, and right arm. The rest of it vaporized, according to the medics.

So I stand here on the *Nineveh's* wide obsidian-black observation deck, alongside Captain Leo Hawthorne, Naval CO of the *Nineveh*, and Rachael. And in front, lined up in formation, is Cronus Squadron, all clad in terracotta dress fatigues. And to the left of them, the entire repair tech battalion and all of the Navy brass on board.

Beyond them, large glass panels show the round horizon of Talmorah, and above that, the scattering of forty-six Republic vessels in high orbit along with us.

Since the ship's coroner staff couldn't free Yuri from the innards of his cockpit, the squadron thought it best to leave the man in there, and instead of a zinc coffin, the remains of his Xenomech would do the job. I mean, it's only the cockpit portion and half of its right arm, but ... it works.

Fitting, I think.

Rachael didn't protest either... but she also added that the mech was now "useless" because Yuri wasn't around to pilot it... that, and she wasn't sending a replacement.

Centre of the floor, the chaplain mentions God a couple of times – talks about tragedy and loss in abstract concepts. And like that, he leaves the podium. As he does, Vaughan breaks formation and slowly steps up and faces us all. Yuri's mech, covered with the flag of the Republic trine, feels like an appropriate backdrop.

"Yuri was my brother," Vaughan says, "and... I wouldn't be here if it wasn't for him."

There's a pause, and he casts his head down for a second... but I gather enough from it.

Shame, mostly.

"He was brave... braver than anyone I've ever known. He was also very kind, but you wouldn't know it when you first met him. Very giving, like a giant rough-around-the edges teddy bear who was always watching out for us all... We all miss him... I miss him," he continues.

Vaughan doesn't cry as he says this.

I saw Lynette wail hysterically in the entrance corridor days ago, and both Serena and Chloeja cussing and pissed to high hell before the funeral... and of course there's Shao-Shi.

In the debrief, Vaughan told me that Yuri was lost on his and Shao-Shi's watch. As Lynette wept, so did Shao-Shi, right alongside her. It's clear he took it pretty hard.

When you're there, and your comrade dies, that kind of thing stays with you.

It's bad when you're not there and hear it secondhand like the rest of the squadron. It doesn't seem real... not really. First he's there, then he's not.

And Vaughan's their captain.

He knows he can't show weakness or that he's hurting. To be honest... if he started weeping, I don't think Vaughan would ever stop. I mean, it was *me* what told them to shove it down... and I've seen what happens when you stop...

It's ugly.

"Yuri," Vaughan says, "from the bottom of my heart, thank you for all that you've done. We will never forget your loyalty or your love, your laugh or your energy... we'll never forget how free you were in life..."

The sound of Lynette sobbing at this reaches me, and I don't blame the girl. She and Yuri were not only squad-mates, they were partnered up together per Titan doctrine – minus Vaughan. If anyone feels the most guilt out of the twelve of them left ... it'd be her.

"Shao-Shi," Vaughan says, "if you would."

"Sir!" he replies.

The kid kneels down, picks up a bottle of whiskey by his feet, and rushes it over to Vaughan. Once received, Vaughan turns and climbs up to top the derelict mech. He stops, opens the bottle, and empties most of its contents into a bowl soldered on top of the flat surface of the cockpit doors.

Vaughan nods at the colour guards, who hoist the flag from Yuri's mech and fold it up into a triangle.

"Lynette," he says, reaching out to her.

She doesn't say anything but approaches him with a mangled face of unwiped tears. From her returning hands, she gives Vaughan a lighter.

"Until we meet again," he says, igniting the bowl.

A blue flame shoots from the chest plate of Yuri's mech, and as it burns, Vaughan climbs down and heads back to the podium. He nods to Yuri's repair tech to his right, who falls out and presses a button on a small console near the mech.

"To our brother, Godspeed," Vaughan says, drinking the last of the bottle.

He suddenly smashes the dang thing against the black polished floor, all while Yuri's mech backs away from the podium and enters a transparent airlock behind.

"Godspeed!" the rest of the squadron echoes, their fists clutched over their hearts.

The airlock seals shut, and that flame stays alight.

Vaughan nods one last time to Yuri's repair tech and falls back in with the squadron.

The tech presses a button on the console and rushes back with his men.

Inside the airlock, blue accelerators light up beneath the mech...

... and Yuri's flame goes out as the airlock opens.

The blue lights in the airlock flash three times, and the mag-strip launches Yuri's mech out into the void. According to Naval send-offs protocol, we send the dead toward a specific point in the Virgo Sphere: the presumed location of where Earth, Holy Terra, is supposed to be.

And that's where the kid's body's going – right back to the origin of every Terran alive.

As Yuri drifts away, Vaughan and the others raise their hands in salute. Out the window, other ships of the 4th and 5th fleet eject twenty-two of their own fallen in the same direction. Some are in downed fighter craft, like Yuri's, and others are zinc caskets. All of them, off on their last journey to the graveyard of the Old Empire.

In the silence I'm all too familiar with, I raise my hand to salute as well.

⋙ ⋘

"Colonel," a steward says, "dinner is served."

1955 hours, right on time.

"Mmm," I grunt, "very good, thank you."

The steward gives a small bow before dipping into the back.

I take a peek at the setup of three tables he and his men arranged in Captain Hawthorn's mess hall. Now, when asked, I *did* say fancy, but the spread looks like the president-general's coming to chow down with us. Or, as Rachael might say, the formality's "*disconcerting*".

There are several forks on the left, and equal amount on the right, and four empty wine glasses to the top right of each place set. The spoons are where they need to be, and each place has a printed name in the centre.

Despite Captain Hawthorne wishing to act as president of this formal mess, I insisted on taking on that mantle. It was our man what got cut down, and *I'd* decide on what was acceptable at these tables, not the Navy or their commissars. Shit, I barely handle Rachael being ours. One's enough.

"Everyone," I announce, ducking back into the fold of the fifteen guests and my twelve, "let's make our way to the mess hall."

"Lovely!" Rachael chirps. "You know, Xhyr, I've never been to one of these before."

"Oh, you'll like it," I say. "It's like a civilian gala, only... more organized."

"Ahhh," she replies, seeming amused.

Not sure how I got roped into having Rachael as my plus one, but we lead the other guests and the squadron into the mess. Everyone leaves half- and quarter-finished glasses of low-proof spirits in the sitting room, which at any other time serves as a study for my pilots.

Once I'm in the dining hall, the Navy officers aren't too far away behind me, and they're followed by Heavy Infantry commanders, and my own godless kids file in behind. I made sure to spread everyone out, with Cronus Squadron dispersed between cadets and colonels of all the branches I invited. Since fighting with the Legion, the formal mess always stood out to me, how rank's left at the door and every soul at my table is a lady or gentleman... equally.

As soon as Vaughan finds his way to my right, everyone else takes their seats immediately.

There's a minor hum of commotion, dispelled when I finally tap the centre table.

"For what we are about to receive, thank God," I say.

"Thank God," everyone solemnly echoes.

Since everyone seems either hungry or despondent, I dig right in. As I lift my head, all the other diners join in with me.

"It's quite the victory, Xhyr," Captain Hawthorn says. "Despite the heavy costs, we're one step closer to the core worlds of the Kingdom."

The *Thriaxian* Kingdom.

"And one step closer to ending the war," a wistful voice adds.

To my left is Colonel Jasmine "Jas" Ptolemy, CO of the 221st Heavy Infantry regiment. From what I heard, there's no more battle-hardened matron than her.

"Something we can all look forward to," I say, "and certainly the Heavies have our gratitude for keeping the vanguard strong on the front."

"Indeed," Jas replies.

Seeing as the table setup was small enough, I didn't elect a vice president for the mess. And also, I didn't want to trouble the squadron... they've got enough on their plate as it is.

"No, Vaughan, it *is* a big deal!" Chloeja stresses in a loud whisper. "What the hell is he doing wearing *those* colours?!"

I follow Chloeja's movements across the table to Commander Lorne Freydas, who happens to be wearing a cord of emerald green and black on his shoulder. The new bobble isn't normally in his Naval dress code, and I ain't ever seen Hawthorn's men fashioned with faction colours on the regular.

"I don't think he knew," Vaughan answers, softer than her. "When have either of you brought it up?"

"Never!" Chloeja says, louder this time. "If I knew he was under the peerage of House Laurier, it'd be doubtful we would have said *anything* to each other!"

As Chloeja not-so-subtly protests, Lynette takes notice at the other side of the table and discretely removes an identical cord of emerald and black from her shoulder. She seems ashamed as she does so.

Oh, of all the...!

I don't wait to tap on the goddamn table.

"Ms. Nadjidhar has been warned," I say to Chloeja so all guests can hear me.

I don't give a shit if her House Tamir or his House Laurier are in the middle of a blood feud; that kind of fuckery *does not exist* at my table!

"*Yes*, President," she replies, cheerfully, and clearly looking to not get fined any further.

⋙ ⋘

The entirety of the mess rolls out much smoother. As far as I can tell, the Naval cadets seem entranced by Horatio's feats of valour; the Heavies are keeping a robust constitution as Chloeja and Xalpha match them shot for shot — in as much civility a formal mess can provide — and everyone seems in as high a spirit as a body can expect at a repast.

Good job, Xhyr.

Supper's ready, and some of the stewards are coming out with decanters of port, while others are coming to collect dirty plates and cutlery. Many of the colonial officers are quite entranced by the whole affair, as I was decades ago. Doubtful they've ever seen so much food on one table, let alone tasted port wine.

Right... time for act four.

"Ladies and gentlemen," I say, raising my glass of port, "His Excellency Vincent DeKierr, President-General of the GUILD Republic."

"Here, here!" the Naval officers roar. "Long may he rule!"

"To His Excellency," Vaughan chimes in.

It's a funny thing. If Vincent were here, doubtful if anyone would remain seated, and yet protocol dictates that in his absence, we all stay put. Funny, and off-putting.

"To absent friends!" Jas speaks up, reaching for her glass. As she does, she accidentally knocks it clear off the table.

Clink!

It shatters, and she draws a contrite expression. "My apologies," she says while ducking below to pick it up.

"No need. Stewar—" I say, cut off by a sudden *thwack*.

A hair above Jas's head, a butter knife tremors back and forth, and it's wedged halfway through the drywall of the wardroom.

All of a sudden, every Titan is on the edge of their seat, steel-eyed and focused on the fallen glass.

But when I check my right, Vaughan remains seated, leaning over the table, his hand outstretched and shaky...

"What the hell was that?" Jas says.

"Steward!" I shout across the table. "Do take better care. You almost knifed our guest in the head."

"My sincerest apologies!" the steward closest to Vaughan says, following my lead.

When I glance back at Vaughan, there's a look of dismay piercing his eyes. The kind that asks that ever-haunting question:

'What have I become?'

Chloeja, who was sitting right next to him, is awash with concern. She's his second, so if she's worried, I'm worried.

"Friends and guests," I say, "let's retire to the drawing room for more refreshments. I'll be with you all momentarily."

Everyone shuffles from their seats, some exchanging glances of surprise or shock... not from the end of the formalities, but from one of my men almost braining a superior officer of the Republic Guard.

Everyone except for Vaughan.

"Son, I need a word," I say to him.

"Sir," he says, with the same kind of expression a dog who bit a passing stranger has.

"To be clear," I say, "you're not in trouble. I just need to sort some things with you. That's all."

"Yes, sir," Vaughan says.

⋙⋙ ⋘⋘

The sounds of Vaughan's footsteps follow me as we walk out to a balcony, overlooking the observation deck from earlier today. There's a clear shot of Talmorah, and a few of the ships left of the 5th fleet are in view.

Once I finally get to the railing, I heave my elbows down on it and pull out a cigar from my coat.

"You want one?" I ask, watching as Vaughan rests against the rail as well.

"No, sir."

"Okey-doke." I take a soft bite of the once light rolled tobacco in my mouth. "So... back at the mess, I could tell you weren't quite yourself."

"I'm... I'm sorry for the knife, sir; I didn't even realise I picked it up."

"Don't worry about that," I say. "I'm sure the doctor's already patching things up with Colonel Ptolemy. I imagine something to the effect of 'combat programming'. Hell, all twelve of you were ready to dance by the time that glass fell... you happened to be the one who reacted. No, what I mean is that your commander is visibly concerned about you. And because she is, so am I. So, when I say you're not quite yourself, I need to know why."

"I'm operational," Vaughan counters sharply, "if that's what you mean, sir."

"I don't doubt it. And you did recently lose a man. I'm not faulting you for your actions because of it. What I mean..." I say, pointing to the rail, "... is that."

Vaughan follows the direction of my hands, cigar and all, to his trembling left hand.

"It happened after the Talmorah drop," he says, "after that dog fight with that new Thriaxian unit."

"Right. New model," I say. "Something we haven't seen on the field yet. Is that why you sent in the req for your X-5 to be modified?"

"That's right," Vaughan says, his visage darker than before. "I need to meet with Doctor Vayne about engineering specs, but if I can at least sense when that unit phases... or makes a jump, I'll be ready."

He's taking this real serious.

"I'm not losing anyone else to this monster," he states, staring me straight in the face.

"I gather." My elbows find their resting spot on the rail, and I take a deep drag of the cigar in my hand. I blow out, peering over at the fading horizon of Talmorah as the ship steadily banks.

"I can be better, sir," he adds.

"Copy that." I stare off into the black stretch of space.

I get what he's saying, and I get he's frustrated. Both Yuri and Shao-Shi got in the way of that demon, according to the debrief, and if Yuri hadn't, it'd be Vaughan we buried today instead...

"Is that all, sir?" he asks me.

"Almost," I reply. "At the eulogy, you mentioned Yuri lived free. What was that about?"

Vaughan shuffles uncomfortably as I shift my gaze toward him, then stops.

"I mean, he lived free as a soldier," he answers. "As a Titan. Yuri lived his whole life on a penal colony, way off on the edge of the Republic, and convicts raised him. When he became a Titan with us on Nostro, for the first time he had an actual family. Yeah, he wanted his citizenship papers granted after service, but while he served under me... he was a free man, sir."

"Hmm," I say to that, "okay."

Satisfied, I salute him, and he returns it. He goes to leave, and halts in his tracks.

"I have a question, sir," Vaughan says.

"Go ahead."

"Have you ever thought about revenge, sir?" he asks.

I choke on the drag halfway through my lungs. "What?"

"For what happened to you when the Legion glassed your planet. Why didn't you act on it?"

My eyebrows raise as he says this. "I have never, nor will I ever, seek revenge for what happened to my family or my planet," I insist, nearing him and pointing to my ear, and I make a circle with my cigar-holding hand, "because the people on my world were terrorists, and they got what they deserved. Are we clear?"

"Crystal, sir."

Fuck. First he ain't got his shit together, now he's tiptoeing around sedition?

"Good, since we're bein' clear-like," I say, my drawl slipping in, "if it's revenge against the Thriaxians an' this Demon of Talmorah, the bastard that killed Yuri... I can help you. Me an' Doctor Vayne both can."

Lordy. I take a good long second to cool down, and as I do, Vaughan bobs his head respectfully.

"... I was going to wait, but High Command's been chattin' with the doctor, and they want that Demon of yours clipped. He's a threat to the sector, an' if he's mobile enough to reach the whole war-front, shit'll get disastrous real quick. And that, Captain, will truly piss off Colonel Ptolemy what with all she deals with on the regular. So instead o' pin-point missions, your primary objective is to shoot down the Demon."

"Roger *that*," Vaughan says, steely and full of purpose.

"There's more to it than that," I add.

He seems puzzled, and before I can put the cigar back in my mouth, it's almost burnt to the ring.

"So far, you've been tagging alien craft. They're in mechs, you can't see them, and you witness them when they die. But in this outfit, at some point, you're going to kill people. As in the Terran kind of people. When that happens, revenge – of any kind – has to be the furthest thing from your mind... because that's the shit that'll eat you up inside. It can't be personal. Your head needs to be in it, yes, but your heart has to be far away."

"Sir?" Vaughan asks.

"No matter who you fight, revenge is an ugly thing. You think you're getting something out of the whole thing, and maybe it feels good in the moment... but soon you realise there's nothing. There's only emptiness, and that spirals you down and gets you more pissed. Afterward, that's all you know: suffering, anger, hatred... and more emptiness." I take the cigar and put it out on the rail of the balcony. "Take it from me. Let go o' that shit, or be dragged by it."

"Hmm," Vaughan grunts, glancing blankly to the left. "Thank you, sir."

"... You sure you're alright?" I ask, seeing him regard me favourably... but those eyes.

They have that same expression he had sparring with Chloeja on Nostro. This time, they're a lot darker.

"I'm operational," Vaughan repeats, same tone as earlier. "You have nothing to worry about... sir."

Chapter 23

Chloeja

Two hours later

"You're too slow; pick up your feet," I say, voice raised as Shao-Shi gets pinned by Ophelia... again.

"Ugh! I-I yield!" he struggles to say, slapping his hand on the mat.

Ophelia loosens her chokehold on him, getting to her feet while facing him.

"Again!" I shout, arms crossed.

Knowing Vaughan, he wouldn't want us to slack off, even on a day like today. So I watch as Shao-Shi gets in position to spar once more, and over Ophelia's shoulder, one sparring ring apart, Oreiga and Xalpha engage in a hand-to-hand match of their own.

As I step back, I take in the full breadth of the training hall.

It's about the same size as four officer's quarters squashed together, lit well from two long fixtures high in the ceiling, and to the right of me is Cronus Squadron's personal mess. It's a small three-stool bar, with a couple of tables and chairs further back, and single replicator fixed to the wall for chow-time.

And there, sitting at the bar, is Horatio, cracking jokes and knocking back Endarian rum with his new friends in the Heavies outfit. Even now, my face tightens into a scowl as I watch him nurse his wounds in languid comfort, but his turn's coming in the ring.

Everyone needs to be on their toes from now on.

"Horatio!" I shout toward the bar. "Pass Oreiga your drink; you're subbing in for him."

"Wha–" he protests, pausing as he sees me raise an eyebrow. "Yes, ma'am!"

A nod is all I give as I stare at Oreiga.

"Fall out, Old Man. Take a break," I order him.

"Ma'am!" Oreiga replies.

Behind me, I have two cups of coffee. Mine is half drunk already, and the other has a polymer cap on top. Still hot and recently replicated.

As the sound of blows and landing punches resonates in front of me, the faint tapping of boots catches my ear to the left. It sounds like it's right before the medic station, where Rachael no doubt is observing all that we do.

The tapping grows into a louder clopping, and out of the corner of my eye I see Vaughan turn the bend, slowly marching his way toward the training hall.

I adjust my stance to face him as he emerges from the dim lights of the corridor. He's wearing his terracotta dress fatigues, which contrasts starkly with the rest of the squadron, who were more than happy to get out of the constricting uniform... myself included.

Although, now that I get a closer look at his approach, his high-neck collar's undone. There's a casual motion in his step, even relaxed.

Maybe he's doing better?

"Atten-tion!" I shout. "Officer on deck!"

Like clockwork, everyone in the training hall stops *everything*. Guests, squad-mates, everyone – and they all face the front, in the same direction I'm in. And as soon as Vaughan enters, Cronus Squadron and the Heavies clap their heels together and salute him. My hand's already raised by the time he sets foot in the hall.

"At ease," Vaughan says with a simple wave of his hand, "and as you were."

Okay, he's definitely still in a funk.

As he walks past me, my gaze falls on the two pairs training... and I don't like how uneasy the squadron acts as they resume their activities. I think they're worried for him too, and it's not like he's had a shoulder to cry on like the rest of us...

"Oh, Captain," I say, grabbing the full cup behind me, before he's out of arm's reach. "Here. I figured you could use a pick me up."

Ah, there it is!

Vaughan's expression softens a little as I hand him the coffee. He grabs a seat, sets his holopad screen vertically on the table, and takes a sip from the cup.

"Mmm," he grunts softly. "You remembered."

Of course I did!

"Well," I say as more of a tease, "it's easy when someone likes cardamom and cinnamon in sweetened black coffee. I don't know too many folks with your tastes."

"Thank you, Commander." Vaughan glances up for a moment before losing himself to the screen.

"You're welcome," I reply, my voice lightening at his words.

Yeah, I'm tiptoeing the line between congeniality and fraternization... but I'd rather act and do *something* rather than nothing, and considering we're under more supervision now than in basic... I'll take it.

Wait.

On the other side of Vaughan's holopad is an inverted schematic with lines of written details and a similar layout to our X-5 Xenomech models... with a couple of notable differences.

"Doctor Vayne approved your designs?" I ask.

"After some arm-pulling, yeah," Vaughan replies, "but she was pretty insistent that I use one of her engineers from the Department of Science and Development. Something about the Titans being 'new to the field' and wanting more control of the hardware specs."

"Makes sense," I say, my brow furrowing.

"Yeah... her project, her rules," Vaughan adds, slipping further into his work.

I come around, peering over Vaughan's shoulder. There's a detailed array of the changes: wing add-ons, integrated pulsar blades into the arm segments of the schematic, and some major adjustments to the shoulder thrusters.

"Are all of us being re-fitted or just your unit?" I ask.

"Only mine," he says quickly, "for extra manoeuvres. Business as usual for the kids; everyone needs to be on top of their game."

"*Indeed*," I stress, "and on that note, it's time to whip the kids into shape."

Lord above, he *can* smile. Good!

"Copy that," Vaughan says with a grin, taking another sip of coffee.

Only three minutes in, and this time, Xalpha body-slams Shao-Shi *hard* on the mat.

Goddamn it...

"Lieutenant!" I shout so hard my voice cracks. "What are you doing?! Your ass has fallen, and now you're dead for the *twelfth fucking time!*"

He gets up, bruises all over his shoulders, appearing very forlorn.

It's pathetic, and I don't have time for this shit.

"Now," I say, approaching Shao-Shi from behind, "square your hips."

I place my hands firmly on his sides, squaring my right side against his back, directly against the three metal contacts of his undershirt.

"Keep your back straight, your stance forward, and deliver your blows with *everything* you've got! Is that understood, Lieutenant?" I ask.

"Yes, ma'am!" Shao-Shi cries, his voice laced with an acrid veneer of defeat.

"Good. Shuffle in," I order, backing up near the tables.

The match starts with Shao-Shi coming in with a strong downward blow, but Xalpha's quick on her toes. I pace around to her corner of the ring, arms folded... as Shao-Shi turtles with his wrists up like walls.

Ugh!

Fuck, I get it. Yuri's dead, and he's taking it badly... it shows.

"Lieutenant!" I bark. "Get out of that shell and *fight!*"

It's no use. Sure, he's sideswiping, trying to catch Xalpha off-balance, but she's good on her dodge.

"Commander," a faint, harsh tone sounds over my left shoulder, "allow me."

I glance over to my left, and there's Vaughan.

And, oh...

Without warning, he quickly but carefully shrugs off his unbuttoned jacket and removes his undershirt, exposing his bare chest...

Oh, my... wow.

"Xalpha, fall in." Vaughan motions his thumb to his right, and she immediately stops.

"Sir!" she says, looking him up and down. I'm not sure if she sees me, but my face tenses into a glare as she does... and either way, she's off the mats before I can snap my fingers.

As Vaughan enters the ring, I catch three long scars that trace the length of his upper back, running through the three chrome ports lateral to his shoulder blades.

When did he get those? Before basic? Not after, that's for sure. He's always been very careful.

The two men square up and shuffle in, but Vaughan has his hands outstretched with his palms facing the ground. He's keeping his distance, circling to the right of Shao-Shi, and it seems like he's providing an opening.

I mean, knowing Vaughan, it's probably a trap of some sort, but the important thing is that he's laying out the welcome mat: something Shao-Shi desperately needs.

"Come on," Vaughan says. "You're a killer pilot, victory marks under your belt. It's nothing you haven't done before. Now come at me!"

"Hyaaa!" Shao-Shi cries, and when he does, it's visceral.

This is strange.

He must be tired, but Shao-Shi is nothing but punches: left, right, one after the other toward Vaughan's solar plexus, and with his force, they'd likely land if Vaughan weren't purposefully weaving around him.

"Faster," Vaughan commands. "Shuffle in fast, like you're approaching a Sentinel."

With an animalistic roar, Shao-Shi charges in, faking out a strike to his side as he doubles in for a shuffle... landing a hit on the left side of Vaughan's chin.

I drop my folded arms.

Ophelia and Lynette collectively gasp to my right, and without looking, I sense everyone's attention pointed directly at Vaughan as he stumbles back, his head downcast.

"Heh..." Vaughan says, holding back a laugh, "...that's more like it."

As encouraged as I am by Shao-Shi's improvement, I can't help but flinch at those words.

As Vaughan collects himself, readying a more offensive stance, Shao-Shi takes only a second to glance at me. And in his expression, it's like he's imploring me to end the match.

"Don't look at her," Vaughan shouts. "Look at me! Your opponent is staring you dead in the face. Imagine your life on the line, right now. What do you do?"

Wordless, Shao-Shi lunges forward, trying to sweep Vaughan's leg and throw him off, but Vaughan pivots left, blocks an incoming blow to the chest, and strikes Shao-Shi with an open palm to the jaw.

Fuck... Vaughan knocked his ass *down*.

Whatever small bits of chatter hung in the air died in that instant.

"Get up," Vaughan says, his voice distant. "Right now!"

Shao-Shi struggles to right himself, blood trickling onto the mat. I wish to God they were sparring in a psy-ring right now... but they're not. It's real.

Even as Shao-Shi squints, moving slower and closing in on himself, Vaughan's glare concentrates with sheer hatred as he approaches Shao-Shi.

"Is this all a game to you?" Vaughan says through gritted teeth.

Vaughan strikes him again, and this time his fist hitting Shao-Shi sounds wet...

"The enemy is out there, and you treat me like I'm the only one who matters!" Vaughan roars. "I haven't trained you this hard, nor has Xhyr, for you to *throw your life away!*"

Shao-Shi's forearms drip with blood, his face twitches, and, even before now, the fight's left him.

I want to interject, to get between him and Vaughan... but I can't. My body tenses. What I'm seeing is *wrong*... but if I break rank or even take those beatings for Shao-Shi, all of that wrath would be on me.

Would Vaughan lose his shit on me too...?

I scan the training hall quickly, and everyone appears as horrified as I feel.

And again... if Vaughan is acting to discipline Shao-Shi, or even make a bloody example of him, there's nothing we can honestly do about it. According to military articles, it's within his right...

... and I hate it.

After one final *thwack*, keeping his fist raised, Vaughan stops.

He glares down at Shao-Shi, who's visibly shaking. His forearms cover his face, hands quivering, and there are tears running down his face.

I think Vaughan notices this... and... for the first time, Vaughan's eyes mist up in our presence.

Finally, he lowers his blood-soaked fist, and it drops like a rock to his side.

"Xalpha," Vaughan says.

"S-sir?" she stammers.

"Take Shao-Shi to sick bay and make sure he's patched up. You're both dismissed."

"Yes, s-sir!" Xalpha replies, scrambling over to Shao-Shi and taking his arm over her shoulder.

Once Shao-Shi's removed, Vaughan slowly gets to his feet and scans across the room at us.

"You're all dismissed to quarters," he says, "and read up on those tactics I sent out. We're going over them in the morning."

He casts his eyes down, trailing the drops of blood falling from his fists and hitting the mats. The sound is rhythmic, and it's tying my stomach into knots.

As one second goes by, followed by another, no one has responded.

"Out. Everyone," I say with a raised, authoritative voice.

"Ma'am!" the rest of the squadron shouts.

The last of the pilots, and even the Heavies behind me, pile out fast. Within seconds, it's just Vaughan and me.

"Captain," I ask, "permission to speak freely, sir?"

Vaughan pauses as he grabs a wet cloth for his hand, his back to me, and wipes the rest of his hand and forearm.

"Sure," he says.

"Uh," I begin, "what the hell was that?"

He glances at me, averts his gaze, and meets up with my line of vision again.

"He's still too soft," he replies, "and I need him battle ready. Otherwise, he's going to get himself or someone else killed."

I blink, unbelieving at his words.

Right. Sure. It's pretty fucking clear that you both have a very similar temperament, and before today I'd have sworn you both were brothers cut from the same cloth.

No... you punished Shao-Shi, beat him to a pulp, because you were taking out any weakness in yourself *on* him.

"Did he deserve to be made an example of like that," I ask coldly, "in front of everyone?"

He hesitates, cradling his bruised hand. "It was necessary," Vaughan says, his expression distant.

"To publicly shame him like that?" I don't care in the slightest that I'm accusing him.

"*Yes*," he says, raising his voice. "This way, every pilot gets the message, not just one. Maybe now they won't all recklessly try to throw their lives away."

"Sir," I protest, "they were *protecting* you. And if I may, we couldn't have hoped to prepare for that new Thriaxian unit, sir. We didn't have the intel, and it was beyond us!"

"It's not enough!" Vaughan yells, his voice echoing throughout the hall. "It's not enough... I can't let go of what happened on Talmorah. If I do..." He trails off, staggering and seeming to search for his words. "If I do, I'm telling myself that Yuri's death is acceptable, and it's not. None of you are supposed to die like that... not while I'm in command."

My mouth drops agape. "What are you talking about?" I take a step forward.

"I'm *their* leader. *Your* leader, Commander... and it should have been me!"

Before I can tell him how stupid, pig-headed, and frankly *weak* his reasons are... Vaughan covers his face, and blood trickles past his fingers, dripping to the mat below.

A sheer look of panic, urgency, and painful regret flashes across his face, and all of this happens in the blink of an eye as he falls forward.

"Vaughan!" I shout, rushing to catch him.

His sweaty, bloodied chest collapses against me, and my breath catches in my lungs as I lead him to the ground.

"M-medic!" I scream.

Once I have Vaughan in my lap, he tenses and convulses against my thighs.

There's no more time.

"Medic!" I holler toward the watch on my wrist. "Man down! Get a gurney to the Titan's mess, now!"

"*Right away*," dispatch replies.

The rattling sound of Vaughan's breaths jar me. So that he doesn't choke on his own blood, I move his head to the left of me, facing the training hall's exit, and all the while pinch below the bridge of his nose.

As he hyperventilates against me, I firmly place my right hand against his back, below his metal contacts, and gently place my left on top of his matted charcoal-brown hair.

"I-It should have been..." Vaughan tries to say.

"No, don't talk." My voice softens again. "I get it. I do. But you need to—"

Before I can finish, I twist my head toward the sound of rapid footfalls, several of them thundering down the corridor toward us.

"In here!" I cry.

In a flash, two medics come with two metal poles and lower them on Vaughan's left and right. A fabric gurney forms underneath him, and they support his neck while one of them reaches out a hand to me.

"Slowly move back, Commander," one of them says, "we've got him."

"Copy..." I breathe and carefully shuffle back.

And, while I'm on my knees, Rachael bursts through the entrance, out of breath, with a holopad open in one of her hands.

"Oh, no, not again..." Rachael says... like she accidentally knocked over a glass beaker...

Chapter 24

Rachael

Drip, drip, drip.

One drop of neuro-inhibitors follows another from a small blue drip bag, flowing down a drip tube into a rubber catheter in my precious specimen's arm. It's a pity, really, that I couldn't simply access one port on the captain's back... but if I did, that might muddy up the results.

As I ready my preparation and insert it into the drip collector, the medication flowing down changes to a beautiful sheen of teal. It's mesmerising, in a way, how the solution interacts with the injection from my hands: a confluence of neuro-agents and stabilizers.

Though ever since the commander followed me into my infirmary half an hour ago, there's been nothing but puppy-dog concern and several grating questions.

But! Despite this, I must be having a *damn good* time, because I'm not deterred in the slightest.

Ask away, Specimen Number Two, ask away.

"For the last time," I say *again*, "the captain's going to pull through."

"You're sure?" Chloeja folds her arms and furrows her brow.

"Of course!" I exclaim. "Oh, I know, he took a terrible reaction to... something... but that's what you and the team have me for! Look."

I gesture to a screen overhead my ailing specimen, showcasing the steady decrease in his beta waves, sufficient oxygen, and, finally, a stable heart rate. That last one took a while.

"Alright." Chloeja relaxes her previously tense shoulders.

"That's a good girl," I reply.

Oh, she *didn't* like that. I may be her superior's superior, but this specimen's not afraid to bare her teeth. I have to admit, I like that kind of tenacity.

"So, my dear," I say, brushing off her disdain, "what exactly happened in the last mission?"

"Was there a piece in the debrief that wasn't clear?" Chloeja asks quizzically, lightening her expression. "Or are you referring to the mental stability of my squadron, ma'am?"

"Oh, no, the debrief was crystal clear. It's the events that happened after the Thriaxian pilot engaged your squadron. I'm assuming it was chaotic, but the specifics in the debrief don't illustrate a cohesive picture. As to the squadron's mental state... remember that I keep close tabs on that."

She draws in and exhales a deep breath, and her gaze darts left and right, seeming to search for something: her firsthand experience, repressed memories, or perhaps filtered information.

"That pilot was relentless," Chloeja says, "and it's a goddamn miracle any of us made it out in one piece. A lot of the details are fuzzy on my end; a lot of the encounter happened between Yuri, Shao-Shi, Lynette, and Vaughan... the rest of us were ordered to evacuate."

"I see," I say, adjusting my glasses, "and what about after that? Before today, how did the captain's detachment seem following the mission on board the *Nineveh*?"

"It affected them," Chloeja says. "I mean, I was livid, but the detachment was visibly wounded. Shao-Shi, for instance, clammed up and seems to have lost some kind of spark he had before. It was pretty clear during training tonight that he wasn't in it."

"No. Based on the captain's actions, I gather he wasn't," I reply.

"Right. And then there's Lynette... she basically spent the last three days crying. She's a lot better now, but she and Yuri were close... so, yeah, I'm thinking it hit differently."

"Hmm... that is concerning," I say.

Chloeja pauses for a moment, hesitating as, I imagine, she thinks on the goings-on of her captain.

"And Vaughan's a fucking mystery." Chloeja glances down at him. "I'm sure he's already told you whatever's rattling around in his head. None of us can really get a read on him."

Yes, our therapy sessions... or as Xhyr would say: "sittin' with the head-shrinker".

To be honest, whatever unravelling I conduct with the captain is minimal at best, and when he does talk, it's not about any core deficits. He's pretty tight-lipped... but again, I'm also biased.

"I've gotten a fair picture of what the captain's encountered as of late," I say, "so for now, it'll have to suffice. I appreciate your input, Commander."

"Ma'am," Chloeja replies.

Unwittingly, I tap my right index finger on the rail of my specimen's stretcher.

"If you would indulge me," I ask, "there are a few things I need cleared up. Would you mind?"

"I'm at the doctor's disposal," Chloeja replies coldly.

"Wonderful! So," I begin, "from what you can tell, has the captain been responding well to the SERUM post-mission, and do you know if he's taking his regimen of medicine?"

Chloeja takes her sweet time to answer and shoots me another sideways glance of assertive deflection. That, and there is much to take stock of when discussing the pilots' performance enhancements, both pre- and post-mission.

To be frank, the SERUM is a very potent drug. Full stop.

Many pharmacists who helped me compile the solution asked if the side effects outweighed the therapeutic benefits... to which I almost smacked their insolent gobs to the ground.

Of *course* the benefits outweigh the side effects!

And what's more, the pilots are fully aware of the high probability of short-term consequences: things like night-sweats, the shakes, and dehydration. Honestly, it's a miracle they're all still alive, the way they drink at mess... goodness...

No, what I keep tight to my chest is the long-term side effects. The ones the pharmacists had the most paramount concerns for.

'*But it dramatically reduces lifespan!*' they protested. '*And the irreversible brain damage!*' they blatted and moaned...

Disgusting... and if only they knew what I seek to accomplish, they would say nothing at all.

Most importantly, at graduation, all of my specimens grasped that the SERUM was *necessary* for mission success. I didn't say the drug was experimental, but, like all of my machinations, some things are better left unsaid.

And again... they're *possible* long-term side effects. The whole experiment is a terra incognita, and we know nothing of how a typical Terran will react to such experimental substances.

But again, my specimen Vaughan is not a typical Terran. Not in physiology, in the nuances of his genetic makeup, or his general performance in battle from the data I collect. And while society would stone him for being a mutant... I find there's a novelty to him.

I wonder, does my precious specimen *need* the SERUM anymore...? A hypothesis for another day, perhaps.

"He's taking them on schedule," Chloeja finally answers, "we all are, ma'am."

"Very good!" I type in a note on my holopad.

Though, as I focus on the shifting of her gaze, the tightening of her jaw as she said this to me... I can tell she's not being entirely honest.

And if Vaughan the specimen *isn't* taking his meds... it would explain much. The drugs themselves are a neat little cocktail of psycho-reactive agents. If he's missed any, let alone one, then the pesky onset of PTSD and insufferable depression is the likely outcome.

"Do try to keep an eye on the captain's drug intake," I chide. "I would personally hate to see him suffer any more than necessary."

"Yes, ma'am," Chloeja returns, teeth clenched.

Hmm. I'm thinking this female specimen doesn't care for me much.

Perhaps it's the paradigm we share: the ardent researcher and the unfortunate military subject, or maybe it has to do with how I treat her precious captain. Yes, that seems the most logical. It's her Vaughan that I tamper with the most and examine like a prized rat in a priceless experiment... like I do right now.

If it's any consolation, I can at least understand why that might make the commander's skin crawl.

"Well, my dear," I say sweetly, "I have a possible theory for the captain's ailing."

"Yes?" Chloeja presses, with much concern for her comrade.

"To be frank, Vaughan is struggling with a complex persona. Being your captain, he's just as much a regular Terran as you and the rest of the squadron." I mute a grin from sprouting on my face.

Heh, right... just a 'regular Terran'...

"And to complicate matters," I continue, "Vaughan seems to wrestle with his desire to engage with his ever-persistent shadow. Truly, a fight for the ages."

Ugh...

Specimen Chloeja squints at my words, not even feigning to understand.

"Could you clarify, ma'am?" she asks.

"Never mind," I say, disappointment heavy on my tongue.

How dull.

"I will say this," I add, "that the captain just needs to best this new contender, and, mark my words, he'll be much more at peace with himself. Those darker feelings he's been exuding surely will dissipate as a result; you'll see."

The specimen Vaughan twitches in his sleep.

If you do dream, young warrior, I hope it lies along the path of serene, complete wholeness.

I bring my head back up, adjusting my glasses and... oh.

Oh, well, this *is* amusing!

With her arms folded tight, specimen Chloeja is the spitting image of defiant. Defensive, her cutting glare evident, as if she would walk right up to me and slap a Republic science officer.

A commissar.

Oh, the girl likely has no idea of the world of trouble she'd be in if she tried. A pretty noble like her would easily face a court martial, sentenced to years of service in a penal colony, stripped of all power she currently possesses.

And if I were to have it my way, this specimen would be a very welcome permanent lab rat in one of my more... private laboratories. Oh, the joys of zero oversight.

"May I be excused, Doctor?" Chloeja asks.

"Yes. Yes, you may go," I say with a gentle wave of my hand.

Whether with sheer vexation or a satisfied familial concern, the girl leaves my infirmary with a terse salute and a sharp step. Now, finally, there are no lingering distractions from my work...

※ ≫≫⟫ ⟪≪≪ ※

Eleven minutes in, and the data collected from my specimen's CNS feedback looks unremarkable.

Perfect in every way.

But, to be sure, I follow the tubes along his right-hand side and inspect their integrity. As I gently tilt his head, it appears the adhesive-fixed electrodes are all well attached to his hair, right above his brainstem.

I wonder... how much more pressure can he take?

Reaching for a transparent-blue visor, I slip it over my specimen's face and attach it to two solid chrome contacts along the wires at the base of his skull.

Once over, the visor comes to life.

Illuminated in softer blue command boxes, lines of code pour from the top to the bottom like cascading rain. The device is a tremendous help with psychiatric rewiring... and frankly, I need all the help I can get these days. The pilots of Cronus have needed this visor increasingly, despite the higher dose of prescription meds... and this specimen has needed it the most.

Oh, how wonderful it would be if it could simply wipe the mind clean of scars...! But it can't... no matter how much I've slaved over the thing or how I've tried to adapt it for military conditioning, it's not a cure-all. Even after thousands of years, the truest therapy lies within... and as of right now, that's not possible in Cronus Squadron. Not enough time, and so much more to do.

It only dampens the effects of mental blocks, allowing the subject to function unimpeded with their day-to-day life. The meds work together with the visor, but alone neither is enough.

"Eugh..." Vaughan groans, tossing in his sleep.

"Easy now, Captain," I say, increasing the intensity on the visor. "The worst of it is over."

This couldn't be further from the truth. I understand what's ahead.

Biologically, the specimen is fine, but what concerns me are the various readouts in his brainwaves.

They're chaotic.

The data I've collected these last two years are telling as well. His EEGs have been steadily showing a gradual deterioration, and I can't have that; I'm so very close!

But his CNS synchronization rates have vastly improved in the same period. In fact, it shows *so much promise* that it almost aligns with the original's baseline data. It seems the more he pushes himself, the more he aligns with his Xenomech's OS.

Yes... very promising.

As I load a REM protocol to the visor, the subject inhales sharply, and his theta waves fluctuate wildly.

"Shhh," I hush, stroking the top of his charcoal-brown hair, "not yet, my precious specimen, not yet."

Like I said to his commander, he's torn between two powerful forces. One is to run away and flee the layers of conflict in his mind... specifically the archetype of this 'Demon', whom he may not be able to defeat. In real life or in the recesses of his subconscious.

And the other is to embrace the bloodshed of his own making.

I've seen this paradigm before in other field reports, but not as closely as I do now.

Finally... the readout on his vitals shows specimen Vaughan slipping into REM sleep, fully adopting the foreign program as his delta waves dance on the screen.

I must say, out of all the squadrons – which I have other specialists supervising for me across the front lines – I'm particularly fond of Cronus Squadron.

"Don't worry," I say. "I'll do my best to see this project through to the end and keep this squadron's captain in working order..."

The flash of an image crosses my mind of the original specimen, who is far from here, closer to HQ on the capital world of Haradrun.

"... within reason." I curl my lips into a smile.

Chapter 25

ΧΗΫR

Two weeks later

Two sliding doors open, and ahead lies the long walk to the war room of the *Nineveh*.

"Don't fret, Colonel," Rachael says all nonchalant-like. "It's a good thing we're being summoned! And, after all of this waiting, I'm sure your men are *eager* to get to work again!"

... A good thing, eh? Good for whom?

"I don't think *eager* is the word I'd use, Doctor," I grumble, fidgeting with a cigar bit from earlier.

"A break from the monotony, then?" she counters, craning her neck at me.

"Yeah. I'm sure Cronus is itching to do *something*. It's hard seeing trained killers get chained to a desk."

She doesn't reply, but she does smile big and stare forward. I fix my gaze on her, and if I were to guess, maybe she shares the sentiment... maybe.

"Halt!" a voice booms ahead of my right ear.

Every bone in my neck snaps forward, and in my line of sight is a sharply uniformed NCO, rifle in hand, and to his left is another equally dressed NCO. Both of them guarding the sealed door ahead.

"Clearance, sirs!" the first Sergeant asks, hand already outstretched.

"A moment, Staff Sergeant," I say, reaching into the left of my jacket. "Here you are."

In my right hand dangles a clearance badge Rachael herself gave me. The second guard scans it with the gun in his hand and stares up at me.

"Thank you, Colonel." The NCO hands me back my photo and clearance chip.

Over my shoulder, Rachael whips out her ID, fixed on a lanyard around her neck, and it flops above the undercut of her black blouse.

"Go ahead and shoot, *Sergeant*," she says, holding onto the lapels of her lab coat.

How in the hell does this dame keep such a cool head?

"A-and thank you, Doctor," the poor NCO stutters.

As the door ahead slides open and we both walk through, she tilts her head to the side and says, "You're welcome!" Her glasses are all a-sparkle, her wide-toothy grin... unabashed.

Of course. Who in the hell would be nervous when you got the Mad Doc of Cronus Squadron at your side?

"You think they'd simply let us through quickly if I had a clipboard?" I ask her, leaning in.

It feels nice to grin when she snorts at my words.

"If we were on base, I'd say *yes, absolutely*... but up ahead, we're going off the map," Rachael says, giving me pause for thought, "and as our dear Shao-Shi reported on mission: here there be dragons."

As the last doors open, a shiver runs down my spine.

The room's dark, save a hanging circular luminescent halo above a polished circular table equal in size to the light above. And sitting down, each with their hands together, are five generals of the Republic Guard.

Two Air Force.

Two Navy.

One Army.

None of these generals are actually here, but their avatars are so lifelike, no one would ever know the difference.

"Please take your seats." A different man down at the far end gestures.

I can't quite make out his features... but as I walk closer to the table and grab the arm of my chair, the man's face comes into focus as he leans into the table.

"Nicholas As'ad," Rachael says for me. "My Duke, you grace us with your presence."

With as much dignity as I can muster, I find my chair and pull in, and as I do, the middle of the table generates a large spherical map of the known universe in hologram. It zooms in, focusing on the Hylii collection of galaxies in the Pavo-Indus Sphere.

The one cosmic point we've bled and died over for these last seven years.

"Let's begin," Nicholas says. "Colonel Talthor, your 223rd regiment has excelled beyond expectations. And with Doctor Vayne's field report on Cronus Squadron's mission success rate... you've done well, to say the least."

"Thank you, Your Grace," I say, bowing my head.

"Now, all available forces are to muster... here," Nicholas says, pointing to the expanded map, "on the planet Hynej."

His focus slowly shifts to the other side of the table, and he fiercely locks gazes with the Army general.

"And that, General Moravir, is where you come in," Nicholas says. "We already have a beachhead established with your 212th and 221st regiments, but they're currently pinned down. Even with all the trench networks amassed, the Thriaxians aren't giving up ground in *this* valley region."

"Why don't we simply glass them from orbit?" General Lydus asks, her jaw supported by her clenched fist, elbow to the table. "We have *both* the manpower and the nuclear arsenal. Then the colonel's pilots can sweep up the remains."

Ah, course, Navy Doctrine 101: if it moves, nuke it.

"Nicholas," an unfamiliar voice intercedes, "I'll take it from here."

Rachael stifles a gasp, inhaling real quick through her nose, hand covering her mouth. And, even though he lingered in the shadows until now, this new man sounds both rough and somehow fair.

Suddenly...

Out of the shadow, coming to the side of Nicholas's avatar at the back of the table, stands the commander-in-chief himself: Vincent DeKierr, the President-General of the GUILD Republic.

"Y-Your Excellency!" I stammer ungracefully, all kinds of flustered.

I quickly get up from my seat and ceremoniously take a deep bow, bending nearly parallel to the ground, hand covering my heart.

While I'm in that position, I glimpse Rachael's legs crossing into a formal curtsey.

The only thing that brings me back is Vincent's upraised hand, gesturing me to rise.

"Enough of that," he says, turning his gaze *directly* at General Lydus, "and dispense with this nonsense of glassing. We need Thriaxian intelligence on Hynej, and the 223rd is going to extract it. End of story."

"My apologies, Excellency," General Lydus says, shame tingeing her expression. The same expression a recruit gets when they're mercilessly chewed out in basic.

Vincent doesn't even pay her any mind. He nonchalantly looks ahead. "Colonel," he says, staring right through me with his sharp steel-blue eyes, "I'm depending on you to muster your pilots past no-man's-land, secure enemy R&D, and, if possible... destroy that minor inconvenience of ours, yes?"

"It'll be done, Excellency," I reply, catching a glimpse of Rachael as I say this.

The woman has the expression a zealot's got, seeing an acolyte talking to God.

She's all awe and wonder, she is.

"Very good," Vincent says, "and in order for your men to get there, the 212th and 221st will stage a terrestrial invasion of enemy lines, assisted by naval destroyers in low orbit."

"They'll be going over?" General Moravir asks, sounding like he already knows the answer.

"They will," Vincent replies. "Even if the result is a very expensive diversion, the ends themselves are invaluable: coordinates leading to the Thriaxian core worlds and their capital of Hal'Darah."

"And with it, the end of the war," Rachael pipes up.

"That's right," Vincent affirms. "Which is why *everything* must go off without a hitch."

"Yes, Excellency!" we all exclaim at once.

"Now, to the generals of this assembly, and to you, Colonel... you're all dismissed. Doctor Vayne, if you'd remain, we need a moment of your time," Vincent says.

As each general disappears from the conference call, their real-life avatars disintegrating into the ether, Rachael nods reverently at her orders.

"Your Excellency." I lean in, bowing again toward Vincent.

The door to the war room shuts behind me, but I don't move a foot more into the corridor.

So... High Command is looking to invade not only the Thriaxian core but also their capital world...

I sigh heavily, bring up my holopad, and flip to the latest intelligence report. The Legion's key concern is that they suspect there's a *massive* concentration of enemy naval craft in the core of Thriaxian space. And unless Rachael's keen on the idea of combining all of her Titan squadrons together, it's... unlikely we stand a chance against them.

What worries me is that, at least on paper, it seems like High Command is planning something.

Well... to hell with it for now. There's an ugly mountain of planning needs doing, and I can't do it worrying here...

"... no, what I'm saying is they'd take Hynej by *themselves*, making a clear shot toward Mar Hylia 41, and they'd already *possess it* if it weren't for that infernal Demon!" Rachael's voice booms behind the door.

... She talking about my men?

I wouldn't dare get closer to the war room... lest any of those three catch me listening in.

In my experience, that's a quick way to an early retirement and an even earlier grave.

So... against my better judgement, I linger. I can just make out their conversation, pressing my ear to the wall near the door, but I can make it out. The bionic implant I got from the Legion still works, after all...

"I trust this nuisance will go away, and swiftly." Vincent's voice carries.

"It will," Rachael affirms.

"Good. Because we have too much on the line to be jeopardized by a single enemy pilot. You know what's at stake. You *know* we're running out of time," Vincent stresses.

Oh, shit, what am I hearing?

Well, I... damn it, well, now I can barely hear a thing! *Come on, speak up!*

"... and you're confident this squadron will retrieve it? After the failures of the other squadrons?"

That's definitely Nicholas. His voice is softer than Vincent's but notably still masculine.

But what is "it" supposed to be...? She never mentioned *anything* about the affairs of the other five Titan squadrons, and now they failed with whatever "it" is... Fuck... damn it, I'm in over my head.

"Dear Nicholas," Rachael assures with her soothing tone, "the Sleeping King under the Mountain is stirring awake in my very squadron. Yes, the other squadrons are not faring well, but I remain... faithful, as it were."

"Then we proceed as planned," Vincent says.

"Oh, shit..." I whisper, clasping my mouth too late.

"Gentlemen, if you'll excuse me," Rachael says.

I've done it now.

Even as I begin to leave to try and undo the threads of my morbid curiosity, the familiar clack of Rachael's stiletto heels approaches. They're not fast, but they are steady.

"I know you're there," she says from behind the door.

No matter what I do, I'm screwed.

If I run, I'm dead.

If I turn around and open that door... I'm dead.

Well... I wanted to listen in, so the price fits the bill, and I ain't going out on my knees.

My lungs fill with air. I spin on my heel, take a step toward the door, and it immediately opens.

And in the war room, the only one left is Rachael... and her back is to me.

She lowers her hands from the top of her leather chair, already pushed in, and rests them right at her sides.

I knew I had a bad feeling at Port Yegevni... and I think that's when the clock started ticking down for me.

"How much did you hear?" she asks over her shoulder.

"Enough," I reply, cementing my fate.

She faces me, her lab coat flowing in sync with her twirl. "Good," she says... smiling... "now we can begin."

Do... do I ask for clarification about what she means? Or is she toying with me?

"Don't I know too much?" I ask, going for the throat. "Aren't you goin' to kill me for that?"

I'm not sure what the hell is going on, but if I'm going out, I'd rather it be now than in my sleep.

Rachael blinks at my words, her face alight with surprise. "Oh, Xhyr, of course not!" she says, most enthusiastically. "I need you."

She rests one arm under her breasts, and the other comes up to rest her hand beneath her chin, fingers splayed across her cheek. A playful smile crosses her lips... and again, not sure how, but I've amused her.

"And what am I needed for?" I ask, even more unclear about her motives.

"Everything..." Rachael broadens her smile.

Chapter 26

VAUGHAN

Six days later

"... You want me to do what?" I ask, hoping I misheard.

In this dimly lit bunker, several meters underground on Terran-occupied Hynej... the woman across from me continues to point to the man kneeling in front of us.

"You heard me, Captain," the woman affirms. "I said I want you to prove your loyalty and put a bullet in this prisoner's head."

My eyes narrow at her words.

Chloeja's in the small sub-bunker room with me, dressed in terracotta field fatigues, and as I shoot her a perplexed expression of confusion, she returns it.

"Ma'am," I say, "Colonel Ptolemy, I don't understand how, or when, my loyalty came into question."

It may have been the night I almost skewered her eye socket with a butter knife, back at the formal mess, less than a month ago. And, judging by the way she received me and my squadron planet-side yesterday... I'd say she was at least a little sore from our last encounter.

"I understand your confusion," Jas Ptolemy says, her voice fluid and almost assuring. "No... I'm not questioning your loyalty to your outfit, corps, or the reverenced name of His Excellency. And... forget about that night at the mess hall. I've been updated on Titan pressures and ticks..."

She trails off as she walks from one end of the room, where the singular prisoner slumps over, and places her hand on top of the black sack covering their head. Their hands are also behind their back, bound with handcuffs... and the area around their arms and torso appears bloody...

"What I'm talking about is your loyalty as a citizen. As a subject of the Republic."

Subject... what is she up to? Why is she slating me, singularly, as this person's executioner?

"Ma'am?" I ask.

"Like I said coming down those stairs," she says, pointing to the exit behind me and Chloeja, "I need both of you for this field court martial. The purpose: to eliminate any risks associated with the mission we're all about to undertake."

I tense as she says this.

"Lives are at stake. The lives of my men, and I need to know I can trust you specifically, Captain." Her cold grey eyes peer deep into my soul.

"The mission's success is paramount to my outfit," I say, glancing back to Chloeja to break eye contact with the colonel, and I snap back to her, "so I'll do what's necessary, ma'am."

Colonel Ptolemy reaches down the back of the prisoner's neck, removes the black bag from their head, and tosses it aside to the left...

... I notice a man's face, hair dishevelled and gleaming with blood.

He stares up at me, at first fiery with defiance... and that fire snuffs out into cold defeat.

"Vaughan..." he rasps.

His eyes are familiar: a soft amber sheen encircled by dark blue... ones that are hauntingly familiar.

"... Commander Kael?" Chloeja says, confirming my doubts.

A lump forms in my throat, and I swallow hard. I've always known Kael to be tough as nails, even if the memories aren't real... but seeing him now, pleading with me... the tables have turned.

"Affirmative," Colonel Ptolemy interrupts my thoughts, "and since both of you are familiar with this officer of the Naval branch, I thought it fitting to slot you two as character witnesses for this court martial."

The muscles in my chest tighten as my fake father winces at her words.

"Colonel Ptolemy," I utter, almost as a whisper, "why is my father being detained?"

"An excellent question," she replies, "deserving of an appropriate answer."

She snaps her fingers, bringing a holopad out of thin air into her reach. She grabs it and draws up a document. It serves as the only luminous object in the room, minus the dim bunker lights on the wall.

"'Commander Kael 634-AFZ, arrested under confirmation of conspiring with the rebel faction the Liberation Front of the Reach, or the LFR, conspiracy to commit treason in a time of war... and frontier smuggling,'" she reads.

That last point hits worse than a violent gut check. I quickly glance over at Chloeja, checking in, and she's as shaken about the whole thing as I am.

If Jas Ptolemy is questioning my loyalty... does she know who I am? Who Mom and Ann'Elise are?

Is this the end of the line?

"Captain," Jas Ptolemy says, "do you understand the charges being laid on this officer?"

"I don't..." I say, trying to buy time. "Can you please tell me how they apply?"

"Very well." Jas, skims over her holopad again. "For the last three months, this commander has smuggled members of the LFR from frontier Republic space to inhabited colonies... assisted in civil unrest, betraying public trust with strings pulled at his previous posting... and aided in plots of terrorism."

My heart sinks as memories of the *Nautilus* come flooding back.

I remember what little kindness Kael offered me and my family... countered by the immense cruelty he and his men inflicted on us and my crew during their invasion of my ship.

"Now, Commander 634-AFZ," Jas says, turning to Kael, "do you have anything to say in your defence?"

"I..." Kael replies. "I did what I did so that my system wouldn't starve. Our replicators have been failing, and everything has been going to the war-front... the rebels had mineral ore for tri-core fusion and parts necessary for repairs. I don't regret helping my people..."

That mineral ore... that powers our Xenomechs... my mech...

"So you're admitting guilt?" Jas presses.

"Sure," Kael says with a tremor of his eyelids.

Jas inhales deeply and collapses the holopad in her hand with a sudden snap of her fingers.

"Very well," she says, "then, by the authority of my position, for the crimes of conspiracy, seditious motives, and behaviour unbecoming an officer of the Republic... Kael 634-AFZ, you are found guilty by this court martial, supported by these character witnesses, and I sentence you to death by firing."

Jas draws a wide-barrelled pistol from behind her, causing Chloeja to jolt forward.

But before she can mouth a word of protest, I throw my arm up and block her from taking a step toward the colonel.

"No," I whisper, my outstretched arm shaking.

"Commander Nadjidhar," Jas says, eerily sympathetic, "I understand you have a history with this man – both men in this room, for that matter, and that this is no simple thing to watch, and least of all for you, Captain. I can't imagine what you're feeling right now."

Jas regards us both, but her gaze lingers on me.

"Colonel..." My tone loses potency and trails off.

"It's a tall order, Captain," Jas says to me, "but I guarantee you, if you follow through with your duties, without objection, I will ensure that your homeworld of Korvingshal VI will be spared any *disciplinary* action. I believe you're aware of the alternative, being schooled in Legion anti-terrorism."

... I am.

Jas is right.

It wouldn't be beyond her power or anyone below her to rip the Korvingshal System apart in nuclear fury. And Mom and Ann'Elise are there...

"No need to punish the loyal for the sins of the father," Jas adds, offering me her pistol, handle first.

Of course I take it, and it weighs heavier than it should.

I examine the side of the barrel; it's exactly the same issue as my own... no difference in make.

For that last fleeting ebb of conscience, my focus lifts from the gun to Chloeja. Her golden green eyes meet mine, and without words, her expression conveys what she'd say out loud if she could:

'*Don't do this.*' She beckons me. '*This is wrong!*'

"Please, please, don't..." Kael pleads between wet, rasping breaths.

And... when Natalia fled, terrified for her life, did his men listen?

No.

Did they listen to Kai's plea for mercy as they beat him to death?

No.

Would they have killed my mother and sister if I didn't stop them? Would Kael have allowed it?

Yes.

The gun in my hand feels *much* lighter now, and with balancing the weight of my squadron and the ruins of my past... following this order is much less of a burden than before.

So when I raise the crosshair of the pistol right above Kael's eyebrows, what little hope remains in his eyes dissipates to nothing.

"N-no," Kael says, his lips quivering, "Vaughan, please, you're my son!"

My thumb flicks the safety off the side of the barrel, my finger barely squeezing the trigger.

"I'm your father..." he adds, his voice broken.

"... I *have no father*," I growl.

One, two blasts of concentrated plasma burn right through Kael's forehead.

Behind me, Chloeja gasps in horror.

Two seconds pass, and Kael's whole body collapses by my boots, face forward. Two charred holes on the back of his head mark where I shot him.

I crane my neck toward Jas, who, for the first time since I've known her, looks impressed.

"Okay," she says. "I trust you."

She extends her arm out, like she wants to shake my hand...

"Good," I say coldly, passing her the gun handle first. "Is there anything else you need from me, ma'am?"

"No, Captain," Jas says, moving past me, "you've done enough. Now, then... I have a regiment to lead. You're both dismissed."

"Ma'am." I salute as she walks away.

As I ascend the steps out of the dark and musty bunker, I glance over my shoulder and see Chloeja staring at Kael's body.

"We need to go," I say, not wanting to linger.

Chloeja takes one last look at Kael... and rushes to catch up with me. "I'm sorry," she says, her voice a strange dance between contrition and mourning.

"Don't be," I assure her. "There's nothing to be sorry about."

It's not like Chloeja gave me the life-or-death choice that put me on this path.

He did... and now he's dead.

Even as I climb the steps back up to the surface, I don't feel anything.

I thought I might, like sadness, personal justice... sadistic pleasure, maybe... but no. Nothing.

No, wait. I *did* feel something, even if it was fleeting: rage.

But strangely enough, not right now. It's like someone flipped a switch and cut the circuits to my gut. My cheeks are flush from the encounter, but not unlike a drop mission... my head is cool.

While I remember who Kael was, as a father of sorts, Chloeja also knows about the memory implants I have... and how my actions might affect me. I get why she's concerned, like I shot my own dad... but she doesn't need to be.

But no... I feel nothing. I wonder if that's normal... for other pilots or other soldiers?

Maybe...

"Let's go, Commander," I say, almost at the top. "We have a job to do."

Chloeja and I emerge from the bunker into beams of light pouring overhead. The first thing that comes into focus is the frame of a trench wall, well maintained, and on either side, men and women almost blending into Terran-sized holes in the wall. Soldiers wear long-wired, thick-tubed inner suits for their power armour and are cloaked with only a thin tarp.

Even when my squadron dropped on the surface days ago, the Heavies' situation had changed little. They'd dug into the trench network and weathered Thriaxian bombardment. Like my Titans, they're eager for that moment to strike, hoping for it, because it's better than anxiously waiting. Less than half an hour ago, Horatio, Chloeja, and I were talking about our next steps, back at the mech bay in Delta Sector of the trench... about what we'd do after the fighting stops and the war is over.

Well... at least for us.

As I march a few steps ahead of Chloeja, I remember Horatio talking about a grand "succession of mantle". Being one of three Nobles in our squad, Horatio had a time adjusting to the rough and tumble that we in the colonies were so familiar with. At least from what I recall in the memory implants.

"*How can they fight like this?*" Horatio said, escorting Chloeja and me to the bunker.

The 'they' he was referring to were the Heavies.

He spent time with them on the *Nineveh* after Yuri died, but I think this was the first time the cold, hard truth about infantry life hit him. And, by extension, what the colonists face daily: that life is not only cruel and short, but by surviving, one becomes strong.

Chloeja, on the other hand, talked about wanting to stay in the military.

"*Are you crazy?!*" Horatio said.

Her rationale was quite the opposite of Horatio's: Chloeja has nothing to go back to. She's the youngest of seven sisters in her family, and she explained that the only thing she'd inherit from her Noble family is an arranged marriage, being a marq's daughter.

"*You forget, Horatio,*" Chloeja said, walking up the down-trench with us, "*the Republic and the Houses are not kind to women unless you already wield power.*"

I stop before the raised terrace of the mech bay.

"Captain?" Chloeja asks, concern miring her voice.

"You said you wanted to be a general," I say over my shoulder. "Well, whatever I can do to make that happen, just say the word."

She scowls, folding her arms. "Tch. I can take care of myself well enough," Chloeja scoffs. "Frankly, I'm more worried about you, sir. Before we... when we got here, you said all you want is to 'go home'. And that's it."

"That *is* all I want," I say, steadfast. "That's all I've ever wanted."

"But you've never been to Korvingshal VI. What would that even look like?"

I pause, turning completely to face her.

"My home's wherever Mom and Ann'Elise are," I explain, "so... I'll sort out their safety there, and take care of my family here... whatever that means."

She nods, smiles faintly, and moves past me, taking a step up toward the terrace of the mech bay. "That'll have to do for now. Just remember I'll be on your ass *when* you make it out of this, knowing full well what you're capable of!"

As she disappears up the steps, a faint shout resonates behind me.

"We're going over!"

It echoes across the back trench, radiating outward, and before I reach the tarmac and jump back into my element, the pilots of the Heavy Infantry shake off tarps, mud, and a collective haze of melancholy. It's as though they recently woke up from hibernation like they were ready for deployment.

Me? I'm always ready.

I march up the steps to the mech bay, where Horatio and Oreiga are checking the gauges on their armour. Chloeja, Xalpha, and Takashi load their rifles, standing by the feet of their mechs.

As I walk by, they salute me.

I nod, moving forward, hands at my sides. I come across a large canvased mech at the very end. Wasting no time, I bring up my holopad from my wrist and press a button labelled 'release'.

In less than a second, several tiny clips disengage at the very top of the canvas and furl downward in a cascade of fabric.

What remains is my X-5 series Xenomech... with some recent additions.

"Looking good, Captain!" Shao-Shi gives a solid shout amid the growing din of the regular and Heavy Infantry march.

And he's right. It *does* look good.

I take a quick walk around, inspecting the new wings installed at the unit's shoulder blades for increased acceleration and shielding. Up top of the shoulders are plasma beam cannons in place of a manual particle cannon, and as I examine the arms of the mech, I take note of where the engineers modified the melee system.

The retractable pulsar blades are exactly like the Demon's design, integrated directly into the unit's forearms.

As a distant air-raid siren blasts, signalling the Heavies to go over into enemy territory, my pilots have mixed expressions on their faces.

Anticipation.

Simmering fury.

Apprehension.

Fear...

Whatever our fates may be, one thing's for sure: our X-5 units serve as both our salvation... and our tombs.

Maybe that's the fate of every pilot who dares call themselves a Titan...

⇢⇢⇢ ⇠⇠⇠

"Careful ahead," I caution over the comms. "It's a steep drop to the bottom, and we're not sure what's down there."

I pull up the controls of my mech, halting right before a low-guarded rail circling a matrix of obelisks made of polished stone and dark chrome metal. They run down a colossal cylinder, and each of them seems to pulse with a soft glow of blue, silver, and pulsing red lines. If I were to guess, they're almost like circuits.

Like the pillars we found on Talmorah.

"*Copy that,*" Oreiga replies. "*Nothing creeping outta the vents yet. Green over here, Captain.*"

We've practiced to death in the simulators and hand to hand on the mats... but I don't feel like we're ready. We've dropped half a kilometre into the surface of Hynej, and like intel suggests, it's an absolute maze.

As I think it goes straight down to the planet's core, the processing towers stop, and below them is a bright yellow hue.

"Cronus 12 and 13," I say, "get a scan on the floor before those towers stop. We'll get a readout from one of the bottom terminals."

"*Copy!*" Horatio booms.

"*What you suppose is down there?*" Oreiga asks. "*Intel doesn't cover it with our sensors.*"

"I'll go look into it. Commander," I order, "see to the core squadron. I'm breaking off, investigating further in."

"*Roger that,* Captain," Chloeja acknowledges, not being subtle about her disdain for me taking a personal risk like this. Her video feed shows up in the corner of my HUD, and the distress on her face is more than clear to me. I step close to the edge of another long fall, with seemingly no obstacles in my way.

"*Sir...*" she continues, flipping to a private channel between us, "*are you faring alright?*"

Why does everyone keep asking me that...?

"Like I said before," I assure her, "I'm fine. Vitals are good. Nothing to worry about."

I fake a smile, trying to reassure Chloeja... but she's not buying it.

"*You're sure you want to go alone?*" she presses.

"I am," I say resolutely, "and I'm not to be followed."

"*Copy,*" Chloeja replies, her video feed showing her bow her head.

The controls in my hands feel stiff, but I ease them forward, giving myself enough of a push so that my Xenomech tilts off the edge and into the yellow abyss.

Left foot pedal, down.

Both thumbs pressing down hard, coasting anti-grav panels softly in descent.

Beep, beep, beep!

"*Proximity alert. Pull up,*" the OS warns.

My own loud, stifled breathing echoes back inside my helmet. I reach back on the controls, press the left pedal harder, and swerve my unit a few hundred metres to the right.

The yellow haze clears, revealing an enormous transparent tank.

In the thick of my descent, large mist vapours rise around the tank, right underfoot of my mech.

"Pilots," I call out across all channels, "I've picked up a massive containment structure below the processing towers."

"*I copy,*" Chloeja says, "*what's in it – can you see?*"

The LADAR sweep and motion sensors don't pick up anything on-screen.

"Nothing," I reply, "except maybe... fluid. I'm not sure if it's the liquid in the tank that's yellow or if there's illumination coming from the containment."

"*Gross...*" Serena pipes up.

"*Yeah, second that,*" Xalpha adds. "*Any bio-matter readouts?*"

"Negative," I reply. "I can't get through the glass; the sensors can't reach it. I'm going down further."

As I keep the rate of descent steady... I hear a low, guttural reverberation. What follows is the outline of a... thing, or creature, slowly coming into view from the yellow cylinder.

"I have a visual," I blurt out. "Sharing on channel."

There are millions of cam sensors spread out across my X-5... but from what I'm seeing, I'm not sure I can trust what they're picking up.

What I see is... ethereal. Like long, wingless dragons covered in circular scales.

"*What the...*" Shao-Shi remarks.

"*The* hell *are those?!*" Xalpha spits out her words.

"*Who cares!? Captain, we're coming down with you!*" Chloeja exclaims. "*If one of those things gets out, it could destroy your mech!*"

"I...! Confirmed," I say, instantly regretting it.

The sound of Chloeja breathing a sigh of relief follows, as well as an increase in the levity of the squad's chatter... maybe I was wrong, trying to do this by myself...

The ground below comes closer, as well as the source of the mist.

Three large waterfalls, a hundred meters in height, collect into a large pool under the yellow tank to my left. Since I'm closer to the bottom, these dragon-looking creatures become clearer on the screen, increasing their movement near the base of the cylinder. From what I can tell, they're tethered – maybe by an umbilical cord of some kind – to a long metal rod in the centre of the tank.

I'm not sure what the Thriaxians are planning, but a single word comes to mind when I watch them slowly writhing in dynamic stasis: Ominii.

If the folklore from the Nomadic Fleet is true... are Ominii Thriaxian in origin?

"*Captain!*" Chloeja shouts. "*There's a service chute running down the anti-chamber wall, and we found a terminal! I'll meet you down at the entrance, and the rest will catch up.*"

"Copy," I reply, navigating toward a landing spot near the basin of the pool.

"*Data transfer should take only a couple of minutes in the chute,*" Shao-Shi adds on the line. "*With the new codes, we'll be up and out in no time!*"

As my mech touches down on smooth stone flooring, an entranceway three mechs in width catches my eye. On the right side of the arch is a large panel with a single opening switch attached.

Like on Talmorah, the dimly lit chute's completely absent of water and instead has several hundreds of meters of wiring along the walls.

My hands move the mech in the opposite direction, toward the closest waterfall.

On the other side of the cistern, along a walkway of polished stone, cascading water ripples like a transparent curtain, revealing lights behind it.

"*Hey!*" Chloeja greets through video while her mech lands forcefully on the other side of the door. It catches a landing bay platform, with the stretch of the chute continuing below.

"Hey." I wave into my screen.

"*Woo! I'm connected with the terminal, Captain; we'll be out in no time!*" Shao-Shi exclaims.

"Good," I say, "and let me know if there's any data as to... whatever *those* things up there are..."

"*Copy that, sir; I'm curious myself,*" he says.

Beep, beep beep!

"*Unidentified unit detected,*" my OS says calmly in my helmet.

Where?

"Commander, are you reading a bogey?"

"*I am,*" Chloeja says, "*but I can't see anything. It's not above; the rest of the squad would've seen it!*"

The HUD isn't showing anything; even the rear cameras show nothing behind me... nothing up to the waterfall and...

Behind me, several small blue lights shine through the waterfall.

A figure about the same height as my unit slowly passes through the cascading water, walking out onto the long stretch of walkway and coming toward me. And as I zero in my aft cameras, focus the image...

"He's here," I say to Chloeja. "I see the Demon."

"*W-where?!*" she replies.

"Listen carefully," I continue, taking one step back. "Stay with Cronus 5. Don't leave until he's done, then get him and everyone else out of here. Await my orders and..."

The words trail off of as I keep a close eye on the Demon, and focus on the panel to the service door.

"And don't follow me," I order, readying my shoulder cannons. "Over and out."

"*Vaughan, wai—!*" Chloeja shouts before I switch off my comms.

Before her unit can reach me and drag me into the chute with her, my fingers release from my controls and shoot two charges into the door panel, sealing it shut.

As I shift the mech around, facing my enemy, he draws a familiar pulsar blade and shield. The water coming off of his mech's shoulders hisses against the pulsar field, and beads of water dance off of the blade.

The joints of my hands ache as they tense around my controls, and as if by instinct, the two pulsar blades at my wrists extend and rage against the dim light around me.

Just *seeing* him makes my hands shake.

Adrenaline courses through my veins, like before, causing my extended arms to tremble. I wait for his next move...

But all he does is extend his shield and ready his blade.

He will not get another chance to cut me down. Not this time.

And not any other time!

"Come on!" I shout.

The G's hit me as my foot slams down on the pedals. Added acceleration from the wings drives me forward, and in seconds, the Demon is visible as a target on the HUD. The echoing sound of my heavy breaths, the thumping of my heart in my ears, and that electric moment when my blade meets his... and I'm actively anticipating where the next five blows from the Demon are going to land.

Horrible screeching, sparks setting patches of the running pool on fire in my periphery... all of it playing concerto to the percussion in my head. And, in minor accompaniment, the soft beeping of an error message on my display, centre to the backdrop of my neon red cockpit:

"*Danger, SERUM dosage output error. Canister damage, warning—*"

The Demon jumps up, taking flight.

I wave my hand over the error, blocking it out as I follow in pursuit.

The upgraded thrusters throw me several more G's into the back of my seat, but unlike before, I'm not crumpling from the added weight.

I push back against the G-force through sheer grit.

"Aarrgh!" I howl.

My mech flies past the haunting outline of one creature in stasis, floating in a sea of yellow, and all while I parry one sword strike after another, the hiss of anti-matter cutting through the air audible through the layers of metal sheltering me...

And it hits me.

That same visceral *rage* from before, in the bunker, courses through me as I trail the Demon out of the massive antechamber. There was nothing... and then it was there, plain as the light of day:

Wrath.

That is what I feel. And that... is what is going to save my family.

As we dodge one horizontal pillar after the other, he brings two blades down on top of me, launching a terrifying volley of lasers toward me...

But I'm ready.

The wings of my mech enclose me like the layers of a cocoon, and one charge after another thunders against the armour surrounding me.

I explode my unit's arms outward, breaking the Demon's shield, and quickly zero in on the torso of his mech, where his cockpit should be. That's where they are with the Sentinels.

My focus narrows down the sights on my HUD, the movement of my fingers roaming frantically against the controls in front of me.

... And there's my opening.

One coordinated volley of missiles, plasma charges, and a guided laser beam bombard the surface of the Demon's mech armour. Even as we dart, weave, and even take cover from each other's blasts in the maze of computerized pillars, I don't lose him. Wherever he goes, I follow quickly. It'd be fine if all he did was attack and return fire... but no. He has to run *like a coward*.

I swear if my soul was an ordnance, I'd pull the pin and destroy us both.

"*Warning. Warning,*" the OS chimes in, "*Approaching surface level. Pull up. Pull u—*"

One pull of the controls, two input commands, and a whiff of alien atmosphere... and the tips of my mech's wings rise skyward, releasing a beam upward.

The display shows the stone framework, metal exterior, and rocky formation of the complex's ceiling completely disintegrate as the Demon and I burst through the disrupted molecules. And what follows is a deafening explosion that licks at the feet of my mech.

Suspended in the air, with no time to think, I pirouette my unit in the air, evading a downward strike.

There's no cover above the surface... and that's probably why he lured me up here.

Even as the Demon spreads the wings of his unit out like a predatory bird, I can't help but laugh.

... Well, this is new.

I haven't laughed in a while. It's weird – as the Demon speeds toward me, everything feels very calm...

"*SERUM output error. Injection levels erratic. Check supply tank—*"

There're errors going off left, right, and centre; like over Talmorah, flashes of red spread out like an infection around my display. But... despite all of it, I can sense him.

Even as he charges in, phase-shifting behind me... I can sense him.

"There!" I shout, shifting in my seat.

From behind, my hands catch the wrist of the Demon's mech and hold tight in a death grip.

The controls in my hands become more like extensions of myself, so when I thrust down, bank, and pivot myself in midair, it doesn't even feel like I'm in a Xenomech anymore.

Another barrage of fire pours out from the Demon mech's shoulder cannons, quickly chipping away at what little shielding I have left... but I've got him.

Even if he phase-shifts away, I'm going along for the ride.

But while I have him in the air, soaring above one trench line after the other... I take my mech's right arm and cut down like an axe until it hits the force field of his shield.

I keep my finger on the charge of the pulsar blade... overloading it.

"This is for Yuri," I say, gruff and low.

A blinding light emanates from my display, followed by a shockwave that knocks me back, and when the horizon finally comes back into the picture, the Demon hangs in the air, hovering above me.

But this time, it's his unit's left arm that's smashed to pieces, not mine.

"Oh, shit..." I check my unit's integrity onscreen.

No. I'm okay.

The screen shows everything on my X-5 is still intact... somehow. All except for the right wing of my craft and right shoulder cannon... the frame's holding together.

In the background, a Terran destroyer falls to the surface of Hynej... landing in a plume of fire. Thriaxian artillery cuts through the air, but my sensors show entire Republic carriers, frigates, and ships of the line pouring through the atmosphere. And with them, emptying drop ships and aerial support. Thriaxian and Terran charges expand in the surrounding air, targeting each other's fighter craft.

Amidst the chaos, the Demon stares down at me, suspended in the air with only one arm. And in it is a flickering pulsar blade on its last legs.

"You're mine." I seethe, readying my controls.

I accelerate up, feeling comfort in the pull of gravity as the Demon spears downward.

"Aargh!" I cry, feral and assured.

With the Demon's shields broken, my blade finds purchase against the upper torso of his mech. I shift my mech right in a fluid cut, and sparks fly in front of me. Then...

BOOM!

A sharp ringing in my ear causes me to squint, and my mech tumbles through the air, my display saturated from the light of the blast.

"*Warning. Warning. Warning...*" the OS repeats until I mute it.

I blink quickly as the visibility takes a while to return... and I see him.

The Demon is plummeting in a spiralling descent toward the Thriaxian lines on the surface. In the air, several Thriaxian Sentinels join up in formation with him. With only me, in the state I'm in, there are too many to take on by myself.

"OS," I say, "status report."

A tiny message on my display asks '*Unmute?*'

"Yeah," I reply.

Alarms of every kind flood my cockpit. The shielding in the top left corner of the screen shows 5% remaining and reactor shielding compromised...

I hit the mute button again.

Despite the state of my X-5, the sensors onscreen show a major Thriaxian withdrawal.

I switch the comms back on and flip to my squadron's channel.

"This is Captain Vaughan 634-AFZ," I say "Anyone still alive?"

My chest tightens as several minutes pass with nothing but static in my ear and onscreen.

Then Chloeja appears.

"*Copy, sir,*" Chloeja says. "*The mission was a success. We collected the data and transmitted it back to the* Nineveh, *per operation specs.*"

On video, she stares at me with her golden green eyes, both relieved and livid. Admiring and unimpressed. I get a visual onscreen. Small video feeds of all eleven of my pilots populate the left corner of my display.

"*Took you long enough, sir!*" Xalpha adds.

"*Did you seriously take on that Demon all by yourself?*" Oreiga chides, his mouth agape on camera.

"*See!? I told you he made it!*" Horatio brags.

"Good," I reply, "and everyone's all in one piece?"

"*Roger that!*" they all say in unison.

I sharply exhale, a sigh of relief echoing back in my helmet.

They're safe. My family, here and far away – they're safe.

"*What about you, Captain?*" Shao-Shi asks. "*Did you get that son of a bitch?*"

... I'm not sure.

"It's not a confirmed kill," I reply, "but I did 'shoot' him down."

"*That's our captain!*" Lynette chimes in.

"*Fuck yeah!*"

"*Got 'em back for Yuri.*"

The voices of my pilots cheer over top of the other, and as they do, my hands shake worse than before. Even though the modifications worked and the planning paid off, I couldn't defeat him... not outright.

But... not one of my pilots died on my watch.

The mission was a success.

I succeeded.

A ragged sigh leaves me, and I turn away from my camera as tears threaten to fall.

"*Sir,*" Chloeja asks me, "*are you okay in there?*"

Still looking away from the display, I sharply sniffle, and then face the screen. I nod softly. "Yeah..." I reply, speaking honestly for the first time in years. "I am."

PART 4

Apotheosis

Chapter 27

Chloeja

Two weeks later

Everyone's on edge. The entire mess hall is quieter than usual. I get we're all bored as hell, but no one's talking about the last mission brief.

"Okay, hear me out…" Xalpha says, sitting adjacent to me at the bar. "You said you don't want to call your folks—"

"I really don't," I say matter-of-factly.

"Right, but," she continues, "but you heard the colonel and saw how stone-faced the captain was… this might be the last major push for us before we get to Hal'Darah. Wouldn't you want to stream a letter back home, knowing what we're up against?"

A chuckle leaves my parted lips. Xalpha's not usually this sentimental.

"Commander?" she presses.

"Lieutenant," I begin, "I'm not sure what's funnier: having every day be the last day, or having the day after tomorrow be more of a last day than the rest."

In two days, we take Mar Hylia 41.

"I see the redundancy," Xalpha replies.

"Right," I continue. "Mind, I'd tell all of you to write home, send a final heartwarming note to your family, friends, and partners… but my *family's here.*"

Two of my fingers tap the table as I lean forward, emphasising the last two words out of my mouth… you'd think she'd get by now that some of us don't really have a home to go back to.

Xalpha visibly sighs, uncomfortable yet resigned.

Good. I'd hate to order her to drop the goddamn subject...

"Commander," Xalpha asks, "what are we looking for on Mar Hylia 41?"

My breath catches, but I maintain strict eye contact with her. She can't have any doubt coming from me, not from her superior.

"A rectangular stele," I reply, shrugging, "like the captain outlined in the exercise."

"I figured," she says, "with five entire divisions converging on the planetary system and two divisions leading a planetary assault... it feels excessive for one stele."

Xalpha's not wrong, and the worst of it is she's not alone in her assessment.

After the hard-won victory on Hynej, a lot of us thought we'd be heading straight for the thick of Thriaxian space, leading a violent assault on their core worlds.

What Vaughan said quashed that... especially after he said High Command was sending us on an errand run for a mystery cube... box... rectangle-thing on Mar Hylia 41.

"I'm sure High Command has its reasons," I assure, while asserting what authority I possess, "and that, like Hynej, we go where the others can't."

"Yes, ma'am." Xalpha casts her gaze to the side.

I nod, pushing myself away from the table, and as I leave, the sound of Oreiga's e-lute trails behind my footsteps out of the mess.

Melancholic notes, that mimicked sound of nylon strings. Wordless in his strumming, the Old Man conveys through song the untold thoughts in his head—and one particular thought that we all seem to think: this is the end of the road.

In victory or defeat, this life is coming to an end. And as much as I want to snap everyone out of it, it's a terrible truth we all have to accept.

I did... I believe I did, anyway.

Ahead of the open bulkhead, stars whiz past to the right beyond an enormous window, just five doors down from the infirmary and our mess hall. The window isn't nearly as large as the ones on the observation deck, where we hold parades and ceremonies, but...

My gaze shifts to Vaughan's quarters to my right.

"Shit," I say.

I haven't been able to talk about Hynej yet.

Not about Kael or anything to do with that incident... no, that ship set sail, and I sure as hell don't know when it's coming back to port.

No... Vaughan still hasn't explained why he locked me out to fight the Thriaxian Ace by himself...

Knock, knock.

My knuckles rap against the metal sliding door to his quarters...

... and nothing.

"Captain?" I call out, inching closer to his door.

Of course, he doesn't have to explain himself. He's the captain... it's not something I would have done if I were leading the squadron. I'd have us work together.

I wouldn't shut everyone out.

"Come in," Vaughan replies.

My posture immediately straightens, and as my hand waves over the command console to his room, the sliding door to it opens.

"Commander," Vaughan greets, our gazes meeting, "please, take a seat."

His voice definitely sounds less distant than in previous days, though he's very much deep in thought.

"Thank you, sir." I salute briefly before finding my usual perch.

It's the closest seat to the door, opposite to an identical one, and separated by a small round dining table. It's also in just the right place to have a decent face-to-face with Vaughan in private.

I cross my legs and turn them elegantly to the side, like I've seen my friend Aryana do many times at many functions. And it's how a lady would sit.

As I sit, I take inventory of my surroundings, look around, and smile.

It's nice to take in how well his bed's made up, how his dress and pilot fatigues are all neatly hung up in an open closet to my left, and how at the far end his shower stall is steamy and recently used.

Then, there's Vaughan, hair slightly damp, sitting at his wide brushed-chrome desk, finished with a transparent laminate.

Sketches hang up on the wall in front of him, pencilled with graphite and charcoal. There are images of the planets where we were deployed, including a large scene of the oceans on Talmorah. On either side, sketches of small spacecraft, destroyers, our hangar, and an artistic outcropping of trees from Hynej stand out.

Near a waste bin by his feet, under the desk, are several crumpled sheets.

One close by, having missed the bin, is partially open, etched with uneven lines... and a scratched-out image.

"Need something?" Vaughan asks.

I crane my neck, my gaze fixated on his dark cobalt-blue irises, and point to the right of my feet. There, Vaughan's lute stands on a tiny pedestal, collecting a modest amount of dust on the rim of the body.

There's no argument from my captain, and no reprimand for not bringing my own – just the beginning of a smile and a gesture of his outstretched hand, palm up with a pencil between his fingers.

"Go ahead," he replies.

Vaughan's lute is almost identical to Oreiga's. It being wooden in frame is a novelty, and it has virtual-sensor strings leading up the body to the end of the fretboard. I've heard him play a couple of times in the mess hall, especially when we're all sparring, but more so on days like today.

My arm extends, and I gently remove the lute from its tiny stand. Adjusting myself cross-legged, I tip the neck of it diagonally to the left and place two of my left-hand fingers along the second and third frets.

With my right hand, I pick the strings.

A gentle melody pours out into the room, and it's a mix of melancholy and longing.

It's like something Yuri used to hum in the hangar and later told me was a folklore sung into prose – about a couple torn apart by circumstance. In the lyrics he described, it almost sounded like a love letter written into tragedy.

Out of the corner of my eye, I see Vaughan stop what he's doing.

A few more strums, accompanied by a few soft hums, and he slowly meets my gaze. I don't catch all of him, shifting my focus back to the frets by my fingertips, and that's absolutely on purpose.

"It's that bad out there?" he asks.

I stop humming but keep picking the strings. "No one's really sure what to do with themselves," I say.

And not for a lack of trying. It's not like we're unaccustomed to the drumbeat of sheer terror parted only by long stretches of boredom.

"We're almost at the end," Vaughan says, "and I get why they're listless. I don't think they planned for a real tomorrow."

"Or the possibility of annihilation before that," I say, "because until now, I don't think they really thought about any sort of end. A few months ago, we all thought we were invincible."

"No," he replies, "and it's not easy to think about. It's why I had a rough time on Hynej explaining what I want, because right now... I only want to get back to my family again. Everything else is too far away."

"Right."

"At least you're sure of what you want. I don't think I'd be okay behind a desk – barking orders; attending meetings... all the politics that Xhyr deals with on the regular."

"Ah, yes," I say, "but I grew up with that. And, when I make it to the top, I'm bringing my allies with me. Seriously... if you stick around, even to command captains of your own one day, remember this: I take care of my own."

"Does it surprise you that I hate fighting?" he says, wincing.

"Not really, no," I reply, "but the truth is you are *really good* at the helm of a mech... and good with a sword."

"I don't enjoy it, though. If I had a choice, I'd leave. And with swords... I learned that for self-defence."

"For yourself?" I ask.

"No, for my family."

"Sooo... not much has changed," I say. "I mean, you do that now."

"*That*, I don't mind," Vaughan stresses, "and gunning down Thriaxian pilots feels different."

"How?"

"They're not Terran."

My hand shifts along the frets, transitioning quickly with the pace of the song.

"That's not what I'm worried about," he says. "It's when there are no more Thriaxians to bury. What then?"

I sigh heavily at his words. "That is the question." I stop myself before we both hop down a *very* dark rabbit hole, and it's one that involves mediating the disputes of noble Houses... and suppressing colonial dissent.

There's a pause, but it doesn't feel uncomfortable. That, and I haven't stopped playing.

... I swear if I weren't in the same outfit as him, I wouldn't have to resort to such trickery...

"Chloeja," Vaughan says, "are they good to fight tomorrow?"

My right hand mutes the strings. "They will be. I'll make sure of it, as I believe you will, Captain."

He nods, glances to my right, and meets my gaze again.

"Captain," I add, "what *are* we extracting tomorrow?"

"High Command wasn't clear on it," Vaughan replies. "They said exactly what I mentioned in the brief: a stele with odd markings on it. Other than that, nothing else."

"Hmm." I don't think Vaughan's withholding anything... I trust he isn't, so if the details are dodgy, it means that Rachael doesn't want us to know the whole picture. And what she could be hiding...? Well, that could be anything.

The stele could be another data bank.

It could be a holy relic... or...

This object could be a Thriaxian weapon. Something catastrophic.

"If everyone hasn't made their peace before the mission," Vaughan says, changing the subject, "maybe they should send a final video-log to their families. The transmitter's open for the next couple of hours."

Before I can answer, a soft chime from the overhead PA speakers rings out.

"*Attention, crew members: the ship's passing through the halo. Prepare for crossing,*" it announces.

Vaughan's brow immediately furrows at this... he's never liked going through wormholes, and he always appears so damn uncomfortable when we do.

There's a brief sensation of unease, but it passes as quickly as it comes, and like every other time, I watch as Vaughan exhales a tense breath, arms folded, his chin slightly lowered.

"A lot of them have." I continue the conversation. "Those who haven't really don't have anyone to write home to."

He raises his face to mine. "Have you sent one yet?" he asks.

"With all due respect, sir," I say, muting the ire of repeating myself, "I'd rather not write home to an audience that neither respects my decision to wear a uniform nor my ambitions for advancement."

"Understood." The concern in Vaughan's eyes betrays the rest of his poker face. "I'm saying, think on it. I sent a video home about an hour ago. I'm not sure how tomorrow's going to end, and because I don't, I'll be operational with no regrets."

"Understood, sir." I restrain a pout. "I will... think on it."

"Good," Vaughan says. "Is there anything else you need?"

I pause. There are several things I want... nothing he could give right now. "No, sir," I reply. "That's all."

"And the squad doesn't need me to come in and give a speech or play that lute?" he presses.

"No, sir. I wanted to keep you informed, considering how close we are to the Thriaxian core."

He nods again, and as he does, I can almost feel him search me. "Okay. As you were, Commander."

Before I stand up, I carefully return Vaughan's e-lute to its home on the ground. "Sir!" I raise my hand in a salute.

Again, his lips curve into the beginning of a smile, and he gently shoos me away with his hand.

As I leave and the flow of air shifts behind me as the door slides shut, a pang of shame runs through me. Frustrated, I run a hand over my face.

Like I have been for the last year and a half, I'm torn.

On one hand, I should toss whatever thoughts I have of Vaughan being *anything* more than my superior officer out the window!

And on the other hand... I should have told him the truth.

I like him. I should have told him I *like him*.

Not Vaughanie, my childhood friend, or the stoic man who leads us all... but the soft-spoken, squishy-hearted Vaughan I've come to know. The one who looks out for us all and bears all... by himself.

"You idiot..." I whisper under my breath.

Chapter 28

VAUGHAN

Mar Hylia 41 High Orbit, seven hours later

From a black dream, my eyes open, and I jolt awake.

The brushed silver above my cabin reflects a bit of light pouring out from flat strip lights along the edges of the ceiling.

"Time?" I ask into thin air.

"*0413 hours,*" a pristine, slightly robotic voice echoes back.

It's pretty early. When I was younger, I'd bolt awake in the early morning, especially when I first arrived on the *Nautilus*.

But this time... something's different.

As I flip my legs over the edge of my bed, a loud alarm cascades throughout my cabin. The ceiling lights above me flip to an ominous shade of red.

"*Red alert, red alert!*" the PA above me sounds. "*The* Nineveh *is under attack! All units to battle stations! I repeat, all units to—*"

My entire room thunders all around me, and without thinking, I force on my leggings and undershirt and shove my feet into my nearby boots. I barely get my dog tags overhead before a violent quake almost sends me to the floor.

As I scramble toward the sliding door to my room, I'm jostled and slam right into it. It opens, sending me tumbling out into the open corridor.

Suddenly... I hear a deafening... blood-curdling shriek.

Not from any person... no Terran could make that sound.

I whimper, hands trembling as I search for the source of the cry. In front of me, there's nothing. Just a large rectangular porthole out into the starry vacuum of space...

All of a sudden, there's a *thud*... followed by a loud *pop*. It almost knocks me on my ass, and an enormous collection of circles instantly obscure the view of the stars... they suction to the other end of the glass. They and tiny spines drag against the porthole, screeching as they do. The grey backdrop of this monstrosity creeps slowly. I want to run away, but I can't.

Screams follow. Terran shouts and cries of terror to either side of me.

Snap out of it. Move, damn you...!

"Move!" I shout to myself.

Without thinking, I run. Bolting down the corridor, I bump others fleeing in every direction.

It's chaos out here. Naval personnel, half- or barely dressed in uniform, race past me.

Come on... think.

First, warn the squadron, and then, to the mechs.

To my right, Chloeja's cabin comes into view... and before I approach it, she springs out, frantically searching around.

"... Vaughan!" she shouts.

"Get to the hangar!" I cry back, motioning my arm forward.

More of my pilots spill out into the corridor, as crazed as everyone around them.

"To the hangar!" I repeat, bellowing as I shove my way forward.

As I leap over the lip of a bulkhead, a low creaking sound groans behind me.

"W-what in God's name is *that?*" someone says.

I stop, do a full one-eighty, and witness in horror as the shape of a tentacle slithers along the row of portholes to my right. In the centre of the corridor, full of rushing Naval personnel, the side of the hull buckles inward.

"Damn it!" I shout, scrambling for the bulkhead seal.

I press it a split second before the sound of howling pressurized air threatens to suck me and everyone else on this side of the corridor in. The last thing I hear before the bulkhead seals and I tumble forward toward the blast doors, is a terrified, collective scream... then silence.

"Ohh," I say, trembling.

No, shove it down, and get up.

My body obeys me, pushing off from the cold floor and moving in the direction of the briefing hall and, beyond it, the hangar.

The crowd's thinning out as I approach, and as I fly through the door, my pilots are waiting for me.

There are seven of us in the room... and no one's clamouring behind me.

"... Where's Serena?" I ask, scanning the room repeatedly.

Lynette tears up, crossing her arms in pain.

I scan over my remaining pilots. Takashi, Rasmus, and Ophelia are missing too.

Chloeja, next to the door of the armoury, glances over her shoulder at me. Her golden green eyes are awash with sadness, and she briefly shakes her head at me.

Just like Yuri... they're gone.

"Damn it..." I whisper, lowering my head.

Again, my hands shake. Tears well up and threaten to fall. I raise my head. "We're out of time. Grab a gun and suit up."

"Sir!" they shout.

Chloeja slams the door panel with her fist, opening the way forward.

As we pour out of the armoury, rifles in hand, the *clank* of our boots hits the catwalk of the hangar. What's missing, though, is the maintenance crew I've come to expect. None of them are here.

"Protocol three," I boom, keeping pace toward my mech.

We've drilled enough to know that means no techs on the floor, no protective suits, and to prepare to fly dirty. It's unpredictable, and the repairs from the last mission might not even be complete yet... but we've trained for that.

We've drilled for almost anything.

"Copy!" they echo back to me in unison.

As another rumble shakes overhead, my hands tremble. We're running out of time.

I fly past Chloeja, Xalpha, and Shao-Shi and into a running leap up to my cockpit hatch. A loud *bang* sends me off course, and I almost fall into the drop bay below. The thirty-seven victory marks flash past me as I grapple onto the ledge of the hatch and furiously key in the release codes.

I hold on to the gangway rail for dear life, and a depressurizing hiss escapes around the seam. The hatch drops in front of me, and I peer down over my shoulder.

"See you planet-side!" I shout to my pilots below.

"Audeamus!" they collectively boom toward my back.

I practically dive into my seat, head first, and reorient my body up and drop my feet to the pedals.

The cries of the ship's crew rattle around in my head as I swing the console up. Recurring images of people being tossed around, sucked out into space... and their shouts of terror mingled with unanswered cries for help.

Forget it. I can't do anything. Not for them.

But I can protect my remaining pilots.

The display in front of me boots up the OS, and the video feed inside my spherical cockpit shows me a harrowing explosion inside the hangar. Following another violent quake, fire pours from above.

My hands rest on the controls, and something dawns on me: this monstrous machine is my only salvation. The other mechs come to life, and I know that it must be the same for the other pilots. When I don't hear the comms, I glance down at my feet.

I pick up the helmet, try to place it over my head and...

"... Shit."

There's nothing to fasten it to. So I reach in and grab a small device and clamp it over the top of my ear.

Immediately, sounds of different fleet transmissions flood my ear as they're displayed onscreen. The comm in my ear focuses in on a ship-wide emergency broadcast:

"*Mayday, mayday!*" Captain Hawthorne pleads. "*I repeat, the* Nineveh *is lost. Requesting escorts! The life rafts won't hold! Anybody! I repeat–*"

The feed cuts out.

"*Take a deep breath in, and hold it,*" the OS chimes.

I draw in a laboured breath, followed by three seat-needles entering my back.

"*Breathe again.*"

The exhale that leaves my lips is sure, controlled, and laced with searing hatred.

I run a command into the console and focus the comms on the local battle group and the squad frequency.

"Manual drop on my command," I say through gritted teeth.

"*Sir!*" they reply.

The OS has already primed the reactor – checks all good. The last command I type is an emergency release of all drop bay mechs, ready to go at the press of a button.

"This is Cronus 1," I say. "Preparing to drop."

A quick sinking sensation grips me as my mech falls through a lake of fire. One that briefly follows me as I'm instantly expelled into the vacuum of space below.

The shoulder thrusters propel me down, faint stars zooming up as I go. And as I follow them, on the top of the concave display is the *Nineveh*, slowly being taken apart by a massive... thing.

What that thing is, or how to describe it, I'm not sure. It's like a mythical leviathan... or a menacing Ominii, like the ones in the tanks on Hynej.

This one has hundreds of giant protruding tentacles, ripping apart panels and using several more to crush the ship. In the blink of an eye and a blinding flash of light, a contracted nuclear explosion is all that's left of the *Nineveh*.

And to the right of it, an enormous Thriaxian carrier emerges out of cloak, with thousands of smaller craft swarming the wreckage. They break off, engaging three Terran starships exiting through three wormholes.

"*Warning, warning,*" the OS cautions, "*SERUM volumes at two per cent capacity. Risk of high-G hemorrhaging and blackout without chemical assistance. SERUM volumes at—*"

I press mute on the prompt and sink further into my seat as my mech nears the surface of Mar Hylia 41.

Beyond the scope of the HUD, the low orbit of the planet's caught in a maze of return fire.

Terran destroyers and battleships send one volley of plasma beams after another at Thriaxian warships. Between them, small fighter craft dart and dodge laser charges, and some Thriaxian pilots crash into Terran carriers.

If that weren't bad enough, large particle beams from Thriaxian orbital batteries fly in front of me. Their targets: the carriers and drop ships in formation.

"*–I repeat,*" Admiral Alvarah cries, "*any officers still alive, proceed with Operation Spear. Any officers still breathing, do you copy?*"

"I copy," I say, synching in, watching as his video feed pops up on my display.

"*Whom am I speaking to?*" the admiral replies.

"Vaughan," I say, flying closer to my pilots in formation, "I'm a captain with the Titans. Cronus Squadron."

"*Copy that, Captain,*" the admiral says, his tone grim, "*you're in the fire now, son. Remember: link up with your men, and keep to the operation. I repeat, Operation Spear is a go. Godspeed, Captain.*"

"Roger that," I say, synching up the logistics panel to my pilots. "Over and out."

The video feed from the admiral flickers out into static, with a distant shout coming from behind him. The signal goes dead.

My hand quakes over the comms button to my squadron. Their vitals are lit on my screen... and I hesitate as I only count six others active onscreen.

"Cronus Squadron, sound off," I call, taking full possession of both controls.

"Hanging in!" Lynette replies.

"All green!" Xalpha says with a forced grin.

"Not dead," Chloeja groans, her unimpressed onscreen.

"Good to go!" Horatio, Oreiga, and Janessa reply in unison.

They're fine...

A wave of relief washes over me... but only for a moment.

Another large particle beam shoots past us, and two more in succession from below.

"Keep tight in formation," I order. "Like I said on the ship, Operation Spear is a go. Stick together, drop together, and fall to ground zero. Clear?"

"Yes, sir!" they echo back to me.

Let's do this.

The HUD shows the distance to the planet's surface deceasing, as we accelerate on a steep arc.

LADAR sensors show the rest of the squadron's mechs forming a triangle formation. Close enough together for blanket-wide shielding.

"*Particle charge detected,*" the OS says, "*brace for impact.*"

Not a moment too soon.

A flick of my wrist, and a wide shield under our feet fans out beneath us. One flash, then two erupt below, and even though nothings hitting us, the shockwave vibrates throughout my cockpit and shakes my controls.

"Cronus 9," I order, "send a downward volley."

"*Roger,*" Xalpha replies.

Out of the corner of my eye, I see her draw her long-range cannon from the side of her Xenomech. Even in the burn of the drop, Xalpha keeps the weapon steady.

"*Firing volley one,*" she shouts. "*Firing volley two!*"

A Terran Destroyer-class ship banks parallel to my port side, accompanied by a sea of drop ships and life rafts. I hope the Heavies have had more luck than us... they're going to need it.

"*Confirmed hit,*" Chloeja says. "*That's one down.*"

"Copy," I say. "That should give them a good head start."

Even though everything's slowly coming together... my hands won't stop trembling.

It doesn't matter. We're going in.

Chapter 29

VAUGHAN

Everything's louder without my helmet on.

The burn from the reactor, the creaking of metal joints, and the sound of particle beams contacting the shields... all of it cascades around me. The blood-red lighting, more ominous without protection, only serves as a reminder of the peril I'm diving into. And what's worse, if I *am* hit in the right place, that's it.

"Evasive manoeuvres!" I order.

Each Xenomech in my squadron fans out, engaging their own energy shields and zigzagging through the air.

The HUD shows a large scattering of Thriaxian forces, thousands of meters below, and all of them are firing upward. As my hands tighten around the controls, every movement I make feels impulsive.

A pulsing red dot blinks in the cartography section onscreen. The target, dubbed "Gaia's Tier" is a citadel of Thriaxian make, and all around me, the Republic drop ships dive bomb toward the surface of the planet. Even as one ship after another is bombed into oblivion, they keep going.

"*For His Excellency!*" I hear repeatedly on the comms.

I'll give it to the Heavies: they're committed.

As explosions dot the horizon, flames lick the edges of my mech's arms on entry, and below, tidal waves crash on onyx cliffs and small charred craters.

Without my suit, the inside of the cockpit is hotter than any other drop I've done. The outer shields will hold... it doesn't help me collect what's left of my nerves.

"Stay with me!" I call to my pilots.

There's no response. Since we fell into the troposphere, all comms have fizzled into static. Visuals onscreen flicker with static at best and go white at worst. At least no one in my squadron has flipped blue.

They're still alive.

"*Captain!*" Chloeja shouts, her comms distorted. "*We're off course, two hundred fifty-three kilometres from target!*"

I double-check the HUD, run the navigation arc... and the ridge *is* horribly far off.

"Shit," I mutter.

Out of the corner of my eye, I see the large destroyer cutting a path for us slowly implode, scattering a huge nuclear fireball hundreds of kilometres away.

"Brace for impact!" I cry.

An explosion rattles me from side to side, causing an unholy groaning outside the cockpit. The roar of the thrusters gets louder as the surface closes in until it erupts in a rage of protest. Anti-grav thrusters kick into full gear, and my mech hovers a couple of meters above the blackened ground.

"*Orders, sir!*" Chloeja asks.

We've lost the element of surprise. They know we're here.

We can't roll up to the top of the citadel, or Thriaxian forces will overwhelm us.

And rows of enemy defences shield the backdoor of the tier.

Come on man, think.

".. *on my position. I repeat, our battalion commander has fallen; the 203rd is being manned by Lieutenant Deckard. We're proceeding through, but we won't last long.*"

"Stand by," I say to Chloeja.

I'm quick to flip the channel, homing in on the 203rd's frequency.

"Lieutenant," I say, intercepting his transmission, "this is Cronus 1. Where are you?"

"*Cronus what? Who the hell is this?!*" Deckard squawks back.

"Captain Vaughan 634-AFZ. I'm with the Titan outfit."

"*You're serious?*" he asks.

"Dead serious," I reply, seeing onscreen as my men drop near to my position, "now tell me, Lieutenant, where are you and your men?"

"*Dropping to sector Bravo, sir,*" he answers. "*I've got Heavies in the air, artillery falling from the sky, but we lost our air support with the* Delgata *and* Corvinos *carrier... my XO's fried. LZ's been compromised. We're on our own.*"

"No, you're not," I say, readying my controls. "We're on our way. Shoot me your coordinates."

"*S-sir!*" Deckard replies.

As I flip the lieutenant's in-air data into my nav screen, I switch comms back to my squadron.

"Pilots," I begin, "shit's fubared. We're off course, but we have an in to the target."

With a quick flurry of keystrokes, I share the recalculated path to the citadel. Everyone's picture shows up onscreen, and they all seem like they get what I'm selling.

"We're linking up with the 203 and the 112," I say, "and we're covering as their escort until we can get to the base of the tier. Clear?"

"*Audeamus!*" they shout.

"Thought so." I push forward my controls and accelerate into the air. "All of you, with me!"

There they are.

"Approaching offensive line," I confirm to my pilots and the 203. "Who's taking point on the rear?"

"*112's covering artillery,*" Deckard tells me, "*but we can't get through. The first wave got blown to hell...*"

"Copy," I say. "We'll get you to sector Bravo."

Flying alongside us are large drop ships and Juggernaut-class Heavy Infantry mechs. They're smaller than us and an easy target for scatter fire. They're mobile, I'll give them that, but their shields are terrible.

"*Hey, who was that?*" another unknown voice chimes in on the line but is marked with Deckard's 203rd regiment.

"*He's a captain,*" Deckard replies. "*He and his pilots are Titans.*"

"*You're shitting me. Is he on now?*" the same unknown voice enquires.

"*Roger that,*" Deckard says. "*It's not every day we get to fly with a Titan, let alone a whole squadron.*"

"Copy," I say. "Who's asking?"

"*Major Quintus, Argyll outfit with the 203rd. You honour us with your presence.*"

"*Yeah, we're sure to win now!*" a younger, more enthusiastic voice adds to the feed.

Who the hell else is listening in on our channel?!

"*Roger that,*" Deckard says with a laugh. "*Captain, you leave the rolling barrage to us. Watch the sky for us, and keep 'em off our ass.*"

"On it." I pull back on the controls. "Cronus 3," I say to Lynette, "take Cronus 6 and 7, tail behind, and cover our flank."

"*Copy!*" she exclaims.

"Chloeja," I instruct, "muster the rest for an intercept run. We're going hunting."

"*Got it,*" she answers, throwing a 'shaka' sign onscreen.

The thrust ramps up as I press forward, dodging massive particle beams from the surface and air.

As Lynette, Janessa, and Oreiga break formation to the rear, the rest follow me up a couple of hundred meters, closer to Thriaxian aerial Sentinels.

"Engage," I order.

On the LADAR map, Chloeja spears ahead, loaded cannon in hand.

Shao-Shi, dual-wielding pulsar blades, takes mark on the train's left flank alongside Xalpha, and Horatio's got my wing. Me, I've got my eye on three hostiles heading for the artillery corps.

One beam flies past my shoulder as I evade it narrowly in a bank.

The pulsar blades on the wrists of my unit extend, hanging outward as the arms drag back.

I swipe up, cutting the first Sentinel in half, blue explosive plasma dancing in the night air.

As the second rolls, turns one-eighty in my direction, Horatio blasts a charge from his rifle, sending the hostile spiralling to the ground below.

"*That's one,*" Horatio says with a grin.

"Only thirty-three million to go," I add.

"*Quick work, sir,*" he replies. "*There won't be any paint left for victory marks when I'm done!*"

"Roger that." My lips twist into a smile.

As the airspace opens up, one downed Sentinel at a time, more drop ships from orbit converge with the train toward the tier. The rolling barrage takes out most of the turrets in our way and completely flattens Thriaxian barricades.

We punched a hole.

And what's more, the base of the tier is only a couple of kilometres away. We've blended in with the train up to this point. They've got this from here.

"Deckard," I say, patching through to the 203 and 112, "Cronus is breaking away. Time to do our part."

"*Roger that, Captain,*" he replies. "*Good luck down there... and thank you.*"

I nod, signing off the comms and securing the squadron's main line.

"Commander," I say to Chloeja, "commence phase two."

"*Copy that!*" she replies, visibly breaking formation from the train. "*Lieutenants, this is it. We covered for the Heavies, and now they're covering for us. Don't let their blood go to waste.*"

"*Ma'am!*" the rest of the squadron echoes, following her toward the target.

I'm the last to leave the onslaught of drop ships converging on the tier. And as I bank my unit right, out of the corner of my screen I see hundreds of drop ships offload their cargo on up the slope of the tier: power-armour-wearing infantry. My rear camera shows a horizontal rain of laser beams cut across the middle of the slope, returning fire from the heavily fortified top of the ridge.

"*Got the entrance on my sights,*" Shao-Shi announces. "*I'm breaching their firewall now. This might take a while, their code is... complex.*"

By the time the base of the tier is only a few hundred meters away, most of the squadron is already defending the perimeter to its entrance.

The proximity gauge rapidly counts down to zero, ending with a sudden jostle and an added creaking of the mech's joints on landing.

Half of the pilots have their rifles aimed at the skies, protecting the others near the door.

The entrance itself is massive. Like with other Thriaxian installations I've seen, the height of the opening is at least a hundred meters tall and about as much wide. But unlike their other military facilities, a translucent barrier of energy seals the door.

"*Anyone get a bearing on* what's *keeping us out?*" Chloeja asks. "*We should just blast through.*"

"*It's alien tech,*" Shao-Shi replies. "*I wouldn't mess with it, Commander. We might blow ourselves up instead.*"

"*Noted,*" she says. "*Let's get in quick. We're sitting ducks as we are.*"

"*Copy!*"

I'm caught between the calm of this respite, scanning the horizon for any Thriaxian expeditionary forces, and the rattling of nerves, coming out in the tremor of my fingers, reminds me of one absolute fact:

I am never *truly* safe.

As I make a sweep, shoulder to shoulder with my men, a single bright star stands out in the blackened haze of the overcast sky above. My camera locks onto the signature, magnifies it...

It's him. The Demon.

"Chloeja," I say, "he's here."

Her face onscreen freezes. "*Shao-Shi,*" she says, "*hurry your ass up.*"

It hits me.

All of that fear and every haunting unknown variable above me disappears... right into a red sea of furious anger.

"Commander, stay with the squad," I command, teeth clenched.

"*Captain?*" Chloeja asks, confused.

"I need to take care of something," I clarify.

There's a pause. And right when I think there won't be any protest, my cockpit rocks as a mechanical arm grabs the wrist of my unit.

It's Chloeja's.

Her video display signals blue, patching me to her private line.

"*You're not going alone...*" she says, steel-eyed, "*... sir.*"

"Out of the question." The incoming bogey quickly approaches as I speak.

"*You don't have to fight him alone!*" Chloeja protests. "*We're out here... I'm out here, fighting for my life* again, *and I can't watch you go off* only to shield us! *Xhyr trained us better than that!*"

I want to say 'fuck off', pull rank... but right now, I don't think she'd listen.

And besides, it's true. I have been shielding them, ever since Hynej.

"What about the lieutenants?" I ask. "There're only six of them left, and I need someone to command them on the ground."

"*The kids are fine,*" Chloeja assures me. "*And if anything else, if things go to shit, Xalpha's a big girl. I'd trust her with command in the interim.*"

The clock's running out. The Demon is only a few hundred kilometres out and gaining speed.

Chloeja's mech lets go of me, and she bolts from the ground before I can stop her.

"Stop!" I shout.

She hovers a hundred meters above me, not taking 'no' for an answer.

"*Also,*" Chloeja adds, "*you still have to protect my ass up there. You promised, and I'm banking on that.*"

Damn it!

I jerk the controls back, shooting up to where she is.

"Pilots," I say, flipping to the squadron's channel, "bogey ahead. Cronus 2 and I are going to take care of it."

The odd gasp comes from Lynette and Shao-Shi, but the rest seem resolved onscreen.

"*Sir!*" they reply.

With the press of a button, I isolate myself to my and Chloeja's line.

"Fine." The muscles in my face contort into a scowl. "Don't do anything reckless. We'll take him down together... for good, this time."

"*Roger that, Captain.*" Chloeja gives a devilish grin.

As much as I hate to admit it, I *do* need her. All those times, I came close, but I can't do this without my pilots.

I can't do this without Chloeja.

Chapter 30

The Demon

Mar Hylia 41 Low Orbit, 30 minutes earlier

The doors before me open, and through a blue-lit hallway, I step out into the hangar.

As I enter, my brothers and sisters await me. All those brave Thriaxian warriors in my charge regard me with admiring glances and their fists held close to their hearts.

There are no words to say as I pass.

The Terrans have come, and now they've even evaded the leviathan guardians of this world. I've tried to stop them, halt their progress to the Matriah... even so, they're here.

My feet carry me to the middle unit along a transparent walkway, one I've become well acquainted with in recent times. I glance up, and the visage of Ix'Nier, my mech, stares down at me.

Every joint held together by electromagnetism, impermeable to damage, connects to form the body of my suit of armour. All of it suspended together but never touching.

With my hand raised, the atoms of the wall to my cockpit separate, creating a hole. The elongated fingers of my gauntlet grip the rim of my helmet, and I put it on.

Code populates the right-hand side of my visor, and a soft blue rain of life-support checks drips down my sights and vanishes through the bottom. Suddenly, my helm mutes a loud pressurizing hiss as it connects to the rest of my suit, and various members of my crew stand by around me.

For the Matriah.

A loud chest thump echoes in unison across the hangar, and even with my helmet on, I can hear it.

One minor leap carries me into the air. With the engines off, a free fall into the heart of my armour sends me directly into the well-lit centre of the cockpit ahead.

With another wave of my hand, the hull of my craft re-seals, each atom recombining into solid matter.

As my hands hover over two orbs on either side of the cockpit, I remember how distressed my second officer was. The Terrans have pushed this far into our core worlds, destroyed our facilities...

... and now they seek to defile one of our sacred temples...

"Everyone," I say, "clear the hangar."

The hull around me turns transparent, fixed with gauges marking reserves of energy for the reactor and weapons systems. Life support and logistics pop up and stay fixed to the bottom right of my helmet's visor. Through the transparent edges and arcs of my mech, I watch as the crew of my ship evacuate behind the blast door to the hangar.

A flick of my fingers activates the ground below me, separating the atoms for a clear drop.

Alright, Ix'Nier... this could be our last battle.

Loud humming erupts above the shoulder clamps anchoring my mech to the hangar.

It launches me down.

Despite that, without the Terran machinations of chairs or straps, I securely levitate in a standing position, suspended by the engineering of my power armour, as the cockpit counters the G-force around me.

Gaining full control of the mech, I peer down at the planet below and make my descent. The orbs hang in the open sphere of the cockpit, floating below my armoured hands, and as I motion my arms forward, a string of landing coordinates stream down my helmet's visor.

Despite our best defences, the Terrans are almost upon the Citadel of Rau'Shaktir. With gaining speed the anti-gravity thrusters at my back launch me closer to the surface. If the reports are true, *he's* there.

The Scourge of Altier.

The same Terran pilot I first encountered on Talmorah.

No matter how many times my people or I have tried to disarm him, prevent him from encroaching further into our space, he's always there. System after fallen system... and now, if he obtains that relic... it's all over.

"No," I say aloud.

This far and no further.

I won't let this spirited madman take *anything more* from us.

Through the troposphere, one Terran battleship fires a sea of particle beams at me, and their fighter craft pour out of the adjacent carriers like a malignant swarm.

No matter.

The concentrated energy at my wrists protrudes into blades, and while I'm at the ready, two particle cannons await a simple flick of my wrist. Whatever the Terrans have to throw at me, let them.

As the destroyer comes closer, I fire a particle charge from my left, tearing a hole through their energy shields. The door's open.

My mech passes through, and with four swift cuts, I fly past the destroyer's keel, leaving behind an imploding mass of metal and fire. In the narrowing view of my rearview, a fission explosion cuts through the air, incinerating the tiny craft darting here and there.

"There," I say, focusing in on a blinking target.

No, more than one.

Two Terran mech signatures are fast on approach. One of them I recognize immediately.

"You..." The words seethe out.

The Scourge did much to augment his mech, even mirroring my armour's design. I'd be flattered if I weren't so insulted.

Blades armed, the orbs in my hand heat up as I increase acceleration.

I fly by the two of them, twist in the air, and send a cover volley of charges right for their ace. The sky lights up, turning the night into day, and it's in this moment I bank right... and swoop up.

He disappears from sight, but my sensors track him regrouping with his comrade.

A single piercing screech in my helm warns me of a rear attack. It's the Scourge's wingman.

I squint, peering into the metal workings of the second pilot's mech and into their cockpit.

There's a woman there, gripping her manual controls and talking. She seems livid.

Zooming out, I bend my right fingers back, activating the quantum flux in the reactor. If I'm going to down these two, I have to be quick.

As I wait, the female pilot dives in, shoots three blasts, and follows up with a wide slash of her blade. I twist my mech around, evading, and return fire.

But the Scourge comes in, blocking the charges with a handheld shield, deflecting it to the side. The way they fight, coming so close to harm's way... they must be hell-bent on their own demise.

"Flux activated." The prompt on my visor notifies me.

Well, if that's your choice... both of yours... then strike at me.

It'll be your last.

As it stands, I can't spare you even if I want to.

It's my life or theirs.

As I move my wrist forward, the flux is engaged. Every subatomic particle in my mech, myself included, shifts through the strings between their crafts and mine, and for a split second, I hop between the veil in dimensions, a quantum drift... to be placed right where I need to be to strike him down.

My blade comes down and makes purchase, cutting through his shields... but bounces off a shot from his wingman's cannon.

Damn.

This isn't the first time a pilot has intervened to save his life. Talmorah comes to mind.

So, if I'm going to take him out, I'll need to take care of her.

The stats pouring down my visor show me the speed and outer G-force straining the metal frame of my mech, but I feel nothing.

"Flux recharged. Activated," my visor advises me.

Once more. One more clean hit, and I've got you.

All three of us dance a mortal step: accelerating, exchanging blows, guarding.

We're only a couple of hundred meters above the citadel, lit underfoot by the combined firepower of the Terrans and my brothers and sisters on the barricades.

While the Scourge is banking left, keen on cutting the outside of my periphery, the female pilot charges in.

Now.

I drift again. My consciousness and recombining matter catch her off guard, and now I have my in.

Right against her shield, pointing directly below her cockpit, is the three-barrelled cannon at my wrist.

Before she can even notice where I am, I fire.

The blast throws me back, and as I deflect a blow from the Scourge, his wingman goes down toward the plateau of the tier. Logistics show a direct hit to her reactor plating. As I guard with my blade, he doesn't follow through; instead, he breaks away, plunging down to follow her.

The female pilot's craft crashes into the plateau, limp like a rag doll. Seconds later, the Scourge hesitates... he drags her off to the side, close to the sealed entrance of the citadel.

If I'm going to exploit the Scourge's weakness, it's now.

I dive my mech down, dive-bombing fast toward him on the surface of the plateau.

My sword's drawn, raised above the head of my mech. But before I can bring it down, the Scourge leaps up and deflects my blade with his.

We accelerate up, flying close enough to take solid swings at one another... but this time it's different.

His movements are erratic. The blows from his blade against mine are tense and furious.

I try to back away, to get a clear shot from my cannons, but he won't let me. We're only a couple of metres apart at all times.

My mech spins in a barrel roll, twisting up, and in a last gambit on my part to blast free.

He gets close, cutting left. But when I try to block, his arm comes up and shoots right under my cockpit.

"Damn it!" I shout.

The transparency of my cockpit crackles, flickering as the optics wires fry against the energy of the blast.

"*Warning.*" A notice flashes red on my visor. "*Citadel has been breached.*"

No... not again.

Even as my screen flickers from the hazy night sky to the opaque dark-tinted chrome sphere from inside my cockpit, I charge forward anyway. I can't let him get away!

Suddenly...

I read: "*Nuclear arms detected.*"

The Scourge launches a torrent of missiles from behind him, coming at me from all sides.

My breath catches. I repel the orbs in my hands and feel the mech around me reverse at high speed, and all the while, the arms of my mech are outstretched, firing every arsenal I have at them.

Contact. The Scourge got me.

Blinding light penetrates through the last remaining optic sensors, causing me to squint.

The surrounding hull shakes violently.

Warning sirens blare, showing the severity of the damage.

When I come to, I find that the hull integrity's compromised.

I'm losing altitude.

The thrusters are torn up, and the whole bottom half of my mech is just *gone*.

"*Reactor compromised*", my visor shows.

I clench my right hand into a fist, blasting the emergency hatch of the cockpit open. Outside the hole, the world outside is spinning wildly. I only have seconds left.

I unclench my fist and stretch out my hand.

"*Ejecting*", my visor reads.

The roar of my overheating reactor overshadows the soft hum echoing around me. But in that one second, a suspension of energy launches me out of my cockpit and into the open air.

"*Suit shielding activated. Brace for impact.*"

Arms raised, legs splayed, I ride the air current down. As I fall, I witness Ix'Nier, right over the top of the citadel, ignite in a burning glow from the reactor.

Another blinding flash hits me, but this time, the light penetrates my eyelids and almost sears my retinas. I have to bury my visor into my arm to stop the pain.

The darkness encroaches again... all but the flying lasers and particle beams meters below me.

Before I crumple to dust on the ground, the shielding around my suit absorbs the shock of the fall, eating up almost all of the power in my suit. The first things to hit the ground are my knees, and with nothing to support the one-point-four tonnes of armour, I fall chest-first down on the charred ground.

"Errgh," I groan, trying to free myself.

No luck.

The only thing that's mobile is the neck joint of my helmet, which is pointing to my left.

The Scourge drags his comrade through the citadel's wormhole entrance. But, before her mech can enter fully, the portal collapses, cutting off its bottom torso.

As blasts erupt around me, making me flinch, I notice in my visor there's enough power to send a message to the fleet.

"Open channel to squadron," I say. "Coordinates listed. I'm down... they broke through." I wince as I talk, unable to move and pinned down by the weight of my suit.

"*We're on our way, Exalted One,*" a voice replies.

"Good," I say. "We need to hurry. The plans have changed."

Chapter 31

VAUGHAN

"Come on!" I shout. "Chloeja, do you read me?!"

Nothing.

The arms of my mech lose their grip on Chloeja's unit, sending me tumbling back. Inside, the cockpit shudders around me.

Even before it stops, I'm struggling to undo the restraints tying me in.

"Let me go!" I cry.

A click follows, and I pour out of my chair, rushing to the emergency release lever.

I slam it down, an explosive *pop* erupts above me, and the door to the cockpit viciously opens wide. I grab the ledge, straining to get topside.

And when I'm finally free, I discover that Chloeja's mech is in shambles. The whole bottom half is sheared in two, and the outside lights are dead.

"Hang on!" As I rush from the bottom half of my mech, I trip over a groove in the unit's hip joint, tumbling forward and hitting a smooth icy surface, elbows first.

Pain radiates across my forearms, but it's drowned out by the panic festering inside my chest. One of my hands reaches past her Xenomech's shoulder and grabs the upper ledge, and I do the same with the other hand. They both ache as I quickly hoist myself up. My feet thunder across the metal plating, echoing all around me.

"Just stay put; don't move!" I'm not sure if she can hear me, but I holler as loud as I can.

It's a small sprint from the shoulder to her cockpit door, but it feels like forever.

"*Commander,*" Oreiga says, "*Captain, you two still there?!*"

"Stand by!" I shout. "Keep pressing through; we'll link up below!"

"*Oh, shit, he's okay... er... copy, sir,*" he replies.

My fingers almost slam into the keypad, furiously typing in the release codes.

I leap out of the way as the door swings open, and when I peer inside, darkness permeates her cockpit.

All the lights are dead.

There's no hum from the reactor.

Chloeja's silhouette is visible from the light above, and she's not moving.

All of it factors through my head in less than a second, and I don't waste the next one.

"Urgh!" I grunt, bolting into the shade of her mech.

My shins sting as I land left of her chair and, with frantic grasping, rip the restraints away from Chloeja's shoulders. The emergency release already expelled the SERUM tubing from her back, and it's lying docile on the floor. Her eyelids are shut, and when I touch her arm, she doesn't respond.

I immediately take her pulse, tilt her chin up, and place my ear above her open mouth.

Nothing.

No breath, erratic pulse.

"M-medic!" I cry, out of impulse.

But there's no one else around. No one else is coming.

Without thinking, I gather her up in my arms and carefully lay her flat on the floor of her cockpit. I clasp both my hands together and start chest compressions. Thirty of them. My arms burn each time I press down, and by the thirtieth, I firmly place my lips over hers and breathe into her, keeping her chin tilted up.

Nothing.

I take another deep breath, clamp down, and give it everything I have.

No response.

"No..." I say, compressing in a timespan that turns seconds into hours. "You're not done fighting. You're going to pull through this!"

An otherworldly terror strikes me as I press down on her chest.

If I stop, she'll die.

Right now, her life is in my hands... I can't stop. I won't leave her behind. My hands release, my lips on hers, my heart going to whatever god will listen.

"Live!" I shout, giving her one more rescuing breath.

As I rise back up... her eyelids tremble and open, and as her golden green irises go wide, her pupils narrow.

Chloeja loudly gasps, like a volt viciously surged throughout her whole body. She convulses, for two seconds, but her chest rises and falls. It feels like a lifetime has passed, but as my fingers find an active pulse against her wrist, I sigh a staggered breath of relief.

She coughs, teary... but she's breathing.

Before I realise it, I'm lunging forward and wrapping my arms around her shoulders.

"...Ow." She slaps me on the side, causing me to bolt back.

Despite the faux pas, I can't help but notice how her gaze won't leave mine. What she means by it, or what's behind them, I'm not sure.

Static erupts in my ear, bringing me and Chloeja to the present.

"*Captain,*" Admiral Alvarah begins, "*are you and Cronus Squadron still active down there?*"

"Copy that," I reply. "We're advancing to the next phase of the operation with what's left of us."

"*Roger that, Captain. We're sending in a fourth wave now. Scanners show you've got some resistance on your tail.*"

"Copy," I say, opening the channel to my remaining pilots, "we'll give 'em hell till then."

"*Roger. Over and out,*" he says as the connection ends with crackling static.

A distant rumble echoes outside of the cockpit.

"Can you move?" I ask.

"Neck and arms... yes," Chloeja says, rotating her head and shoulders, "but legs are shit."

"Copy." I swoop down.

"C-Captain," she stammers, "what are you doing?"

"Getting us out of here," I reply.

She gives a quick yelp as I scoop her up, keeping my hands under her knees and around her shoulders.

I hold her close, and we escape the darkness behind us.

My feet land on the smooth crystalline floor below, and I double-time it to my Xenomech.

"Hey!" Chloeja protests. "I-I can probably walk; let me down!"

"No time," I counter. "Hold tight."

She does as I say, wrapping her arms behind my neck as I use my right hand to climb up the thigh of my mech, the maw of my cockpit in sight.

"Hang on," I say, leaping down. "Things are going to get rough ahead."

We both land near the edge of my seat, and I rest her on the edge of it as the reactor starts up.

I keep one hand on the left-hand control and another on her shoulder. I gently press down on two buttons, and the mech rights itself. Once level, I reach down and pull Chloeja up, setting her down in my lap. Her head rests against my upper right shoulder, and her soft hair brushes against my bare skin.

"There's nothing to fasten to in here," I say, strapping myself in, "so don't let go."

I glance down, and watch her nod with trusting eyes.

I seal the cockpit shut, straining my already pained forearms as I pull the lever downward, and press my back into the seat.

"*Take a deep breath in, and hold it,*" the OS says through my earpiece.

My lungs expand, and the discomfort of three needles enters the ports on my back. The map to the object, already illuminated on my HUD, guides my path.

"*Breathe again.*"

Chapter 32

CHLOEJA

... What the hell is happening?

"Hang on tight," Vaughan says again.

My arms tighten around his neck as the hum of the reactor burns into a steady roar.

I let out a gasp as the mech ploughs forward, zeroing in on one warp gate after another. The entire facility is one enormous maze.

"*Hostiles confirmed!*" I hear from my earpiece. "*Blades ready. We'll converge on the central chamber!*"

That's Oreiga.

"Copy," Vaughan says. "We're on our way."

"*Is that the commander?*" Oreiga adds, looking me up and down onscreen.

"Yeah," Vaughan replies. "Chloeja's hurt. Her mech's torn to shit, but she's riding with me."

"*Roger that!*" Lynette says.

His muscles tense and release against the back of my head with every shift of his controls.

Out of the corner of my right eye, I see the HUD track Sentinels, and with the flick of a button, the hostile units disappear into a rage of fire in our wake.

My brows slowly crease into a frown, and I piece together the events of the last few minutes.

"Oh," I say in a soft whisper.

He *scooped me up*, tossed me in here, and now my ass is *in his lap*. His arms almost seem to barricade me from the oncoming assault, the bare skin of his biceps warm to the touch.

What the...?!

We pass through a sudden explosion, dive through a barricade, and jump through another portal.

"Don't let go," Vaughan cautions me, his voice firm but caring.

Oh, no, I won't.

"Got it." I wrap my arms tighter around his neck.

And on top of that, this is the first time I've seen Vaughan fight from *inside the cockpit of a Xenomech*. I've never been this close.

Looking up, I notice every inch of his face is plastered with determination. His gaze is intense. Passionate.

As we dip down, falling through a vertical air duct, I can't ignore the weakness in my neck.

"Ugh," I grunt.

I want to rest my head against him. I want to do more.

But... that would be right between his shoulder and chest. What would Vaughan think?

I sigh.

When have I ever cared? Really? When the hell did that start?

I don't second-guess myself. I take what I want.

And right now, while he's fighting for our lives, that's *exactly* what I want.

So that's what I do.

Thump

I don't peer at the HUD. Against the surface of his chest, I can barely make out our port side, and with every sharp movement Vaughan makes, I jostle more.

But I don't care... I honestly never have, and should never have.

What grabs my attention, however, is the SERUM gauge muted in the far-left corner of the display.

My eyes grow wide as I reread it: the reserve tank measures at 0%.

With my head pressed against his chest, I gaze up at him, astonished. Horrified, and in awe.

He's doing this *all on his own*. He's fighting G's, the limitations of Terran processing, and every jellyfish bastard we come across... he's a badass.

For the first time in years, I genuinely feel safe. And not because of my might – because of his.

"Brace yourself," Vaughan says.

I gasp, press deeper into his chest, and block out the world.

The toned muscle of his arm holds me tight, right along my waist.

A thunderous quake erupts all around me. But after it stops, he doesn't let go.

Right...

My stomach twists in knots, and I think back to every time I never told Vaughan how I really feel.

Yeah, I followed protocol, didn't stir the waters. I wasn't direct and kept his secrets safe.

What the hell is wrong with me? I hate this. My tear ducts sting, and my vision's obscured and watery. I can't remember the last time I was *this* happy... and so very fucking sad.

How many times did I stop myself from doing what I wanted? Like when I clearly saw that Vaughan needed me? When he was weak, suffering, or plain stupid?!

Too many.

And to top it all off, will I ever get a chance like this again?

Not as long as I serve under him...

Tears roll down my cheeks, and I only have myself to blame. I should have been braver. Honest. Bolder.

"I'm so stupid..." I blurt out, softer than a whisper.

"Hey," Vaughan asks, his voice gentle, "are you okay?"

God, why do you have to speak so sweetly, you asshole?!

And no! Far from it!

"Yeah," I lie, "it's only my chest. It hurts from before."

Okay. A half-truth.

"I'm sorry..." he says, both concerned and contrite.

"N-no, don't apologize," I reply, off my guard. "You saved my life. Again."

I glance up for a second, and he beams down at me.

"Of course I did," Vaughan says, full of conviction.

No, don't say it like that! Not unless you mean it! The way he speaks hits harder in this moment, and he could say anything and it would feel great.

My cheeks are flush, wet with tears... and we're flying into the jaws of death.

Great.

"Vaughan...?" I ask, but suddenly stop myself.

What's onscreen overshadows my moment of courage: the end of a long drop as we enter a large anti-chamber with an enormous shrine-like structure in the centre.

"Yeah," he says, "I see it too."

... Not what I meant. But, yeah.

The target is down there, only a few metres away.

"Captain! Resistance is thin down here; we have a clear shot to the package!" Janessa's cherub face pops up on the screen as she says this, I crane my neck to see for myself.

There're *dozens* of Thriaxians down there, standing near the shrine! But they're barely wearing any armour.

The mech's targeting system jumps everywhere onscreen, zeroing in on their ground forces... but when I turn to Vaughan's hands, they're still. His fingers hover above the buttons for the cannons and any of the new features his mech has.

He's hesitating.

"Vaughan?" I ask.

"... Why aren't they firing...?" he says.

Plasma charges rip through the air, coming from the rest of our squadron.

Purple blood from the Thriaxians splatters across the alabaster surface of the shrine's plateau, but nothing's being shot back at us.

They raise their hands.

A haunting, echoing sound reverberates inside my head. It's jarring and almost makes me sick.

[*Come no closer. We mean you no harm.*]

... That came from my head! That serene, otherworldly voice came from *my mind*.

"*The hell?!*" Xalpha spits.

"*D-did you hear that!*" Shao-Shi adds.

"*They hack our comms?!*" Oreiga shouts.

I snap my head up at Vaughan, and he's not saying anything. He's shook.

Even with all of that, Janessa charges ahead, rifle drawn.

"Wait!" Vaughan cries. "Cease fire!"

"What?" I ask, sensing the tremor of the mech touching down on solid ground.

"They're unarmed," he says, wincing.

His hands shake again... It's worse now than before.

"Hey—" I try to reassure him.

"Stay here," Vaughan says, lowering his mech to kneel, "and whatever happens, don't move."

"Sir," I say, nodding.

He unbuckles his restraints, and his soft hands hoist me up, rotate me ninety degrees, and sit me in his seat.

The hatch to the cockpit opens, and in front of me, a soft blue-grey light hangs in the air. I can't determine where it's coming from, but there's a shallow pool of purple blood surrounding a pile of Thriaxian bodies.

Vaughan leaps down, staying in my line of sight, approaches a prone Thriaxian combatant, and kneels. He gets closer, side arm drawn, inspecting the body with a saddened expression.

"They're priests..." he says, holstering his gun.

[You must...] I hear, watching the Thriaxian reach up a shaky, long-fingered hand at Vaughan.

Vaughan reaches down, both hands pressed against the Thriaxian's open wound to stop the bleeding.

"*Sir!*" Xalpha cries. "*What are you doing?!*"

He raises his hand toward her mech, preventing her from approaching.

"This is wrong," Vaughan says. "They didn't do anything."

The Thriaxian priest narrows its eyelids, seemingly in pain. [What lives will die...] it says, [and what is dead shall live.]

Vaughan's face goes pale, his arms trembling.

He backs away as far as his arms will stretch while keeping them pressed against our enemy.

That same priest moves its arm to Vaughan's right, pointing maybe fifty metres away.

In the centre of this shrine, is a large rectangular object. It's dark, tinted with bronze, and seems to be marked with inscriptions, but I can't make them out this far off.

The Thriaxian's arm drops, and Vaughan gasps.

"Xhyr said it might be a weapon," he says, "or a power source of some kind. Rachael wouldn't say."

"Captain?" I ask.

"But," Vaughan continues, "if it really is such a powerful artefact, why is it being guarded by priests?"

I open my mouth, hoisting myself closer to the edge of the open hatch... and a sudden shiver runs over my body.

Vaughan *immediately* gets up, arms at his sides. He's clearly shocked. And he turns away from me, toward the object ahead.

A soft howl blows past the maw of Vaughan's cockpit. I peer further out of his mech, and a gentle wind current brushes along my hair, blowing behind me.

The willowy clothing on the dead priests flows and ripples toward the middle of the room, and as the wind grows stronger, Vaughan moves toward the artefact.

"Captain!" I holler.

Nothing. He keeps walking.

"Ngh." I wince, shoving myself out of the mech and collapsing onto the ground. "No, wait!"

The wind grows stronger. I can't get to him.

"Vaughan!" I yell, heaving my arms forward to catch up, and my useless paralyzed legs refuse to budge.

"*Captain, wait! What are you doing?*" Lynette adds, her voice tinted with fear.

The monolithic structure lights up, its etchings coming into sight. They're like hieroglyphs, written in a language that doesn't appear human in origin... or Thriaxian.

As he approaches it, the thundering of several pilots' boots comes from behind me, Shao-Shi, Xalpha, and Oreiga rush past me, rifles in hand.

"Vaughan!" I scream as I loud as I can, struggling to move my legs, arms burning.

Before they can get to him, Vaughan raises his hand and...

... he touches it.

Oreiga grabs Vaughan by the shoulder, followed by Shao-Shi... and both of them fly back several metres in an enormous blast of white light.

My arms tremble, but I keep crawling. Only a few more metres...!

As I move, all the light from the object concentrates at the point where Vaughan's hand is. The wind picks up, causing me to stumble toward him.

"Ahh!" I shriek, tripping over Oreiga.

We're all being dragged toward it, except for Vaughan, his feet being firmly planted to the ground.

As I'm an arm's reach from Vaughan's boots, the howling gale dies.

Stuck in a fetal position, I stare up at him and watch as he crumples to the ground.

Oh, God...

"Commander..." Xalpha groans, on her knees, "what the *fuck* was that?"

I don't answer. I keep moving.

"Vaughan!" I cry.

I scrape my wretched body forward and grab a hold of him.

I'm not knocked away.

"Come on," I say, "you're stronger than this. Stronger than *any* of this!"

I lean over, press my ear to his mouth.

"He's breathing," I blurt out.

"Captain?" Lynette says, not far behind.

"O-oh shit..." Shao-Shi stammers.

I don't lift my head up. The rhythm of his heart against my chest is comforting. And I try to stifle a sob, but it's no use. Tears roll down my cheeks, and my chest hurts worse than before, but I *really* don't care. He's alive. That's all that matters.

As I lift myself up, his eyelids are shut and moving back and forth. Like he's dreaming.

"No, *seriously*," Xalpha stresses, "what the hell did I just see?"

I shake my head. "I-I'm not sure. I told him to stop, and he just kept going. And he *fucking touched it*. What... I don't... how can he...?"

No one answers. And as I glance over my shoulder, every one of our pilots stiffens.

"Commander," Oreiga says, pointing his rifle away from us, "we've got company."

I look past him, and on the perimeter of the shrine, the loud hum of mech reactors grows in the darkness. As if appearing from thin air, Thriaxian Sentinels step out of cloak and slowly approach us. Twenty in total.

They encircle us, and all I can think to do is to shield Vaughan below me.

Then I remember: in the event of capture, same as the Legion, we were surgically installed with a chip behind our ear. Press it for ten seconds, and it completely shuts down our CNS.

Lights out. A quick alternative to captivity, torture, and spilling military secrets.

As I reach for mine, it hits me: Vaughan's might not work. The same might go for Oreiga and Shao-Shi, who got knocked back when they touched Vaughan.

Suicide's not the answer.

So I draw my pistol and arm it.

"Lieutenants," I say, staring each of them in the face, "it's been an honour."

Oreiga nods, rifle at the ready.

But before any of the other pilots arm themselves, that *same* sensation from before overtakes me.

The same haunting echo from before resonates in my mind.

[Stay your hands,] it says, [you will not be harmed.]

Against my better judgement, caught between a rock and a hard place... I do as they say.

Chapter 33

VAUGHAN

One Hour Later

"*Wake up*," a gentle feminine voice whispers.

I'm standing on the surface of an endless sea. On the horizon, sparse clouds move with a strong wind, set on the backdrop of a soft azure sky.

In front of me is a woman. Her very long platinum waving hair obscures her face, blowing to my right.

"*Vaughan...*" the same voice says, like she's whispering right in my ear, "*...wake up.*"

I blink, feeling my world shift, distort, and blend into a consuming darkness.

⋙ ⋘

The darkness snaps away, and in its wake, I stare up at a ceiling of illuminated lines, similar to a circuit board, giving off soft blue and green. They seem to pulse, as though the light itself is alive. It's like what I've seen...

In a Thriaxian facility.

Bolting up to a sitting position, I find myself in a bed. Soft sheets cover me, and my wrists are bound with what appears to be handcuffs woven together in a solid beam of energy. The plus side is that I'm still wearing my uniform.

[Ah, you are awake. Your companions were worried, but the Exalted One assured us you would recover.] I hear in my head.

Who said that?

[I did,] it says.

I freeze.

No one's in front of me, and as I scan the room from left to right, I find my answer.

To my right is an unarmoured Thriaxian, and covering the bottom half of its face is what seems like a canister of water... maybe something to breathe from. Its skin is a light purple, long tendrils protrude from the back of its head, and it has eyes that are almost Terran in appearance.

[You are very astute,] it replies, [and 'it' is a 'she', thank you.]

"Where are they?" I ask aloud, sternly, disregarding her words. "Where are my pilots?"

The shackles are tight around my wrists, and I raise them up, not taking my gaze off this Thriaxian.

[Calm yourself,] she says. [I was given orders to treat you and your companions well. I am the Ini'Shir of this vessel... you might call my title a 'captain' of sorts.]

"They're safe?"

[They are, and they will stay that way. Those are my orders.]

I sigh, dropping my hands.

The Thriaxian woman rises from her chair. [Can you stand?]

Pausing, I wiggle my toes and shift my legs in bed. I shimmy off the comfortable mattress and plant myself down, my boots contacting smooth polished ground.

[Good,] she replies, [and if you are well, I will need you to come with me. The Imir-Tarshau has requested your presence. That was one of the stipulations of your care. That, and those of your pilots.]

"... Who?" I ask.

[The 'Warlord of a Thousand Fleets', our Exalted One and my commanding officer...] she says, trailing off in my thoughts.

"Is something wrong?" I press.

[You have a history with him. I have been informed that the two of you fought several battles against each other, wielding what you call 'Xenomechs'. Recently, his armour was torn asunder in your last fight, before you entered the citadel.]

The Demon.

[Indeed,], she adds, [though it must be providence, since he refers to you as the 'the Scourge.']

Her words hit me like a gut-check... I'm their boogeyman.

"Could you... not read my mind, please?"

[I wish it were possible, but I am afraid I cannot. We are all susceptible to different brainwave frequencies, and it is how we have evolved to communicate with one another.] She extends her hand out toward me, her elongated fingers touching together. [Will you come with me?]

"I will," I say, squaring my hips, "but before I meet with your commanding officer, I must see that my pilots are safe."

[Of course,] she says with a reverent bow. [The Imir-Tarshau expected as much.]

I try to keep up with the wide gait of the Thriaxian guiding me, but it's not easy.

From where I started in the medical wing, the corridors wind and twist organically to different sections of the deck. As alien as this place feels to me, there is a hint of the familiar here: the way the *Nineveh* used to be structured for my squadron, and how the living quarters were so close to everything.

... and the same way the *Nautilus* used to be filled with greenery.

The silver and blue trim of the corridors contrasts nicely with ferns and small trees, with leaves pocked with holes, and as I examine one plant closer, there's chlorophyll rushing through what seem like veins on the surface of the stems, like a river, and venation itself is translucent to the naked eye.

What catches me off guard are flowers and ferns that are *very* familiar. Lilies, well-manicured climbing ivy, and fluffy moss on the rock bed of ornamental fountains. These species of flora appear *identical* to ones I'd find on the *Nautilus*. And unlike the *Nineveh*, the width of the corridors leaves a welcoming impression, like the expanse of a temple.

"Why is this ship so open?" I ask. "Wouldn't a ship like this be filled with water?"

[The Imir-Tarshau prefers it this way,] she replies, not lacking in serenity.

In fact, everything about the way she and other passing Thriaxians move shows a world of grace and elegance, one I have never seen in everyday life. And this isn't even their natural environment.

They're like ageless mysteries, inhabiting an inhospitable void.

[Here we are,] she tells me, [your companions are through this door.]

It opens with a gentle wave of her hand, and beyond it...

"Vaughan!" Chloeja shouts, her eyes wide.

"Captain!" Shao-Shi and Lynette join in.

My squadron... they're all here. Sitting in a well-furnished common room, moving and alive.

"We didn't think you'd wake up!" Oreiga adds.

They rush over. Lynette takes the lead and nearly knocks me back as she grapples me into a hug.

I brace myself... and accept it.

"We didn't know *what* was going to happen!" Lynette stresses.

Her arms tense and suddenly release.

"I-I'm sorry, sir," she says, dodging a swooping clap on my shoulder from Xalpha's hand.

"Forget it," I say, sporting a grin.

In the back, Chloeja watches our pilots circle around me, her arms crossed loosely across her chest. There's an unmistakable smile on her lips as the others clamour around me.

"Chloeja," I say, "you're standing."

"Yeah," she replies, "they, uh... fixed me. I can't say how, but they did."

[As promised,] the Thriaxian assures me, [your companions are safe.]

"Right," I say over my shoulder. "Just give me a moment."

The Thriaxian nods, taking a step back into the corridor.

"Sir?" Shao-Shi asks.

"Their CO wants a word with me," I explain, "It's partly why we're still here."

Chloeja's eyes flash at me.

"Captain, it could be a trap," Xalpha cautions me.

"Possibly," I say, "but not likely. They could have offed us at the shrine, but they didn't. However, if the worst happens... the commander's in charge."

While her objection is plastered across her face, Chloeja nods. She knows what to do, and I trust her to do it... in whatever manner an escape is even possible.

"But none of you worry about that," I add, wrestling with my fears and resolve. "I'll be right back."

They're all visibly uneasy, but regardless, they stand at attention, raising a salute.

I return it, about-face, and take a single step into the corridor. The door seals behind me.

"I'm ready," I say, feeling my left-hand tremor... but not my right.

⋙ ⋘

[Apologies. I am not permitted to enter,] the Thriaxian explains, stopping before a twenty-foot-tall door. [The way is through here. It was a pleasure to meet you, Vaughan.]

"Thank you." I nod.

With a simple bow, she backs away and walks back down the corridor.

Bang!

Behind the door, the sound of metal hitting stone echoes toward me.

Two sliding panels retract into the wall, revealing an enormous hall. In it, two rows of armoured Thriaxian infantry stand at the ready, each holding a long pulsar-bladed halberd up to the arched ceiling above. They stand on either side of a burgundy carpet that leads up to a wide and raised chair. In it sits a figure in a distinctive suit of power armour.

[You may enter.] I hear, this time, a harsh masculine tone.

The first few steps I take are surreal. Behind the Thriaxian guards, expansive panels open up to a black canvas, dotted with twinkling stars. In the distance, Thriaxian vessels of all makes come into sight.

As I get closer, off to the right, a familiar planet emerges on a curved horizon.

It's Mar Hylia 41.

"We're in orbit," I mutter to myself.

The seated figure rises from his chair like a feudal lord with a guest in his throne room.

Even though he's only a stone's throw away, this unique Thriaxian stands higher than eight feet, a fair bit taller than the other Thriaxians in the room. Not including the raised steps leading up to him.

The doors behind me shut loudly.

"You surprised me..." the Thriaxian in front of me says, his synthetic voice garbled by his helmet. "I didn't think someone like you, who fought as viciously as you have, would show such empathy to one of our priests."

Every muscle in my body tenses as he approaches.

This is the same man who killed my pilots, who almost killed me several times in the last few months... including today, down near the surface.

He takes one last step forward, stopping as my eyelids tense furiously.

It's fair game. He has my men, and he may have stolen our X-5s. If he wants to interrogate me here, fight me in hand-to-hand combat for his amusement, away from my squadron... there's nothing I can do about it. The bonds on my hands tighten, and I can't help but pull against them.

But...

With a flick of his long armoured fingers, the bonds disappear.

I grasp at my left wrist with my right, glancing down for a second, and snap my gaze back up.

"What do you want with me?" I ask, confused.

"Hm," he grunts.

He places his hands on his helmet. A loud hiss escapes the bottom edges, and he removes the aquatic apparatus from the rest of his armour. For the first time, I see the Demon's face.

The one who has been my nemesis in this war. This "Imir-Tarshau": the Thriaxian "Warlord of a Thousand Fleets", the very object of my waxing and waning madness and the reaper of my comrades. The fiercest Thriaxian soldier they possess... and...

"You're Terran," I blurt out.

Chapter 34

SEAN

"What do you mean?" I ask, cradling my helmet.

"I mean, you're *Terran*," the young captain repeats, "and I don't understand why you'd fight your own people!"

Oh, kid...

I catch myself from laughing, pursing my lips and turn away.

Even when I make eye contact again, he doesn't seem to comprehend who or what I am. And to be fair, he really has no idea.

[Exalted One,] Vaikinos, the head of my guard, says, [what shall we do with them?]

The young pilot searches the room, trying to figure out which one of my guards uttered this.

I pause, scratching my chin, catching my reflection shining back at me from the visor of my helmet.

The same weathered features I've accumulated over the years – smile lines, stress creases, and grey hairs lining my sandy-blond hair. What hasn't changed in two decades is the brightness in my light grey-blue eyes.

"With the whole of the Terran squadron?" I clarify.

Vaikinos steps out of formation and stares directly at me, his H2O canister at his mouth bubbling.

The sound of my metal-covered hand clicking against my helmet rings up to my ears while I weigh the scales of how to process my enemy's forces.

Hm. What harm could it do?

"Let them go," I say.

Vaikinos stares at me, and the young captain seems even more unsettled.

[My Imir-Tarshau, is this your command?] Vaikinos asks, double-checking my orders.

"Yep," I say, having decided.

The young pilot's mouth hangs open, unbelieving.

"Oh," I add, "and before we release them, I want to speak with this one. And while I'm away... treat the rest of his squadron like you would a representative of the Matriah. You know, the royal treatment."

[As you wish,] Vaikinos replies, bringing his right fist to his heart.

There's a moment of silence, followed by the young captain staring at his feet. Vaikinos bows and leaves the hall.

"Is that your name?" the captain asks. "Imir-Tarshau? Or is it a title?"

"It's a title," I say, waving my free hand. "No, my name is Sean."

"Sean?" he repeats.

"Yes. Spelt with an 'ea' instead of a 'haw'," I reply. "How about you? We've been calling you the Scourge of Altier this whole time. So what do I call you?"

"Vaughan," he says. "My name is Vaughan."

"Hm. Very well." I place my right hand over my chest. "It's an honour to meet you face-to-face."

Vaughan nods, looking awkward as all hell. I can't blame him.

"Okay," I begin, "I think a walk around the ship is in order. I assume you have questions."

"And then some," Vaughan replies, glaring at me.

Maybe I should have changed. The sound of my metal boots echoes horribly down the hallways. Vaughan keeps pace, walking alongside me to my right.

"How is any of this possible?" he asks.

"That's a little vague," I say, "but I think I get what you mean. Like you said in my audience chamber: what is a Terran doing commanding *a thousand Thriaxian fleets*? I paraphrase, but you get my meaning."

"Right," he replies, occasionally staring off to the change in scenery.

In the small time we've travelled, we've passed by a shrine to the En'kiir, one of the Thriaxians' patron deities. Or, as I've heard some human fleets call them, the Ominii.

"You were laughing before," Vaughan says, glaring up at me. "How is any of this funny?"

"I'm sorry; it's ironic," I reply, "that because I'm human and I defend an alien species, that somehow makes it strange. But you fight for a space-faring pro-Terran government... and you're not even Terran yourself, are you?"

Now he seems confused *and* threatened.

"Don't worry," I say, shaking my head, "it's not like I'm going to blab to your superiors about the medical info we collected. Somehow, I feel like they wouldn't even let me through the front door."

Ah, thank God. Finally, this kid's loosening up!

"That is true," Vaughan says, tension melting from his face.

"Honestly, the story of how I got here is, uh... complicated." I scratch the back of my head with my armoured gauntlet. "It might actually take a few days to explain."

"Okay," he replies, "but why are you letting us go?"

"Ahh..." I sigh, "... that."

Oh, boy... how do I even start?

"The short answer is you're not a threat to us. Not right now, anyway."

"And the long answer?" Vaughan asks.

"Well... our primary concern was a war of attrition from the humans... er, Terrans. For a time, our borders were far enough away that we didn't really need to worry about an invasion. And..."

Vaughan glances up at me, quizzically. "And?"

"Your people developed stronger mechs, especially your X-5s. Tie that in with the program that made you and your pilots, and we started losing ground. What we *weren't* expecting was how you mostly targeted our holy sites. All across Thriaxian space. So we changed up our strategy of defence for total war. It was pretty clear at that point that your President-General wanted something specific from us."

"... Defence!" Vaughan repeats, stopping in his tracks, "Your people *actively* attacked our colonies, bombed civilian craft, and threatened the sovereignty of our borders! You nuked the Silesia System to hell!"

I glare down at him, unflinching. "We did no such thing."

"That's a lie!" Vaughan shouts, banging his fist against the wall.

Frustrated, my cold metal gauntlet pressed to my face, I let out a sigh. "That's something you're going to have to find out yourself," I say calmly. "Don't take my word for it."

I lower my hand and walk again, glancing over my shoulder.

"From where I'm standing," I add, "I have no reason to fight you. Or any Terran. That's why, with the shrine as it is, your people no longer pose a threat to us, because your people have no reason to attack us. From our side of the war table, we've won. For now, anyway."

"How did you gain a victory over us?" Vaughan counters.

"Not over you," I reply, "but in defending against you. Even if you secure the relic itself, I won't stop you."

"So we can ... take it?" he asks.

"With my blessing," I assure.

God, he'd be terrible at poker. He's not even subtle about his suspicions.

"Okay. Don't trust me," I say, "but also don't be surprised if your Congress signs an armistice with the Thriaxian Kingdom, at least within the next forty-eight hours. Truly. I'd stake my life on it. And, about the relic, I'm sure the priests would have a word with the princes and the Matriah, but for all I care, you could melt it down and turn it into a cannon."

There's a long pause, interrupted only by the loud *clack* of my metal exoskeleton echoing around us.

"Okay," Vaughan says, "but what *happened* down there? What happened when I touched it?"

Wait, he did *what*?!

"Oh, when you activated it?" I say, barely keeping myself calm.

"Right. What was that energy?"

Oh shit oh shit oh shit oh shit oh shit!

"That," I say, stalling for time, "was energy stored in the artefact. When you released it, it no longer posed a threat of falling into Terran hands."

"Oh."

"Yeah. You might want to keep that to yourself," I caution, turning a corner. "Now, out of curiosity, what possessed you to touch it in the first place?"

Vaughan glances away to the right and faces forward. "I don't think I had a choice, and all I remember is one of your priests reached out to me, pointed at the artefact... and the rest is hazy."

Hmm.

"Sean," he begins, "*why* was that energy there to begin with?"

"That... I can't say," I reply solemnly.

And as I expect him to protest, he stops talking.

The hallway opens up to the cartography room, filled with navigators fussing over their spherical star charts. From this far away, several of my crew relay fleet positions to the comms deck... and, of course, everyone's holding their breath for the Terran High Command, waiting for diplomatic terms. I'm not worried though. The Terrans'll have what they need within the hour.

Vaughan stands on the edge of the open circular room, and he seems like he's fixed on one particular thing or one of the Thriaxians moving about.

"Everything okay?" I ask.

"... Are there more than one of you on this ship?" he asks.

I blink at his words. "How do you mean?"

"I mean," he says, facing me, "do you have any more Terrans working on your ship? She's not one of mine."

"No..." I say. "I'm the only one on this ship. My family and I are the only Terrans in the Kingdom, and they're several megaparsecs from here."

"Wait, then who—" Vaughan stops mid-sentence. "She's gone."

"Who's gone?" I raise an eyebrow.

"There was a woman, right there!" He points to an open section of the room. "She had platinum-blonde hair, braided long, and was wearing one of your people's uniforms."

"Huh," I grunt.

Vaughan sighs, scanning the room over again. "Never mind," he says, defeated.

Well... that is interesting.

Breaking the silence, a notification shows up on the screen on my wrist.

"The hangar's ahead," I say, changing the subject. "From what my subordinates say, your squadron's taken to how our repair techs work our machines."

※≫≫ ≪≪※

When I suited up today, I didn't think I'd pass by this same hallway, side by side with my nemesis.

Life is strange that way.

And when Vaughan takes a few steps ahead of me, though I can't make out his expression, his head moves all across the wide expanse of the hangar.

"How do they stay up that way?" He points to the levitating Sentinel units.

"I couldn't tell you if I wanted to," I say. "I'm not sure how half of this tech works."

Up above, several of his pilots fawn over repair equipment and marvel at our mechs up close. I guess I'd react the same if I were on a Terran ship... and not getting shot at.

Before I can take another step forward, Vaughan rushes up the stairs to the catwalk above, met with cheers for his safe return. It's nice.

I follow far behind, climbing up the stairs.

"... and that's how they repaired the commander's unit! You should see the ring they used; it recombined it like it was tossed into a replicator!"

"We're still not sure if it even moves now," a sharp feminine voice counters.

"No, no, that's just it!" an excited masculine voice replies. "They did a remote test, and *it works!*"

"Well, House Yin will be happy if you both can figure out the patent," Vaughan adds.

As they all come into view, they all face me, shocked.

"Captain!" the oldest looking of the seven blurts out. "They captured another one! How long have they kept you here? How have you—"

"Oreiga," Vaughan interrupts.

"Oh," I say, "going on twenty-three years now or so. Earth years though, not Thriaxian time. For them, it'd be more like, uh... ten months."

"This is Sean." Vaughan introduces me. "He's the commanding officer of this vessel."

It's good that he leaves out that I'm their "Demon of Talmorah". I'm not sure how they'd all take it.

"Seriously?" the familiar-sounding woman replies. "That can't be."

"It's true," Vaughan says. "And right now, he's our host."

I nod and take inventory of his crew.

They all appear cautious as I approach, but again, that's to be expected.

Before I explain my plans to release them, I catch Vaughan staring at one specific X-5: the one with the mechanical wings. On closer inspection, I find he's staring at the number of victory marks on the side of the unit. Thirty-seven in total. And, when he turns back, there's a notable sadness darkening his face.

And as much as I want to reassure him, to help remove some of the festering guilt, it's not my place.

As cordial as I've been, I'm still their enemy.

Either by my hand, or by my men's, we slaughtered their people.

"The repairs on the last X-5 should be finished soon," I say, "and I'll make sure to take you back once it's ready."

⋙ ⋘

The last mech hovers above me, hoisted by a metal, half-circular anti-grav cranes. There's a large wormhole active in the hangar, connecting directly to the shrine by a portal-generator, and their Xenomechs gently passes through the portal and teleports instantly back to the shrine. Moments before, the Terran pilots crossed through ahead of their units.

"That should be it," I say, surrounded by twenty of my guards at the bottom of the hangar.

Vaughan stands a good foot in front of his men, sombre as all hell.

The rest of his pilots don't seem any better. Of course, we *did* stow their weapons away inside their mechs, and to add to it, my captain insisted I escort them out with a small platoon. More tension.

[*The risk to your safety is too great,*] she said. [*If Terran forces intercept you, the likelihood of capture is too high.*]

Very true.

Vaughan, though... he has questions, and it's plain as day on his face. Millions, probably. And on top of that, there's something different about the way he looks at us.

At me.

In the audience chamber, he not only seemed ready to fight but to die.

And now, I can't help but feel like he doesn't want to leave.

One of his pilots leans in and starts talking to Vaughan. I can't really make out what he's saying.

And, I'm not sure what it is – maybe my morbid curiosity – but I examine the other side of the wormhole's ellipsis and witness the remains of the artefact.

It's tilted on its side, where before it hovered, only to be seen by the most devout of our priests. The soft blue glow it emitted is now absent from the inscriptions and illustrations.

No doubt. The reports were correct. It's gone.

"Captain, I must insist! We can't simply let him go!" I hear, and I snap my head forward.

"I said no," Vaughan interjects, staring down the pilot he called the 'Old Man' back in the hangar, "They kept their word, and they could have easily killed us. And they didn't."

As I observe the Terran pilots, my guards have already armed the cannons stored in their wrist armour, prepared for a confrontation.

"Oreiga's right," Chloeja, the same woman I downed hours before, adds. "We can't simply do nothing. There's too much blood on his hands."

They don't know I'm their Demon, but they are aware that I'm a Thriaxian officer.

And, yeah. She's right.

"I—" I try to say...

A massive rumbling from above cuts in.

[Exalted One,] my Ini'Shir, Orakyn, says, [we have no more time. They've come for the artefact.]

Vaughan and his men stare directly at me, full of intent to enact their justice on me, a Thriaxian officer... but with no actual means. I understand their reasons... maybe because they can't stomach letting their enemy go free.

"You're right," I say, "there is blood on my hands... and I'm sure you can't forgive now. But maybe one day you can."

While the other pilots are insulted, Vaughan's face betrays him again.

"When next we meet," I say, more to him than anyone else, "I hope we won't be enemies."

As soon as I retreat to the portal, a loud scuffle of boots screeches behind me.

"How can I trust anything you've said?" Vaughan asks, with fleeting hints of desperation.

"You can't," I say, "but like I mentioned, you should find out the truth for yourself."

"Based on what you said, I'm not sure what's true," he replies.

I wince. His words hit harder than I thought.

That, and the rest of his men share confused expressions. Not good for PR.

"What do you know for certain?" I ask, hearing a far-off explosion above. "What do you remember?"

"*Very little* before I became a pilot." Vaughan's brow creases. "Nothing is certain. Not any purpose I had before or my n—"

He was going to say 'name'. *They took that away from you too, didn't they?*

As he says this, Chloeja turns to him, her face awash with concern.

"Well..." I say, followed by a sharp inhale. "Time's against me right now, but I can say this."

Two more explosions echo throughout the spherical chamber of the shrine.

"You're not what you remember. You're what you *do*." As I finish, I raise my hand.

The loud pulsing sound of my men's rifles arming sends the pilots a step back.

"For saving face," I explain, "since we can't let them think you let us get away. That wouldn't be good."

That, and it's a good thing we scrubbed the cameras and black boxes on their X-5s.

I turn around and step toward the portal. Before I step through, I take a moment. "So, Vaughan," I say over my shoulder, "what are you going to do?"

As another, more violent explosion rocks the plateau, I step through the gate, and the metal *clank* of my boots lands on the surface of my bridge.

When I glance back, the blurred shadows of Terran reinforcements pour down from above the holy site. They advance, causing boulders to crash onto the walkways of priests and their acolytes.

And enshrined in the middle of the watery, distorted image of the gate, staring back from the other side, is Vaughan. While everyone else takes cover or converges to the aid of their soldiers, he stands still.

Shook, maybe, but the path is before him.

The space-time rift collapses into nothing. Both of our worlds severed, and maybe forever.

[Exalted One] Orakyn, says, [we have connected to the Terran High Command. They await your presence in the war room.]

I inhale sharply and breathe out.

"Okay. Captain, maintain defences with the other admirals in our sector. This shouldn't take too long."

My crew regards me admiringly, hopeful in my resolve. And, with any luck, maybe this time the Terrans will accept a ceasefire.

In the dimly lit war room, with gun-grey walls and a circular table, a figure stands across from me. As I approach the hologram, Vincent DeKierr's features come into focus. I notice, like our previous encounters, that the President-General of the GUILD Republic dresses in the formal attire of his station. And, I watch as he raises an eyebrow, seeing me for the first time without my helmet.

"Your Excellency," I greet.

"Exalted Imir-Tarshau," Vincent replies, "I've received word that you wish to parley a ceasefire?"

"That's correct," I answer, keeping my composure, "provided that you're satisfied with our terms of surrender."

Vincent stares down at a holopad in his hand and reviews my request.

"And," I add, "I've been told your forces have secured one of our holy relics. Is this true?"

As I play dumb, he smiles confidently at me.

"Yes, it's true," Vincent replies. "The Key is in our possession. Does this change your stance on a ceasefire?"

"It doesn't." I shake my head. "Let's end this."

Vincent types on his holopad, and it disappears. "Oh, we will," he says, "on the condition that you will remove your forces from the Mar Hylia System and allow us to transport the relic to Terran Space."

I pause for effect... force a conflicted expression, and re-engage with Vincent. "I agree. As part of the ceasefire, we won't stop you from taking the relic, and all Thriaxian forces will withdraw from the system. Are we in agreement?"

"We are. I'll send word to my war council, and my military will be ordered to cease fire." Vincent says.

"I will order my fleets to do the same. And if you're willing, my Matriah wishes to negotiate a formal peace treaty with the Republic."

Vincent glances to his right, then back at me. "This is something we can discuss in the days to come. For now, I'm sure you agree that we've shed enough of each other's blood."

"Agreed, your Excellency," I say, burying my ire.

He and I nod at each other, and as a holopad appears in thin air above my hand, I sign above the dotted line, agreeing to the terms. And, as the translucent page collapses with my finished signature, Vincent stares at me like he has all the trump cards in his hand. The expression of a man who has crushed his opponent...

... but unlike Vaughan, I'm really damn good at my poker face.

"We'll keep in contact as our nations hammer out a proper treaty," Vincent says, "but until that time, Terran forces will be held at bay by this armistice, effective immediately."

"As will our Thriaxian forces," I say. "Until then, Your Excellency."

Vincent and I bow respectfully at one another, and his lifelike avatar opposite to me disappears. As soon as it does, I march through the war room's exit, stepping onto the bridge.

"Captain," I order, "send an urgent order out to the fleet. Tell them there's a ceasefire in effect."

[Of course!] Orakyn replies.

"And," I add, "bring up the admirals, and send word to the Matriah. Tell them it's urgent."

Orakyn nods, giving orders to her staff on the comms deck.

In a matter of seconds, Orakyn waits at the semi-circular table of the helm.

Alright. Let's rock.

"Put 'em on." I rest my hands against the rail of the upper deck.

The lower admirals appear as projections, surrounding the hollow circular table alongside Orakyn and me. And, in the centre, a regal female Thriaxian appears, dressed in fine flowing garments and adorned with accenting jewellery. I approach her, stepping into the centre of the semi-circle, and drop to one knee, bowing reverently.

"Honoured Matriah." I venerate the sovereign of our Kingdom, bowing my head.

I wait three seconds, lift my head, and I'm greeted by her matronly gaze.

"And to my esteemed admirals. Before I continue, have all of your forces cease fire."

A wave of discomfort sweeps through my ranks, but each officer nods unquestioningly, and as I peer out past the observation screen at the front of the bridge, every ship of every fleet stops firing.

"My admirals, and my beloved Sovereign, I bring news of the front."

[*Tell me, Exalted One,*] the Matriah replies, her resonating voice serene and patient, [*what has become of the Citadel of Rau'Shaktir?*]

I rise to my feet, and my admirals seem nervous.

"The Terrans have invaded the shrine," I say regretfully, "and have taken possession of the Netzah Key."

A look of terror crosses my Matriah's eyes, her hand covering her tiny mouth, and my admirals share an expression of abject disgust.

[*Heresy!*] one of them cries out.

"However," I interject, "one of the Terrans made contact with the Key... the infamous Scourge, no less. And, when my forces investigated the relic, we saw that its dormant power is gone."

While my admirals murmur amongst each other, the Matriah's face flickers with relief. [*Then... it chose him,*] the Matriah replies.

I bob my head at her, scanning my gaze over my military subordinates.

"There's more," I add, hushing the murmurs in the room. "I spoke with the Terran leader, Vincent, and he agreed to a ceasefire. On the condition that we retreat from the system and that they take the Key, the Terrans won't advance further into the Kingdom."

The Matriah tilts her head gracefully toward me.

"All of you," I say, motioning to my admirals, "fall back to Hal'Darah. I'll speak more with you there."

I watch as my fifteen admirals thump their chests, fists over their hearts, and their avatars fade away as quickly as their ships blink out of Mar Hylia 41's low orbit.

Now it's only the Matriah and me.

[*Sean... Can we trust this young Terran?*] she asks. [*Or... will they use him against us?*]

I shake my head, raising my hand level to my chest to alleviate the Matriah's concerns. "Vaughan's in *her* hands now," I explain. "Whatever his fate holds, she's with him... and she has been with us since the beginning."

An otherworldly peace seems to wash over her.

[*I trust your judgement,*] she replies. [*Now... return to your family. They worry about you.*]

I glance at the floor of the bridge, trying to keep my composure, and look back up at her.

"As you command, my Sovereign."

And just like that, the Matriah disappears too.

I clear my throat and straighten my back, looking to Orakyn.

"Prepare to fold space," I order.

[To which destination, Exalted One?] Orakyn asks.

"We're going home." I point straight ahead.

Chapter 35

VINCENT

DeKierr Estate, Republic Capital of Durranir, Planet Haradrun – 5 minutes ago

I'm not sure what I find more amusing: watching the Thriaxians send yet another petition to cease hostilities... or the fact that a Terran leads their military. Either way, I can't help but smile as he asks me if we've gained their holy relic.

"Yes, it's true," I say, my hands held comfortably behind my back, "the Key is in our possession. Does this change your stance on a ceasefire?"

The Imir-Tarshau shakes his head. "It doesn't," he replies. "Let's end this."

Looking down at my desk, I watch a brief clip from central intelligence. The expeditionary pilots of Cronus Squadron are being escorted out, and, in the hands of Juggernaut mechs, the Key is being moved to the surface.

"Oh, we will," I assure him, "on the condition that you will remove your forces from the Mar Hylia System and allow us to transport the relic to Terran Space."

My brows crease as the Imir-Tarshau pauses and looks as though he's weighing the pros and cons of my terms...

Are you seriously *having second thoughts?*

"I agree," he says, finally. "As part of the ceasefire, we..."

Ugh. Yes, yes, get to the point.

"... Are we in agreement?"

"We are," I reply. "I'll send word to my war council, and my military will be ordered to cease fire."

"I will order my fleets to do the same," he says. "And if you're willing, my Matriah wishes to negotiate a formal peace treaty with the Republic."

I'm not against it. I have what I want... nevertheless, I crane my neck toward my chief advisor, Nicholas As'ad. He sits in the corner of my dimly lit, stately congressional office, perched stoically in his formal robes as he listens in. As I look at him, he bobs his head in agreement.

"This is something we can discuss in the days to come." I turn back to the Imir-Tarshau. "For now, I'm sure you agree that we've shed enough of each other's blood."

Ha, there it is. A crack in my opponent's mask.

He quickly glances to my left; I can sense a flicker of defiance to my words.

"Agreed, Your Excellency," he replies.

To seal our agreement, I port the ceasefire document to him at his coordinates and nod as it materialises in his hand. Contented, I watch him sign, and it disappears on his end, now filed away with the central intelligence desk of the Legion.

After all, why *would* I want to keep fighting? The Key is mine, and the Thriaxians have yet again come to me to offer peace. No matter the lives spent, the war goal is met.

I've won.

"We'll keep in contact as our nations hammer out a proper treaty," I say, "but until that time, Terran forces will be held at bay by this armistice, effective immediately."

The second the last word leaves my mouth, I glance at Nicholas, who is already sending a message to my generals to cease fire.

"As will our Thriaxian forces," the Imir-Tarshau says, his voice calm and level. "Until then, Your Excellency."

We give each other a slight bow, a typical courtesy, and the second I rise, I terminate the comms transmission on my desk with the wave of my hand. As the very Terran military leader of the Thriaxians disappears from sight, the large windows of my office change from opaque to transparent. The morning light pierces through the high ceiling, illuminating the ornate copper and terracotta accents of the office walls, the polished granite of my desk, and the dark blue carpet of the room.

Moreover, it sheds light on Nicholas's quizzical expression.

"Hmm..." I hum. "Well, my friend, what do you make of that?"

"I think it's strange that the head of the Thriaxians' military is a Terran, for one," Nicholas muses, sitting with a leg drawn up over his lap, "and... it's a little off-putting."

"How so?" I ask.

"Think about it," Nicholas says, leaning forward. "We've been fighting the Thriaxians for eight years now. And the moment we have their relic, they don't put up a fight to take it back. My question is why? Why give up when the stakes are the highest now?"

I raise my hand and slowly shake my head. "It's *because* the stakes are so high that they back off. Think on this: if you had the potential to destroy the universe a thousand times over... and your enemy takes it from you, how would you react?"

"True." Nicholas's eyebrows rise momentarily. "But that begs the question, why wouldn't they use it on us?"

"It's because it's a holy artifact to them," I explain, turning to the window, seeing a bird's-eye view of Durranir, "and thankfully for you and every living Terran... I'm not that sentimental."

As I look over my shoulder, I watch as Nicholas grins.

"Granted. So, this Imir-Tarshau... what's his story?"

I shrug my shoulders casually. "Likely another colonial rebel without a cause... or maybe a member of the Nomadic Fleet who fancies himself a revolutionary by fighting for the enemies of the Republic. He's a novelty, I'll admit, but in terms of interest, *his* is fleeting for me. Wherever he came from, I couldn't care less. I only concern myself with his willingness to capitulate."

"I couldn't agree more," he adds, "and forgive my question, but when I ran his facial recognition... he didn't show up in the Citizen's Registry."

Now my brow furrows.

"Oh, like he's from one of the Lost Colonies in the Virgo Sphere? Or worse, one of those mythical Thetians?" I ask, keeping in a mocking laugh.

Nicholas takes a deep breath. "It's a possibility," he says, "though, like you said, his willingness to capitulate speaks volumes. More to the point, it speaks to how little of a threat he poses."

"Exactly," I reply, "and with the Netzah Key, we're one step closer to achieving our goals."

Nicholas bows his head reverently. And, as I take another calculated step to the centre of the room, the sheer potential of the artifact fills my mind.

The power of God.

The unprecedented might to force the powers within the Republic into submission... like the emperors of the past, who ruled the Old Empire from Earth.

"My friend," I begin, "we have much to celebrate."

Nicholas rises from his seat and respectfully bows toward me.

"Of course, Your Excellency," he says. "With an end to the war, and your war goal achieved, drinks are in order!"

I bob my head and lead the way out of my office, and we step out into a grand and lavish corridor. Ahead, high pillars of marble and alabaster tower over us and other dignitaries within the Hall of Congress. As I walk, the dark magenta robe pinned to my left shoulder flows from me.

"Only four more to go," I say to Nicholas, hearing his footfalls quicken to catch up, "and then we won't be subject to the scrutiny of the Houses any longer."

"Yes, Your Excellency," he replies, "though, if I may... what narrative will we tell the public? About how the war concluded?"

"The same as we always intended," I begin, "that the infamous Thriaxians, who 'attacked our colonies' and 'invaded Terran Space', were so beaten into submission by our valiant forces that they lost the will to fight. And of course, I'll give special consideration to the survivors and fallen pilots of the Xenomech Division."

"The people need their heroes," Nicholas says glibly.

That they do. And, by propping said heroes up, we demonize the Thriaxians even more.

Truly, it's a win-win.

As we walk toward Nicholas's office with the promise of celebratory brandy in mind, I stop in my tracks. To my left, between the open ivory pillars of the corridor, I peer out toward the gallery of the House Council.

"Hang on a moment," I say, getting Nicholas to stop. "I think she's sitting in today."

Without a reply, he turns the corner and accompanies me over to the balcony of the gallery. We enter through an open archway, bordered by two marble pillars, and we stop at rail of dark quartzite. Over the edge, three stories down, standing in the front row of three resplendent desks before the Speaker is a woman, orating to the Houses.

My adopted daughter and, perhaps, the only ray of light in my life.

Michelle speaks gently, confidently, concisely with her words. Then, when you least expect it, she exclaims her argument, her hand gestures animated, if not forceful and determined, and, at the same time, elegant and poised. Her waist-length crimson red hair sways as she moves, and the meaning in her body language speaks to the passion of her convictions.

"She's giving the opposition a run for their money today," Nicholas notes, "and, not that I can make out what she's saying, but no one's interjected. You have to admit, she's getting better at this."

I glance over at the other sixteen Noble House members present. As she stops, there's a roar of applause, drowning out the few voices that argue against her.

"Truly, she honours House Laurier and House DeKierr with her service," Nicholas adds.

"Michelle's earned it," I reply, "and that's the point. Nothing's been handed to her, and her own merit speaks volumes about what a model woman of the Republic represents and what any citizen can do... if given the chance to shine."

If anyone deserves my affections, it's her.

I think of the rest of my family, grimace, and sigh.

"Yes... if only my son weren't so fucking useless, I'd be a proud parent entirely," I bemoan.

"Mihail continues to languish?" Nicholas asks.

"As a Noble oft does... regrettably. He's a begrudging soldier and a worse politician."

The Speaker stands up, likely bringing a new bill to the House, and as he does, I watch as my daughter disappears through the main entrance below.

"Let's keep going," I urge. "I'd like to forget about my son's failings and celebrate our victory while I'm still in a convivial mood."

Nicholas nods, gesturing me to take our leave.

As we re-enter the corridor, I think on the positives of actual recent military achievements. And the Titan program comes to mind.

"What do you think of my idea, Nicholas? To expand the Titan Division?"

"It's a shift," he replies, keeping to my right, "especially since the branches of the infantry have been a longstanding model for the army."

"Oh, a tradition to be sure, but there's no progress without innovation," I counter. "And with the war over with the Thriaxians, we're going to need solutions to problems at home."

"Agreed," he says, "but wouldn't you say Titan pilots are too specialized for expanded ranks?"

I smile. "Not necessarily. It's true that it takes a special kind of soldier to pilot an X frame. But, if Cronus Squadron serves as an example, it shows the merit of our fighting men matched with our state-of-the-art technology. It's a tempting gambit with a promising reward."

Now it's Nicholas who grins. "I take it you don't wish for the good doctor to spearhead such an enterprise?"

"Certainly not. Doctor Vayne and Colonel Xhyr know far too much about the relic. We'll have to start from scratch if we're to proceed. Besides, the Legion has a copy of the project's data, making those two quite expendable."

Mere steps away from Nicholas's office, he stops and looks at me squarely, wearing an icy-cold expression.

"I trust you know what needs to be done," I say meaningfully.

"Of course, Your Excellency," he replies. "I'll have the Legion take care of them. They should still be on the *Ozymandias* light craft if Daniel's intelligence is up to date."

"Good. It's best to tie up loose ends such as these, wouldn't you agree?"

"As Your Excellency commands," Nicholas says. "And, if I may be so bold, do you wish the same for Cronus Squadron's pilots?"

I shake my head. "No, that's unnecessary. Besides, none of them are aware what the Key is or what it's for. And, from what we've pulled from the transmission on their black boxes and surveillance, none of them have come into contact with the Key."

As Nicholas opens the door to his office, the look he gives me shows his understanding.

"We'll leave them as they are," I add, stepping through, "as heroes of an unfortunate war."

Chapter 36

Rachael

Mar Hylia 41, High Orbit, Lower Decks of the Nineveh, 3 Hours Ago

"Where now?!" I shout, running as fast as I can in my heels down a red-flashing corridor.

"Left!" Xhyr shouts, rifle in hand, taking a sharp corner.

The raid sirens almost seem to blare louder, and out of the corner of my eye, I spot life rafts from the *Nineveh* spewing out the side of the ship, visible from an open window to my right. All of them dropping to the planet below, or caught up in the maelstrom of particle beams slicing through the vacuum of space.

"W-why the hell are you running in those?!" Xhyr gasps, his voice almost shrill.

As he looks over his shoulder for a moment at me, I return his look with a questioning pout... I hear the *clack* of my stilettos echoing as we run. "Oh, I'm *so sorry*; I wasn't expecting to abandon ship so quickly!" I shout back.

Before Xhyr can issue me a rebuttal, the corridor quakes around us, throws me off-balance, and my body crashes against the wall to my left.

"Ow," I grunt, reaching up, and feel Xhyr's rough fingers on my hand.

"Come on, woman!" he roars. "We're gettin' the fuck out o' here!"

I quickly bob my head, and he hoists me up like I'm made of paper, and we keep running... and Xhyr has yet to let go of my hand. Hmm.

"Here!" he shouts, slamming his fist against a side panel to an escape vessel chute.

A door quickly parts from the middle, and we barrel inside.

As he seals the entrance shut, I wobble to the co-pilot's seat and flip on the comms channel, searching for an active signal.

"*Mayday, mayday!*" I hear. "*I repeat, the* Nineveh *is lost. Requesting escorts! The life rafts won't hold! Anybody! I repeat—*"

The transmission dies.

"Buckle in," Xhyr cautions me. "Shit's about to get real ugly."

No sooner does he say this than the hull above us roars violently. I scramble to fasten myself in, like I imagine my poor specimens are now... if they're still alive...

"The pilots!" I exclaim. "W-what if they didn't make it off the ship?!"

He doesn't answer. Instead, he disengages the ship from the *Nineveh*; my heart drops into my heels... then...

"Ahhh!" I scream, grabbing hold of my restraints.

The craft we're in shoots off like a plasma charge, the keel of the *Nineveh* disappearing in seconds. And ahead, a violent torrent of enemy particle beams rains down on the surface of Mar Hylia, cutting through the space between Terran and Thriaxian warships.

"You holdin' on?" Xhyr asks.

"Y-yes!" I say, my voice several octaves higher than normal.

He grunts, twisting the ship sideways, evading a beam that almost hits our ship. The G-force isn't terrible, but seeing the approaching planet swerve viciously is... nauseating.

"They'll be fine," Xhyr says, his voice softer. "I know my men. They'll make it through this."

Despite the clear and present danger, the approaching low orbit battlefield, and my stomach engaged in somersaults, his assurance makes purchase. I can't help but smile, even a little.

"*Can anyone hear me?*" The comms channel picks up a voice.

With a frenzied flip of my hand, I open the comms, revealing the name of the ship we're on: the *Ozymandias*.

"Yes, I read you!" I reply "This is Doctor Vayne of the *Nineveh*! Who am I speaking to?"

"*This is Admiral Alvarah of the 27th fleet. What's your position?*"

I look at Xhyr and frantically shrug my shoulders.

"Tell 'em we're separated from the battle group, approaching low orbit." Xhyr strains, manipulating the controls of the ship.

As I relay the information verbatim, Admiral Alvarah sighs.

"*My condolences,*" he says, and my breath catches, "*both for the destruction of the* Nineveh *and for your predicament. If you can, make it to the 54th fleet's coordinates, centre of the battle group. And... if it's any consolation, your 223rd broke through Thriaxian defences. Honestly, it'll take an act of God to get a pilot to escort you; most of our forces are engaged in operation.*"

I gasp.

"Operation Spear is still...?" I ask.

"*Copy. If your men survived, they're in the fire now. Godspeed to you and your navigator.*"

It's a miracle we have enough forces to deploy for landfall. And!

"My specimens..." I say. "They're alive. Well, some of them are."

The channel cuts off. A second later, Xhyr sighs, his gaze fixed on the shifting horizon beyond our ship's observation window.

"Hang on," Xhyr says. "I'll get us there in one piece."

As much as I appreciate the gesture, statistically our odds are improbable.

The map on my comms HUD shows a path between hundreds of allied and enemy destroyers, millions of fighter craft, and every arsenal imaginable, firing in every direction.

The *Ozymandias* twists, spins, and banks in every which way, evading particle beams larger than the diameter of our ship. All the while, my knuckles go white as my hands grip my restraints.

"You're a bloody madman, Xhyr!" I exclaim, holding on for dear life.

And an admirable one, at that.

As more Thriaxian destroyers appear below our horizon, the comms deck at my console flickers to life, and a garbled voice emerges from the static.

"*Hey,*" a relaxed, masculine voice says, "*the hell are you doin' way out here?*"

"W-we're escaping our ship's wreckage, you dolt!" I say, suppressing a visceral scream.

"*Huh. Okay. You folks need an escort?*"

"Oh, of all the... yes! Where are you, and whom am I speaking to?" I ask.

"*Currently, five hundred clicks from your coordinates,*" the voice replies, almost nonchalantly, "*an' it's Captain Eckhart. Hyperion Squadron. I'm with the Titans.*"

"No shit..." Xhyr stresses. "Wait, why ain't he on the surface?"

"Who the hell cares?!" I snap.

"*Hmm?*" Captain Eckhart asks.

"N-no, not you! Yes, please, we're easy targets out here."

"*Copy that,*" he replies. "*You proceed to your destination; leave the rest to me.*"

Within seconds, an X-5 Xenomech slowly drops into view, near the top of the ship's right-side window.

"Fuck," Xhyr says, "I'll take it. If he's a Titan, there ain't a better wingman than that."

"Heh." I nervously laugh.

But, true to his word, the Titan pilot shields our flank from Thriaxian fighters and deflects particle beams with equal return fire... I've always seen reports and video feeds... but to experience it like this...

It's breathtaking.

And before I can catch my breath again, the planetary horizon gets bigger, and so do the number of Terran vessels, huddled together in a defensive formation.

"*Righty-o,*" Captain Eckhart says, "*welcome to the 54th's rearguard. And this, my nameless friends, is where I leave you. More shit to blow up an' all that.*"

"Yes, well, thank you," I say over the comms. "I'll put in a good word for you."

"*Oh, thank you!*" the captain replies. "*That'd be good because I, uh... definitely need it. Over and out.*"

What a peculiar man.

And, as Xhyr and I watch the lone Xenomech fly off into the fray... it hits me.

Oh, God. We made it.

"Heh." I laugh. "Ha, hahaha!"

What an exhilarating rush!

And when I turn to Xhyr... he looks at me, stunned. "I don't think I ever seen you laugh before," he says, finally looking relieved.

As the flash of distant particle cannons erupts in the distance, Xhyr pops his head up from a hatch on the floor.

"Hey," he says, "there's a small hangar down there. You could easily fit, I dunno, one or two mechs there, at least."

I regard him, hoist my thumb up, and continue to pace as I have for the last hour, thirty-four minutes, and fifty-three seconds. And all the good that counting does... they might as well be years.

Is this what it's like for my specimens? To wait, battered by belligerents one second and have time freeze the next?

How awful...

"Rachael," Xhyr says, his drawl coming out in full force, "there ain't nothin' we can do. Like I said, we trained 'em well, an' prepared 'em for the unknown."

"Easier said than done," I retort. "I've waited years for this. Years! And not knowing anything only exacerbates the entire situation!"

I breathe shallow, quick breaths, my head low and toward the floor.

... Xhyr gently places his hand on my shoulder, and I look up at him.

"It'll be okay," he says, empathetically.

My nerves aren't any less unwound... but again, it's very much appreciated.

Beep.

He and I snap our heads to attention, both of us poised toward my terminal.

We share a look, and I bolt from his hand, landing unceremoniously in my seat, my white lab coat flitting behind me.

"It's from a Lieutenant Deckard," I read aloud. "Two field reports."

Xhyr rushes over, hovering over my shoulder.

"The 203rd broke contact with Cronus Squadron during the invasion of Gaia's Tier... resumed contact, unsuccessful. Suspected pilots are... MIA." I blink, slowly sinking back in my seat. "Ohhh," I bemoan.

"What about the other one?" Xhyr asks. "You said there's two o' them."

I gasp, bring up the second report and...

It triggers the comms channel directly to Colonel Ptolemy's line.

"*Doctor Vayne,*" the colonel greets, "*belay the first message I sent you. We recovered seven of Cronus Squadron's pilots and have secured your stele.*"

My mouth drops. "My specimens!" I cry.

On the colonel's video feed, there's a scattering of Heavy Infantry and, behind them, the unique X-5 that belongs to Vaughan.

"A-acknowledged," I say, breathless.

Xhyr chuckles, patting my shoulder. "I knew they'd make it through." He folds his arms as I look up at him.

They made it. My precious specimen made it... and they got the relic!

Before I can jump up and squeeze Xhyr exuberantly, a sudden flash erupts in the distance. Then another.

"What...?" I say.

I stand and look to Xhyr, who seems as perplexed as I am.

Out of the ship's observation window, Thriaxian ships across the horizon simply... blink out of existence in rapid succession.

"Those aren't explosions," Xhyr says, awed. "I ain't ever seen anythin' like it."

If that's how the Thriaxians travel, it's rather elegant. A stunning display of interstellar travel... and, admittedly, a pang of jealousy hits me in the chest.

Xhyr speaks more with Colonel Ptolemy about the safety of his pilots, and in the background of her transmission, I hear her men chant my precious specimen's name like a fabled demigod from when Terrans ruled an empire on Earth.

So, with a giddy stride, I walk over to the far side of the bridge, to a desk with another open terminal. After all these years of countless research, planning and preparation... it's all led to this.

I log in with my security clearance, open any pictures of the Netzah Key and... they're not there.

In fact, nothing's there.

The folder's empty.

My chest constricts, confusing lines of thought conflicting in my mind.

"Xhyr..." I turn away from the terminal and walk over to him. "I'm sorry to pull you away, but can you assist me?"

He throws me a questioning look but ends his conversation with Colonel Ptolemy and follows me to my terminal.

"It's gone," I say, partly in shock.

"What do you mean, it's gone? Can we even access sensitive intel from this light craft?"

I pinch the bridge of my nose, sighing heavily.

"The data can be accessed on *any* military vessel. I-I don't understand. Where could it have gone? Who could have sanctioned this?!"

Xhyr leans in, inspecting the last updated log.

"Says here the last person to make changes to this archive was... Nicholas."

"Nicholas As'ad?" I laugh. "Why would he..."

Oh.

No. No, that's not possible. Vincent, my sovereign lord – he wouldn't... would he...?

"No..." I say. "He did. My god has forsaken me."

I look away from the blank screen and out into the vast space of the *Ozymandias's* bridge. "He's taken what I have offered him on the highest altar... only to rain fire down upon me... It's all over now," I say, listlessly.

"Whoa, whoa, whoa. Step back a second. What are you talking about?" Xhyr is clearly as confused as I am.

Vincent. He betrayed me.

I keep a hand on the desk if only to keep me standing.

A terrible, constricting knot forms in my stomach, followed by a stinging pain in my tense brows.

I won't let this insult go unanswered. I'll...

And then Xhyr places his hand on my shoulder... and two free-falling tears run down my cheeks. My lips quiver, and any vestige of composure melts away.

I look back at him over my shoulder. His face is marred with worry. Behind those eyes, a world of empathy stirs like a vast ocean... and maybe something more.

"The, uh... truth of it is," I say between a couple of pathetic sobs, "Vincent stole my work. And, as you've suspected, we know too much."

He rubs my shoulder and thoughtfully darts his gaze from side to side.

Xhyr served in the Legion. He knows their tactics and espionage protocols.

He knows what's about to happen to us... and yet... he looks down at me, determined.

"It's a long shot," he says, "but I've got an idea."

As I stare at the blank data drive on my screen, I hear the loading of a pistol magazine.

Off by the corner of my desk, Xhyr slams the magazine in, loading his gun.

"We've got maybe three minutes before they burst through here," Xhyr says, "and beyond that..."

"Hmm. I'm not worried."

Though as I stare at my now blank canvas, a single tiny data cube hangs from my neck, suspended by a simple silver necklace.

I reach behind the nape of my neck, undo the necklace's bonds, let it hang from my loose grip, and dangle it before my eyes. It's translucent green, a centre of living digital matter, and it sparkles against my desk lamp.

I shift from it to Xhyr, who walks toward me.

I move alongside the left edge of my desk, and I seat myself on top of it, crossing my legs.

I swing the bobble like a pendulum. As he stops about a foot or so from me, a thought comes to mind.

"Tell me, Xhyr. If you had the weight of the world in the palm of your hand, what would you do with it?" I ask.

I can tell by the way he looks, with his brow furrowing, that he doesn't understand.

"Or rather, the fate of one man? A certain blue-eyed specimen we're both fond of?"

It's almost endearing how he tries. But as he hesitates to answer... the moment passes. Whatever secrets could have been exchanged between us are gone.

"Never mind," I say as sweetly as I can, clutching the cube in my hand.

Ah. Disappointment spreads across his face, and he goes to move back to his post.

"Wait," I say, reaching out. "Care for a drink?"

My left hand searches for the nob of my desk's side drawer, and once found, I open it.

I retrieve a small bottle of whiskey. And once placed, I lean in again for two small tumblers. Cube still in hand.

I don't waste any time in pouring us each a glass. There's so little of it left. I hand him one and reach for mine, raising it up.

"To the future," I say, clinking his glass.

As I drink deeply, I savour the burn. Its complexity. How unique it is.

As if on cue, comes a loud bang on the door behind Xhyr.

Sparks quickly fly on all edges of the bridge's exit, and a second thud brings the sliding door down. Fanning out right behind Xhyr are the ones His Excellency sent. Our executioners. Our own angels of death.

With a sudden lunge, I wrap my arms above his shoulders, clasping my fingers behind his neck… all while Xhyr readies his pistol.

As I lean in closely, I bring my lips to his ear. "You were always my favourite."

I let the empty glass slip from my hand and fall.

It shatters.

Chapter 37

VAUGHAN

Mar Hylia 41, Bravo Sector, 10 Minutes Earlier

"*You're not what you remember. You're what you do.*" I play the words again in my mind.

After a long stretch of nothing but darkness, the glimmer of a breaking dawn comes into sight.

With escorts above and below us, I shoot through to the light at the end of the tunnel, emerging out into the open air. On my screen, the targeted Thriaxian ships start disappearing into thin air, erasing their signatures. And below is a newly formed hole at the top of the citadel's entrance.

"*Standby, Captain,*" I hear on the escort's frequency. "*We have clearance to land on LZ Kappa. See you folks on the ground.*"

Pulling the controls back, I punch in a code to the landing zone, and off to my left, the rest of Cronus Squadron vectors their course along with me.

As the aft thrusters do a quick burn, large swaths of Heavies dot the area around makeshift landing pads. People setting up camp, clad in power armour, look up as we make our descent.

"*They look excited,*" Chloeja says over the comms.

"I'd be too," I say, "if hundreds of Thriaxian ships simply up and left."

"Yeah, that," she agrees, "*and if what you said about Sean is right, we're probably going home.*"

Home... Holy shit, it's actually over. I can go home! I can see Ann and Mom again!

But what would I say to them, after all this time? Without anyone censoring my video letters, where would I even begin with everything that's happened to me? With Ann'Elise looking more grown up in each transmission she sends and the life Mom has lived on Korvingshal VI... it's like our lives are as far apart as the cosmic distance between us.

Before I can dive deeper into my troubled thoughts, the cockpit shudders as my mech touches down and springs upward. As everything stops moving, I hold in a sob as my eyes sting.

Before I even power down, there's an ocean of people standing from their camps and clasping their hands to their mouths like they're shouting.

I open the hatch.

As I step out onto the open metal ledge, I grab the handle to my lead, and I peer out.

Fifty-eight feet below, tens of thousands of Heavy Infantry rally around our mechs, and start cheering loudly. In no time, there's a sea of eager Terrans clamouring by the feet of my X-5.

Some look mangled, others have missing pieces to their armour, but they're in high spirits.

"Hey! Hey!" A man moves up toward us from below.

He's dressed to the nines with an impressive model of power armour, minus the helmet, and he's joined in by others, fitted in an identical regimental blue tone.

"Which one of you is the captain?!" the first man bellows, drowning out the other soldiers.

"Him." Far off to my right is Chloeja. She's standing up on her perch, same as me, with a generous wind blowing against her messy short hair.

Then it hits me. She's pointing at me.

"*That's* my captain," she says, beaming proudly.

My cheeks burn, and my arms and legs tremor, followed by a sudden surge of butterflies in my stomach.

And I can't simply close the hatch door and hide. It'd make things worse.

"Hey, that's him! That's the guy!" the man below exclaims.

Wait... is that...?

"Deckard?" I call out. "Lieutenant Deckard? With the 203?"

"*Yeah!* See, he remembers me!" Deckard calls to the others. "But that's him! That's the guy who led us up the tier! He did that! That's *Vaughan!*"

Deckard looks like he might have a heart attack...

"That's the hero of Gaia's Tier!" Deckard exclaims, raising his hands up.

The voices below meld and chaotically holler out different cheers... until all I can hear is one word:

"Vaughan! Vaughan! Vaughan!" they shout, over and over.

Yep. It feels weird. I mean... I didn't earn this, right? Not to *this* scale!

And yeah, I made the call to aid the 203 and the 112 up the tier, but... I'm no hero. I don't feel like one.

I squint as the sun rises further above the horizon, tinting the purple sky with orange, its rays obscuring my vision. I lift my right hand up for some cover, splaying my fingers out. It... sort of helps with all that cheering, too.

And with my hand right up in front of me, my thoughts become... heavy. Fuzzy almost, like when I first stepped off at Port Yegevni years ago. As my whole body continues to tremor... my hand stays still.

Vaughan, you dummy.

That's the same hand that touched... the...

"*Vaughan...*" a voice whispers crystal clear: a soft, wistful, and... familiar voice of a woman. It felt like it was right next to me, like she was standing right next to my ear... I mean, if a whisper could drown out an entire chant.

No. It didn't drown it out. It muted it.

"What the...?" I say.

As I look back to the ground, everyone has stopped moving, and when I snap my head toward Chloeja, so has she. In fact, the very dust kicked up by landing mechs hangs in the air above the ground.

Frozen in time.

"*Vaughan,*" she says again, sharper this time. Whoever she is.

A trail of embers flits down and across from the left.

As I turn my head, I spot her.

On the left shoulder plate of my Xenomech is a woman, lithe in build, with long flowing platinum-blonde hair, at the tips of which, embers appear and scatter into the air. And the blue dress she's wearing flits and flutters in a gust of wind, decorated with ornate white-threaded inscriptions leading down her crossed legs.

The same woman standing on an endless sea in my dream.

But... how? No wind touches the surface of my hand or brushes past my face.

She sits there, looking down at me.

And then she smiles... and starts bouncing her crossed legs up and down against the surface of her perch.

"*Vaughan,*" she speaks, melodically and poised, "*what do you see?*"

Not knowing what to do or what to say, she shoots me a knowing look. She gracefully raises her right hand up, palm facing her. And with an elegant flick of her wrist, she extends a hand out in front of her.

Having lowered my hand, I look at the palm on my right hand.

On it, nine dots are forming a circle, with a tenth in the centre... nine are blacked out, with the one in the middle tinted white. I look back up at her, and she widens her eyes slightly... I think she wants me to mimic her.

So I raise my hand up, palm facing me. One of the black dots illuminates blue.

Confused, I look back up at her.

She continues to smile, palm back toward her... and again, she flicks her hand out away from her.

As I play along with her, I mirror the woman without looking at my own hand.

"*What do you see?*" she repeats.

I blink, confused, but I do as she says and look forw—

"W-what?"

Blood.

Blood cascades down my hand, past my wrist, and flows down.

"**How they pray for the blood to cease running.**" Kinsharla's words spring to life in my head.

When I look down, in place of the soldiers below, there's an ocean of blood crashing against the feet of my mech.

Beyond it, on the ground, the terrible red ocean spans the horizon, overshadowed by the dimming of the morning sky into night.

"**Your path is marred by shadow.**"

Stars appear. They choke out the light of the sun, expand in brilliance, and fade into nothing.

"Urgh!" I gasp, trembling.

This isn't real! This isn't real!

My left hand clasps my right, trying to stop the blood from flowing.

I blurt out a loud sob, shutting my eyes tightly, and a sudden wave of nausea hits me. It hits hard.

"This is all in my head," I say, wincing. "I've seen too much shit, and now I'm seeing things!"

Smoke fills my nostrils. A terrible heat rises toward my feet.

"Argh!" I cry.

Did she do this?! How?!

I open my eyes again, bracing myself for the horrible sight from before...

It stopped.

There's no blood at all. The sickening sight is gone.

My hand is still outstretched, shading me from the light.

There isn't a single star in the sky, and the orange sky gives way to a soft baby blue.

I snap my head up and to the left... and...

She's gone.

"Where the hell is she...?" I whisper.

What... what did I witness?

Dust sweeps by me, the wind blowing past. There's no smoke, no scorching heat... and everyone below is back.

My hand stays raised, and I'm barely keeping it together.

As I do everything to fight my weakening legs and shove *everything down* as far as it will go, the horrifying images and Kinsharla's words meld together...

But then, a line I heard today breaks through all of it:

"*So, Vaughan*" – Sean's parting words resonate in my mind – "*what are you going to do?*"

An otherworldly calm settles over me. It doesn't take away from what I saw, but it keeps me standing.

The chant of my name roars below me like a rising tide.

Acknowledgements

I would like to express my deepest gratitude to my editor, Laura Josephsen, who provided incredibly helpful developmental feedback, improved my writing and gave me a better appreciation for the English language. This endeavour would also not have been possible without the skillful talents of my sister and book cover designer, Angela Adair, who painstakingly worked to pull all the ethereal images of my story, and etched them into reality. Thank you as well for reading and giving feedback on the first draft of my book.

A very special thanks goes to my parents, Jonathan and Maurine Adair; my sister Sarah Adair Thibault; my cousin David Thomas; my family friends Daniella Barsotti and Franco Fragomeni, and my fellow writing colleagues Aaron Grierson and Hayden Morgan for all of their much appreciated long suffering and hard work as beta-readers for this book. All of your very meaningful insights and reflections helped me shape my story into what it is now. I would also like to extend my sincerest thanks to Drew Hazlewood, another treasured writing colleague who helped me with research on military customs, physics, and the combat mechanics that brought much of the novel's tension to life.

S.J.S. Adair first started writing at the age of eight, and worked as a technical writer at the age of eighteen. He's originally from the Ottawa Valley, and resides in the Bay of Quinte. Currently, he's pursuing an education in counselling psychology, to become a licensed psychologist in the field of crisis and trauma. He is an avid nerd of space operas, military science fiction, Yoshinkan Aikido, and the venerable genre of mecha anime. In his lifetime, he has survived cancer not once, but twice, and doesn't know the meaning of giving up. *Dirge of Titans* is his first novel.

Manufactured by Amazon.ca
Bolton, ON

39797335R00194